the American Literary Anthology / 3

the American Literary

Selected by Donald Barthelme, Joyce Carol Oates,
Max Steele (fiction); Denise Levertov,
William Stafford, Reed Whittemore (poetry);
Richard Ellmann, Brendan Gill, Dwight Macdonald
(essays and criticism)

Edited by George Plimpton and Peter Ardery

Anthology / 3

*The Third Annual Collection of the
Best from the Literary Magazines*

THE VIKING PRESS / *New York*

Acknowledgment is hereby made for permission to reprint the following:
Adventures in Poetry: "Paris by Night." This selection is reprinted from the
book *A Nest of Ninnies* by John Ashbery and James Schuyler. Copyright
© 1969 by John Ashbery and James Schuyler. Used by permission of
E. P. Dutton & Co., Inc.
Angel Hair #3: "Invitation Au Voyage II" by John Wieners. Copyright ©
1967 by Lewis Warsh.
Apple: "1966" by Dick Lourie. Copyright © 1968 by David Curry.
Beloit Poetry Journal: "Adjust, Adjust" by Christopher Bursk. Copyright
© 1968 by *Beloit Poetry Journal.*
The Brown Bag: "House of Blue by the River's Curve" by James Apple-
white. Copyright © 1968 by James Applewhite.
Camel's Coming: "For Poets" by Al Young. Copyright © 1968 by Richard
Morris.
The Carleton Miscellany: "An Exhibit of Paintings by George Inness" by
Robert Grant Burns. Copyright © 1968 by Carleton College. The text
has been revised for this volume.
Cassiopeia: "Taking Heart" by David Bromige.
Caterpillar: "The Student's Testimony" by Jerome Rothenberg. Copyright
© 1968 by Jerome Rothenberg. "Rilke's Sixth Elegy Transposed" by
George Quasha. Copyright © 1968 by Clayton Eshleman.
Chelsea: "Westward and Up a Mountain" by Elaine Kraf. Copyright ©
1968 by de Palchi Corporation.
Chicago Review: "Human Relations" by Emmett Jarrett. Copyright © 1968
by *Chicago Review.*
The Colorado Quarterly: "Preparation" by Sandra McPherson. Copyright
© 1968 by the University of Colorado, Boulder, Colorado.
Confrontation: "New England Love" by Lynn Strongin. Copyright © 1968
by *Confrontation* of Long Island University.
Contemporary Literature: "The Depraved Angel of *Marat/Sade*" by Sybil
Wuletich. Copyright © 1968 by the Regents of the University of Wis-
consin.

Ephemeris: "Beginning of Lines: Response to 'Albion Moonlight'" by Mary Norbert Körte.

Fire Exit: "The River" by Sam Cornish. Copyright © 1968 by *Fire Exit.*

Folio: "A Man's Life" by Del Marie Rogers. Copyright © 1968 by Adele Sophie de la Barre.

Hanging Loose: "Thin Ice" by Jim Harrison. Copyright © 1968 by Emmett Jarrett.

Hollow Orange, 1967: "It's Raining in Love" by Richard Brautigan. Copyright © 1968 by Richard Brautigan.

The Hudson Review: "Guitar Recitativos" by A. R. Ammons. Copyright © 1968 by The Hudson Review, Inc.

Kayak: "The Lost Angel" by Philip Levine. Copyright © 1968 by Kayak. "Against the Evidence" by David Ignatow. Copyright © 1968 by David Ignatow. Reprinted from *Rescue the Dead,* by David Ignatow, by permission of Wesleyan University Press.

The Kenyon Review: "James Agee: A Memoir" by Robert Fitzgerald (abridged version). The unabridged version was published as an introduction to *The Collected Short Prose of James Agee.* Copyright © 1968, 1969 by The James Agee Trust. "A Memoir" Copyright © 1968 by Robert Fitzgerald. Reprinted by permission of the publisher, Houghton Mifflin Company.

The Little Square Review: "Our Willows" by John Skinner. Copyright © 1968 by John Skinner. "My Father's Hands Held Mine" and "Because This Is the Way Things Are" by Norman H. Russell. Copyright © 1968 by Norman H. Russell.

New Mexico Quarterly: "The Garbage Wars" by Donald Finkel. Copyright © 1969 by the University of New Mexico. "Indiana I: Three Bad Signs" by Eugene McCarthy. Copyright © 1968 by The University of New Mexico Press.

Northwest Review: "The Image Waits" by Warren Carrier. Copyright © 1968 by the University of Oregon.

The Outsider: "The Walnut Tree" by Elizabeth Bartlett. Copyright © 1968 by *The Outsider.*

Partisan Review: "International Love" by Alan Friedman. Copyright © 1968 by *Partisan Review.*

Poetry: "Sonnet" by Hayden Carruth. Copyright © 1968 by Modern Poetry Association. "The Wings of the Nose" by Michael Benedikt. Copyright © 1968 by Michael Benedikt. "For a Russian Poet" by Adrienne Rich. Copyright © 1968 by *Poetry,* and from *Leaflets, Poems 1965–1968* by Adrienne Rich. Copyright © 1969 by W. W. Norton & Company, Inc. Reprinted by permission of W. W. Norton & Company, Inc., and The Hogarth Press, London.

Poetry Northwest: "10. (from *Window Poems*)" by Wendell Berry. Copyright © 1968 by the University of Washington. Reprinted by permission of *Poetry Northwest* and Harold Matson Company, Inc. "Poem Beginning with a Line Memorized at School" by Roderick Jellema. Copyright © 1968 by the University of Washington.

Prairie Schooner: "Flighty Poem" by John Pauker. Copyright © 1968 by the University of Nebraska Press.

Quarterly Review of Literature: "O they left me" by Jonathan Greene and "Mozart in Nova Scotia" by Richard R. O'Keefe. Copyright © 1968 by *Quarterly Review of Literature.*

The Quest: "Cantata for Saint Budóc's Day" by Ramon Guthrie. Copyright © 1968 by *The Quest.*

Renascence: "The Dry Salvages: Topography as Symbol" by John D. Boyd, S.J. Copyright © 1968 by *Renascence.* Lines from "Ash Wednesday" in

Preface

This third volume of the *American Literary Anthology* appears at a time of widespread interest in small magazines and their role in the history of American literature. Selections from such magazines as *Pagany*, which published Conrad Aiken, Ezra Pound, and Gertrude Stein in the early thirties, can now be found in book form. And many of the influential journals of the twenties and thirties, such as the *Dial, Broom,* and *transition,* are now being reprinted in their entirety. Without question this atmosphere has encouraged the success of the *American Literary Anthology,* a project which seeks to reward and preserve the best poems, essays, and stories in the small literary magazines of today.

The aims of the Anthology, which were set forth at the time of its inception in 1966, were: first, "through wide distribution of the Anthology to give greater circulation to work that originally appeared in magazines with limited circulation"; second, "to supplement the small payments usually made to authors by such magazines—paying grants of $1000 for prose material, $500 for each poem"; and third, "to reward the magazines which had the perspicacity to publish the selections in the first place with grants of $500 and $250 to individual editors for use in the development of their magazines." Nine publishers continue to offer their cooperation to the Anthology program (i.e., to publish the book at cost). They are Atheneum; Doubleday; Farrar, Straus and Giroux; Harper and Row; Little, Brown; Macmillan; New

Directions; Random House; and, of course, the present publisher, Viking, whose name was drawn from a hat by Malcolm Cowley at a ceremony in February 1969.

The publisher for the first volume, Farrar, Straus and Giroux, was chosen by Marianne Moore at a similar ceremony in December 1966. Anthology / 1, which appeared in an edition of 4500 hardcovers and 3000 softcovers in June 1968, has sold out, and the second volume in the series was published by Random House in February 1969. Encouraged by the favorable early reviews (*Publisher's Weekly* called the book "A really fine and varied survey, sophisticated, sensitive, wide-ranging"), Random decided to increase the run to 5000 hardcovers and 5000 softcovers. At this writing Anthology / 2 has nearly sold out and a second edition is being considered.

On the whole, the program has fulfilled its early promise. To date grants have been made to 78 small magazines and to more than 150 writers. The recognition and the money bestowed by the Anthology have helped a number of the writers find publishers and enabled many of the magazines to survive. In addition the yearly volumes continue to serve as a valuable record of a body of American writing which has all too frequently passed undocumented.

There have been a number of complaints against the program, however. The most persistent have been those made by the smallest independent magazines which must compete with the larger, subsidized periodicals. (Magazines submitting to the Anthology must have circulations below twelve thousand, a ceiling high enough to admit many of the better-known scholarly journals.) As one reviewer pointed out, the magazines contributing prose to the volumes were not in the main "tiny mimeographed affairs of the heart, but the more established reviews and quarterlies." Only the poetry selections, he found, showed "a greater proportion of obscure authors and magazines." On investigation the causes for this imbalance became clear: most of the smaller magazines are devoted primarily if not exclusively to poetry, hence their smaller showing in the prose categories. With this in mind we have increased by fifty per cent the number of poems in each volume in hope that more of the available grant money may be directed to those magazines most in need of it.

Certain small-magazine editors, however, would have us go much further. They argue that the anthologies, instead of trying to select the "best" published each year, should avoid qualitative judgments altogether and merely *reflect* whatever that year may have produced. Leonard Fulton, the editor of *Small Press Review*, writes, "The making of an anthology should begin not with just a desire to have an anthology and then seeing what's around to put into it, but rather with a knowledge of what *is* around and then attempting to get a fair representation of that." In the *administration* of the program we have embodied this spirit from the beginning, carefully choosing readers appropriate to each magazine, small-magazine editors for "little mags," graduate students for academic quarterlies, and so on. And as a result our judges each year contend with a mountain of material representing every conceivable school, however obscure.

But from here on the decisions belong to the judges alone, guided only by their standards of quality and taste. (If only Mr. Fulton could hear some of their reactions! Anthony Hecht, who resigned as a poetry judge for the present volume, criticized our sending him piles of what he termed "the careless and militantly third-rate" submitted for "a cultural Poverty Program for Underprivileged Poets.") We are well aware of the literary eclecticism and the sympathy toward innovation that is essential to a project such as this. But we also feel that if the Anthology is to be of lasting value, we should assure that quality, not representation or promotion, is our final consideration.

Some acknowledgments are in order. For their help in assembling the nearly one thousand magazines read for this volume, we are indebted to Linda Feick of the Coordinating Council of Literary Magazines and to Leonard Fulton, editor of *Small Press Review* and Chairman of the Committee of Small Magazine Editors and Publishers (COSMEP). To cull through these magazines we were assisted by ten readers: Kirby Congdon,

Stephen Donadio, Clayton Eshleman, Caroline Herron, Natalie Lehmann-Haupt, Ron Padgett, William Sharfman, Harvey Tucker, Lewis Warsh, and Ann Hancock, our editor at The Viking Press. We also thank Francine Ringold of *Nimrod* magazine, which first published Norman Russell's poem "My Father's Hand Held Mine" in 1967. In Washington, the National Endowment was represented by Carolyn Kizer, the Director of Literary Programs, and her assistant Marilyn Yarbrough.

In the second *American Literary Anthology* (Random House, 1969) two poems were printed incorrectly: Richard Brautigan's "It's Raining in Love" and John Wieners' "Invitation Au Voyage II." These may be found corrected on pages 390–93 of the present volume.

George Plimpton
Peter Ardery
Directors,
The American Literary Anthology

Contents

POETRY

Contents /   xiii

ESSAYS AND CRITICISM

the American Literary Anthology / 3

JOHN ASHBERY AND
JAMES SCHUYLER

◑

Paris by Night

from *Adventures in Poetry*

I

"I have just spoken to the concierge," Dr. Bridgewater said. "He informs me that this evening's performance of *Tartuffe* is sold out."

"Then it's *Le Soulier de Satin*," Fabia said with ill-disguised pleasure.

"That too is sold out," Dr. Bridgewater said, shading his eyes against the harsh glare from the ceiling fixture. "The only thing he has seats for is something called *Ali Baba*—a musical comedy I believe."

"Is it some kind of children's entertainment?" Mrs. Bridgewater asked plaintively. This drew a coarse and rather knowing guffaw from Victor.

"Hardly," Dr. Bridgewater said, glancing reprovingly at his son. "In fact, children—those under the age of eighteen at any rate—are not allowed in."

Fabia joined Victor at the window. Outside, the rain fell ruthlessly on the Quai Voltaire, the Seine, and the greenery beyond. "Well, I couldn't care less about that stuff," Victor said. "Anyway, I have an appointment with my pen pal, Paul Lambert."

"Just who is this person, Victor?" Mrs. Bridgewater asked. "I mean, I know you've corresponded with him through the years, but do you have any idea what his background is?"

"His father," Victor said, "is an *avocat*."

"A lawyer—an attorney," Dr. Bridgewater explained.

"Except," Victor added, "in France there isn't anything shady about it. It's more like being a judge."

"How old is he?" Mrs. Bridgewater asked.

"In his middle thirties, I think," Victor said.

"What kind of work does he do?"

"Tests sports cars," Victor continued imperturbably. "Before they leave the factory. He also drives them around to different parts of the country where there are going to be auto races."

Dr. Bridgewater sat down heavily on the bed where his wife was stretched out with—as she put it—her feet up. "Is all this true, Victor? Or are you merely tormenting your mother?"

"Oh well," Mrs. Bridgewater said, crossing and uncrossing her ankles, "as long as he doesn't race them, I suppose there's no harm in it."

"*La Grande Maison de Blanc,*" Fabia said, reading the name off the side of a passing truck. "He sounds pretty horrible to me and I intend to avoid meeting him at all costs."

There was a sharp tap at the door, which immediately opened. A maid entered carrying a large basket of fruit. "*Monsieur-dame,*" she said as she withdrew.

Mrs. Bridgewater took a small envelope from the top of a pineapple and read the note inside. " 'Welcome to my country —or rather, *Soyez les bienvenus,* since you must speak French now that you are here. Please do me the honor of being my guests at dinner Thursday night. R.S.V.P.' (signed) 'Claire Tosti.' Oh dear," Mrs. Bridgewater went on, "and it was Mrs. Kelso who had her to dinner. Still, how very thoughtful."

Fabia examined the notepaper. "Engraved," she said thoughtfully, and began to hum a little tune.

"No, Victor," Mrs. Bridgewater said, "I wouldn't eat any of that—at least not until I've had time to wash it all thoroughly."

"I'm getting sick of this claustrophobic atmosphere," Fabia said. "Why don't we take one of those boat rides along the Seine? Even Victor would enjoy that."

"In the rain?" Victor said.

"The top part is glassed in," Fabia explained patiently. "Look, there goes one now."

"I," Mrs. Bridgewater said, "am not going to budge until dinner. Who would have dreamed that a little thing like the Sainte
Chapelle could be so taxing?"

"I certainly wish Alice were here," Fabia said. "She at least
has some get-up-and-go to her."

"*That* she certainly has," Mrs. Bridgewater said. "In fact, I
expect we'll be running into her any day now—loping along the
Champs-Élysées with that peculiarly aggressive gait of hers."
Victor looked inscrutable.

"Wasn't that a card you got from Alice this morning?" Fabia
asked him. "It looked like her writing. And besides, no one but
Alice would choose a view of the Chrysler Building."

At this the telephone made a loud rasping sound. Dr. Bridgewater cleared his throat, picked up the receiver, and said, in his
chestiest tone, "*Oui? Oui . . . Oui . . . Mon fils est ici.*" He
hung up and turned to Victor. With the air of one diagnosing
cancer, he said, "A Mr. Lambert is coming up."

"Good grief," Victor said. "I could have met him in the
lobby."

"I don't think . . ." Mrs. Bridgewater was beginning, when
suddenly the door burst open. A dark heavy-set man of thirty-
eight, with bushy but receding hair and wearing a black suit and
raincoat, advanced into the room.

"Well, Victor," he said, or rather, roared, "at last we meet!"
He bore down upon the startled youth and slapped him on the
shoulder with a massive paw. "And you must be Victor's parents
and sister, about whom I hear so much," he added, beaming at
the others.

"Well," Mrs. Bridgewater said, struggling to her feet, "this is
a surprise."

"You must excuse my impatience," Paul said, "but I have
been waiting so long to see Victor, to embrace him. We are pen
pals, you know."

He spoke with a strong American accent, pronouncing Victor
"Victer."

II

"Paris!" Claire said somewhat superfluously. Under a heavy June sky, the city was looking more than usually maleficent. Mrs. Bridgewater, refusing to step out onto the balcony, gazed apprehensively at the scene from the relative safety of the living room. To the right rose the stern contours of the École Militaire; on the left, the Eiffel Tower plunged into low-hanging clouds.

With a gesture that seemed likely to sweep them into the void, Paul Lambert pointed to some trees. "There," he said, "was the home of Blériot, the famous airman."

"That house there," Claire added hastily, indicating an imposing granite pile just opposite them, "belonged to Sacha Guitry. You may not have read his books and plays, but you have probably seen his films."

"The exterior," Dr. Bridgewater said, "is François Premier, though somewhat bastardized." After a noncommittal pause, the group edged its way back into the living room.

"Oppressive, isn't it?" Claire's sister Nadia said. "The night air, I mean." As if in reply, a bolt of lightning lit up the park below and almost at once thick sheets of rain began to fall.

Dr. Bridgewater turned to her as though to the business of the day. "I understand, Mademoiselle, that you are an *antiquaire*."

"Yes," Nadia said, smiling pleasantly. "I am in the antiques business."

"Ah," Mrs. Bridgewater said. She peered about at the comfortable but nondescript furnishings of the room as though there were some point she had missed.

Nadia seemed to sense her difficulty. "Many of my clients are Americans," she continued encouragingly.

"Somehow," Fabia was saying to Claire, "I hadn't expected Paris to be quite so much like Florida."

"Yes," Claire said, "here, too, we have rain." She switched her attention to Mrs. Bridgewater. "I see you are admiring the Charles X prie-dieu. It unfolds to become library steps."

"How convenient," Mrs. Bridgewater said.

"Hasn't most of the good stuff been gotten to already?" Victor asked Nadia.

"Uhmmmm," Nadia said, as she considered his question and the possibility of an answer, but Claire got there first.

"Styles come and go," she said, "in antiques as in all things. In fact, Nadia has launched some herself—for instance, the current rage for English brass fenders."

Mrs. Bridgewater gasped and hastily took some nuts from a dish that declared itself a souvenir of the Trocadero.

"Remember those firedogs we saw in the window at Madeleine Castaing's?" Dr. Bridgewater murmured confidentially to his wife.

"Madame Castaing is one of my closest colleagues," Nadia said, a shade reprovingly. "Of course it was she who started the vogue for *la mode anglaise* just after the last war. And yet I find all those tartans and antlers a trifle—how shall I say?—lugubrious."

A far-off tinny sound was heard through the abating rain. Claire winked mischievously at Dr. Bridgewater. "Ah—the secret guest."

Dr. Bridgewater goggled. A moment later the maid ushered a humid figure into the room. It was Irving Kelso.

"Dr. Bridgewater, I presume?" he said with a broad grin and outstretched hand.

Everyone expressed shock, but in fact, no one was too surprised. It had appeared likely for some time that Irving would win the salesman-of-the-year award from his company, which took the form of a round-trip ticket to Paris. Even before the Bridgewaters had left New York, he had hinted darkly at running into them in Harry's Bar, or some such.

When Victor had spelled this out for Nadia and Paul, the latter asked, "And just what is it this company makes that he sells so well?" His face bore the expression of one who every now and again dips into *l'Humanité*.

"Oh what difference does that make?" Claire said. "The point is, he's here. But what—" she scanned the depths of the vestibule—"have you done with Mme. Kelso *mère*?"

Irving looked grave. "Well, you know—or I guess actually you don't—Fluffy passed away. I was really glad of this chance to get Mildred out of the apartment and away from all the associations. She's at the hotel, lying down. It was a pretty bumpy flight."

"Poor Fluffy," Claire said. "I always remember him."

There was a moment of respectful silence, in which Paul and Nadia joined with puzzled expressions, not certain that they were registering enough emotion. Finally Claire resumed her role of Mistress of Revels. "You must be absolutely parched," she said, taking a martini from a silver salver held out by the maid and offering it to Irving. "Here, try this on for size."

"But, Mr. Kelso," Nadia said, "you need not gulp. There is yet time for another wee drop."

Esperanza, the maid, continued to circulate with the pitcher of martinis. Claire glanced at it warily, as though able to judge the degree of dryness. "How are they?" she asked of Victor, who was on his third, in tones of sincere concern. "It is the one thing we French, with all our experience of wines and cognacs, never seem to be able to do right."

"They taste fine to me," Victor said. "I like the kind of gin you get over here, or whatever it is."

"I'd like to ask you a question," Mrs. Bridgewater said to Nadia during a lull in the conversation. "A friend of mine back home has asked me to bring her some old prints—something she can have framed to hang in the living room. Do you know where I could get some?"

"What kind of prints?" Nadia asked.

Mrs. Bridgewater frowned. "Her living room is done in pleasantly muted tones, with a few heirloom pieces mixed in."

Nadia smiled understandingly. "I think a few *vues d'optique* ought to fill the bill. I shall keep my eye open for you."

Meantime, Fabia was saying to Paul, "In other words, you enjoy all the excitement of a dangerous sport, without running any of the risks."

"Say, that's quite a smell coming from the kitchen," Irving said to Claire. "What is it?"

"I persuaded Esperanza to make her famous *arroz con pollo*," Claire said. "It's really the thing she does best."

At the sound of these words, Victor placed his martini glass on the piano, kicked aside a small scatter rug, and brought his heels down smartly on the parquet. "*Olé!*" he shouted. "*Olé! Olé!*"

Esperanza hastily announced dinner.

When it was over they returned to the salon. The rain had stopped, and above the dripping trees a few stars could be seen between the clouds. Claire flung open the doors to the balcony, and a gust of wind tore through the apartment. When Paul and Victor had succeeded in closing them, they rejoined the others, who were grouped around a small coal fire in a grate.

"I believe I read somewhere—perhaps in Anatole France," Dr. Bridgewater said, "that the Paris weather is as fickle as a woman."

"Actually the weather is always terrible here," Nadia said, "especially in the month of June. And we Parisiennes are faithful in our fashion," she added kittenishly.

This sally appeared to leave Dr. Bridgewater somewhat at a loss, and Claire interposed the suggestion that they go out to a near-by cabaret. Mrs. Bridgewater replied that she had always wanted to see the Lapin Agile, and wondered if it was still open. It was not so very long before they were there and seated at the best table, while a guitarist bent over Mrs. Bridgewater and serenaded her with a song from the Belle Epoque, which neither Claire nor Nadia showed much interest in translating.

"Do you travel a lot?" Paul asked Irving Kelso.

"Yes and no," was the reply.

"I don't get it," Paul said, frowning.

Irving, who was afraid he might have offended the foreigner —for so he thought of him—hastened to explain. "I mean—I'm constantly on the move between New York and Dayton, Ohio —but I don't know if you'd call that travel. A trip to Paris on the other hand . . ." He rolled his eyes suggestively and made a gesture traditionally associated with French chefs.

Paul nodded. "I understand," he said. "As we say here, 'It's the icing on the cake.'"

"That's funny," Irving said. "My mother often says that, though she knows no French."

"That's funny," Paul said.

Victor, whom the Beaujolais at dinner had decidedly not rendered less boisterous, downed his *cerises à l'eau de vie*, spat out the pits, and plunked his glass on the table. "*Garçon—on a soif!*" he thundered.

He received a look of brief surprise from his companions, perhaps for his unexpected command of idiom.

The waiter brought fresh drinks for everyone, though the others had scarcely touched theirs. The guitarist, meantime, had struck up a jangling lament. Turning to Nadia, Fabia murmured, "If we give him some money, will he go away?"

"I'm afraid he would be terribly offended," Nadia said. "But after the next song, he *will* be expecting a little something." Fabia relayed this to her father, and the situation was dealt with accordingly.

They did not long remain in peace, however. A grizzled octogenarian wearing a smock and beret and carrying a large pad under his arm soon approached the table with an offer to sketch Mrs. Bridgewater's portrait, and, at the doctor's insistence, did so.

Irving now began to mellow to the scene. After tugging on his drink and releasing a smoke ring, he turned to Paul and said, "Tell me, Paul—is this where the Paris artists congregate? Or is it just an act they put on for the tourists?"

Claire dipped her fingers in her drink and playfully flicked a few drops at Irving. "Do not play the philistine," she said. "No artists have been sighted in this district since the Bateau Lavoir sank."

III

"Do you find it's harder to bear your friends' little idiosyncrasies when you're on a trip?" Alice asked. "I suppose it's the same principle that makes you go out of your way to be friendly to people you'd hardly speak to at home."

"On the liner I did have a feeling," Fabia said, "that the Bridgewater family was taking part in a revival of Tolstoy's *Resurrection*."

Victor exhaled a puff of smoke, which was quickly wafted over the boat railing in the direction of some trees bordering the river. "These are more like cigars than cigarettes," he said. "Except you don't inhale with cigars."

"I am a veteran smoker," Paul Lambert said, "since thirteen. But I never inhale. In that way I maintain my health."

"What's the point of smoking if you don't inhale?" Victor asked.

"Sometimes I have the feeling that I've seen all this before," Alice said.

"You did—from my car, a few minutes ago," Paul said, with a laugh. "Paris is a very small city," he added in a more serious tone. "You see the statue of the Zouave on that bridge? We have the habit of measuring the water level with it. When the Zouave has wet feet, the level is high."

"Is *that* the one," Victor said. "I nearly missed it."

"That street over there should make you feel homesick," Paul continued, obviously beginning to warm to his task. "It's called New-York. I have an aunt who lives in it. Her name is Marie-Louise but we all call her Loulou."

"Is that the aunt who owns the Théodore Rousseaus and the Diazes?" Fabia asked.

"No. Aunt Eulalie is more a cousin of one of my grandmothers. She lives at Rennes. Well, near it."

Alice frowned. Perhaps she wished the conversation would take on a more personal character. But she said nothing.

"A *centime* for your thoughts," Victor said, resting his elbows beside hers.

Alice's frown deepened slightly, but she made an effort to overcome her annoyance. "I was just thinking about the movie we saw last night. I hated it—except for the last five minutes."

"*Esquimaux Gervais!*" Victor cried in a falsetto voice. "*Esquimaux Gervais!*" A number of people—French, no doubt—turned to stare at him.

"Do you like the French ice cream better or the American?" Paul suggested to Fabia.

"You like anything," Victor said, "that's about a woman walking down a long empty road."

"It's getting rather chilly out here," Fabia said as though in reply to Paul's question. "Shall we go in?"

Just then an unseen hand caused some klieg lights to shoot their beams up into the trees. *"Comme c'est féerique,"* Paul said in a solemn voice.

"That's a dumb remark, even coming from you," Alice said, though her tone seemed to disguise a certain admiration for Victor.

Victor spoke more confidentially. "Listen, Alice, I wish you'd tell me: what did Marshall say when you said you weren't going to the Adirondacks?"

Alice shrugged.

"Yes, we may go in if you like," Paul said. But no one seemed in a hurry to move. Without warning, a rocket climbed high into the sky, where it exploded. Paul turned a complacent face to his American friends. "With the renewed interest in promoting tourism, every day is Bastille Day."

Everyone waited for another rocket, but none was forthcoming. Instead, from a loudspeaker harrowingly close at hand, there began to issue the strains of "Musetta's Waltz."

"Would anyone like a Coca-Cola?" Paul asked.

"I'll get them," Victor said, and went charging off.

"I wouldn't mind one of those jaw-breaker ham sandwiches you seem to feature over here," Alice said. "And a glass of soda water."

With an open glance, Fabia appraised Alice's robust figure. "Don't you want to save some room for the onion soup? According to Baedeker, hearty helpings are the rule at Les Halles."

"In this country," Paul said, "it is possible to eat and eat without ever gaining any weight." Alice exhibited her profile to the night.

Victor came back with some small bottles of what appeared to be a powerful orange dye. "They ran out of Coca-Cola," he said apologetically.

"Just a minute, sir, your change, please," said a waiter who had been pursuing Victor. He seemed startled when Victor accepted it, and walked angrily away.

Alice yawned and shuffled her feet. " 'Stand close around, ye Stygian set,' " she said. "Doesn't this *bateau ivre* ever dock?"

Paul looked crestfallen. "I guess boats are not much fun," he said. "Would you like to go to some night clubs? I could take you to one in Montmartre that is frequented by gangsters."

"Anything," Fabia said, "so long as we don't wind up at another Akim Tamiroff festival. However, I am determined to visit the site of *Les Funambules*."

"I'm not sure I know where that is," Paul said.

"Frankly, I'd settle for a hot bath and the English weeklies," Alice said as the boat crunched to a stop next to a dock. "But—*vive l'aventure!*"

A. R. AMMONS

◑

Guitar Recitativos

from *Hudson Review*

1

I know you love me, baby
I know it by the way you carry on around here certain times of
  the day and night
I can make the distinction between the willing and the unre-
  fusable
That's not what I'm talking about
That's not what I need
What I mean is could you just peel me a few of those grapes
  over there
I want to lie here cool and accumulate
Oh say about half a bunch
That's what I need—flick out those little seed—
Just drop them in here one at a time
I'm not going anyplace, baby, not today
Relax—sneak the skin off a few of those grapes for me, will you?

2

Baby, you been stomping round on my toes so long
they breaking out in black and blue hyacinths,
well-knit forget-me-nots
Geraniums are flopping out over the tops of my shoes
tendril leaves coming out along the edges of my shoelaces

Gladioli are steering out of the small of my back
strumming those cool stalks up my spine

Zinnias radiating from the crock of my neck
and petunias swinging down bells from my earlobes
All this stomping around on me you been doing, baby,
I'm gonna break out in a colorful reaction
I'm gonna wade right through you
with the thorns of all these big red roses

3

I'm tired of the you-and-me thing
I am for more research into the nature of the amorous bond
the discovery of catalysts for speeding-up, wearing out,
    and getting it over with
or for slowing it down to allow long intervals of looseness

Baby, there are times when the mixture becomes immiscible
and other times we get so stirred up I can't tell
whether I'm you or me
and then I have this fear of a surprising reaction in which
we both turn into something else

powdery or gaseous or slightly metallic
What I mean is this whole relationship is, lacking further
knowledge, risky: while there's still time, why
don't you get yourself together and I'll

get myself together and then we'll sort of shy out
of each other's gravitational field, unstring the
electromagnetism, and then sort of just drop this
whole orientation, baby

4

I can tell you what I think of your beauty, baby,
you have it, it's keen and fast, there's this
glittery sword whipping about your head all day
and, baby, you make people snap—you condescend

and a surprised little heart splatters or you turn your
cold head away and a tiny freeze kills a few
cells in some man's brain—I mean, baby, you
may be kind but your beauty, sweetie, is such

many a man would run himself through for
hating your guts every minute that he died for you

5

You come in and I turn on:
freon purrs and the
refrigerator breaks out with hives of ice:
the Westinghouse portable electric fan flushes
my papers all over the room:
the waffle-iron whacks down sizzling imaginary waffles:
one paper glues itself and billows to the back of the fan,
my nerves nervous as newspapers.

I tell you, you are a walking calamity
And when you sit down there is hardly less activity:
the alarm clock breaks out raging its held cry
and the oven in the kitchen sets itself for broil:
I mean the gas-jet in the incinerator bloops on
and, frankly, the mechanisms in my legs—I hope you
      never find out—jerk:
Oh, beauty, beauty is so disturbingly nice.

JAMES APPLEWHITE

House of Blue
by the River's Curve

from *The Brown Bag*

Riding with the roiled sheen of the river
      we in a canoe
coasted haunting bends
         with that current.

Over a clay bank it carved against,
      from far upon cloud-touched sky,
a white house hollow with windows and light
         looked back at us.

Fields were lazy and rich before;
      curved corn
         raised itself
without a fieldhand in sight.

The house in its standing oaks shone clear;
      a lane ineffably familiar under the trees,
winding its length back into me,
               touched beneath memory.

Landscapes, green lawns, stirred unseen.

It seemed I held the jugs for our water
      one in each hand; in one shone a circle

which lapped each step.
            The sand path led

through an atmosphere,
            with fields' depth, breath of the river,
like part of the live far sky
      brought incredibly blue and rare to earth.

When I came close to the wooden steps
      the blue morning glories that twined
a latticed railing held my eyes,
            held to me dew from early dawn.

The porch with grain scrubbed white as lint
      answered my footsteps
            hollow, familiar.
I rapped on the flimsy screendoor frame.

Linoleum held yellow light and worn red flowers.

A pump in a sink in the kitchen
      stung my nose with well water and iron.
Its handle curved
         like a snake or a river.

My eyes paused, stared into the electrically
      vacant spout as if drawn by a spark.
I clinked one jug onto speckled enamel
        and pried the handle.

A crystalline sensation
         rang through the house in a shiver.
My hand under a petal of water
      froze to the bell-round glass.

I knew sun-color of her hair from the sound
      of her voice, from the cleanly smell

of a cotton frock
                    the scrubbed white flesh of her arms.

She knew me well. We talked for a timeless
                hour; while she was gathering lunch
I forgot my brother by the river.
                                    From corners,

from the worn rug and print cotton drapes,
                dust in sunlight behind the flowered sofa,
scents of the past
                        came real to touch me.

The house of thin boards lithe to weight
                moved sensitively around me.
                                            I felt it

balance, with sky's cold drift,
                the diurnal arc of sunlight stealing
across a tin roof that creaked by degrees.

We walked through the company parlor
                where a cabinet jingled.
                                    Musty
with plush upholstery, the room opened
                one wide window onto low fields and river
curved blue beyond.
                        Barred across the sky
and the sun-flashing torso of water
                were glass slats set as shelves.

The skin of my neck prickled with recognition;
                my feelings handled with an accustomed grasp
those shapes of recollection
                                sharp below thought.

A curled dry leaf in a vase of azure glass
                enclosed one autumn day I'd held my kite

(the twine a curve from the new moon's rim)
        deep in a sky of transparent stone.

A crystal waterglass with its twisted twig
        was the spring day I'd climbed
in a sprouting pecan tree
            with my cousin.

Broomstraw in an earthenware jar
        curved the cold walk of myself,
                my brother,
toward home with a shining duck we'd killed
           through fields dust-pale in the moonlight.

Tears blurred my sight of the chunks of quartz,
        driftwood knots and the figurines,
that one agate marble in its amber jar.

Who was she to have collected again
        those objects of feeling lost out of pockets
down scattered trips
          into so many waters?

I heard the steps of another man's presence;
        when I stood still they ceased.
              I wondered—
had her husband returned from the fields?
        I turned to show her my questioning face.

"You are the beloved image of my only son,"
        she said, her eyes on me and into my life.

"And our father?"

           "He tends the fields unseen.
The curved corn, the river,
           are arced from his strength.

The air which fills this house and the fields
        burns blue and rare with the flame of his love,
of which the emblem is the grace of dew."

"I saw it on the blue morning glories,"
        I said.

                "That color he has given to me."

"And why is it you
                who fish stones from the river?"

"He completes himself like the sun's circumference;
        merciful as the moon, I nurse all broken arcs,
draw to me wandering water which stumbles
        only toward his circle in turning,
                                in glances.
I keep in this house the broken, imperfect
        bends from your course till he fits them together.
I have the loop of your kitestring, sway
        of broomstraw,
                both toward the moon my mirror."

She gestured toward a mirror tall as my height,
        silver with an horizon faced through the door.
It held the lane I must travel backward,
        knowing and guessing,
                        under green trees.

I stepped to go, then turned again to the reflection.

In the middle of my body
                        I saw a child in a field of grass.

Above my shoulder was her head's silhouette
        on the sky, long hair falling

                              in the curve of a hood;
The look of her face was horizon's blue.

We rounded the bend with brown flow ridged by speed.
        My brother looked back at me. Our eyes
fell wistfully to the emptied jugs;
                              we'd both

had our dream in sight of that house, been caught
        from the instant of turning,
                              returned.
We'd neither one waited in the canoe ashore.

JOHN D. BOYD, S.J.

◗

The Dry Salvages:
Topography as Symbol

from *Renascence*

Cape Ann in Massachusetts is one of the more plentifully documented areas of the country in tourist literature and in books of local color and history. Details of historical and literary interest are carefully noted in brochures and guide maps. Kipling's *Captains Courageous* and James B. Connolly's *Gloucestermen* are rightly remembered. Summer visits of minor New England literary figures are duly recorded, and reference is ubiquitous to the Reef of Norman's Woe off the Magnolia side of Gloucester Harbor, immortalizing Longfellow's "Wreck of the Hesperus." Yet one looks in vain for any notice of Cape Ann's most distinguished literary event, T. S. Eliot's *The Dry Salvages*, despite his explicit note preceding the poem: "(The Dry Salvages—presumably *les trois sauvages*—is a small group of rocks, with a beacon, off the N.E. coast of Cape Ann, Massachusetts. *Salvages* is pronounced to rhyme with assuages. *Groaner:* a whistling buoy.)" [1] I found a recent visit to the museum of the Cape

[1] T. S. Eliot, *Collected Poems 1909–1962* (New York, 1963), p. 191. All references to Eliot's poetry are quoted from this edition by permission of Harcourt, Brace and World, Inc. I am especially indebted to Mrs. Henry Ware Eliot, Jr., the poet's sister-in-law, for information about several details of his life, shared in a gracious interview with Fr. J. Robert Barth, S.J. I must also thank Fr. Barth, who very obligingly helped me in several ways, Mr. W. H. Bond of the Houghton Library at Harvard, for permission to quote from the Henry Ware Eliot, Jr., Collection, and Mr. Wallace A. Bruder of the United States Department of

Ann Scientific, Literary and Historical Association in Gloucester no more rewarding. Apart from a few of his published books, the Sawyer Free Library in the same town has only a small collection of photos of Eliot and a drawing by his sister. Even the detailed and very readable *Saga of Cape Ann* of Melvin Copeland and Elliott Rogers (1960) passes the poem over in silence, though it does speak of the danger to navigation offered by the rocks for which Eliot named the third of his *Four Quartets*.

In a more directly academic context, however, two studies have recently appeared which do deal to some extent with the Cape Ann background of the poem. These are Herbert Howarth's *Notes on Some Figures Behind T. S. Eliot* and Samuel Eliot Morison's "The Dry Salvages and the Thacher Shipwreck." Though both speak of the poem in a general way, Howarth's interest is largely biographical and Morison's one of regional history and nomenclature. Neither is concerned with the subject of this paper, namely the strong intrinsic connection between the Cape Ann topography and the Eliot poem.[2] The better known commentators on the poem have regularly been satisfied with a general reference to the Cape Ann background and its influence. Although *The Dry Salvages* is not really a descriptive poem but mythic and depth-symbolic in its ultimate concern, nevertheless I believe that the details offered here and the interpretation suggested should enrich the reading of the poem.

Commerce for some valuable geodetic and naval information. Finally I wish to thank the following for certain incidental information and suggestions: Mrs. Margaret Ferrini, Dr. Walter J. Bate, Jr., Frs. Vincent Blehl, S.J., Edwin Cuffe, S.J., James Finley, S.J., William Power, S.J., and Robert Tobin, S.J.

[2] Herbert Howarth, *Notes on Some Figures Behind T. S. Eliot* (Boston, 1964), pp. 113–21; Samuel Eliot Morison, "The Dry Salvages and the Thacher Shipwreck," in *The American Neptune*, XXV (1965), 233–247. I originally completed most of my research independently of these two studies, but have since found them valuable, especially Morison's careful search into the origin of the name of the Dry Salvages. In the course of the paper, however, I shall have reason to differ on some minor details with both of them.

I tend to agree with Miss Gardner's passing comment about Eliot's Cape Ann experience that has been transformed in the poem: "As always when he writes of the sea the poetry has great freedom and power; and in this poem, for the first time in the Quartets, the natural imagery is used boldly and beautifully, and, as it were, for its own sake. The landscape of *The Dry Salvages* is a landscape remembered, for this poem is not about the present, but about the past as it is known in the present, in our consciousness of it through memory." [3] The scenery of the poem, though of the sea, which "is the land's edge also," is not quite the same as that of Dover or even of Cape Cod, but uniquely that of Cape Ann. Eliot's early impressionable years in the neighborhood and his experience of later visits surely called profoundly, yet uniquely, to what Jungian depths the images of the sea have for us all. And the poet in him then fetched us the broader and more universal meaning which his poem achieves. Miss Drew has wisely observed: "The poet's own experience flows into the poem through the identification of the river with the Mississippi, and the rocks and sea with the New England Coast. But the tone changed from that of purely personal introspection to that where the poet is the individual interpreter of general human experience." [4] In a broader context Albert Cook offers a pertinent reminder of what is true of all symbolism: "All symbolism must start from actual facts and symbolize them, rather than combine them in merely logical patterns." [5] The topography which I identify here has in itself a biographical interest for students of Eliot. But, more important, without being either "affective" or "intentional" in my criticism, I wish to claim that both cumulatively and in detail this topography offers evidence of being a peculiarly realistic basis for the symbolism of the rocks and the sea in the poem, and that these symbols have a peculiarly realistic structure and character precisely because of

[3] Helen Gardner, *The Art of T. S. Eliot* (New York, 1950), p. 170.
[4] Elizabeth Drew, *T. S. Eliot: The Design of His Poetry* (New York, 1949), p. 177.
[5] Albert Cook, *The Dark Voyage and the Golden Mean* (Cambridge, Mass., 1949), p. 21.

Eliot's Cape Ann experience, later recollected within his Christian point of view, which governs the poem's development.

Eliot has spoken warmly of his impressionable years spent in both areas of the United States which are celebrated in this poem, Missouri and Massachusetts—"The river is within us, the sea is all about us." His family, he says, "guarded jealousy its connections with New England; but it was not until years of maturity that I perceived that I myself had always been a New Englander in the South West, and a South Westerner in New England. . . . In New England I missed the dark river, the ailanthus trees, the flaming cardinal birds, the high limestone bluffs where we searched for fossil shell fish; in Missouri I missed the fir trees, the bay and golden rod, the song sparrows, the red granite and the blue sea of Massachusetts." [6]

In another interview reported in the St. Louis Globe Democrat Eliot gives a slight edge to his Missouri impressions: "Of course my people were Northerners and New Englanders, and of course I have spent many years out of America altogether; but Missouri and the Mississippi have made a deeper impression on me than any other part of the world." [7] Yet it is clear, for our present purposes, that The Dry Salvages reflects much more of the Cape Ann days than those spent in the West. At all events, we need only recall what Eliot wrote in The Use of Poetry and the Use of Criticism to guess through metonymy how rich and pervasive his memory of Cape Ann days was. Here he speaks of "the experience of a child of ten, a small boy peering through sea water in a rock-pool, and finding a sea-anemone for the first time." [8]

EAST GLOUCESTER. T. S. Eliot (1888–1965) likely first saw the

---

[6] Quoted from an interview reported by Cristian Smidt, Poetry and Belief in the Work of T. S. Eliot (London, 1961), p. 4.

[7] From an interview with M. C. Childs in the St. Louis Globe Democrat (1930), by permission of the Harvard College Library.

[8] T. S. Eliot, The Use of Poetry and the Use of Criticism (London, 1933), pp. 78–79. The strong impact of memory upon imagination is stated in more general terms in this same context: "There is so much memory in imagination that if you are to distinguish between imagination and fancy in Coleridge's way, you must define the difference between memory in imagination and memory in fancy."

Cape Ann region when he was five years old, in 1893. In all he would have spent nineteen summers in the area, including the summer of 1911. These spanned the years of his grammar and prep schools, his undergraduate days at Harvard College, and the year he was a graduate student and teaching-fellow at Harvard University. After that time he visited the neighborhood only for a few days in 1915, when he returned from abroad, and again in 1960.[9]

The Senior Eliot had a house built especially for the family on Edgemoor Road in East Gloucester. This included a fireplace made from bricks carried from their St. Louis home. On the occasion of the first American edition of *The Dry Salvages*, Eliot's brother, Henry Ware Eliot, Jr. (1879–1947), sent a letter to the Sawyer Free Library in Gloucester, which reads in part: "My brother spent some 20 summers [a round number, I take it] as a child and a youth at Eastern Point where my father had a house on the top of the hill back of the old Beachcroft hotel. The poem reflects a very deep affection for these scenes." [10] The house still stands on Edgemoor Road, now owned by the Cahill family. The road was named for the large moor it bordered, still partially there though partially built upon, but in those days it swept spaciously down to the sea. The Eliot house commanded a 270-degree panoramic view: northwestward and westward to the Gloucester Harbor and beyond in the direction of Boston, then, moving counterclockwise, southwestward toward Eastern Point Lighthouse, then southward and eastward over the entire expanse of the Atlantic Ocean, past what is now the Jesuit Eastern Point Retreat House (where I first conceived an interest in this topography), then northeastward and northward over Brace's Cove, Bass Rocks, Thacher Island, Straitsmouth Island, and ultimately to Rockport, off which lie the rocks that give

[9] I am following Mrs. Henry Ware Eliot, Jr., on these dates; see note 1 above. Professor Howarth says Eliot first came to Gloucester in 1895, and that he lived at the Hawthorne Inn until the Edgemoor house was built in 1897, p. 113.

[10] *Gloucester Daily Times*, Feb. 27, 1942, by permission of the Harvard College Library.

their name to the poem. This sweep becomes much more than mere topography when one remembers its issue in:

> the sea is all about us;
> The sea is the land's edge also, the granite
> Into which it reaches, the beaches where it tosses
> Its hints of earlier and other creation.
>
> . . . . . .
>
> The sea howl
> And the sea yelp, are different voices
> Often together heard: the whine in the rigging,
> The menace and caress of wave that breaks on water,
> The distant rote in the granite teeth.

This granite is everywhere along the shore and even well back from it. Eliot, we have seen, remembered its red color, caused by oxidation when the rain and the waters spray it. A picture is extant in the Henry Ware Eliot Collection at Harvard of the Young Eliot playing on a large slab of such granite directly outside the Edgemoor house.

In three poems, the last section of *Ash Wednesday*, the Cape Ann section of *Landscapes*, and in the latest, *The Dry Salvages*, Eliot shows an interesting gradation in his attitude toward the sea. In the first of these childhood memory is alluring, as on a halcyon day, as Miss Gardner says, "looking on it there with longing as on a world hard to renounce." [11]

> (Bless me father) though I do not wish to wish these things
> From the wide window towards the granite shore
> The white sails still fly seaward, seaward flying
> Unbroken wings
>
> And the lost heart stiffens and rejoices
> In the lost lilac and the lost sea voices
> And the weak spirit quickens to rebel
> For the bent golden-rod and the lost sea smell
> Quickens to recover
> The cry of quail and the whirling plover
> And the blind eye creates
> The empty forms between the ivory gates
> And smell renews the salt savour of the sandy earth.

[11] Gardner, p. 170.

In the autumn this neighborhood is alive with goldenrod, and in
the spring with lilac and with the many birds Eliot affectionately counts in the second of these poems. In it, while the materials are still from boyhood memory, his judgment is firm with
resignation and realism:

> Follow the feet
> Of the walker, the water-thrush. Follow the flight
> Of the dancing arrow, the purple martin. Greet
> In silence the bullbat. All are delectable. Sweet sweet sweet
> But resign this land at the end, resign it
> To its true owner, the tough one, the sea-gull.
> The palaver is finished.

The dense litany of birds in this entire section of *Landscapes*
reminds one of the mixture of birds' and children's voices in the
first part of *Burnt Norton*. It seems quite likely that the idea
originated in this East Gloucester terrain. At present there is a
large bird sanctuary of the Audubon Society at Eastern Point,
two miles from the Edgemoor house. At all events, in *The Dry
Salvages*, the third of these poems, the sea becomes the vehicle
of his most realistic response to life. For all its beauty, it is the
primeval and all but insurmountable threat to mankind, to his
entire human condition, needing a redemption well beyond the
devices of childhood imagination:

> It tosses up our losses, the torn seine,
> The shattered lobsterpot, the broken oar
> And the gear of foreign dead men.

THE DRY SALVAGES. Turning from the Eliot house to the near-
by main road, Atlantic Road, going generally northward—"If
you came this way,/Taking the route you would be likely to
take"—you would travel about ten miles to Rockport, a small
fishing village of colonial origin, now shared with the artists.
About a mile and a half offshore, at approximately 42° 40′ 20″
N., 70° 34′ 06″ W., lie the rocks which gave the poem its name.
They are at the center of swift currents, and, as one can observe
on Chart 243 issued by the Coast and Geodetic Survey of the
Department of Commerce, the waters about them are quite
shallow, at times only about three fathom deep. These cold facts

are enough to indicate their danger to ships at sea. *The Saga of Cape Ann* of Copeland and Rogers has the following comment:

> The hazards of navigation in the neighborhood of Thachers and Straightsmouth are rendered substantially more serious by the Salvages—the "savage rocks"—which lie outside Straightsmouth. The Little Salvages are about a mile offshore and the Big Salvages [The Dry], a half-mile farther out. On a clear day the Big Salvages glisten in the sun, whitened by the droppings of myriads of gulls, but in stormy weather those ledges have brought disaster to many a ship.[12]

Although the authors of this passage give no indication of being familiar with Eliot's poem about the rocks, their account echoes the realism of the poet's description:

> And the ragged rock in the restless waters,
> Waves wash over it, fogs conceal it;
> On a halcyon day it is merely a monument,
> In navigable weather it is always a seamark
> To lay a course by: but in the sombre season
> Or the sudden fury, is what it always was.

This topographical realism will have serious import in the second part of this paper for interpreting this central symbol of the poem. It will be an important point of return.

THE GROANER. A central concern of the poem is life as a voyage. The Dry Salvages have frequently been the scene of hazard and of wreck to many returning from fishing ventures on the Grand Banks or to those coming to our shores from across the sea:

[12] Melvin Copeland and Elliott Rogers, *The Saga of Cape Ann* (Freeport, Me., 1960), pp. 132–33. Straitsmouth and Thachers (Thatcher, Thatcher's) are islands due south of the Salvages, with important beacons on them. Thacher is unique in the country for having twin lighthouses. Only one of them is now in use, however. The beacon on the Dry Salvages of which Eliot speaks in his prenote, though there while he was a resident and when he wrote the poem, is no longer there. It was removed through Notice to Mariners 26 of 1945. There is, however, a lighted bellbuoy about a thousand yards N.E. of the rocks, established through Notice to Mariners 44 of 1935. I am grateful to Mr. Bruder for this information.

O voyagers, O seamen,
You who come to port, and you whose bodies
Will suffer the trial and judgment of the sea.

Actually many ships make landfall within sight of these rocks, and then sail along the coast till they round the Eastern Point Lighthouse and are safely inside the Gloucester Harbor. They pass by much of the panoramic sweep described above, and heed "the wailing warning from the approaching headland." *The Saga of Cape Ann* describes this important station:

> For the seafarers of Cape Ann, Eastern Point has always been an outstanding landmark. Located at a sharp angle on a rocky shore, it indicates dangerous rocks and reefs to be shunned and marks the entrance to Gloucester Harbor from the east, a point to be rounded to reach a haven of safety in foul weather.[13]

In 1812 the station had a beacon and lantern, which were replaced in 1831 by a modern lighthouse. In 1904 a breakwater, the Dog Bar Reef, was built westward from the point with a small light at its end. It acts as a powerful breakwater for the harbor, offering safe anchorage after a difficult entry (it is at the opposite side of the harbor from the Reef of Norman's Woe). Though constructed of many granite slabs twelve ton in weight, this wall was recently broken through at one point by a winter storm, reminding us that the sea as well as the river keeps "his seasons and rages." A further defense against the sea's ravages was installed about 1880, Eliot's "heaving groaner/Rounded homewards." A notation in *The Saga of Cape Ann* corroborates that this is the spot Eliot had in mind: "As an additional aid to navigation a whistling buoy [Eliot's very phrase in the prenote] was placed, in 1880, in the ocean off Eastern Point." [14] Today it, or its successor, heaves and groans even on a relatively calm day.

---

13 Copeland and Rogers, p. 69. Morison places the Groaner east of Thacher Island, "and the 'wailing warning' of the diaphone on Thacher's itself." I prefer to think of both of these at the voyage end, rounding Eastern Point, partly for the sweep of the terrain involved, mentioned earlier, and its consequent inclusion of the entire voyage, and partly because Eliot speaks of the "wailing warning from the approaching *headland*," whereas Thacher is an island. Morison, 234–35.
14 Copeland and Rogers, pp. 69–70.

An interesting bit of minor literary history surrounds the early days of this buoy. Copeland and Rogers record that Elizabeth Stuart Phelps was one of the more distinguished early summer residents of East Gloucester. A minor literary personage, she opened her home, "Old Maid's Paradise" on Grapevine Road, to literary celebrities and a few boarders. Longfellow is said to have first seen the Reef of Norman's Woe from her cottage. The noise from the groaner, however, annoyed Miss Phelps "who was then suffering from a nervous ailment." Subsequently to her complaints the United States Secretary of the Navy gave orders "to have the buoy taken up in May and put out again in October." This occasioned a sort of town-and-gown conflict with the year-round fishermen, who claimed that the solution endangered their safety. Shortly afterward, however, the problem was solved from an unexpected source. Miss Phelps soon married the Reverend Herbert Ward, a clergyman sixteen years her junior, who had been a boarder at her cottage during the summer, while a sloop he had commissioned was being built. *The Boston Record* summarily commented: "Since her marriage Mrs. Ward is much better, and the officer who had to remove the buoy has put it back with the assurance that next summer he will have no orders to disturb it." [15] The buoy still whistles and groans.

THE SHRINE ON THE PROMONTORY. From the Dog Bar Reef referred to above one can view the town of Gloucester encompassing the harbor and rising above it like a huge scallop shell. Dominating this view is the church of the Portuguese fishermen on Prospect Street, the Church of Our Lady of Good Voyage. The original structure was built in 1893 but destroyed by fire in 1914. It was replaced the following year by the present building, modeled on a church on the Island of San Miguel in the Azores. It is finished in white stucco with blue-capped twin towers, one of which houses a 31-bell carillon, the first in this country, installed in 1922.[16] The church is tastefully decorated in nautical

---

[15] *Ibid.*, p. 70.
[16] Kitty Parsons, *The Story of the Church of Our Lady of Good Voyage* (North Montpelier, Vt., 1945), pp. 7–11; Howarth, p. 118.

fashion. Outside between the towers stands a life-size statue of the Lady sustaining a fishing vessel in her outstretched arm. Inside over the main altar is another statue of her holding the Christ Child in one arm and a ship in the other. The windows, too, depict various scenes and aspects of her life, frequently including the ubiquitous ship as symbol. Her features are somewhat swarthy and Portuguese. These windows are the gifts of captains and seamen. The rear tribune displays five model ships, two of them Gloucester schooners, together with a life preserver, gifts of "Thomas Fortune Ryan of Virginia." Though Eliot was more familiar with the previous structure, he had opportunity to see the new one during his visit in 1915.

The "Lady whose shrine is on the promontory" has as pervasive a presence in the poem as she has in the church's *décor*, and, indeed, in the Christian tradition. Eliot's reference to Dante's *Paradiso* (xxxiii, 1), "Figlia del tuo figlio," shows her as the paradoxical context of God's Incarnation, "of whose human substance God was made man, the timeless taking the temporal to itself." [17] Her presence in the Christian tradition as Star of the Sea has the proportions of an archetypal image. The well-known ninth-century hymn, still used in the Roman Liturgy, the *"Ave Maris Stella,"* reflects this imagery. Because she is God's human Mother (*Dei mater alma*) she is also a Star (*maris stella*) to the redeemed on the sea of life (*iter para tutum*), leading to the "heaven-haven of the/Reward" (*felix coeli porta*). Eliot uses this same pervasive image; and when the sea bell becomes the angelus bell, the complicated themes of the poem receive a taut clarity. It is interesting to note that by the identification of these two bells the entire expanse of the sea, from the Dry Salvages and beyond to the harbor, is united, and becomes the redeemed arena where the fishermen must struggle, leaving and returning to harbor many times before reaching the heaven-haven of the reward. [18]

[17] Grover Smith, *T. S. Eliot's Poetry and Plays: A Study in Sources and Meaning* (Chicago, 1956), p. 283.
[18] Herbert Musurillo, S.J., *Symbolism and the Christian Imagination* (Baltimore, 1962), pp. 133–34. The hymn *"Ave Maris Stella"* occurs

GLOUCESTER. Gloucester has long been famous as a fisherman's town. Though the volume of trade is considerably lessened to-day and the town depends as well upon tourists and permanent summer guests, it still sustains a substantial fishing community. Fishermen of various sorts come and go day and night, for short trips to the lobster beds along Cape Ann or for long hauls off the Grand Banks of Newfoundland. The town is alive with history and with its own contemporary concerns, concerns of "those/Whose business has to do with fish." This fits the dominant mood of the poem, which deals with ultimates only through the daily round of the commonplace. Here one will find lobster pots, shattered or whole, oars, broken or pliant, and "every lawful traffic," as indication of the on-going quality of human life. Though fish processing is mechanized, the name of Gorton still greets one as a familiar American trademark. One readily thinks of the fifth stanza of the second section of the poem:

We have to think of them as forever bailing,
Setting and hauling, while the North East lowers
Over shallow banks unchanging and erosionless
Or drawing their money, drying sails at dockage;
Not as making a trip that will be unpayable
For a haul that will not bear examination.

Here too, as in other New England towns, one finds an occasional "widow's walk," a mute reminder of the terror of the sea. It is a porch high atop a house, where an anxious wife would pace while awaiting the uncertain return of her husband at sea. In the publisher's preface to the 1928 edition of James B. Connolly's *Fishermen of the Banks*, written according to Haworth by Eliot, we read: "There is no harder life, no more uncertain livelihood, and few more dangerous occupations" than that of the fishermen. And: "Gloucester has many widows, and no trip is without anxiety for those at home." [19] This awareness enters

---

in Vespers common to the feasts of the Blessed Virgin Mary in the *Breviarium Romanum*.
[19] Howarth, p. 117; James B. Connolly, *Fishermen of the Banks* (London, 1928), pp. vii–viii. Howarth also speaks of a widow's walk on the Edgemoor house, which at present, at least, is no longer there, p. 114.

the theme of the poem, when he speaks of these "anxious worried women":

> Trying to unweave, unwind, unravel
> And piece together the past and the future,
> Between midnight and dawn, when the past is all deception.

The Portuguese fishermen of Gloucester also hold a memorable fiesta in June, marked by the solemn blessing of the fleet, as well as a "Crown Service" at the Lady church on Trinity Sunday, begun in 1902, in thanksgiving for a rescue from a disaster at sea. The beliefs of these fishermen mix easily with their daily round of work, as the names of their boats well suggest. Finally, from the Gloucester Harbor the famous statue of the Gloucester Fisherman peers out to sea with a look that has about it something of the archetypal eternity of the Scriptural quotation on its base: "They that go down to the sea in ships" (Psalm 106, 23). Though it marks three hundred years of Gloucester's lifetime (1623–1923), one feels that it marks "a time/Older than the time of chronometers."

The topography of Cape Ann is very beautiful and attractive. "On a halcyon day" it can even tempt one to romantic reveries about the sea. But the beauty of Eliot's poem is of a far deeper sort, a poignant and at times almost terrifying beauty of "the hardly, barely prayable/Prayer of the one Annunciation." It leads us to revise any too easy notion of the beauty of the sea we may have formed and of the other hidden forces in life which Eliot has it symbolize. Like the river, the sea is

> ever, however, implacable
> Keeping his seasons and rages, destroyer, reminder
> Of what men choose to forget.

We can never quite become "worshippers of the machine," when even within the past few years at least four shipwrecks have been recorded in the neighborhood, that of the *Ohio*, a fishing trawler, off "Mother Ann" (a rock formation, resembling an old woman's face, just north of the Eastern Point Light), that of a pleasure craft off the Reef of Norman's Woe, and those of the tanker *Lucy* and the Navy minesweeper *Grouse* on the Salvages themselves. This "realism" of fact, I believe, has effectively entered the tone and structure of the main symbols which Eliot has incorporated in his poem.[20]

To stop, then, at the mere recital of topography would be like having "had the experience but missed the meaning." Yet the meaning of the symbols which rise out of the topography enjoys a peculiar character precisely because, as Miss Gardner has already been quoted as saying: "The landscape of *The Dry Salvages* is a landscape remembered." I suggest that this symbolism, especially of the sea and the rocks and of the plight of the fishermen, has a peculiarly realistic quality. I use the word "realistic" largely in an epistemological context, with, however, psychological and anthropological overtones. This quality refers to structure, theme and tone. Further, transforming and intensifying this realism is a structure best seen as deriving from a Christian imagination—an "approach to the meaning restores the experience/In a different form."

It is commonplace to say that Eliot's poetry is deeply indebted to the French *Symboliste* tradition. It is also commonplace to say that this tradition, as its theory and practice developed from Baudelaire through Rimbaud and Valéry, became more and more self-enclosed and private in tone and meaning. The strong idealist tendencies of its epistemology and its premises of the poet's isolation from society are well known.[21]

Whatever Eliot's rather rarefied and complex epistemological interests in his Harvard days, such as we find in his recently published thesis on F. H. Bradley, *Knowledge and Experience*, by the time of the *Quartets* his Christian belief had surely directed his imagination toward a more communal realism. This seems clear enough from the tenor of these poems, and in the preface to *Knowledge and Experience* we note: "Forty-six years after my academic philosophizing came to an end, I find myself

[20] I am grateful to Mr. Lorne G. Taylor of the United States Department of Commerce for some of this information. Also see Morison, 233. Copeland and Rogers speak of the long history of wreckage that has attended the Gloucester fleet, p. 119.

[21] William Wimsatt, Jr., and Cleanth Brooks, *Literary Criticism: A Short History* (New York, 1957), pp. 590 ff.

unable to think in the terminology of this essay. Indeed, I do not pretend to understand it." [22]

The strong realism at the heart of Eliot's theme of Christian redemption of time, which pervades the *Quartets,* involves a permeating sense of a transcendent God as the measure of man's meaning, of an objective eternity making sense of man in time. As the four poems progress, the realism involved in this redemption becomes more and more explicit with something of a conelike comprehensive intensity, "at the still point of the turning world." The imagery of *The Dry Salvages* carries with it a rich empirical memory of the physical realities that constitute its raw material. The immediacy of the rocks and the sea and of the fishermen's lives is intensified in poetic transformation, and presents a greater sense of physical reality than, say, the imagery in *Burnt Norton.* In this respect the tone deriving from much of the symbolism of *Little Gidding* is more spiritual or, to use a poor word, more mystical in its reference, reflecting the realm of Grace and the Resurrection; spiritual, yet in a manner quite different from the speculation of *Burnt Norton.* One thinks of the opening passage of *Little Gidding* that begins: "Midwinter spring is its own season," and ending: "Where is the summer, the unimaginable/Zero summer?" At all events, I find a unique sense of the empirical in the dominant imagery of *The Dry Salvages,* and I believe it is due in good part to the impact of the topography just reviewed.

But this realism, Christian as it is, can, perhaps, be more sharply understood if read in the context of the traditional Christian notion of Incarnation as the pattern of human redemption. I am suggesting that the pattern of the Incarnation and of its implications for human redemption has an analogue in the very structure of the symbolism of the rocks and the sea, as well as in what is said of the plight of the fishermen.

As an orthodox Christian, Eliot believed that Christ, the God-Man, is a Divine Person eternally subsisting in his Divine Nature, but also subsisting in the created human nature He as-

<hr>

[22] T. S. Eliot, *Knowledge and Experience in the Philosophy of F. H. Bradley* (New York, 1964), p. 10.

sumed in time. Because of the latter He became capable of human activity and experience. Further, He offered his redemptive sacrifice and rose from the dead in his human nature, although these were actions of a Divine Person. Though this is neither the time nor place for a long discussion of this central mystery of Christianity, it should be noted that the orthodox believer has always jealously guarded the unity of the Divine Person of Christ in both natures, yet the independence or nonconfusion of these natures with each other. The Athanasian Creed reflects this faith of the Church against such a doctrine as Monophysitism, held by Apollinarius of Laodocea, which taught that in Christ the Divine Nature absorbed the human nature into itself.[23]

The theological and psychological implications of this seemingly rarified subject are substantial. If the life of the redeemed is modeled on the pattern of Christ and his redeeming activity, it is important to note that the human has not been bypassed or absorbed into the divine. For the redeemed the human situation must be embraced entirely as it is; and though it is redeemed, graced, and in a very meaningful way divinized, all its human implications, including the effects of sin, must be faced squarely. Hence all the antihuman or escapist forms of Christianity are not considered orthodox in this context. Christ brought the human and the divine together, in fact united them in his person; but he did not confuse them, nor have either of them cancel the other out. The victory of the divine was not at the expense of the truly human. Human realism, then, is the key to Christian realism; and the Christian imagination, which can reasonably be predicated of Eliot in this poem, will reflect this pattern. In his essay on Christian imagination, *Christ and Apollo*, Father William Lynch sums up the theological basis in the Incarnation of this imaginative Christian realism in the following comment:

The theologians have their own vocabulary, sometimes with divine sanction: St. Paul seems to attribute the ascension of

[23] Louis Bouyer, of the Oratory, *Dictionary of Theology*, transl. Rev. C. U. Quinn (New York, 1965), p. 311. The Athanasian Creed occurs on Sunday at Prime in the *Breviarium Romanum*.

Christ into Heaven causally to His descent into the earth, and generally we ourselves will be stressing the great fact of Christology, that Christ moved down into all the realities of man to get to His father.[24]

Further, this incarnational pattern is invariably paradoxical both in the light of the incomprehensible meeting, though without confusion, of the human and divine in us, and in the light of the defects and limitations that characterize our persons and our human situation.

I believe that some such approach as this is needed to describe the peculiar structure of the symbolism of the rocks and the sea in *The Dry Salvages*. The on-going daily life of the fishermen (really of all men) is redeemed from the frustrations of isolated time by a proper union with the still point through the "hardly, barely prayable/Prayer of the one Annunciation." Yet, for all that, redemption is not rescue through escape but through immersion in the human in imitation of Christ's archetypal, redeeming act; and the inevitable paradox involved is something of a hither side of the central paradox in Hopkins' *Wreck of the Deutschland*, that of God's mercy in His mastery. The central description of the rocks, the Dry Salvages, shows this most clearly:

And the ragged rock in the restless waters,
Waves wash over it, fogs conceal it;
On a halcyon day it is merely a monument,
In navigable weather it is always a seamark
To lay a course by: but in the sombre season
Or the sudden fury, is what it always was.

When one reads this passage in connection with the prayer of the Lady on the promontory and the fishermen's (and our) hardly, barely prayable share in it, this pattern of Incarnation emerges as quite essential to the poem's theme and its somber tone. To be sure, the pattern is quite somber and lacks the fuller implications of Resurrection, which must wait for the last Quar-

---

[24] William J. Lynch, S.J., *Christ and Apollo: The Dimensions of the Literary Imagination* (New York, 1963), p. 28.

tet. "The tolling bell . . . rung by the unhurried/Ground swell," though now the "sound of the sea bell's/Perpetual angelus," is still a warning to mariners that the "ragged rock . . . is what it always was."

A recent interpretation of this passage seems unaware of this important dimension, rooted as it is in the text and in the topography and theology here outlined. C. A. Bodelsen observes: " 'The ragged rock in the restless waters' is the Faith. 'On a halcyon day it is merely a monument' (i.e., regarded as a venerable cultural heritage). 'In navigable weather it is always a seamark/To lay a course by' (i.e., in normal times it is a guide for right conduct). But 'in the sombre season/Or sudden fury, is what it always was,' in times of distress and despair it remains our only refuge." This interpretation turns Eliot's symbols into allegory, misconstruing both structure and meaning. It leaves the incarnational tension of the timeless and time very slack indeed, and avoids the basic paradox of the rocks and the sea as saviors through danger and destruction. Bodelsen appends a note to this passage about the name of the rocks, implying, I think, the same misunderstanding. "The very name of the rocks, the Dry Salvages, calls up the ideas of a firm foothold in a troubled sea and of salvation." [25] But more of this point in a moment.

From a slightly different vantage point Malcolm Ross seems to corroborate my claim that these symbols are incarnational in pattern (he uses the word "sacramental") and peculiarly topographical in source:

The great achievement of Eliot's *Four Quartets* is, of course, in the sacramental re-possession of nature and time, things, and history. In these poems the sacramental act is consummated through, and by means of, contemporary sensibility and

[25] C. A. Bodelsen, *T. S. Eliot's Four Quartets: A Commentary* (Copenhagen, 1958), p. 91. Another reading which seems to miss this structure of Incarnation and paradox in the symbolism of the rocks, turning the poem to a mystical and pantheistic mood it does not profess, is that of Krishna Sinha, *On the Four Quartets of T. S. Eliot* (Devon, n.d.), pp. 71–72. "The rocks have their own symbolism: Christ, moments of agony, the periodicity and permanence of Nature. Nature itself is God."

contemporary knowledge. . . . In *Dry Salvages* . . . you get
a fine illustration of the recovery of authentic Christian symbol. The river and the sea of this poem are actual river and
sea. You could get wet in them. They exist in their own
unique right. . . . Yet this is not descriptive nature poetry;
this is not Masefield. In Eliot the river is a river. But it rises,
through psychological and anthropological allusion, to ethical
and spiritual levels of meaning for the life of the person, just
as Eliot's sea, actually and sensuously known at one level, is
also at another level the symbol of the motion and the intention of history. And beneath its chaotic and complex rhythm
beats "the unhurried ground swell, measuring time that is not
our time," and touching both exterior nature and interior man
with inscrutable but perpetual benediction.

I would say that Eliot as a Christian sacramentalist has, in
the *Four Quartets*, overcome the fragmentation of contemporary culture by reabsorbing the natural or cosmic myth in the
historical symbol. And I would say that he has done so in the
terms proper to our moment in time.[26]

There remains one final remark about the name of the rocks,
the Dry Salvages, and its import as title of the poem. Though
somewhat related to each other, there are two problems here,
not one; namely, the historical origin and meaning of the name
of the rocks, and the meaning Eliot wishes it to have in the
poem. Ultimately, only the latter is a literary problem.

Both these problems involve a set of homonyms. Our English
word "salvage," "to save," derives from the Latin "*salvare*,"
meaning the same. Our word savage, "a wild man," however,
derives from the Latin "*silva*," "the woods," through the adjective "*silvaticus*" (Late Latin "*salvaticus*"), describing wild men
or savages who haunt the woods. A perusal of the entry *savage* in
the Oxford English Dictionary shows a variant of the mor-
pheme "savage," namely "salvage," which also has analogues in
French, Italian, Portuguese, and Rumanian. This variant was in
common usage in seventeenth-century English. Hence we get a
set of homonyms: *salvage—to save* and *salvage—*the variant of

[26] Malcolm Ross, "The Writer as Christian," in *The New Orpheus:
Essays Towards a Christian Poetic*, ed. Nathan A. Scott, Jr. (New York,
1964), pp. 91–92.

savage—a wild man. In 5b of this same entry, *savage*, we read in particular of "the salvage man"—a "conventional representation of a savage in heraldry and pageants."

Professor Morison has studied the problem of the regional name thoroughly and convincingly. He first disposes of Eliot's suggestion in the prenote (and with the acquiescence of the poet, as we shall presently see) that the "Dry" derives from the French *"trois"* (pity it is not a question of German influence!). Morison shows that maps do not begin to use the word "Dry" until 1867, "when any derivation from *trois* would be far-fetched." Champlain and the French charted the area in the seventeenth century. Rather, the word "dry" is not in uncommon use along the Atlantic coast for ledges bare at high water, which is the case of the Dry Salvages in contrast with the Little Salvages, which are covered twice daily.[27] As for the word "Salvages" in the name, after a detailed study of maritime histories and maps Morison strongly favors calling it a seventeenth-century variant of "Savages," probably named for Indians in the neighborhood, with a possible but not too probable influence of the French equivalent *"Sauvages"* through the work of Champlain.[28]

But more important for our purposes is the second problem, the import Eliot wishes the name to have as title of the poem. His prenote should be taken as part of the poem, a hint at the imaginative inference intended in the title. (We recall here the poetic importance of the other three titles of the *Quartets*.) Whatever Eliot's inaccuracy about the origin of the rocks' name, his imagination was attracted to the explanation he gave. He wrote in 1964 to "Cousin Sam" Morison:

> I imagine that it was to my brother [Henry Ware, Jr.] that I owe that explanation of the title, and I seem to remember that the rocks were known to the local fishermen as the "Dry Salvages." But I myself can give no further explanation and it may be that mine owes more to my own imagination than to any explanation that I heard.[29]

27 Morison, 236.
28 *Ibid.*, 236–43.
29 *Ibid.*, 246.

In the light of the densely paradoxical structure of all the *Quartets* and especially of the argument for the paradoxical Christian realism outlined in this paper, it is not farfetched to think of Eliot as wanting us to keep in mind the paradox deriving from the violent opposition between "salvage" as "savage" and "salvage, to save." The natural danger of the rocks makes the comparison with wild men realistic enough.

Further, in this connection it is intriguing to speculate that there may be a hint here not only of the Christian paradox, but also of a transformation into it of the pagan practice of the *apotropaic*. Did Eliot, perhaps, fancy the name of the rocks having its origin in a euphemism, in the practice of warding off evil and avoiding sinister reference by using a kind or favorable name? It is a teasing temptation, at least, to see such a practice as germane to the various forms of fortune-telling and magic, which Eliot rejects in the last section of the poem as false ways of dealing with the redemption of time. Christian realism has always rejected the magical, replacing it with the sacramental, which is something quite different. It would be easy in the context of Christian realism to transform the apotropaic into the genuine paradox of salvation. At all events, this paradox seems implied by the title to reinforce what the poem's theme is surely saying, that men are salvaged through the savagery of the rocks and the sea; find mercy through this mastery.[30]

"Old [and not so old] men ought to be explorers." In the present case topography has had its reward for at least one explorer, who found the image of journeying, so dominant in the *Quartets*, especially satisfying; and who is pleased to have a refreshed sense of the impact of a region upon a poem and of a poem upon a region, and in a sense to have known them both for the first time.

[30] The paradoxical middle ground of faith sought by Christian realism between gnosticism and the praeternatural, described by Eliot in *East Coker* as "So the darkness shall be the light, and the stillness the dancing," has an interesting analogue to this last passage of *The Dry Salvages* in G. K. Chesterton's *The Ballad of the White Horse*. The archetypal symbolism of light and darkness and of the sea finds interesting echoes in Eliot, in the stanzas beginning, "The men of the East may spell the stars." The Blessed Virgin is speaking to Alfred. *Collected Poems* (New York, 1946), pp. 216–17.

ELIZABETH BARTLETT

◐

The Walnut Tree

from *The Outsider*

It was the year the walnut tree went mad
with a forty year passion;
every night, for weeks, it tapdanced on the roof
and played ecstatic drums
until by morning, the ground was littered
with the wild folly of its joy.
It was almost a kind of hysteria
that nothing seemed to satisfy,
not sun or stars, nothing, except to revel
in orgasms of delight.
It was a daily race to keep up with it,
to rake leaves and gather nuts;
with dark-stained fingers and an aching back
to cull and grade, clean and stack.
The boxes and baskets soon overflowed,
and when there were no neighbors left,
walnuts took the place of bread, meat, cheese.
I thank you, Lord, the owner said,
but spare us a flood after a dry summer,
this is excessive reward.

The following spring, the tree leafed poorly,
half the branches sick and bare.
Everyone had a different remedy,
diagnoses disagreed:
too much water, not enough water, zinc

starvation, suffocated roots.
Hormones, thought the owner, and if pills
would do the tree any good . . .
but before the summer could involve it
in still another romance
with birds, clouds, moonlight, the song of the surf
and the latest calypso,
the leaves turned brown and quietly dropped off;
brittle hands clutched at the sky;
while the owner went about nursing shoots
that in the next forty years
might recall the madness and the passion,
might revive the savage drums.

◑

Fable of the
Third Christmas Camel

from *Tennessee Poetry Journal*

(The following poetic fragment, evidently an overlooked scrap of the Dead Sea Scrolls, was recently discovered near Jerusalem, stuck to the bottom of an empty bagel can. We offer here an approximate translation into modern English of this invaluable historical document.—Ed.)

I went all the way
But on the return trip
I gave the caravan
The slip

One desert night
Quit Balthazar
With all his frankincense
And myrrh

And humped away
Across the sand
It was dawn when I came
To this strange land

And found this family
Living here
Without a camel
Because they were poor

So I stayed with them
Carried their hides
Gave the kids
Free camel rides

Sat with the baby
Worked with the man
Sang them ballads
Of Ispahan

Carried the water
Pulled the plow
Loved my neighbor
Who was a cow

I like it here
I'm staying with them
As I wanted to stay
In Bethlehem

With that other
Family I knew
Which proves Effendi
That passing through

The eye of a needle
Is an easier thing
For a camel
Than a king

MICHAEL BENEDIKT

◑

The Wings of the Nose

from *Poetry*

The wings of the nose
I sense them fluttering
Making a passenger
Out of the whole olfactory system
And the brain flies along just for fun
Where are you going O wildest of widely wandering wings
Where are you taking us, my Sweetie and me?

"I am taking you someplace where you will like it
I am trying to find a place where you can rest
   and enjoy the most important sense of things of all, which
   is mine.
Haven't you given up the other pleasures yet?
   Touch, which is just an irritation
   Taste, which I view with distaste
   Hearing, which is there just to put a strain on you
   Sight, which is something I have never quite been able to see
Just in case you haven't
                   come with me now
                      aloft in my sensational flying machine
Spend all your time
Wandering with me all day long, not to the places you want to
   go, but to places you can't resist going
Let your schedule of appointments be organized by waftings
   O follow follow

So you will say
At the end of the day
The odor of decay
Is the best and strongest and sweetest:
The smell of fire on bone;
Of rich earth."

◑

The Shark

from *The Yale Review*

On the steel deck it looked dead until it was kicked. When that happened the dry body would flop. The mouth would fall open, backing into the underbody to display the thousand serrations of needle teeth in banked triple tiers. There was a cut, now baked dry, back of the head. The bone structure of the mouth was punched in one spot where it had been hit with a chisel. A wire ran through the hole replacing the hook. It was bent to a piece of twenty-one thread. The shark was small, about three feet, but in a way it was a record. It had been alive for six hours.

It was Gamper's shark. Its longevity made him proud. He knew that they did not often live long, that like rabbits suffering stroke from a single pellet sting, sharks did not often live much past the catching. Gamper had set himself the task of keeping this shark alive.

He gave the shark a jerk with the line. His face was impassive except at the moment of the jerk, when it held a snarl. "I'll kill this sorry damn thing if it takes all day," he announced generally.

Behind him another man lounged at the rail of the cutter, taking advantage of the shade. The shark lay in the bow, on the sun-heated plates behind a winch. The metal was very hot. A man could not walk about the deck with bare feet. Through a near-by hatch came the desultory sounds of a card game, mingling with the experimental plucking of a guitar.

"Hit me," a voice said. "Stand," the voice said. Then in a conversational tone the voice lifted. "Gamper, how's your fish coming?"

The man standing at the rail stirred. Gamper turned to him, a tough grin on his weathered face that was small and exactly proportioned but not pleasing. "Let's put him back over," he said.

The man, Fernandez, stood without moving. The Gulf of Maine heat that could be dispelled by the slightest breeze lay oppressive about the anchored cutter. Her rail aft was festooned with yellow drying loops of manila line. The line was still damp and steaming from the tow of the broken-down vessel the night before. When the line was dry it would be flaked out on the fantail for the next search and rescue.

"Sunday," a player's voice said. "Last day of patrol. I bet we catch a job and don't get home."

"Don't even think it," another voice warned.

"Bet we do. It happened last five times out of seven. I kept count."

"So, quit counting."

"Bet on something else," a third voice suggested. "Two-bit pot on how long Gamper keeps his fish alive."

"Why not," the second man answered. "Make out twenty minute slips and draw for a quarter." The voices sank to a drone. Fernandez had not moved. Gamper looked at him hard. He gave the line a tug.

"Let's put him back over."

Fernandez attempted a look of dignity and contempt. "You put him over."

"Not alone. He's still got some stuff."

"Then get a gun from Cap and put him out of his misery. You had your fun. Now shoot him."

"Pee on his misery." Gamper twitched the line. The body gave a jerk. "He's still got some stuff. He's not done yet."

"You mean cooked." Fernandez stood up to leave. He was ship steward's mate, the junior man. He had no authority. "You're a big man, Gamper. You're a hero. Put him over yourself, and I hope he takes your arm."

"Don't push it."

"Then kill him. You had your fun." Fernandez stepped through a hatch into the shaded heat of the passageway. He disappeared into what seemed absolute darkness after the glare of the deck and sea. Words from the card game greeted him. He was asked about the execution, twitted about the shark. They suggested to him that if he did not buy it for the wardroom mess the crew would be stuck. The man experimenting with the guitar motioned to him.

"No."

"Sure," the man said. "All you Mex play guitars."

"Texas."

"All right. All you Texans play guitars." The man motioned again. Fernandez sat beside the man to show him a chord. Through the passageway came another flop. Fernandez found the chord and hit it hard.

"That Gamper is a natural damn louse," he said.

A quartermaster looked up. Shark, guitar, and card game had been uninteresting. He was reading a magazine. Now he yawned and stretched like a cat. "Naw," he said. "Gamper ain't any meaner than you. Gamper's scared."

"Scared? It's just a garbage shark. Why scared?"

"All guys are scared of sharks. Gamper's just showing it."

Another thump sounded on deck. Then Gamper's voice said, "Okay, fishy, I'll put you over myself."

A man rose from the table. "This I gotta see. If he's such a hot shark now's the time for him to prove it." He went out. There were several thumps. The card game continued undisturbed. The man who had gone out to observe returned.

"Snugged the line and his head up hard to the rail, threw a bowline around the tail and pitched him over. Like to broke its back, but hell, you can't bust shark bones. Then he unhitched the line and dropped him. Easy."

"What do you mean, scared?" Fernandez asked again. The quartermaster had resumed his reading. He grunted and did not answer.

"That girl was sure to hell crying." A player picked at a former discussion.

"Well, the other woman was there. Maybe she helped."

"The old guy sure God wasn't her daddy."

"Next time she'll say no to a boat ride. She ain't fresh meat no more."

"What do you mean, scared?" Fernandez asked again. "Garbage sharks don't hurt anyone." The quartermaster stirred, irritated.

"You've seen bodies come up. You've snagged bodies. Well . . ." He motioned with a thumb to the hatch. "He don't understand."

The men pretended indifference. A silence fell. Occasionally a man asked for a card. The deal passed once, indifferently. Most of the men had seen bodies. They are a part of a Coast Guard's experience, perhaps the worst part. Each man had his own mental picture of how bodies come to the surface, tossed and eyeless as the salt water washes in the scavenged eye sockets. The fingers and toes are gone, along with the lips. If the clothes are torn the soft body parts are gone and the bloat and stink wells out of the holes.

They are lifted out with a wire basket, like a stretcher. The basket is dragged under them with lines. They are netted by the basket because otherwise the body might pull apart. The smell is very bad. Bodies are stored under canvas on the fantail. If it is a really bad one the smell permeates the ship and men get sick. When that happens the cooks keep only coffee going. A few men eat sandwiches as a brag. Scavengers hover over death. If a shark finds a body the body does not rise. The shark is the king of all scavengers. The men had seen various things.

A player stirred, then gave a conscientious chuckle, deliberately trying to break the mood. "Best job I ever heard was a fella evacuated a cat house."

"Naw." Another man forced a grin.

"Sure. Gibbs, seaman. Knew him at the lifeboat station. He had a letter one of the women wrote to the newspaper."

"Why? What did he do to her?"

"Good letter, I mean. A bosun mate and Gibbs were out in a thirty-eight picket. The boats brought it right through a flood to the window of the house. Old Gibbs went in there and started carrying out whores and their stuff in a forty-knot blow. They didn't even think the boat would make it. Brought her in with the spaces looking like a combination cat house and dime store."

"Life and property, man. But he must of made out."

"I reckon later. The girl really branded his tail with that letter. Everybody knew what she was and razzed Gibbs."

"Hey, hey, look at him go!" The players looked at each other, reacting against the edge of hysteric hatred in Gamper's voice.

"That jerk."

"At it again." The quartermaster put down his magazine. "You'd foul up a free lunch, Gamper," he was trying to yell him down. "You'd screw up the Last Supper."

The voice from the deck was a hiss. "It was pretty screwed up without me."

Fernandez stood up. "That flushes it," he said. "I'm getting a gun." He turned and went down a short passage where a ladder led to the bridge.

The quartermaster stood up. "He's scared too. All guys are scared of sharks. . . ."

"Shut up," a voice said.

The quartermaster grinned. "Have it your way. If there's going to be a shoot-out I think I'll watch." He stepped through the hatch and stood at the rail. The other men looked at each other, played out the hand, then rose and went out on deck.

Looking over the rail, they could see the shark plunging hard against the line. He would plunge, be brought up hard, then allow himself to surface gradually, gathering strength for his next hard dive. The heat was intense. The men loosened or took off their shirts. The shark rolled his white belly and dived hard. He was a tough shark.

A voice spoke nervously. "Worst I ever had was one we got two years ago. Worked it off a cutter instead of a boat like we should of. Back must have been busted. He fell right in half. God!"

"Why don't you club him?" a man asked Gamper. "That's the way to kill a shark."

"Don't suffer enough."

Another voice spoke. It was tense. "Worst I ever had wasn't

even wet. We were on harbor patrol. This old party waved us in
to an island. He was drunk as hell, and four of them had borrowed somebody's island for a weekend tour. Two men, two
women, all about fifty or better. Their boat drifted or something. Anyway, this guy says he's got a sick woman, but she
wasn't. She was dead as a nit. Sitting at a table, naked and
weighing maybe three hundred pounds. When we lifted her
there was this real bad look on her face. Bareass dead, man, and
looking like she was staring at the center of hell!" He paused
apologetically. "You just don't forget one like that," he said.

A bell sounded inside the cutter.

"Calling the engine room," the voice was a protest. "If it's a
job . . . Who was that jerk that was counting?"

"If it's a job they'll tell us." The quartermaster looked up.
The bridge was silent. "Gamper, you better get rid of your
shark. If we got a job . . ."

Fernandez came through the hatch without a gun. "The old
man says to club him. He won't give me any gun."

Gamper looked at him. "Was that an order?"

The steward looked as if he wanted to lie. The men's faces
told him that they could read him. "No," he said. "But do
something. Radio is working one."

"Hell."

"Worst I ever had," another man was beginning eagerly, imposing his story against time, "was blue. He was stealing lead
cable from a government island and overloaded and floundered
in a White squall. I think it scared him blue, and then he died."

"In the water they change." Gamper pretended interest.

"Naw—this one was fresh. We got the grapple in his left eye,
and he was dark blue, shooting out red when he came up. I still
dream . . . The hell with it. . . ."

"Stand back," Gamper announced. "I'm bringing him back
up." He started hauling in on the line. A chief bosun mate came
through the hatch. "Story time?" he asked.

"I'll tell you one, chief." The quartermaster grinned.

"I'll tell you one. We got a sinker working. Trawler. The
water is getting ahead of his pumps."

"In this calm?" The quartermaster was indignant. "How far off?"

"Some of them things leak in drydock." The chief was grinning at the indignation. "He's five and a half, six hours off."

"Sea's good,"another man said. "We ought to get him."

"If the tide change don't bring wind." The chief turned. Gamper had the shark level with the rail. The chief looked at it, then looked at Gamper. "Games," he said. "Bad luck on Sunday. Get rid of it."

"Bad luck to let one go." Gamper was suddenly angry. He bounced the line.

"Depends on how you let it go. You screwed away a whole day with that thing. It takes two minutes. Take a turn in that line, then shag below for some of that scrap from the new shoring. Put a couple nails in." Gamper went.

When he returned, the chief took the nailed-together pieces that looked like a kite frame. He attached a wire to the nails, then with a line hoisted the shark's tail and twisted the wire onto the tail. The frame would drag about two feet behind.

He took a knife from his pocket. "You have to mend this line," he told Gamper. He lifted the tail level with the rail. With the knife he made several fairly deep cuts in the white belly. "Needs to bleed a little," he explained. The blood oozed red and waterish from the cuts. Then the chief let the tail drop so that nothing but the head of the shark appeared beside the rail, the eyes dull, lethargic, and unaccusing. With the precision of a striking gull the chief picked twice with the knife and the eyes popped. The body drummed against the side of the cutter. The chief cut the line and the body fell to the water. The shark dived and tried to swim deep. The blocks floated just below the water's surface.

Gamper checked his watch. "Made it a little over seven hours, anyway," he said to no one.

"Might make it for a couple more," the chief said. "The little fish will eat out his belly. Now you deadbeats get to work." He turned and went forward to where the anchor detail was assembling. There was a rumble, and the stack belched black, then the engine settled to a steady throb. "Power on the winch?" he asked.

"We got it, chief." The winch began to make turns. There was the slow rattle of chain in the hawsepipe. The sun was very hot. The anchor detail wiped sweat and cursed the hot deck. The cook stuck his head through the hatch and told Fernandez to make fresh coffee. Fernandez stood as if he did not hear. He stared after the chief.

"Sea's good," the quartermaster said to no one in particular. He started to walk forward to the bridge ladder, then hesitated. A puff of air was faint, it might have been the ship moving now that the anchor had broken ground. The quartermaster sniffed at the air with the studied, judicious manner of a man privy to bridge secrets.

"Sea's good," he repeated. "Awful good. . . . Don't know what that jar-head means. This tide won't bring no change."

10. (from *Window Poems*)

from *Poetry Northwest*

Rising, the river
is wild. There is no end
to what one may imagine
whose lands and buildings
lie in its reach. To one
who has felt his little boat
taken this way and that
in the braided currents
it is beyond speech.
"What's the river doing?"
"Coming up."
In Port Royal, that begins
a submergence of minds.
Heads are darkened.
To the man at work
through the mornings
in the long-legged cabin
above the water, there is
an influence of the rise
that he feels in his footsoles
and in his belly
even while he thinks
of something else. The window
looks out, like a word,
upon the wordless, fact
dissolving into mystery, darkness

overtaking light.
And the water reaches a height
it can only fall from, leaving
the tree trunks wet.
It has made a roof
to its rising, and become
a domestic thing.
It lies down in its place
like a horse in his stall.
Facts emerge from it:
drift it has hung in the trees,
stranded cans and bottles,
new carving in the banks
—a place of change, changed.
It leaves a mystic plane
in the air, a membrane
of history stretched between
the silt-lines on the banks,
a depth that for months
the man will go from his window
down into, knowing
he goes within the reach
of a dark power: where
the birds are, fish
were.

DAVID BROMIGE

◐

Taking Heart

from *Cassiopeia*

Take me in again, how did I ever doubt
you were right for me, your mouth
beyond reproach, telling me you love me,
lovely, I am, your body is
an ocean, in its own way, saying the same—

so you lose, once more, giving me courage
to go away into the love of others,
lakes & rivers, surely
they will welcome
a body all of salt.

❶

Edgar Poe: Style as Pose

from *The Virginia Quarterly Review*

There should no longer be any question—indeed, there probably never should have been a question—that Poe is one of our major writers. Yet in the august company of Hawthorne, Melville, Emerson, Thoreau, and Whitman, he alone is likely to have his credentials repeatedly challenged, as if he might actually be an impostor. Whatever their deficiencies as writers, his great contemporaries inescapably possess the bearing of serious artists. Poe, however, although he grandiosely proclaimed a theory of pure art, betrays an air of pretentiousness, posturing, and even downright fraud. To be sure, he has his devoted followers who see him as he wished to be seen: the embodiment of the Romantic Artist as Victim. And he has the sturdy corps of academic specialists and defenders seeking to protect his honor and reputation. Finally, he has more than his share of psychoanalytically minded critics seeking to define the nature of his threatened ego.

For Poe's life cast him in the role of victim—victim of orphanage, of an insensitive foster father, of alcohol, of grinding poverty, of a hostile and materialistic society, and finally of a villainous literary executor, one Rufus Griswold, whose present claim to immortality is his energetic effort to defame Poe. Small wonder that his admirers identify with his victimization, that scholars defend his sullied honor, and that psychoanalytic critics seek the primal psychic wound which bled into his art. Yet accompanying this figure of Poe is a disturbing set of contrivances which seem almost designed to provoke precisely such a response. There is in almost everything he wrote or did a certain shameless dramatization, a tawdry theatricality, which should remind posterity—if it needs reminding—that he was indeed the son of traveling actors. In other words, Poe's life constantly presents itself as if it were as much act as action, and it is difficult to escape the conclusion that at the end of his life Poe, like the diabolical narrator of "The Cask of Amontillado," deliberately trapped his hated enemy Griswold by naming him his literary executor. If so, the unsuspecting Griswold fatuously rose to the bait, producing the intensely hostile obituary which has never ceased to bring a host of scholars to Poe's defense to pronounce Griswold's distortions the act of an unprincipled scoundrel.

If there is something contrived about Poe's life, there is also something contrived about his art. This exposure of contrivance is not an error into which Poe occasionally lapses; it is an integral aspect of his identity as a writer. Aldous Huxley had the quality clearly in focus when he cited Poe as the example par excellence of vulgarity in literature. "Was Edgar Poe a major poet?" Huxley rhetorically asked himself, and confidently replied, "It would surely never occur to any English-speaking critic to say so." Despite the monolithic assurance of his English instincts, Huxley was troubled by the extreme praise fairly lavished on Poe by Baudelaire, Mallarmé, and Valéry. It was in fact the French praise in the face of Poe's patent vulgarity which struck Huxley, as it has struck many another critic of Poe, as a paradox deserving critical attention. How could this poet who thrust himself forward in the world of letters like a gentleman exhibiting a diamond ring on every finger—how could such a man, wondered Huxley, be taken seriously as a great writer? Huxley concluded that the French, while they recognized and admired the refinement of Poe's substance, were by virtue of the language barrier blind to the essential vulgarity of his form.

After thirty years Huxley's remarks still retain a singular aptness. They are as hard to explain away as that French praise which so troubled Huxley. For Poe is vulgar, if by vulgarity is meant the deliberate effort to achieve sensational effects in order to shock the sensibility of the audience. Henry James had Poe's vulgarity thoroughly in mind when he remarked that "an enthusiasm for Poe is the mark of a decidedly primitive stage of reflection." So did Paul Elmer More when he observed that "Poe is the poet of unripe boys and unsound men." So did James Russell Lowell when he found Poe three-fifths sheer genius and two-fifths sheer fudge. And so of course did Emerson when he scornfully referred to Poe as the jingle man.

Even Allen Tate, the most sympathetic and perceptive of Poe's critics in our own time, is reduced to the following admission when confronted by Poe's style:

> I confess that Poe's serious style at its typical worst makes the reading of more than one story at a sitting an almost insuperable task. The Gothic glooms, the Venetian interiors, the ancient wine cellars (from which nobody ever enjoys a vintage but always drinks "deep")—all this, done up in a glutinous prose, so fatigues one's attention that with the best will in the world one gives up, unless one gets a clue to the power underlying the flummery.

Tate speaks of Poe's style at its typical worst because he realizes just how much this worst is typical of Poe's writing. For Poe's style is so ridden with clichés that it seems always something half borrowed, half patched. And not in the worst stories only is this evident, but in the best. Here are the opening sentences of "William Wilson."

> Let me call myself, for the present, William Wilson. The fair page now lying before me need not be sullied with my real appellation. This has been already too much an object for the scorn—for the horror—for the detestation of my race. To the uttermost regions of the globe have not the indignant winds bruited its unparalleled infamy? Oh, outcast of all outcasts most abandoned!—to the earth art thou not forever dead? to its honors, to its flowers, to its golden aspirations?—and a cloud, dense, dismal, limitless, does it not hang eternally between thy hopes and heaven?

But why go on? William Wilson sounds like a fugitive from an asylum devoted expressly to the maintenance of ineffectual heroes escaped from sentimental and Gothic romance.

It is of course possible to argue that this language is William Wilson's, not Poe's. The truth is, however, that all of Poe's narrators are remarkably similar—are in effect a single narrator who tells, under various names, practically all of Poe's stories. There is really no fallacy in equating this narrator's style with Poe's style so long as one does not go on to insist that Poe's narrator is Poe. For insofar as the narrator embodies Poe's narrative style he is just so much the style and not the man.

As style, the narrator is characterized by an excessive impersonation of the conventions of learning and literature which produces an effect of intellectual and literary posturing. Moreover, the narrator's literary or "narrative" posture is never separate from but invariably a part of his intellectual arrogance. These twin postures are not an accident of Poe's style but its essence. It is not too much to say that, for Poe, style was pure pose. In a world where style is pose, there are necessarily going to be some momentous transformations. Symbol in such a world becomes anagram, form becomes rationale, imagination becomes impersonation, cause becomes effect, and creation becomes invention.

To recognize such transformations is to begin to grasp the terminology for describing the world of Edgar Poe. It is not surprising that Poe's genius, which first displayed itself in excessively rhythmic poetry, moved next to the extravagant improbabilities of sensational fiction, on to formulate a poetics of short fiction which elevated the traditional oral tale to the status of written art, before realizing itself in the invention of a new form —the detective story—which Poe characteristically and accurately termed the tale of ratiocination. For Poe had, from the very outset of his career, passionately believed that true genius was to be equated with originality, and he never ceased to celebrate the notion that in art as well as in experience the true excitement was the thrill of doing something utterly new.

His first move toward extreme originality was in the realm of poetry, where, by intensifying rhythmic effects, he sought to placate the esthetic censor and thereby release images of horror and morbidity along an overrefined sound track. Whereas Emerson was making American poetry in New England by threatening the sound of English poetry with sense, Poe was making it in Virginia (though he typically exhibited his Bostonian identity on the title page of his first book of poems) by threatening the sense of English poetry with sound. For Poe, following Coleridge, meant to numb the reason with rhythm, until truncated dream images could flow into his lines and embody his forms. This whole poetic process, which both released and transformed the repressed dream life, Poe was accurately to call the "rhythmic creation of beauty."

If in the creation of poetry Poe assaulted reason, in the invention of his fiction he impersonated reason, ultimately making the very action of his invention the *rationale of discovery*. His progress toward this invention is in one sense difficult to plot, for his single narrator leaves the illusion of a completed consciousness successively revealing itself rather than a changing awareness undergoing development. That is why "M.S. Found in a Bottle," a very early story, is indistinguishable from Poe's "mature" style. For Poe's fiction was never a way toward invention so much as it was invention itself and any one of Poe's best tales could be used to exemplify that fact. Thus, the four tales which I have chosen to illustrate Poe's act of invention are not the only stories which could be used, but they represent his finest effort and afford maximum vision of the revolution he wrought in literary form between 1837 and 1841—that remarkably fertile period of his life which began shortly after his marriage to Virginia Clemm and ended with the writing of "The Murders in the Rue Morgue."

II

The Narrative of A. *Gordon Pym*, long neglected even by Poe enthusiasts, is a work which our age has with justifiable pride rediscovered. The recovery of Melville and *Moby Dick* from relative oblivion in many ways made Poe's forgotten story more accessible. After all, "Pym" begins as a whaling voyage and pursues themes and symbols similar to those of Melville's masterpiece. No one remembering Ishmael's meditations on the whiteness of the whale can fail to be struck by the apparition looming on the scene in Pym's last sentences:

> And now we rushed into the embraces of the cataract, where a chasm threw itself open to receive us. But there arose in our pathway a shrouded human figure, very far larger in its proportions than any dweller among men. And the hue of the skin of the figure was of the perfect whiteness of the snow.

Yet seeing Pym in relation to Melville has little significance unless he is first seen in relation to Poe. For Pym epitomizes the Poe narrator, and to define Pym is to define once and for all the narrator who compulsively thrusts himself upon our consciousness, forcing us to dissociate from rather than to identify with him. He is not the observer but forever the *actor*, and his experiences come more and more to seem the hallucinations of a madman. Instead of watching what a central intelligence is observing—as we do in the fiction of Hawthorne and James—we are brought round to the position of watching the narrator himself.

This narrator, who is at once fulfilled and defined in the person of Arthur Gordon Pym, has inevitably been identified with Poe, critics having noted that Pym's name is a consonantal echo of Edgar Allan Poe, as indeed it is. The fact that Pym's forebears had investments in Edgarton is but one more coy invitation Poe planted to reinforce the relationship. Yet Pym is not Poe, and the difference between them defines their relationship as much as the similarity. Who is Pym? He is clearly an anagram of Imp. And here the anagram is no simple trick to induce a teasing meaning but a connection the imagination must make if it is to define Pym and Poe. Pym is at once the Imp of Poe and the Imp of the Perverse—and perversity constitutes the root of his identity. His only motive for launching himself toward the grand fantasy of a polar vortex is a perverse desire to go to sea which intensifies in proportion to the resistance it encounters. This desire leads him first to a preposterous outing in his sailboat, the *Ariel*—a freak, Pym calls the episode—culminating in his being thrown into the sea. Miraculously rescued by a passing whaler and saved for greater adventures, Pym proceeds to stow away on the whaler *Grampus*, emerges from the hold to discover that the crew has mutinied, helps put down the mutineers with another mutiny, only to be among a handful of survivors of a storm which whelms the ship. Riding the inverted hulk of the *Grampus*—it cannot sink because of the empty oil casks in its stowage—Pym and three companions face death at sea, managing to escape starvation by the radical means of eating one of their number. Even after this morsel of sustenance, one of them dies—Pym's long-time companion, Augustus Barnard, who expires horrendously on the first of August—but at last the two remaining souls, Pym and his Indian companion, Dirk Peters, are picked up by the *Jane Guy* bound for south latitudes. Gaining strange dominion over the captain of the *Jane Guy*, Pym persuades him to sail ever southward until they reach the island of Tsalal [alas, at last], where seemingly friendly natives trap and bury the entire crew in a man-made avalanche. Pym and Peters once more survive, however, and after almost starving on the island, they finally commandeer a native canoe and cast off from Tsalal toward the south. The farther south they go the warmer and whiter the water becomes, until at last they are caught in a current drawing them irresistibly toward a roaring polar cataract. The narrative abruptly breaks off with the description of the shrouded figure rising in their pathway.

The identity of this mysterious figure invites such intense speculation that the nature of Pym's narrative is likely to be forgotten. His story as it unfolds is one of the most absurd, arbitrary, and capricious tales ever written. Poe himself—after, and probably because, the book failed to sell—pronounced it a silly book, and there are many times when the entire account veers between being a practical joke at the expense of the reader on the one hand and a parody of the sensational adventure tale on the other. It is well to remember in this connection that Poe began his career writing burlesques and all his life long could never quite keep from assuming poses which evidently struck him as howlingly funny but which are usually incredibly labored. Yet if his "pure" burlesques are failures, the burlesque element makes its presence felt at the heart of Poe's tales of terror, among which *Pym* stands as one of his more illustrious successes. Indeed, the burlesque impulse operates in the context of terror as an embodiment of the spirit of the perverse and absurd. Thus Pym himself is the Imp, which is to say the demon tricked out in comic form. He has no tragic sense; he cannot really change. All he can do is experience sensations which in turn produce imaginings—imaginings, Pym says at one point, "of the dreadful deaths of thirst, famine, suffocation, and premature interment." These are what he calls the "prominent disasters" in his path, and the entire narrative insistently exposes him—or rather, he insistently exposes himself—to the very fears his imagination excites in him.

It is just here that Pym's perversity is located, for in seeking to excite himself with fear, he reveals that fear itself is a desire which he is wishing into actuality. Thus insofar as Pym is a character, he is voraciously trying to shock himself into life with sensation. But insofar as he is narrator he is trying to shock his audiences into life. He seeks always the effect, the lurid thrill, the further excess in an effort to excite his reader, making every Poe story seem something of a performance—stagy, exhibitionistic, vulgar.

The reader's sense that the Poe tale is something of an act is what makes him suspicious of the grandiose interpretations the stories perversely invite. Yet it is foolish to dismiss the stories as simply hoaxes or burlesques on the basis of such a suspicion. The perversity in *Pym* does not diminish the force of the story; rather it defines the central action. For Pym's perversity and the voyage to the South Pole are one, a turning of the world upside down. And what is a voyage to the South Pole but a turning of the world upside down, a treading of the turning globe until its bottom is precisely on top? As the bottom comes up, so does Pym's perversity. Thus the action of the book revolves around mutiny in the community—mutiny against the father in the family, against the captain in the ship, against man in the world, against God in the universe. The mutiny in the community is accompanied by the emergence into full consciousness of Pym's twin fears: burial alive and cannibalism. These fears are the excitements Pym perversely seeks throughout the voyage and they are at the same time the effects he, as narrator, shamelessly exploits.

A typical example of his exploitation is in the first nightmare episode when, buried alive in the hold of the *Grampus* while the mutiny rages above deck, Pym finds himself at the threshold of starvation. Such a situation would be adequate for the author of an ordinary thriller, but we are dealing with the incorrigible Poe, who can never resist the excess. By absurd fiat, he intrudes into the narrative a dog named Tiger, who, it develops, though Pym's oldest and dearest friend, in his present famished condition threatens to devour his beloved master. Despair gives Pym the strength to extricate himself from Tiger's jaws and deliver the reader into the ultimate discovery of the situation:

> In this struggle, however, I had been forced to drop the morsel of ham-skin, and I now found myself reduced to a single gill of liqueur. As this reflection crossed my mind, I felt myself actuated by one of those fits of perverseness which might be supposed to influence a spoiled child in similar circumstances, and, raising the bottle to my lips, I drained it to the last drop, and dashed it furiously upon the floor.

This last touch, which from a psychoanalytic viewpoint appears to be the hallucination of a dipsomaniac, in the course of the story serves as the absurd and hopeless gesture of perversity which saves Pym, for the sound of the breaking bottle leads Augustus to rescue Pym from his premature grave.

He is saved merely to be exposed to more absurd extremities: to suffer more savage fits of hunger until he at last participates in cannibalism, engaging—along with Augustus and Dirk Peters —in the grisly business of eating their companion Parker (the perversity in the matter of eating Parker occurs immediately after the feast, when Pym remembers the whereabouts of an ax, enabling the still famished party to hack its way into the ship's storeroom containing an abundance of supplies); to endure the even more literal burial alive upon the island of Tsalal; and to suffer the headlong plunge into polar regions which, instead of growing colder, grow ever warmer.

It is possible to interpret this voyage to the South Pole as a disguised journey into the Black Belt of the Southern United States. In such an interpretation the white figure emerging at the end is a symbol of the white race which Pym and Peters embrace, and the deepest fear haunting Pym throughout the voyage is the rebellion of the blacks. This racial tension is present again and again in Pym, but it is unnecessary to go so far as Sydney Kaplan, who, in his interesting introduction to a recent edition of *Pym*, concludes that the book is in reality a pro-slavery tract disguised as an adventure. Not that Poe, as one of our revered major writers, should be defended from the crime of embracing such a sentiment. He had enough editorial instinct to flatter the peculiar institution sustaining many of the most influential readers of his *Southern Literary Messenger*; he had enough antagonism to New England life and letters to hate the abolitionism and transcendentalism which sustained the anti-slavery movement; and he had enough fierce contempt for the mass of mankind to have found much to admire in the institution of slavery. But the fact remains that it is the adventure and not the pro-slavery sentiment which is paramount in *Pym*, transcending any symbolic referent or political belief which may have impelled the author of the narrative. Pym, the Imp of the Perverse, is exploring the possibilities of perversity, and his narrative inverts the world, rendering experience into fantasy and fantasy into experience. His narrative enacts, in the last analysis, the absurdity at the root of the psyche. The huge white figure who—and the fact is important—intercepts Pym's frail bark is neither God nor Devil so much as it is an excessive *deus ex machina* to get Pym out of his narrative and at the same time perversely arouse the reader to absurd speculation. It is finally the ghostly identity of riddling perversity itself which Pym's insistent self-consciousness has disclosed.

That self-consciousness, emerging in an endless sequence of exhibitions, not revelations, constitutes what is at once the character and narrative of Arthur Gordon Pym. In Pym, the Imp of the Perverse, Poe's genius—which inevitably gravitated toward burlesque, parody, invective, hoax, and exposure—found its embodiment and complete fulfillment. Pym is the discoverer who embarks upon a new departure from the old forms and the old psyche; at the same time he is the demon possessed with a perverse desire for departure. Neither tragic figure nor mere hoax, he is the Imp embodying the demonic in the figure of the almost Joker.

III

In "Ligeia," "The Fall of the House of Usher," and "William Wilson," stories following hard upon *Pym*, Poe explored the perverse world he commanded. Each of the three stories discovers its reality—which is to say its effect—in perverse disintegration of the psyche. In each story the narrator witnesses or enacts a crime which will be so thrilling in its effect as to shock him not to death but to life. Moreover, the disintegration and the crime emerge along burlesque patterns, the stories wrecking the forms upon which they prey.

"Ligeia" was, to the end of Poe's days, his favorite story. On different occasions he picked it as his most successful effort in the short-story form. The best way to define its tone is to come to grips with the notorious epigraph of the story.

> "And the will therein lieth, which dieth not. Who knoweth the mysteries of the will, with its vigor? For God is but a great will pervading all things by nature of its intentness. Man doth not yield himself to the angels, nor unto death utterly, save only through the weakness of his feeble will."

So it runs, proudly exhibiting itself as a passage from Joseph Glanvill, the seventeenth-century mystic. Scholars have searched through Glanvill in an effort to locate the passage, but to no avail. Thus in anthologies, the passage is almost inevitably footnoted as not apparently in Glanvill and possibly spurious. Yet the passage has a haunting authenticity about it, as if it could come from Glanvill; at the same time it has the slippery cadence of a Poe impersonation.

In that shadowland between mimicry and authenticity Poe's genius dwells. The entire tone and action of "Ligeia" have about them the same air of being somewhere between a new departure and a rank impersonation. Almost everyone is familiar with this story in which the endlessly resurrected Poe narrator tells of his undying love for the lady Ligeia. Having met her, married her, and lost her through wasting death, he marries the lovely Lady Rowena Trevanion of Tremaine while still in the throes of grief for the lost Ligeia. Ligeia, the haughty dark lady of his imagination, reincarnates herself in the very form of Rowena, finally resurrecting herself like a triumphant vampire in the closing sentence of the story.

Even on a first reading of the story, Ligeia seems increasingly to be a hallucinated image of the narrator's fevered consciousness. He begins his narrative by observing that, so perverse is his memory, he cannot for his life remember when he became acquainted with this woman who has loved, married, and haunted him. But the fact that she is likely an hallucination, far from diminishing her reality, makes her an aspect rather than an object of the narrator's imagination and at the same time causes the narrator to become an object of the reader's curiosity. The whole maneuver is one of Poe's favorite gambits, which he relies on so repeatedly that it has the force of a necessity.

Yet Poe was right in liking "Ligeia," which is at last a masterpiece, if by masterpiece is meant the triumph of form in action. For the action of the story is the narrator's account of his attempt to remember Ligeia. The only way he can recall her is through the shabby Gothic décor with which he surrounds the Lady Rowena Trevanion of Tremaine. Only by killing Lady Rowena, the blond and blue-eyed empty beauty out of Sir Walter Scott, can the narrator resurrect his lost Ligeia. Through the disintegration of the Lady Rowena and the rank artifice of Gothic machinery surrounding her, the fragile yet dark intensity of Ligeia is brought to life. This does not mean that Ligeia is the vital dark lady of mythical power and passion, the profound reality lurking behind the façade of the lovely Rowena. She is the repressed will, the diseased passion, lying beneath the sterile image of Rowena. Though her name relates her to the mythical sirens, she has suffered a long descent and is in her way as absurd as the blond and blue-eyed Rowena. What the story marvelously succeeds in doing is to define the relation between the two empty traditions Poe inherited and burlesqued: the Gothic world of vampires and the romantic world of maidens.

"The Fall of the House of Usher" enacts the entire collapse of these traditions. When the Gothic machinery of the house of Usher tumbles into the tarn at its base, it carries with it the last extremity of the romantic artist in the person of Roderick Usher. But this time the narrator, instead of assuming the pose of central actor, comes to the aid of his dying friend and in the process manages to become Usher's accomplice in burying the lady Madeline Usher alive. The closing action of the story, in which the lady Madeline claws her way out of her tomb to kill her brother, is even more insistent in its burlesque than "Ligeia." Whereas "Ligeia" extravagantly burlesqued Gothic and sentimental traditions in the persons of Ligeia and Lady Rowena, Poe here goes so far as to manufacture as part of the action an overt parody of Gothic romance. After the burial of the Lady Madeline, the narrator, attempting to quiet the high-strung Usher, takes down the "Mad Trist" of Sir Launcelot Canning, one of Usher's favorite romances. As he reads the impossible prose of that archaic production, the action of the narrative not only begins to conform to but luridly exceeds the ponderous Gothicism of the "Mad Trist." In this excessive impersonation of a prior degenerate form Poe literally invents a burlesque romance as a means of exposing Usher's utter degeneration. For Allen Tate, this last piece of flummery is the tastelessness which alienates the adult from the story he identified with as a child. Yet surely the ending is a full exposure of the play upon which the story is built. For Usher is, in the last analysis, the artist— the sick artist gradually dying in the stifling environment of the Gothic house he haunts. Having fed upon its own decay, his imagination at last betrays itself in incest and madness. Both he and Ligeia are the decadent artists who haunt the narrator; they are his madness, his disease, and the rather sick and banal correspondence poems which each has written—and which Poe inserted grandiloquently at the center of each story—reinforce their impotence.

In "Ligeia" the maddened narrator had destroyed the blond and blue-eyed lady of romance who had repressed, distorted, and driven underground his will, which in turn took its revenge in the form of the aggressive fantasy of Ligeia. In "The Fall of the House of Usher" he brought down the House of Usher along with the pale, sensitive artist who was in turn victimized by all the degenerate traditions embodied in the house, the sister, and his art. But in "William Wilson," instead of figuring forth the drama of repression in terms of an attempt to murder a wife or bury alive a sister, the narrator directs his attack completely upon himself in an effort to kill his conscience. Thus instead of preying upon the form of the Gothic tale of sensation, "William Wilson" takes the form of a parable in which there are two William Wilsons. They are in actuality twin aspects of a single consciousness, and the story itself is, as Thomas Mann noted, the classic example in fiction of the phenomenon of the *Doppelgänger*. In the story, the narrator William Wilson [Will-I-am—Will's son] relates how his dissolute and profligate life ultimately evoked a haunting figure in the person of a schoolmate also named William Wilson who, in a typically Poesque turn, attempted to break his will. The scoundrel narrator tells of trying to put down his emergent antagonist by means of practical jokes, hoaxes, and banter, but his conscience retaliates by imitating, by impersonating, and finally by invading his consciousness. Hounded mercilessly throughout Europe by his double, the narrator turns at last and kills his conscience only to see in a mirror the shattered image of his self-mutilation.

The murder of the conscience is the crime of the Poe narrator pushed to its furthest degree. It is the crime of Pym, of the murderer of Rowena, of Usher, carried out explicitly against the self. The earlier narrators had attempted to bury their guilt in the person of the "other"; Wilson also tries, but discovers that the "other" is relentlessly himself. Having killed the other Wilson, he presumably sinks into a life of total profligacy, out of

which he at last emerges to recall the story of his demise in its
earliest form.

If we take the narrative as simply a parable of a man attempting to kill his conscience—and I am not at all unwilling to do
so—we nevertheless need to see what form the conscience assumes, what assaults it makes upon the ego, and what stratagems
the ego employs in dealing with it. First of all, the other Wilson
appears not as a figure haunting the narrator with guilt, but as a
rival, a competitor:

> In his rivalry he might have been supposed actuated solely by
> a whimsical desire to thwart, astonish, or mortify myself; al-
> though there were times when I could not help observing
> with a feeling made up of wonder, abasement, and pique,
> that he mingled with his injuries, his insults, or his contra-
> dictions, a certain most inappropriate, and assuredly most un-
> welcome *affectionateness* of manner. I could only conceive
> this singular behavior to arise from a consummate self-conceit
> assuming the vulgar airs of patronage and protection.

Clearly the narrator, embarrassed by his own vulgar name,
insecure, highly competitive, and ambitious, projects upon the
other Wilson the series of imagined insults, contradictions, and
rivalry. His strategy of dealing with his rival lies in jokes, banter,
wit, and impersonation. He burlesques his double. Through
this impersonation of each other the two Wilson's establish the
relationship which unites them. The other Wilson is gradually
brought to life through a scandalous and perverse impersonation
of his muted voice. He comes to assume the form of a conscience by virtue of the narrator's increasingly excessive attempt
to destroy himself in an effort to evoke as much as to evade his
conscience. The narrative denies the piety of the parable by disclosing that the conscience actually preys upon the destruction
of the self. Suicide becomes the only action capable of sustaining the illusion of morality and conscience.

IV

"William Wilson" completes Poe's portrait of the distintegra-
tion of the self. From the destruction of Lady Rowena, Madeline

Usher, Usher, the House of Usher, and William Wilson—from the very crime attending their ruin—C. Auguste Dupin emerges. If Roderick Usher is the creative artist in impotence and decay, Dupin is the resolvent artist reconstructing the world from the crime which haunts it. He is in fact the perfect foil to Usher; for while the narrator watches and assists Usher in burying his guilt, he accompanies Dupin in the process of discovering the criminal. "The Murders in the Rue Morgue," the first story in which Dupin appears, is by all odds the best of the three tales of ratiocination, though it is clear why Poe and many readers have preferred "The Purloined Letter" for its neat compactness. In "The Murders in the Rue Morgue," however, there is the energy of a form springing into existence fully armed.

Dupin has inherited the world William Wilson left behind him. Wilson's memorable flight from his double had taken him through all the capitals of Europe. From Oxford he had escaped to Paris, thence to Rome, then to Vienna, on to Berlin, and finally to Moscow, returning at last to Rome, there to kill his conscience in the Eternal City. Into a world without a conscience comes Dupin, a night-going isolatoe, an aristocrat fallen on evil days and living his life out in proud solitude. The world he enters, the world of day, has been victimized by a crime the police cannot solve. Faced by the brutality and dismemberment of it all, they are morally obsolete and psychologically impotent. But Dupin, working alone and through the powers of ratiocination, succeeds in discovering the criminal—an orangutan escaped from his master, a sailor who had captured him in the East Indies. The ending has about it the inveterate Poe sham, yet here again as in his best stories Poe makes the extravagant device simply one more part of his power.

But the chief power assimilating the implausible denouement is to be found in Dupin's solution to the mystery. Dupin discovers the criminal by reconstructing the world in the terms of the crime. What this first detective story reveals is that to understand and make sense of the modern world—the world of crime —one must be able to imagine a crime *without* a motive. This particular motivelessness, this perverse violence which Baudelaire recognized as Poe's disclosure of an exception in the moral order, man must discover about himself if he is to solve the crime which keeps him in chains. Unable to accommodate itself to a crime without a conscience, the world perforce depends upon an imagination grounded in relentless reason. Such a mind Dupin eminently possesses, being a poet and a mathematician. Reversing the laws of cause and effect, motive and consequence, Dupin works forward from the effect toward a new cause instead of backward toward an old one as the police are doing. Instead of assuming the necessity of a motive, he makes the crime and its effect his own motive for imagining the killer into existence.

The recognitions leading Dupin to his solution are worth noting. He realizes immediately that all the witnesses thought the sounds they heard coming from within the room of the crime were an alien language. The Italian, the Englishman, the Spaniard, the Hollander, and the Frenchman all thought the killer a foreigner. Though not one of them recognized any words, or sounds resembling words, each ascribed an alien humanity to the screams of the beast. From just this clue Dupin's intuition of the crime takes its shape. His intuition is in reality his suspicion, and from it he investigates the premises. Finding that there are no apparent means of entering or leaving the murder room, he nonetheless reconstructs the scene in terms of his original suspicion. Thus, when he sees the windows sealed from within, he insists to himself that this must be an appearance. By a process of facile logic he imposes his own reality upon the appearance, making the scene conform to his suspicion of it. When he tries the window and it fails to open, he simply adds to the situation a secret spring, which he says "must" be concealed. Observing a nail which secures the window, he "knows" something is the matter, for his imagination has eliminated all other possibilities. He touches the nail and it drops neatly in his hand. By means of his leaps of spurious logic, he invents a plausible reality containing the beast he has intuited at the outset of his investigations.

But his reasoning is only half the story. There remains the

other half of the act, the narrator. His relation to Dupin is almost exactly the same as his relation had been to Roderick Usher. Dupin is his double. The two figures occupy the same quarters; by day they remain closeted in great Gothic chambers as if they were living in the House of Usher and dreaming Gothic fancies; by night they emerge to exercise their reason. Dupin's first such exercise is, interestingly enough, to "read" the narrator's mind by means of a series of highly faked deductions. The whole thing is almost a burlesque exhibition, the two figures playing the part of extravagant pretenders at solving crimes, but it is brought off with such confident audacity that the illusion of ratiocination is flamboyantly sustained. Pretense is in fact part of the game, for Dupin's entire method ultimately comes down not only to the tenuous reason he exhibits, but to his capacity to identify with the situation. He reads the narrator's mind by means of identification, or inner impersonation, just as he understands the Minister D—— in "The Purloined Letter" by imitating in the loneliness of his chambers the facial gestures and appearance of his antagonist.

As for the actual crime, it is the perfected, not the present action of the story. The present action is the narrator watching Dupin's mind re-creating the crime. Dupin is constructing beneath the rapt gaze of the narrator the world in terms of original crime to be solved, not original sin to be redeemed. The narrator's relation to the reconstruction is made fully clear when Dupin, after describing the extraordinary agility required to enter the windows of the murder room, emphasizes again the peculiarly shrill and harsh quality of the murderer's voice.

> At these words, a vague and half-formed conception of the meaning of Dupin flitted over my mind. I seemed to be upon the verge of comprehension, without power to comprehend— as men, at times, find themselves upon the brink of remembrance, without being able, in the end, to remember.

The narrator is at the same point in relation to the comprehension of the crime that the narrator of "Ligeia" occupied in relation to the memory of Ligeia. As Dupin re-creates the crime he draws forth from the recesses of the narrator's awareness the *knowledge* of the crime which he and all of Europe refuse to know. The form the narrative assumes throughout this phase of the story is quite rightly that of the Platonic dialogue, for Dupin is a Socratic midwife bringing to birth from his dense interlocutor the idea not of original sin but original crime.

The fact that the killer is an orangutan is the extravagant detail which assimilates the bizarre under the rubric of reason. It is the absurd denouement resulting from the blindness of a world going on the old morality and the old assumptions, a world which must evoke a detective from the world of the imagination to save it. At the level of appearance, the fact of a sailor walking down the streets of Paris with an orangutan is absurd; but at the level of reality Dupin brings into apprehension, the alien orangutan escaped from its keeper has an import startlingly relevant. In the absurd appearance lies the reality that the failure of the imagination has released the beast—all that is alien to reason—into the center of what seems to be life but is really death. For the murders take place upon the street of death in a society whose imagination has died. The beast, the murder, and Dupin are all that are left of life.

These then are the terms of Poe's invention. And it is an invention, not an extension of older dramas such as *Oedipus* and *Hamlet* (both of which can be seen as forerunners of the detective story). For Dupin's motive in reconstructing the crime is *pleasure*. It is a puzzle which he takes delight in solving. The older motive—of saving the kingdom and discovering the self—is relegated to a most incidental position. The only hint that Dupin is interested in conventional morality comes when he observes that since Adam le Bon, the chief suspect of police, once did him a slight favor, he is glad to return it. Yet even here, it is simply a matter of aristocratic manners, not a moral issue.

Dupin operates outside the law. He does not take the law into his own hands as a host of later detectives have learned to do; he is instead indifferent to the law. He is not interested in punishment—there is nothing to punish in this instance—but in the sheer satisfaction of solving the enigma, and he significantly appears upon the human scene at the moment when the great discoveries in modern mathematics were being made. He himself is a mathematician. But he is also a poet, and he represents a discovery for the literary imagination, just as the form in which he appears is itself an invention—a new organization which releases power. Moreover, his deductions are impersonations of mathematical reasoning. In the tales of terror, Poe had impersonated romanticism and Gothicism, dramatizing their relationship and enacting their inward collapse upon each other; in the tales of ratiocination he impersonated reason restoring order to the stricken world. If the tales of terror depicted madness as the extremity of sanity, the detective stories disclosed sanity as the extremity of madness. Dupin's discovery was no more real than Usher's disintegration; it was a complementary gesture capable of exposing equal reality.

Exposure is inevitably the mode of revelation for Poe's impersonative genius, for impersonation itself exposes rather than conceals the mimicry of imitation. What Poe succeeded in doing was to realize the possibilities of impersonation. Thus his fiction, which began in parody and burlesque, the dependent and parasitic modes of impersonation, ended in the invention of a new form, the independent mode. To see that Poe's invention lay in the act of impersonation is to understand why his critical theory took the shape it did. To the impersonative imagination, reality lies not in sense, but in sensation, not in motive but in act, not in cause but in effect, not in experience but in art. Thus Poe in his critical theory emphasized the craft rather than the motive of art, and exposed the wheels and pinions of the artist's workshop which, he rather extravagantly contended, artists before him had tried to conceal. This insistent effort to expose the artist lay behind Poe's inveterate suspicion of plagiarism among his contemporaries. Much more important, it was an aspect of his relentless effort to exhibit the principles of fiction and the rationale of verse. After all, the elaborately conscious artist of Poe's criticism is the counterpart of the art in Poe's tales. Both artist and art expose the tricks, the devices, the craft of the imagination. The form of the short story, as Poe discovered it, at once exploited and exhibited the possibilities of narrative fiction: exploited by assimilating the terror of Gothicism and the sentimentality of romance; exhibited by impersonating the forms and fantasies of Gothic and sentimental tales, thereby disclosing that the desire for an exciting or moving "story" arises from a universal awareness that life as ordinarily lived is a living death from which the victims wish to be shocked into life.

Poe's "art," which converted the traditional form of the tale of terror into the conscious form of the short story, reveals that terror is the illusory life into which man perpetually flees in an effort to escape the living death he cannot acknowledge. This larger terror, this perversity, is the recognition which Poe's form enacts. Since the recognition is enacted through impersonation, the faces of terror and sentiment inevitably assume lurid, grotesque, sensational, morbid, and ludicrously exaggerated postures, inviting a cultured audience to shrink from their vulgarity. But to reject Poe's art is to forgo and drive underground the power of his discovery. T. S. Eliot's careful tribute to this underground current which, emerging in the poetry of Baudelaire, Mallarmé, and Valéry, flowed back into Eliot's own verse, has shown clearly, if patronizingly, how Poe made his way back to American shores in poetry.

His power has come back much more recently in fiction in Nabokov's *Lolita*, which might well be entitled *The Return of Edgar Poe*. For Humbert Humbert is, among other things, the Poe narrator come back to America after a hundred years of exile. His first wife Annabel somewhere behind him, he invades our shores not in search of Virginia Clemm but of a nymphet equally young. His entire pilgrimage, as Elizabeth Phillips showed some years ago, has innumerable echoes and suggestions of Poe. The very form of the book is Poesque, particularly in the trick of presenting a narrator who is a madman pleading to a jury for his life. To see the presence of Poe in *Lolita* is not to deny all the other literary sources Nabokov so masterfully impersonates. Rather, it is to affirm that in Nabokov's love affair with the English language and Humbert Humbert's travestied invasion of America the figure of our own Imp of the Perverse has returned from exile.

◖

An Exhibit of Paintings
by George Inness

from *The Carleton Miscellany*

1844, age nineteen, you began:
valleys, trees, rain, sunsets,
the spot of light, the long summer, the velvety look—
never to abandon them.
Picture after picture, the trick is there:
black lump rising on the right,
expanse to the left,
spot of sun halfway back—
passing shower after *passing shower*,
approaching storm after *approaching storm*,
sunset after *sunset*.
Even in the one snowscene
a sunset shines through square cloths
being hung by women at a washline.
Winter has left the trees clean
and thin as chicken bones,
but you give us roundness—the roundness
of women, the roundness of clouds,
roundness of fluffy sitting birds,
roundness of snow heaped on the ground.
The line is bent where the woman holds it down.

Always stepping from frame to frame,
frowning, shoulders hunched, fingers to cheeks or lips,

we cross our feet in a most ungraceful ballet:
Sir, our pantomime of wanting to see,
wanting to know, hoping.
We come to the museum looking maybe for grace
while our steps quack at us.

In 1882 the spot of light begins to move.
From melting sunsets, 1885
a day moon over a blossoming orchard.
In 1891 the proscenium is gone,
the sun is eclipsed by clouds,
the light no longer pooled like mercury.
Who might have warned us of this?

1894.
The sun has become a searchlight in the orchard—
old orchard, meaning
grass, graze,
without ladders and hands, without songs—
a white sun looking in, not away.
too holy, maybe, to be seen directly,
shining from behind trees to the left,
where we might not have looked.

Master, that sun is you,
looking in the world's woods, the same woods!
At last you found a sunset more than sunset,
orchard more than orchard,
picture more than picture,
that stand in this museum corner
revealed at last to those of us
who in our own lives look and look
for the same shining,
the wordless heart,
the birdless woods where light goes in.

CHRISTOPHER BURSK

◐

Adjust, Adjust

from *The Beloit Poetry Journal*

I was born committing suicide,
holding my breath; they had to drag me kicking
out of this damp garage, this airtight inside,
the gases I struggled back to
until the doctors slapped me alive
and shouted: survive, survive.

After Hiroshima, turning four,
I battered my head at the master bedroom door;
every night I dreamt I was a child burning at that town dump
at the world's edge, Japan;
and every night my father yelled: be brave,
behave, behave.

I ripped his set of Plato at eight,
the year my mother was put away at Boston State,
and war was fought in some darkness called Korea;
all winter, I played dead in the corner
while my teachers clapped:
adapt, adapt.

Grandmother took me in till I was ten;
with her best silver carving knife I locked her with me
in the den, all night, clinging to her bathrobe, demanding
to cut our wrists in a lovers' pact;

her only promise I could secure
was: endure, endure.

I threw tantrums into eleven;
I couldn't sleep; McCarthy lashed out at reds in the nightmares
where he held me witness; they nailed grandmother up for
   heaven,
that year; I pounded my fingers bloody on the pews
while the minister spit:
submit, submit.

I counted my bones, waiting to be dead;
at thirteen, an invalid in this nursing home, my bed,
I watched the homemakers of Arkansas rail at Negro girls
between commercials, curse the first graders
whom they tried to storm,
shrieking: conform, conform.

At fifteen, in South Station where I ran away,
every week, I bedded down on papers inksmudged with the
   blood
of freedom fighters, left in heaps in Hungary to decay,
while old men rubbed against my thighs,
lulling me to them with the hum
of: succumb, succumb.

I couldn't. Even with sleeping pills,
razor blades, I couldn't. While the U.S. played chicken
in the hills with atom bombs, I gave up my body like sixteen
   years
of hardened clay to be molded slippery
under the touch of my girl's hand and thigh
while she moaned all night: comply, comply.

Why couldn't I? When the world lapsed wide
and elastic into too much, too bright space when Kennedy died
and the roads wore bald; and the yards stretched between houses,

and the towns gleamed like chrome, I drove into walls,
day after day while the police barked:
obey, obey.

Can't you bleed? Coward, can't you die
while wrists are cut, throats slit, those children, all suicides,
are gassed in Vietnam; at twentyfour can you only cry
while men shoot themselves to death
in the DMZ, and your analyst coughs: you must
adjust, adjust.

GRACE BUTCHER

◑

Some Sort of Death

from *Trace*

The heron
steps
            slowly

along the edge
of a certain dream

shattering two skies.

            Dark soft weeds
            move with the water

            dark with slime
            my hair still growing
            . . . even now.

The heron
walks
            across my eyes

His strange feet
change my face
                        easily

            I need no form.
            This lake is enough.

I have two skies
although they break
and break
        where herons walk.

GUY A. CARDWELL

◑

Time of the *Fermeture*

from *Shenandoah*

Professor and Mrs. Gilmore went to the apartment of their new
friends with at least slight feelings of trepidation, but the evening went very well, everything considered. The Steinbergs lived
in an old building near Censier-Daubenton. They were *au troi-
siéme* and there was no *ascenseur*. Although Mrs. Gilmore was
very fit, she insisted for the sake of Mr. Gilmore, who showed
his age, that they pause several times for breath on their way up,
always prudently near a *minuterie,* so that they wouldn't have to
fumble their way in the dark. When they left, Mr. Steinberg
had to walk down with them to let them out. By then the *concierge* had gone to bed, and the outside lock was complicated.

Like so many young people of the Gilmores' acquaintance,
the Steinbergs had no notion of the way things should be done.
They invited the Gilmores—Mr. Steinberg had met Mrs. Gilmore at the automatic laundry on Place Monge a few days
earlier—to come at eight-thirty or nine o'clock, after the Steinbergs' two children were in bed. Thirty years earlier anyone
teaching at a respectable college would have known that the
thing to do was to invite people for cocktails or for cocktails and
dinner, not for some kind of nondescript occasion involving
conversation after dinner, perhaps with highballs or beer, followed at ten-thirty or eleven by cheese and rye bread and coffee
(what an hour for coffee!). But the Gilmores were not at all
surprised. College faculties had become completely vulgarized,
mainly since the Second World War, and not just in the sciences. The social sciences were dreadful, but they always had

been, and Jews had gotten in everywhere. The humanities were almost as bad as the sciences. They sometimes seemed worse, if only because one expected more of young men who taught English and French and Latin, or even history, for that matter. Mr. Gilmore had explanations for this, which Mrs. Gilmore did not attempt to carry in her head—she considered him to be perhaps too tolerant on some topics. Not that Mrs. Gilmore objected to such persons as individuals—it was just that they shouldn't be on college faculties or, of course, in society. She liked people and was interested in them, much more so than Mr. Gilmore, especially since he had lost touch, she often thought, and she could get along with almost anyone. Irish cleaning women and Negro maids were always devoted to her. Good servants know what quality is, and they respect it.

Mrs. Steinberg turned out to be a tall, dark, handsome young Jewess who spoke almost no French and was very lonely. She was interested in art (although she seemed to know comparatively little about it), and she certainly did not know how to dress. Mr. Steinberg did not even wear a necktie. He wore some kind of dark sport shirt and a sweater, and his shoes were in need of polish, but he had a good deal of information about French politics, as he should have had, for that was his subject, and that was why the Guggenheim people had given him a fellowship to come to Paris to write a book.

Even if Mrs. Gilmore had not enjoyed telling Mrs. Steinberg about museums and certain important things to see in them (Mrs. Steinberg was so eager that she got a pen and paper and made copious notes), she would have been glad to have given the evening to this visit on Mr. Gilmore's account. Always on her mind, now, was the problem of making sure that he was occupied, was not too bored. As she sat talking with one part of her mind on the conversation and the other part alert to make sure that Mr. Gilmore was enjoying the evening, she had to place a hand on her heart when she thought again of the vicious and underhanded way in which the new president of the University had arranged to force Mr. Gilmore out of the chairmanship of his department. Her heart thumped so vehemently that she felt surprised that no one else could hear it, and again she was proud that Mr. Gilmore had reacted to the president's insulting actions (the president was an overriding almost illiterate boor) by resigning three years before the usual retirement age.

Of course the Steinbergs had neither brandy nor Scotch. They brought out rye bread and cheese and offered the Gilmores either beer or "a very good bottle of Graves." The Gilmores took the Graves, which wasn't very good and must have been kept on a shelf over the stove. The Steinbergs apparently were not accustomed to having or serving wine: they drank beer. But over the drinks the conversation was rapid, and Mrs. Gilmore thought that everyone had a good time. The Steinbergs were so lonely that they would have been pleased to have any company, no matter whom, and they were genuinely eager to hear many of the little things about food and museums and theater and music that the Gilmores could tell them.

The Steinbergs carried the conversation in an almost lively way for a few minutes—although they were really not a witty couple—telling about the dreadful first apartment they were in. They spoke in rapid alternation; it was like a passage of stichomythia. They had rented this place before leaving Indiana, through the kind offices of a colleague who had seen it only once and at night. It was the only place they thought would be at all suitable that they got any word about, although Mr. Steinberg wrote dozens of letters. It cost much more than they could afford, and it was very far out in the *banlieue*. It took Mr. Steinberg nearly an hour to get to the Bibliothèque Nationale. Mrs. Steinberg never got anywhere; she was absolutely isolated. The man who owned the apartment was a complete eccentric. He cared nothing about keeping it up. He had put call bells in each corner of every room. There were wires, some of them bare, with sparks jumping from them, running all around the ceilings. The Steinbergs spent their first three weeks in Paris trying to clean the apartment and wrapping the wires with tape as a protection against being incinerated. The place was filthy. They were on hands and knees much of the time. And they could not get rid of—it was the first time they ever contended with them

—the roaches. At last—it was a terrible business—they got a lawyer and managed to break their lease.

Mention of the roaches reminded Mrs. Gilmore of New Orleans, and she told about the four years they spent there, "temporarily sold down the river," she laughed, "before they called Ronald back to be chairman at the University. Oh, that climate! Like equatorial Africa! I hope I never have to bear anything like it again! But one of the worst things was the roaches. Did you know that they were one of the first of created things? Like the gingko. Indestructible! I set the maid (we had a maid six days a week in those days) cleaning in every corner. I put out deadly poisons. But as fast as I killed them new batches hatched out. Or I brought new ones to the house with the groceries. The little hard brown ones were impossible to get rid of. They came up the water pipes. The big black ones were the most spectacular."

As she talked, Mrs. Gilmore had not been conscious of leading up to the "big black ones" until the words were out. Then she was aware that she had done something that she hated when she observed other wives doing it: she had fed lines to Mr. Gilmore; she had cued him in.

He took his cue and told his story—superbly, Mrs. Gilmore thought. He adapted it exactly as was necessary for the Steinbergs, and they loved it.

"It was our first important dinner party," Mr. Gilmore said. "We had done the little house entirely over—it was like a small, rather old-fashioned jewel. I understand that Paracelsus explains the rhythm of generation and putrefaction, though how he would account for our society, which, to me, seems all putrefaction, I don't know. At any rate, it was time for that small house to live again, and we gave it new life. Everything was fresh and clean, clean, clean. We invited the president, the dean, and a member of the board, a very stately gentleman he was, whose wife was related to Mrs. Gilmore. Mrs. Gilmore had all the silver polished and got out her best damask tablecloth and her biggest, finest damask napkins."

The tone taken by Mr. Gilmore was perfect. It had just the proper edge of delicate irony directed at himself and Mrs. Gilmore—the Steinbergs had probably never eaten from a damask tablecloth, nor had their parents or their grandparents *ad infinitum.* Badly told, the story could have made the Gilmores seem pretentious, could have made the Steinbergs feel condescended to. But Mr. Gilmore had been a department chairman for more than thirty years, had handled all kinds of persons, and knew beautifully how to deal with them, even now, if he concentrated and put his mind to it.

"I got one of the waiters from the Faculty Club at the University to come pass drinks and serve at the table." With a few motions of his hands Mr. Gilmore suggested the white-jacketed Negro, the good drinks, the good talk. "I must say that everything proceeded swimmingly—that is, until I finished carving the *filet* and sat down. As I picked up my napkin and started to taste my wine, I raised my eyes. Our dining room was oddly shaped, as so many rooms were in those old New Orleans houses. Half of it, shaped like half of an octagon, projected from the house, and lighted the room during the day with its long French windows. That night, perched on one of Mrs. Gilmore's new valances near the ceiling, at the far end of the room from me, eying me with his obtruding, glittering obsidian eyes, formidably waving his long antennae, like Milton's Satan, this cockroach exalted sat! I watched him in silent horror, and he watched me, positively nodding and becking at me, like one of Chaucer's pigeons on a barn. I looked at Mrs. Gilmore, but of course the creature was behind her, and she didn't have the faintest idea of what was going on. I glanced at our guests, but they had seen nothing and were quite tranquil. I had almost made my mind up to forget the roach when I was shocked to see that he was beginning to spread and agitate his wings, very gently at first, but clearly with malign intent."

At this point the Steinbergs gasped. "Wings!" said Mrs. Steinberg; "I didn't know they had wings."

"Ah, yes," said Mr. Gilmore; "I am no expert on roaches, but I can assure you that at certain stages, at least, some of them have wings. At any rate, there I sat, like a character in a tale by Hoffmann, absolutely frozen, while that creature, all of four inches long, folded and unfolded his wings. At last he rose on his hinged, accordion-like hind legs. I gave a muffled cry, and everyone, everyone but Mrs. Gilmore, turned and looked up at the valance, following my eyes."

"I couldn't look," Mrs. Gilmore said; "I could only see Mr. Gilmore's face and that held horror enough for me."

"He was a thoroughly histrionic beast," said Mr. Gilmore. "As soon as he had our complete attention, he made his grand entrance. He projected himself out into the room on a long glide, swooping down near Mrs. Gilmore's head, passing between the lighted candles in the candelabra at each end of the table like some daredevil pilot of the first war diving through the Arc de Triomphe, then rose behind me to alight on the valance at that end of the room. Everyone laughed, and the spell was broken. He was part of the fauna of the country, and those New Orleans people were accustomed to his kind. I stopped thinking of him as a filthy, antediluvian horror and accepted his flight as symbolic of mysterious passage, of our brief journey, as another version of the sparrow that flies through the banquet hall in Bede's story of the conversion of Edwin."

A few minutes later Mr. Gilmore did something that was rare for him. He had been talking about efforts that he and friends at the University made during the early 1920s to stimulate interest in literature, and, looking first at Mrs. Gilmore, he recited one of his poems.

"I never pretended to be a poet," he said. "I wrote only four or five poems. This one, as you will see, is somewhat imitative, but I rather liked it at the time, partly because of the family connection. It is drawn after one of Mrs. Gilmore's relatives, but I mean it to be only gently satirical." He recited in a soft, husky, slightly unnatural voice:

"Her ways and manners without flaw
    adapted were to all
the situations one must meet:
    the hunt, the church, the ball.

Her lares and penates, though
    in foreign judgments odd,

seemed sane to us—first, children;
   then came family, husband, God.

In July she sought out the hills,
   spent August by the sea:
no matter how arthritis pained,
   she moved impeccably.

She listened to the gentlemen,
   went ha-ha over tea
with father's friends, but with her own
   responded hee-hee-hee.

Her sensitivity was precise,
   her tone, indeed, perfection—
knew how to treat a neighbor's maid,
   when open to correction.

She died before her husband, lies
   by her father and her ma;
with her she tinkles hee-hee-hee,
   with him, laughs ha-ha-ha.

Aye, when she died she knew her role,
   went, dazzling brow unworried,
to rest in high Episcopal ground.
   That's all. Short horse, soon curried."

Mrs. Gilmore did not like the poem as much as she did the anecdote. The next day as she prepared to go out she reflected that Paracelsus and the Anglo-Saxon sparrow were new items. Ronald was not like the duller academic storytellers she knew. He changed his tales to suit the circumstances, and he tended to revise them, whether or no, as he went along. She had thought he was careless of reality, but he once explained when she protested a revision that he simply didn't remember the original and had to improvise. And now his memory was getting worse. This story about the winged roach he must have told six or eight times in the past twenty-five years, and there were several others she knew as well. Perhaps she should try to make opportunities for him to tell his stories. It was essential that she do as many things as possible to keep him interested. It wasn't easy to think of Ronald as not alert and alive. That night in New Orleans he had been just thirty-two years old—certainly one of the youngest chairmen in the United States. His hair had been yellow—rippling yellow. He looked like the brother of Flora in Botticelli's "*Allegoria della Primavera*"—a long pale face, long eyes, and long hands that he waved a good deal as he talked.

Retirement wasn't going nearly as well for him as it was for her. She had her amusements and her little occupations, but he was not doing the writing he had always said he wanted to do. He went to the library four days each week and stayed there from ten until five, eating lunch at one or another of the little restaurants he liked. At home he got out notes and puzzled over them from time to time. But the truth was that in eighteen months he had not written twenty pages, and she suspected that he thought this feeble little start toward a book was no good. At the University the young men had run in and out of his office; he had discussed their problems with them; he had talked with the graduate students; and he had dictated letters for an hour or two every day. It wasn't easy for him to change his entire way of life. The theater and concerts were not enough, and there simply were not many people for him to talk to in Paris. She wondered if perhaps they should consider moving back to the United States, though never back to the University. Perhaps Ronald was like Antaeus; perhaps the soil, the American soil, would give him vitality again.

This was one of Mrs. Gilmore's two major shopping days. She approached Mouffetard from Lacépède and across the Place de la Contrescarpe, as though she were entering a stage from the wings. It seemed to her that there was a momentary pause, that for an instant the high buzz was stilled. She stepped out in Mouffetard, everyone moved, and the musical humming was resumed.

Mrs. Gilmore felt the elation that was usual for her when on Mouffetard. She advanced with exact, confident, ceremonial steps, much as Fonteyn might approach Nureyev to place her hands exquisitely behind his head, only to turn in a moment enticingly away, the working leg moving easily. Then she drifted forward in a sublime kinetic tracery. Madame Bugniet, momentarily unoccupied, saw her coming and burst into her usual song: *"Tapez dans les camemberts!"* Madame Bugniet's voice held the roar of avalanches. "Hello, there, *ma petite dame,*" she bellowed; "you weren't here on Friday."

Mrs. Gilmore smiled apologetically. "I was in bed with a bad throat. My husband bought what was essential right in the neighborhood."

"That's all right, dear. You don't look too bad, today."

"Il ne faut pas se plaindre," Mrs. Gilmore said.

"I've got something you'll like," Madame Bugniet continued, almost affectionately.

Mrs. Gilmore nodded appreciatively. With two small packages in her *filet,* she next threaded her way across the street to consider the *gibier.* "Such a treat," she thought. "We've nothing like this at home." It was just here that she had once been buffeted, caught up by the throng, and lifted positively off her feet.

Her eyes fell on the *sanglier.* The whole magnificently ugly thing was there, hanging snout down, its coarse hackles—black, gray, and russet—standing all ferocious and bristly, *hérissés,* down its back. What a terror, snorting about in the thicket, charging you! But thrilling, like having your partner put his great hand behind your back and swing you up and straight out over his head, only one of your legs gracefully tucked up, you white and still and finally sliding slowly, slowly down. So the proud beast. After his initial flight the turning, the charge, the *grand échappé* in fifth position *sur les pointes* in the air as the fatal lead enters; extreme tension in buttocks and thighs before the soft unraveling of all.

"No, thank you," she said; "he's beautiful, but I won't reserve any. My husband doesn't even like *chevreuil.* Are they always *panard,* like that? I'll take four *cailles.* There are only two of us, but Monsieur likes to eat well, as you know, and he never puts on a pound, so why not?"

For a second meat, Mrs. Gilmore consulted with her butcher at the big *boucherie.* He picked a *faux-filet* for her. "Take this one," he said knowingly. *"C'était une bonne bête."* As he passed her the meat, Mrs. Gilmore slipped fifty centimes into his hand. With butchers these small attentions are important.

Back across the street, a little farther down, at the best *poissonnerie*, her eyes fell on a basket of *tanches*, fat, gray-green and bronze, and so freshly caught from the ponds of the Somme that they were still jumping—like so many Nijinskis or Fedeyechevs or indignant small water gods. I must try them, Mrs. Gilmore thought, but not now. We'll have the *cailles* tomorrow, but tonight I'll have a little treat, *sole à la meunière*. Perhaps next week when that girl comes I'll have *sole Marguery* for lunch. The soles are so darkly pretty and when skinned so deathly pale, like some otherworldly mucous membrane.

Turning away with two soles in her *panier*, she stood a moment, quiet and happy, looking down the busy street. Oh, Mouffetard, Mouffetard, she said to herself, I wish I were a poet. Straight road to Rome; straight road from Rome to Paris! Colors, sounds, odors. Faces, names, voices. People I know who know me. I am rich. She shivered slightly and drew the delicious network of associations about her. I love you, Mouffetard, she whispered. When I die they can recite the stupid old poem:

> *Ci-gît, dans une paix profonde,*
> *Cette dame de volupté,*
> *Qui, pour plus grande sureté,*
> *Fit son paradis en ce monde.*

Her last call was on Monsieur Jo-Jo. He was her favorite. The butcher was very polite, calling her madame; Madame Bugniet was aggressively friendly and said *ma chére* and *ma petite dame*; but Monsieur Jo-Jo was a law to himself. He was about eighty and tiny and wizened and conducted his business from a little pushcart. He had a familiar word and a pet name for each of his regular customers. *La gosse* he usually called her, and she felt young all over. Today he urged pears on her—Passe-Crassanes—and a pineapple from the Azores. They were exactly right and quite reasonable, he said, the same quality that he supplied to the Tour d'Argent. Mrs. Gilmore had often wanted to ask him if he really supplied the Tour d'Argent, and now, first looking to see whether she were delaying anyone, she summoned up her courage.

"Is it true or a joke," she asked, "what you always say?"

"What do you mean?" Monsieur Jo-Jo said.

"About supplying the Tour d'Argent."

"It's no joke! Don't you think I have my connections? One has to have them, of course, and mine are very good. When you deal with me, you get the best that can be had in this world."

"All right," said Mrs. Gilmore. "Thank you. I'll take two of the Passe-Crassanes and a medium-sized pineapple. Choose the pears for tonight and tomorrow and the pineapple for Thursday."

She had everything she needed, and she turned away from Mouffetard by the little church of Saint Médard to take a bus home. Mouffetard was wonderful, but it was exhausting—struggling against the crowds, following the argot, making the decisions, the whole pattern unfolding in a great hurry—no hesitating, no looking back, with so many crowding in behind you at the busier stands.

When she got off the bus, she hesitated. She didn't want to arrive at the apartment until shortly before one. That would give her just time enough to put her purchases away, to prepare sandwiches, and to get to Madame Petit's just after the one o'clock *fermeture*. She would dawdle a bit. She began to look in shop windows along Linné, naming objects to herself in order to continue to build vocabulary and to practice her pronunciation, which was excellent, because of the two years she had spent at school in Switzerland when she was a girl.

Château Rauzan-Gassie, 1957, she read. That should be good, if you like the slightly metallic taste, the tannic taste of a Margaux. My father liked good wine. He was a person of distinction. Both of my grandfathers were persons of distinction. When my husband resigned from the chairmanship, that was the End of an Era at the University. Is *Beurre Bleu* better than the butter I buy on Mouffetard? If it is, I would still buy on Mouffetard. What will he do when people stop writing to him and there is no one for him to write to? Every day he writes to people he doesn't care about. *Poulet nantais* really is the best *poulet*, unless *poulet bressan* is better. I have never been disappointed in it, but then I always examine it very carefully. The girl who is stopping over on her way to Rome to talk to him about her dissertation. He will be terribly excited. We must have something special for her lunch. The sole; some Chablis, too?

I should be afraid to go into that bar. Those loud, rough voices. Or to visit Madame Geneviève, *la cartomancienne patentée*. I believe they said she is *Baoulée*. Chicken blood over wooden idols? Vegetables in a *filet* and her pink panties always hanging from her window. *Cette robe là est de tissu perse. Étoffe perse* or of *bleu canard* suits me very well. One of the good things about France is the deliveries. Three times a day. Of course the early mail is nothing but second-class things. What are second-class things *en français? Les imprimés*. The *facteurs* are very nice. Should we subscribe to more periodicals? It used to be that he couldn't keep up with the *Wall Street Journal*, the *Times Literary Supplement*, PMLA, and *The New Yorker*. I don't know how this place dares call itself the Grand Hôtel of anything. *Complet*. How do they do it? Now he finishes them off the day they come. I can't stand *Marie-Claire* or *Paris-Match*. *Réalités* is an authentic *tour de force*, he says: nothing presented as though it were something. We won't get that. Uncle John would have liked to read that *guide du zoologiste au bord de la mer*. He knew the names of shells and said Poe was a plagiarist. *Histoires d'amour de l'histoire de France* could be amusing, but I must remember not to spend. Falling in love was easy. He used to be so wonderful on the tennis court, reaching everywhere. That meat is *not* fit for a king. No matter how you cook it. Blood tells. Intellectual interests are a great help. In spite of his scholarship, does he? We must invite the Steinbergs in once or twice, without the children. More, and they could become boring. But good for a letter or two after they go home. *Tirage le jeudi*. Do they use a blindfolded child? Madame Petit buys them. I must not forget to go back to the Jardin des Plantes on Saturday at three-thirty for the next lecture in the series. Three-thirty, but earlier for a good seat. The Basque language, a fascinating topic, but we are not yet up to the Basque. There are too many *Indo-Européenne* languages for me to be interested in all of them. Six divisions, *Indo-Iranien* through *Slave.* Four is the one: *Celtique—Gaélique d'Irlande et d'Écosse, langues brettoniques du pays de Galles et de Bretagne. Pré-Indo-Européenne* vestiges in French. Fascinating. Sexual words, but I couldn't understand them. Hunting calls, and I know nothing of them. Words in some old songs. Could I? Like tu-whit to-whoo? toorelay, toorelay? Or whatever they are? *Marrons entiers au naturel* are tasty, if you like them. Those or *bégonias* for Madame Petit? Not today. That nice woman with the boxer had trained him to go to the gutter. Here and on the rue des Arènes, especially, one must be careful. What did she say? *C'est dégoutant.* No discipline. He would die if he knew that I buy our dried soups from a *boucherie-chevaline.* But here I am home again, and at just the right time.

After putting her purchases away, Mrs. Gilmore got out cheeses and bread and butter and mayonnaise and made three sandwiches—one for herself and two for Madame Petit. Then she opened the cookie tin and took out four brownies—two apiece. At five minutes past one o'clock, with sandwiches and brownies in a little basket, she went out again. Three houses down the street, she rapped sharply on the locked door of the *marchande de couleurs.* In a moment Madame Petit opened the door. Mrs. Gilmore slipped quickly inside, and Madame Petit pushed the door to before any unwanted customers could arrive.

Madame Petit walked first down the narrow aisle, past toppling piles of plastic buckets and counters overflowing with kettles, teapots, liquid wax, vases, thermos jugs, and flashlights, past rows of red-painted containers of gas for cooking, past the drum of alcohol *à bruler,* to the neat little downstairs back room, just big enough for them and the furnishings. "Ah, madame," cried Madame Petit, slipping off her blue *tablier* and putting on a sweater, "If you knew how I wait for these luncheons on the days that your husband goes to the library! I don't know what I did before you came to live in Paris!"

These meetings were snatched from the press of commerce by Madame Petit, from household duties or rounds of shopping, galleries, and museums by Mrs. Gilmore, but the participants never took the occasions lightly. Madame Petit was careful to have a few blossoms on the table or a sprig from a flowering shrub, and Mrs. Gilmore tried always to bring with her something special. Today it was the brownies. Madame Petit adored them.

Plates and teacups were already in place on the table, and water was almost at the boil on the stove. Chirping like a bird, Madame Petit took a tomato from her tiny refrigerator and got things ready for tea. "It isn't as though I were a native of Paris," Madame Petit said. "What's left of my family is all in Caen, and Monsieur Petit's family hates me because I am better than they are and have a little money. These men," she changed the subject abruptly, "they think we can't live without them, but it is they who can't live without us."

"I should not like to have to live without Monsieur Gilmore," said Mrs. Gilmore. "I enjoy taking care of him; he is very good."

"I know, he isn't like Monsieur le Roi," said Madame Petit, using the ironic title she often gave her husband. "Monsieur Gilmore is different. He is quiet; he never disturbs one; he is a gentleman. On the other hand, Monsieur le Roi is something like a fiend. His nerves are out of order. Only two nights ago, if you will believe it, he was roaring and screaming at me so that I thought the whole neighborhood would wake up. He tore off his nightgown and threatened to go out like that just to make a scandal."

"Really screaming?" asked Mrs. Gilmore. Monsieur Petit was a coarse, blackly hairy man, and she associated him for a moment with a snorting, squealing *sanglier*, a great dancer fit for a queen with bacchic knees, all shaggy, burning the wild air at the head of his prancing rout.

"Truly," said Madame Petit. "And that isn't all. You know how he couldn't rest until he got another position, because being a waiter in a café kept him on his feet too long for a man of his age? So a cousin helped him get his present position as a museum guard? Now he doesn't like being a guard and blames me because I said he should try it. The work is too confining. It is too solitary. There is no companionship. As soon as you get accustomed to one set of rooms in one museum, they move you to another set of rooms or to another museum. What do you think of that? No adaptability!"

"That *is* too bad," said Mrs. Gilmore, sipping her tea. "This is that good Lapsang Souchong. You are spoiling me."

"Ah!" said Madame Petit. "I know you like it; so I get it. But you are the one who is spoiling me. These exquisite cakes!" She nibbled with restrained eagerness at the beautifully soft, crusty brownie.

"What will Monsieur Petit do?" asked Mrs. Gilmore. "Look for another position?"

"He doesn't say," replied Madame Petit, "and frankly I am not sure that I care. *J'en ai marre, à la fin, moi,* if you will permit me a small vulgarism." Madame Petit always spoke *avec rondeur* to Mrs. Gilmore, with an air of openness appropriate to dear friends. "I could bring myself to kick him out, if I weren't so used to putting up with him."

"Perhaps he will settle down in the new job," Mrs. Gilmore ventured. "The screaming is probably just nerves."

"The screaming," said Madame Petit indifferently, "that's nothing; that's normal." She protruded her lips and made a vigorous poohing noise. "I have discovered that he has a new reason for not coming home at one o'clock so that we might have dinner at the standard hour. I find that he has gotten himself a regular mistress, a Vietnamese, only twenty years old, and, if you will pardon the expression, a real slut."

Mrs. Gilmore caught her breath, and her mouth hung slightly open. She told herself that anyone could have knocked her over with a feather, and at the same time there popped into her head a crude phrase she heard when a girl—"arse over teakettle." But what she said was, "Oh no! That can't be!" and she thought, Ronald mustn't know of this.

"Ah, yes!" said Madame Petit firmly. She looked at the clock on the shelf above the stove. "I have until three-thirty, if you

can stay that long. Just hold on a second, and I'll tell you all
about it."

"Please do," said Mrs. Gilmore. "That is really something to
talk about."

The little gas heater threw out good warmth, and the tea that
Madame Petit poured was fresh and hot. What with the differences between inner and outer temperatures and the steam that
came in lively jets from the spout of the boiling kettle, the one
window was fogged over and the outside world excluded. The
atmosphere was cozy, glimmeringly intimate. Mrs. Gilmore's
mind was crowded with mixed, floating impressions. That ill-
bred, ugly, blue-jowled, rumbling, not unattractive beast of a
man doing elevation steps and a *cabriole derrière*. With a Vietnamese slut fit for a king, no doubt, as his partner. The ritual
dance, the movements so old, so fixed, so beautiful. Norman
and Parisian phrases rose like bees from *demi-plié* position,
swirled in allegro passages, ubiquitous as Jews, leaping like fish.
The dancing words attended images of a boar with hind legs
delicately, angularly crossed, skeletally bony, resembling aged
Mr. Gilmore, who, youthful tennis racket in hand, rose minc-
ingly from his Mouffetard meathook, bleached ribs exposed to
view. Mrs. Gilmore herself magically appeared as the White
Horse of Uffington, symbol of ancient power, commanding in
bursts of furious energy the entire stage: steam, roach, sparrow,
Monsieur le Roi. The music sang to her, "To be Rome! To live
forever!"

Madame Petit poured again through her pretty little silver
strainer, and Mrs. Gilmore joined gracefully in the social rite,
inclining her face over her tea to capture the small, warm fra-
grance of it. Private twists of steam ascended from each cup.
Two sympathetic heads, one just streaked with gray and frowsily
bushy, the other white and well groomed, bent closer together.

WARREN CARRIER

The Image Waits

from *Northwest Review*

The image waits
in ambush
in dream:

the long gun
gleaming like a Cadillac
under streetlights

held against my head
by me.
It comes in other

cars, in sunlight
screaming curves
on long stretches

going all out.
In movies
the outlaw hero

trapped in canyons:
I'll take as many of you sonsofbitches with me
as I can.

Always the barrel
the world looking,
like father,

into the locked room
of my head
with a black bang.

◗

Sonnet

from *Poetry*

Cry, crow,
caw and caw, clawing
on black wings over hot black pines. What's
one more voice?

This morning the spring gave out.
No water in pipe, hustled to spring, peered
in and saw three salamanders, very pallid;
saw water-level below pipe-end.

No more syphon. What's that? What? *And*
the brook is polluted.
                   Weather going to pot,
each year drier than last, and hotter.

What's the trouble? Long time, 25 years, was I
mad.
      Won through, does anyone know?
      Hey, crow, does anyone know?
I see a chance for peace! What about water?

ROBERT FITZGERALD

○

James Agee: A Memoir

from *Kenyon Review*

I

The office building where we worked presented on the ground floor one of the first of those showrooms, enclosed in convex, nonreflecting plate glass, in which a new automobile revolved slowly on a turntable. The building bore the same name as the automobile. It had been erected in the late twenties as a monument to the car, the engineer, and the company, and for a time it held the altitude record until the Empire State Building went higher. It terminated aloft in a glittering spearpoint of metal sheathing. From the fifty-second and fiftieth floors, where Agee and I respectively had offices, you looked down on the narrow cleft of Lexington Avenue and across at the Grand Central building, or you looked north or south over the city or across the East River toward Queens. As a boomtime skyscraper it had more generous stories than later structures of the kind, higher ceilings, an airier interior. Office doors were frosted in the old-fashioned way, prevalent when natural daylight still had value with designers. In a high wind you could feel the sway of the building, and thus contact of a sort was maintained with weather and the physical world. In our relationship to this building there were moments of great simplicity, moments when we felt like tearing it down with our bare hands. Jim was vivid in this mood, being very powerful and long-boned, and having in him likewise great powers of visualization and haptic imagination, so that you could almost hear the building cracking up under his grip.

He was visited on at least one occasion by a fantasy of shooting our employer. This was no less knowingly histrionic and hyperbolic than the other. Our employer, the Founder, was a poker-faced strongman with a dented nose, well-modeled lips, and distant gray-blue eyes under bushy brows; from his boyhood in China he retained something, a trace of facial mannerism, that suggested the Oriental. His family name was a New England and rather a seafaring name; you can find it on slate headstones in the burial grounds of New Bedford and Nantucket and Martha's Vineyard. The Founder had that seacoast somewhere in him behind his mask, and he had a Yankee voice, rather abrupt and twangy, undeterred by an occasional stammer. A Bones man at Yale, a driving man and civilized as well, quick and quizzical, interested and shrewd, he had a fast, sure script on memoranda and as much ability as anyone in the place. He had nothing to fear from the likes of us. Jim imagined himself laying the barrel of the pistol at chest level on the Founder's desk and making a great bang. I suppose he saw himself assuming the memorable look of the avenger whom John Ford photographed behind a blazing pistol in *The Informer*. It is conceivable that the Founder on occasion, and after his own fashion, returned the compliment.

The period I am thinking of covers '36 and '37, but now let me narrow it to late spring or early summer of '36. Roosevelt was about to run for a second term against Alf Landon, and in Spain we were soon to understand that a legitimate republic had been attacked by a military and Fascist uprising. One day Jim appeared in my office, unusually tall and quiet and swallowing with excitement, to tell me something in confidence. It appeared very likely that they were going to let him go out on a story of tenant farming in the deep South, and even that they would let him have as his photographer the only one in the world really fit for the job: Walker Evans. It was beyond anything he had hoped for from *Fortune*. He was stunned, exalted, scared clean through, and felt like impregnating every woman on the 52nd floor. So we went over to a bar on Third Avenue. Here I heard, not really for the first time and certainly not for the last, a good deal of what might be called the theory of *Let Us Now Praise Famous Men,* a book that was conceived that day, occupied him for the next three years, and is the centerpiece in the life and writing of my friend. It may occur to you that if he had not been employed in our building and by our employer (though upon both at times he would gladly have attracted besides his own the wrath of God), he would never have had the opportunity of writing it. That is true; and it is also true that if he had not been so employed, etc., the challenge and the necessity of writing it might never have so pressed upon him as for some years to displace other motives for writing, other ends to be achieved by writing.

II

The native ground and landscape of his work, of his memory, was Knoxville and the Cumberland Plateau, but his professional or vocational school was one that for a couple of years I shared. You entered it from shabby Cambridge by brick portals on which were carven stone tablets showing an open book and the word VERITAS, a word—not that we paid it then the slightest attention—destined to haunt us like a Fury. The time I am thinking of now is February of 1930. On a Wednesday afternoon in the dust of a classroom I became sharply aware for the first time of Mr. Agee, pronounced quickly Ay-gee. We had been asked each to prepare a lyric for reading aloud. The figure in the front row on my right, looming and brooding and clutching his book, his voice very low, almost inaudible but deliberate and distinct, as though ground fine by great interior pressure, went through that poem of Donne's that has the line "A bracelet of bright hair about the bone." It was clear that the brainy and great versing moved him as he read. So here, in the front row, were shyness and power and imagination, and here moreover was an edge of assertion, very soft, in the choice and reading of this poem, because the instructor for whom he was reading did not belong to the new School of Donne.

After this, Agee and I would sometimes have a Lucky together and talk for a few minutes outside Seaver Hall in the bitter or sweet New England weather. Seniority was his, then and for that matter forever, since he was a year older and a class ahead. He lived in the Yard and we had no friends in common. Older, darker, larger than I, a rangy boy alert and gentle, but sardonic, with something of the frontiersman or hillman about him—a hard guy in more than the fashion of the time—wearing always a man's clothes, a dark suit and vest, old and uncared for, but clothes. His manner, too, was undergraduate with discrimination. He was reading Virgil that year under a professor whose middle initial had drawn down upon him the name of Pea Green William; Agee grimly referred to him strictly as Green. In the Seaver classroom with a handful of others we gave our attention to English metrics as expounded by our instructor, the Boylston Professor, who had set his face against Eliot and Pound. Faintly graying, faintly blurred, boyish and cheerful, mannerly and mild, he turned back to us each week our weekly sets of verses with marginal scrawls both respectful and pertinent.

Far away from college, in the realm where great things could happen, great things had in fact happened that year: works of imagination and art in newly printed books. These we pored and rejoiced and smarted over: *A Farewell to Arms*, most cleanly written of elegies to love in war, in the Great War whose shallow helmets, goggled masks, and khaki puttees were familiar to our boyhood; *Look Homeward, Angel*, the only work by an American that could stand with *A Portrait of the Artist as a Young Man*; and *The Innocent Voyage*, from which we learned a new style of conceiving childhood. We were also devoted to Ring Lardner and to all the Joyce that we knew. But "The Waste Land," which had made my foundations shift, had not affected Agee in the same way, nor did "Ash Wednesday" seem to him as uncanny and cantabile and beyond literature as it did to me. Here we diverged, and would remain divided in some degree, as he desired in poetry something both more and less than I did, who chiefly wanted it to be hair-raising.

In the Harvard *Advocate* that year there were poems by J. R. Agee, but to my intolerant eye they seemed turgid and technically flawed. I did not see until several years later the highly mannered and rather beautiful "Epithalamium" that he wrote in the spring. "Ann Garner" was a more complicated matter. This longish poem appeared in the quarterly *Hound & Horn*, still known that year by the subtitle, "A Harvard Miscellany," and edited by the princely Lincoln Kirstein, then in his last year as an undergraduate. Kirstein had known James Rufus Agee as a new boy at Exeter four or five years before, and there is a passage on Jim in his book, *Poems of a Pfc.*, finally published in 1964. "Ann Garner" had been written, in fact, while Jim was still at Exeter in 1928. Boys in prep school do not often write anything so sustained, and it is clear from one of Jim's letters what an effort it had been.

What brought me fully awake to Agee as a writer was not this poem, callow even in its power, but a short story in the April *Advocate*. Two boys hunting with BB guns in the outskirts of Knoxville got some infant robins out of a nest and decided they must be "put out of their misery," so while the mother bird flew shrill and helpless overhead they did the deed with stones. In puzzlement, in awe, in fascination, in boastful excitement—in shame, in revulsion. The younger boy threw up; the boys went home. That was about all, but the writer fully realized and commanded his little event. When I reread this story after thirty-three years I saw that he had put into it some of the skills and passions of his life: sympathy with innocent living nature, and love of it; understanding of congested stupidity and cruelty, and hatred of it; a stethoscopic ear for mutations of feeling; an ironic ear for idiom; a descriptive gift. Significantly, too, the story intimated a pained interest in the relation between the actuality of birds and boys—kicking and gaping both—and the American institution of "Church" or weekly Christian observance. The two hunters, parting uneasily after their crime, agreed to meet at Sunday school.

III

By simply descending a flight of steps and pushing through a turnstile, for a nickel you could leave the university behind and set off for the big-city mystery of Boston, where wine in coffee cups could be drunk at the Olympia or arak at the Ararat on Atlantic Avenue; then other adventures would follow. If the Yard was our dooryard, Boston and neighborhood were the back yard we explored. We lacked neither opportunity nor time for our excursions and for a good deal of what we had to concede was Young Love. As for the university, it could be contented with a few classes a week and a few sleepless nights before exams. It is remarkable that Agee and I both talked of breaking for freedom, but we did, and he even had a plan of bumming to the Coast that spring on the chance of getting a movie job. If he had, the American cinema might have felt his impact twenty years sooner. I reconcile myself to things' having turned out as they did. He waited until summer and went west to work as a harvest hand and day laborer in Oklahoma, Kansas, and Nebraska.

Jim had been briefly in England and France in the summer of his sixteenth year, on a bicycle trip with his boyhood and lifelong friend Father James Flye. Although he never returned to Europe, he had absorbed enough to sharpen his eye and ear for his own country. He was American to the marrow, in every obvious way and in some not so obvious, not at all inconsistent with the kind of interest that some years later kept us both up until three in the morning looking through drawings by Cocteau, or some years later still enabled him to correct for me a mistranslation of Rimbaud. He took Patrick Henry's alternatives very seriously. Deep in him there was a streak of Whitman, including a fondness for the barbaric yawp, and a streak of Mark Twain, the riverman and Romantic democrat. What being an American meant for an imaginative writer was very much on his mind. His summer wandering fell in, so to speak, with his plans.

Two short stories written out of his working summers appeared in the next year's *Advocate*. They are the last fiction he would publish until *The Morning Watch* in 1950. In both stories you may feel the satisfaction of the narrator in being disencumbered of his baggage, intellectual or cultural, urban and familial and social, and enabled to focus on the naked adventure at hand. The stories are pure fiction in the usual way of pure fiction, as much so as stories by Hemingway, their godfather. My point is that to conceive and feel them on his skin he had deprived himself of all the distraction that he liked—company, music, movies, and books—and had lived in lean poverty. To write them, and almost everything else that he had to work on for any length of time, he took on destitution by removing himself from class bells, Thayer Hall and his roommates, and holing up in the *Advocate* office for days and nights until the job was done. Advocate House at that time was a small frame building up an alley, containing a few tables and chairs and an old, leather-covered couch, all pleasantly filthy; and there were of course places round about where you could get coffee and hamburgers or western sandwiches at any hour of the night. A boardinghouse bedroom or an empty boxcar might have been still better.

Did he ever draw any conclusions from all this? He certainly did. He never forgot what it meant to him to be on the bum, and he managed it or something like it when he could. His talent for accumulating baggage of all the kinds I have mentioned was very great, as it was very endearing, and he spent much of his life trying to clear elbowroom for himself amid the clutter. But on the question as to whether he had any business coming back to college that year, his third and my second, the answer is yes, and the best reason was Ivor Armstrong Richards.

In the second semester, on his way back to Magdalene, Cambridge, from a lectureship at Tsing Hau University in Peking, Richards paused at Harvard and gave two courses, one on modern English literature and the other carrying on those experiments in the actual effects of poetry that he had begun at Cambridge and had written up in *Practical Criticism* (1929). Jim and I attended both courses and found ourselves at full stretch. Though he appeared shy and donnish, Richards was in fact intrepid and visionary beyond anyone then teaching literature at Harvard; when he talked about our papers he sometimes gave me the impression that he had spent the night thinking out what he would say in the morning. By pure analysis he used to produce an effect like that produced by turning up an old-

fashioned kerosene lamp, and he himself would be so warmed
and illuminated that he would turn into a spellbinder. When he
spoke of the splendors of Henry James's style or of Conrad facing the storm of the universe, we felt that he was their companion and ours in the enterprise of art.

Richards' exacting lucidity and Jim's interest in the "Meta-
physicals" are reflected in a poem in octosyllabics called "The
Truce," printed in the *Advocate* for May 1931, the first poem of
Jim Agee's that seemed to me as fully disciplined and professional as his prose. I not only admired but envied it, and tried to
do as well. The image of the facing mirrors fascinated him and
made its last appearance in his work twenty years later, in *The
Morning Watch* and his commentary for the film *The Quiet
One.* There is an echo in "The Truce," as there is also in one of
the sonnets, of a great choral passage ("Behold All Flesh Is As
the Grass") in the Brahms *Requiem,* which he sang that spring
in the Harvard Glee Club; the surging and falling theme stayed
in our heads for years.

Along with his stories, "The Truce" would be evidence
enough—though there is explicit evidence in one of his letters—
that in the spring of 1931 Jim held the English Poetic Tradition
and the American Scene in a kind of equilibrium under the spell
of Richards, and lived at a higher pitch, but at the same time
more at ease with his own powers, than in any other college
year. He was elected president of the *Advocate* and thus became
the remote Harvard equivalent of a big man on campus. We
still saw one another rarely aside from class meetings, but had
now one or two friends in common, including Kirstein and a
superb girl at Radcliffe, a dark-eyed, delicately scornful being
who troubled him before she troubled me; I can still see his grin
of commiseration and tribute.

IV

In the world at large where the beautiful books had happened,
something else had begun to happen that in the next few
years fixed the channel of Jim Agee's life. I was in England in

'31–'32 and saw nothing of him that year, when he got his degree, nor in the next year, when I was back at Harvard to get mine. What gradually swam over everyone in the meantime was an ominous and astringent shadow already named by one cold intellect as the economic consequences of the peace. Worse evils and terrors were coming, but at the time this one seemed bad enough, simple as it was. People had less and less money and less and less choice of how to earn it, if they could earn any at all. Under a reasonable dispensation a man who had proved himself a born writer before he left the university could go ahead in that profession, but this did not seem to be the case in the United States in 1932. Nowhere did there appear any livelihood appropriate for a brilliant president of the Harvard *Advocate*, or any mode of life resembling that freedom of research that I have sketched as ours at Harvard. Hart Crane and Vachel Lindsay took their own lives that spring. Great gifts always set their possessors apart, but not necessarily apart from any chance to exercise them; this gift at that time pretty well did. If a freshman in '29 could feel confined by the university, in '32 it seemed a confinement all too desirable by contrast with what lay ahead —either work of the limited kinds that worried people would pay for, or bumming in earnest, winter-bumming, so to say. Agee thankfully took the first job he could get and joined the staff of *Fortune* a month after graduation.

During the next winter, back in Cambridge, where my senior English tutor was studying *Das Kapital* and referred to capitalist society as a sick cat, we heard of Jim working at night in a skyscraper with a phonograph going full blast. Thus a writer of fiction and verse became a shop member on a magazine dedicated by the Founder to American business, considered as the heart of the American scene. It is odd and, I think, suspicious that even at that point in the great Depression Jim did not live for a while on his family and take the summer to look around. Dwight Macdonald, then on the staff of *Fortune*, had been in correspondence with Jim for a year or two and had bespoken a job for him on the strength of his writing—which incidentally included a parody of *Time*, done as one entire issue of the *Ad-*

vocate. The man who was then managing editor of *Fortune* was clever enough to recognize in Agee abilities that *Fortune* would be lucky to employ, and he would have had it in him to make Jim think he might lose the job if he did not take it at once. I do not know, however, that this occurred. What else Jim could have done I don't know either; but again at this time there was the alternative of Hollywood, and there might have been other jobs, like that of a forest ranger, which would have given him a healthy life and a living and left his writing alone. Now and again during the next few years he would wonder about things like that.

At all events, he hadn't been on *Fortune* three months before he applied for a Guggenheim Fellowship, in October 1932. Nothing came of this application, as nothing came of another one five years later. In the '32 application, he proposed as his chief labor the continuation of a long satirical poem, *John Carter*, which he had begun at Harvard, and said he would also perhaps finish a long short story containing a "verse passacaglia." The title of the story was to be "Let Us Now Praise Famous Men." For opinions of his previous writing he referred the judging committee to Myron Williams, an English teacher at Exeter, Conrad Aiken, and I. A. Richards. For opinions of *John Carter* he referred them to Archibald MacLeish, Stephen Vincent Benét, Robert Hillyer, Theodore Spencer, and Bernard DeVoto. Phelps Putnam, he said, would also be willing to give an opinion. If awarded a fellowship he would work mainly on the poem, "which shall attempt a diversified and comprehensive reflection and appraisal of contemporary American civilization and which ultimately, it is hoped, will hold water as an 'Anatomy of Evil.'" He would work on it "as long as the money held out," and he thought he could make it last at least two years. It is a fair inference from this that in October '32 he did not yet know that he would marry Olivia Saunders the following January. Both in October and January he must have considered that he had a good chance of a Guggenheim. On his record he was justified in thinking so. Yet in the last sentence of his "project" for *John Carter* his offhand honesty about the prospect of never finishing it may have handed the Guggenheim committee a reason for turning him down.

The two long sections that he got written, with some unplaced fragments, have been printed in *The Collected Poems of James Agee*, recently edited by myself. His hero, never developed beyond conception in the poem as it stands, would have owed something not only to Byron's Don Juan but, I think, to the Nihilist superman Stavrogin in *The Possessed*, a novel we were studying with Richards in the spring of '31—greatly to the increase of hyperconsciousness in us both. Jim's fairly savage examination of certain Episcopalian attitudes and décor—and, even more, the sheer amount of this—indicates quite adequately how "Church," "organized religion," etc., in relation to awe and vision, bothered his mind. Another value, almost another faith, emerges in the profound respect (as well as disrespect) accorded to the happy completion of love. When Jim spoke of "joy" he most often meant this, or meant this as his criterion.

V

Moderate ambitions may be the thing for some people at some ages, but they were not for James Agee, and certainly not at twenty-three. To make "a complete appraisal of contemporary civilization," no less, was what he hoped to do with his long poem. Now the Founder, Henry Luce, with his magazines, actually held a quite similar ambition, and this accounts for the mixture of attraction and repulsion in Agee's feeling for his job. Attraction because *Fortune* took the world for its province, and because the standard of workmanship on the magazine was high. Also because economic reality, the magazine's primary field, appeared grim and large in everyone's life at that time, and because by courtesy of *Fortune* the world lay open to its editors and they were made free of anything that in fact or art or thought had bearing on their work. Repulsion because that freedom in truth was so qualified, because the ponderous and technically classy magazine identified itself from the start, and so compromised itself (not dishonestly, but by the nature of things), with one face of the civilization it meant to appraise; whatever it might incidentally value, it was concerned with power and practical intelligence, not with the adventurous, the beautiful, and the profound—words we avoided in those days but for which referents none the less existed. At heart, Agee knew his vocation to be in mortal competition with the Founder's enterprise.

Nevertheless he had now three uninterrupted years of it. One blessing was the presence on *Fortune* of Archibald MacLeish, a Yaleman like the Founder and one of the original editors, but also a fine artist who knew Jim for another, respected him, and helped him. MacLeish in 1932 was forty and had published his big poem, *Conquistador*. Being experienced and distinguished, he could pick the subjects that appealed to him, and, being a clearheaded lawyer-turned-poet, he wrote both well and efficiently. His efficiency was a byword on *Fortune*. Requiring all research material in orderly sequence on cards, he merely flipped through them and wrote in longhand until five o'clock, when he left the office. Often enough other people, including Jim, would be there most of the night.

I had a brief glimpse of the scene when I got to New York in the summer of '33. The city lay weary and frowsy in a stench of Depression through which I walked for many days, many miles up and down town, answering ads, seeing doubtful men in dusty offices, looking for a job. MacLeish got me an interview with a rather knifelike *Fortune* editor who read what writing I had to show and clearly sized me up as a second but possibly even more difficult Agee, where one was already enough. Staring out of the window reflectively at Long Island, he told me in fact that the Founder had taken a good deal from Agee, allowing for Agee's talent, but that there were limits. Back in MacLeish's office I waited while he, the old backfield man, warm and charming as ever, called up Jim. Jim came in and we poets talked. One subject was Hart Crane, whom Archie had once persuaded *Fortune* to take on for a trial. Hart had been completely unable to do it. It did not cross my mind that this had any relevance to me. I felt elated over my visit, and Jim took me home to dinner.

The basement apartment on Perry Street had a back yard where grew an ailanthus tree, and there under the slim leaves we sat until dark, he and Via and I, drinking—I imagine—Manhattans, a fashion of the period. After dinner we went to the piano and sang some of the Brahms *Requiem*. Then he got out his manuscripts, read from *John Carter*, and read a new poem, a beauty, "Theme with Variations" (later he called it "Night Piece"). *Fortune*, I suppose at MacLeish's suggestion, had assigned him an article on the Tennessee Valley Authority, and in the course of preparing it he had gone back that summer to the countryside of his boyhood: hence, I think, this poem. In that evening's dusk and lamplight neither of us had any doubt that we shared a vocation and would pursue it, come what might. We were to have a good many evenings like it during the next three years while that particular *modus vivendi* lasted for Jim Agee as office worker and husband.

Jim must have thought *Fortune* would have me (*Time*, instead, had me, but not until February of '36), because at the end of August, when I was temporarily out of town, I had a letter from him that concluded: "I'm wondering what you'll think of a job on *Fortune*, if you take it. It varies with me from a sort of hard, masochistic liking without enthusiasm or trust, to direct nausea at the sight of this symbol $ and this % and this *biggest* and this some blank billion. At times I'd as soon work on Babies Just Babies. But in the long run I suspect the fault, dear *Fortune*, is in me: that I hate any job on earth, as a job and hindrance and semisuicide."

His TVA article appeared in *Fortune* for October. Soon after this Luce called him in and told him that he had written one of the best things ever printed in the magazine. It was characteristic of the Founder to acknowledge this; it was also characteristic of him to indicate, as Agee's reward, the opportunity to write a number of straight "business stories" whereby to strengthen his supposed weak side. The first of these concerned The Steel Rail, and, according to Dwight Macdonald, the Founder himself buckled down to coach Agee in how to write good hard sense about the steel business.[1] Eventually Luce gave up and the job

[1] A story later got around that the Founder for a time considered send-

went to someone else, but the article as it appeared in December retained traces of Jim's hand: "Caught across the green breadth of America like snail paths on a monstrous plantain leaf are 400,000 . . . steel miles. If, under the maleficent influence of that disorderly phosphorus which all steel contains, every inch of this bright mileage were suddenly to thaw into thin air . . ."

VI

During that fall and winter and the following year we pretty often had lunch or dinner together. I would call for him in his lofty office, or would look up over my typewriter in the newspaper city room, where by that time I worked, and see him coming down the aisle from the elevator. He would approach at his fast, loose, long-legged walk, springy on the balls of his feet, with his open overcoat flapping. We would go to a saloon for beer and roast beef sandwiches. I wish I could recall the conversations of those times, because in them we found our particular kind of brotherhood. Both of us had been deeply enchanted and instructed, and were both skilled, in an art remote from news writing, an art that we were not getting time or breath to practice much. You would underestimate us if you supposed that we met to exchange grievances, for of these in the ordinary sense we had none. We met to exchange perceptions, and I had then and later the sense that neither of us felt himself more fully engaged than in talk with the other. My own childhood enabled me to understand his, in particular his schooling at the monastery school of St. Andrew's in Tennessee. We were both in the habit of looking into the shadow of Death. Although we came of different stock and from different regions, we were both Catholics (he, to be precise, Anglo-Catholic) by bringing-up and metaphysical formation; both dubious, not to say distressed, about "Church"; both inclined to the "religion of art," meaning

ing Agee to the Harvard Business School. "That story," Luce wrote to me in 1964, "is quite plausible—though I do not actually recall it. A problem in journalism that interested me then—and still does—is to combine good writing and 'human understanding' with familiarity with business."

that no other purpose, as we would have put it, seemed worth a damn in comparison with making good poems. Movies, of course, we talked about a good deal. My experience was not as wide as his, my passion less, but we admired certain things in common: Zasu Pitts in *Greed* and the beautiful sordidness of that film; the classic flight down the steps in *Potemkin*; Keaton; Chaplin. We saw, sometimes together, and "hashed over," as Jim would say, the offerings of that period: the René Clairs, the Ernst Lubitsches; *The Informer*; *Men of Aran*; *Grand Illusion*; *Mayerling*; *The Blue Angel*; *Maedchen in Uniform*; *Zwei Herzen* . . .

Many-tiered and mysterious, the life of the great city submerged us now, me rather more, since I had no eyrie like his but all day long spanieled back and forth in it and at night battered at my deadlines. Whatever other interests we had, one became fairly constant and in time inveterate: the precise relation between any given real situation or event and the versions of it presented in print—that is, after a number of accidents, processes, and conventions had come into play. The quite complicated question of "how it really was" came before us all the time, along with our resources and abilities for making any part of that actuality known in the frames our employers gave us. Those frames we were acutely aware of, being acutely aware of others. Against believing most of what I read I am armored to this day with defenses worked out in those years and the years to follow. Styles of course endlessly interested us, and one of Jim's notions was that of writing an entire false issue of the *World-Telegram* dead-pan, with every news item and ad heightened in its own style to the point of parody. Neither of us felt snide about eyewitness writing in itself or as practiced by Lardner or Hemingway; how could we? We simply mistrusted the journalistic apparatus as a mirror of the world, and we didn't like being consumed by it. Neither of us ever acquired a professional and equable willingness to work in that harness. For him to do so would have been more difficult than for me, since he had a great talent for prose fiction and I had not. After being turned down for the Guggenheim, in fact, he thought of trying to publish a book of his stories, and went so far as to write a preface for it. But he dropped the idea and instead, with MacLeish's encouragement, he gathered the best of his old poems together with some new ones to make a book. In October 1934, in the Yale Younger Poets series, in which MacLeish and Stephen Vincent Benét were then interested, the Yale Press published *Permit Me Voyage*.

VII

Of how I felt about Jim's book then, it is perhaps enough to say that at bad times in the next year or two I found some comfort in being named in it. So far as I can discover, none of the contemporary comments on it, including the foreword by MacLeish, took much notice of what principally distinguished it at the time: the religious terms and passion of several pieces. In two of his three pages MacLeish did not refer to the book at all, being engaged in arguing that neither of the current literary "programs," America Rediscovered and Capitalism Be Damned, mattered in comparison with *work* done. As to Agee, "Obviously he has a deep love of the land. Equally obviously he has a considerable contempt for the dying civilization in which he has spent twenty-four years." But he said nothing of the fact that Agee's book appeared to be the work of a desperate Christian; in fact, he concluded that by virtue of the poet's gift, especially his ear, and his labor at his art, "the work achieves an integral and inward importance altogether independent of the opinions and purposes of its author."

This was true enough, but some of the poems were so unusual in what they suggested as to call, you might think, for a word of recognition. One gusty day years later, as we were crossing 49th Street, Jim and I halted in the Radio City wind and sunlight to agree with solemnity on a point of mutual and long-standing wonderment, not to say consternation: how rarely people seem to believe that a serious writer means what he says or what he discloses. Love for the land certainly entered into *Permit Me Voyage*; contempt for a dying civilization much less, and contempt here was not quite the word. It could even be said, on the contrary, that a sequence of twenty-five regular and in some cases truly metaphysical sonnets rather honored that civilization, insofar as a traditional verse form could represent it. The most impressive things in the book were the "Dedication" and the "Chorale," and what were these but strenuous prayers? They could have no importance, because no existence, independent of the opinions and purposes of the author.

A sense of the breathing community immersed in mystery, exposed to a range of experience from what can only be called the divine to what can only be called the diabolical, most intelligent in awe, and most needful of mercy—a religious sense of life, in short—moved James Agee in his best work. If in introducing that work the sensitive and well-disposed MacLeish could treat this motive as unmentionable, that may give some idea of where Agee stood amid the interests and pressures of the time. It must be added that those interests were also his own, and that those pressures he not only profoundly felt but himself could bring to bear.

Four years at Harvard had complicated out of recognition his youthful Episcopalianism (he preferred to say Catholicism), but he hated polite academic agnosticism to the bone. In one *Advocate* editorial as a senior he had even proposed Catholicism as desirable for undergraduates. The poem *John Carter* was to be an "anatomy of evil" wrought, he said, by an agent of evil in the "orthodox Roman Catholic" sense. At twenty-five, after two years in New York, he published an openly religious book of poems. MacLeish was not alone in ignoring what they said; the reviewers also ignored it. It was as if the interests and pressures of the time made it inaudible.

Inaudible? Since I still find it difficult to read the "Dedication" and the "Chorale" without feeling a lump in my throat, I do not understand this even now. If he had been heard, surely a twinge of compunction would have crossed the hearts of thousands. But the book itself, Jim's poems in general, remained very little known or remarked during his lifetime, and for that matter are little known even now. One reason for this, I am well aware, is that in the present century the rhymed lyric and the sonnet for a time seemed disqualified as "modern poetry." Jim was aware of it, too; so aware that his sequence ended with a farewell to his masters, the English poets: "My sovereign souls, God grant my sometime brothers/I must desert your ways now if I can. . . ." The concluding poem in the book, the title poem, was indeed a conclusion, but it enfolded a purpose. "My heart and mind discharted lie"—with reference, that is, to the compass points, religious, literary, and other, within which at St. Andrew's, at Exeter, at Harvard, and in New York he had by and large lived and worked. This was more than the usual boredom of the artist with work that is over and done with. He turned away now from Christian thought and observance, and began to turn away from the art of verse. Yet his purpose was to rechart, to reorient himself, by reference to the compass needle itself, his own independent power of perception, his own soul . . .

VIII

Everyone who knew Jim Agee will remember that in these years there grew upon him what became habitual almost to idiosyncrasy: a way of tilting any subject every which way in talk, with prolonged and exquisite elaboration and scruple. He was after the truth, the truth about specific events or things, and the truth about his own impressions and feelings. By truth I mean what he would chiefly mean: correspondence between what is said and what is the case—but what is the case at the utmost reach of consciousness. With philosophy dethroned and the rise of great realists, truthtelling has often seemed to devolve almost by default upon the responsible writer, enabling everyone else to have it both ways: his truth as truth if they want it, or as something else if they prefer, since after all he is merely an artist. Jim Agee, by nature an artist and responsive to all the arts, took up this challenge to perceive in full and to present immaculately what was the case.

Think of all that conspired to make him do so. The place of

Truth in that awareness of the living God that he had known as a child and young man and could not forget. The place of truth at the university, VERITAS, perennial object of the scholar's pains. New techniques for finding out what was the case: among them, in particular, sociological study, works like *Middletown* in the United States and *Mass Observation* in England, answering to the perplexity of that age, and the "documentary" by which the craft of the cameraman could show forth unsuspected lineaments of the actual. Then, to sicken and enrage him, there was the immense new mudfall of falsehood over the world, not ordinary human lying and dissimulation but a calculated barrage, laid down by professional advertisers and propagandists, to corrupt people by the continent-load. Finally, day by day, he had the given occupation of journalism, ostensibly and usually in good faith concerned with what was the case. In the editing of *Fortune* all the other factors played a part: the somewhat missionary zeal of the Founder, a certain respect for standards of scholarship, a sociological interest in looking into the economic condition and mode of life of classes and crafts in America, an acquiescence in advertising and in self-advertisement, and, of course, photography.

The difficulties of the period were, however, deepened by an intellectual dismay, not entirely well-founded but insidious under many forms: *what was the case* in some degree proceeded from the observer. Even literary art had had to reckon with it. To take an elementary example, Richards would put three Xs on a blackboard disposed thus ∴ to represent poem, referent, and reader, suggesting that a complete account of the poem could no more exclude one X than another, nor the relationship among them. Nor were the Xs stable, but variable. VERITAS had become tragically complicated. The naïve practices of journalism might continue, but their motives and achievements, like all others, appeared suspect to Freudian and Marxian and semanticist alike; and of what these men believed they understood James Agee was (or proposed to make himself) also aware. Hence his self-examinations, his ambivalences on so many things. As he realized well enough, they could become tedious, but they were crucial to him and had the effect that what he knew, in the end, he knew with practiced definition. It must be added that the more irritated and all-embracing and scrupulous his aspiration to full truth, "objective" and "subjective" at once, the more sharply he would know his own sinful vainglory or pride in that ambition, in those scruples; and he did. Few men were more sensitive to public and private events than he was, and he would now explore and discriminate among them with his great appetite, his energy, his sometimes paralyzing conscience, and the intellect that Richards had alerted. I am of course reducing a long and tentative and often interrupted effort into a few words.

I named three books arbitrarily as stars principal in our first years at Harvard; I will name three more, arbitrarily again, to recall the planetary influences after graduation. In the spring of '34 Random House published *Ulysses* for the first time legally in America, and if we had read it before, as Jim and I had, in the big Shakespeare & Co. edition, we could and did now read it again, in a handier form suitable for carrying on the subway. Or for the Agee bathroom, where I remember it. Joyce engrossed him and got into his blood so thoroughly that in 1935 he felt obliged, as he told a friend of mine, to master and get over that influence if he were ever to do anything of his own.

Céline's *Voyage au Bout de la Nuit* was our first taste of the end-of-the-rope writing that became familiar later in Miller and later still in Beckett. Malraux's *Man's Fate* had another special position. This story, with Auden's early poems, counted as much as the Russian movies of Eisenstein and Dovzhenko in swaying Jim toward Communism. The attraction in any case was strong. The peaceful Roosevelt revolution had only begun; there was a real clash of classes in America. I had myself, in a single day of reporting, seen the pomp of high capitalism to be faded and phony at an NAM convention in the Waldorf, and the energies of laboring men to be robust and open at a union meeting. On one side of his nature Jim was a frontiersman and a Populist to whom blind wealth and pretentious gentility were offensive. Besides this he had the Romantic artist's "considerable contempt" for the Philistine and for what were then known to us as bourgeois attitudes. For poverty and misery in general he had a sharp-eyed pity. The idea of a dedicated brotherhood working underground in the ghastly world held his imagination for several years—spies amid the enemy, as Auden had imagined them; at the same time he had no great difficulty in seeing through most of the actual candidates for such a brotherhood, including himself. The Party fished in vain for Agee, who by liking only what was noble in the Revolution liked too little of it.

IX

In May 1936, some time before the great day of the assignment in Alabama, Jim and I journeyed to Bennington to read our verses to the college. In that budding grove he was almost inaudible, as usual when reading his own or other poems, but then as a kind of encore he did a parody of a Southern preacher in a hellfire sermon, and this was more than audible: it brought down the house. You do not hear much of his parodies. You do not hear much, either, of his mimetic powers, great as they were, though years later he had a bit part as a "vagrant" in one of his movies. At the time I am thinking of, one of his best acts was a recital of "When the lamp is shattered" in the accent and pitch of rural Tennessee.

We saw a good deal of one another all that spring—by this time I was married and working for *Time*—but by midsummer he was gone into the deep South with Walker Evans on the tenant-farmer job.

Jim's passionate eye for the lighted world made him from boyhood a connoisseur of photography, and among all photographers I think the one who moved him most was Mathew Brady. The portraits and Civil War photographs by Brady were a kind of absolute for him, calling him and sounding in him very deeply. Another near absolute was the photography in Von Stroheim's *Greed*; he especially loved the burning-white powdery kind of sunlight produced by the "orthochromatic" film of that period. These kinds of studied finality and fiery delicacy in images of contemporary existence he found above all in the photographs of Walker Evans. Their work together made them collaborators and close friends for life.

After the summer in Alabama I should guess that he got his *Fortune* piece done in September or October, and I remember it hanging fire in the autumn, but I can't be sure of these dates. Why did the magazine in the end reject the article that the editor, knowing Agee and therefore presumably knowing more or less what to expect, had assigned him to write? Well, one reason was very simple: the editor was no longer the same man. He was no longer the same man because *Fortune*'s repute in the Duquesne Club and the Sky Club and the Bohemian Club—in those places, in short, where subscribers met—had been damaged by what appeared to subscribers as a leftward drift in the contents of the magazine. In 1935 Jim's piece might have been printed, but in 1936 the new editor, not much liking his duty, did his duty and turned it down.

Now all hands at last had more than a glimmer of a fact I have alluded to earlier—that Agee's vocation, at least at that point, was in competition with *Fortune*. It appeared that the magazine, committed of course to knowing what was the case, had had the offhand humanity and imagination and impertinence to send an ex-president of the Harvard *Advocate* into the helpless and hopeless lives of cotton tenant farmers, but that it did not have the courage to face in full the case he presented, since the case involved discomfort not only for the tenants but for *Fortune*. Well and good, this gave him his chance to show *Fortune* and everyone else how to treat the case: he would make the assignment his own and produce a book about the tenant farmers. His friend Edward Aswell at Harper induced that firm to offer Agee and Evans a contract and an advance, but for the time being Jim did not accept it, fearing that it might affect the writing.

In 1937 he was in and out of the *Fortune* office on three jobs. The most interesting took him to Havana on an excruciating Caribbean "vacation cruise," of which his narrative, appearing in September as "Six Days at Sea," was a masterpiece of ferocity, or would have been if it had been printed uncut. He had become grimmer about American middle-class ways and destinies, and would become grimmer still. His inclination to simple cleanliness, for example, turned to anger for a while as he discerned meanness and status and sterility even in that.

In the good poems of this period, the one to his father in *Transition*, the one called "Sunday: Outskirts of Knoxville," and some of the lyrics in the *Partisan Review*, he did things unachieved in *Permit Me Voyage*. But most of the topical poems in quatrains, published or unpublished, are not so good. He never did as well in this vein as in the epigrammatic "Songs on the Economy of Abundance" that he had sent to Louis Untermeyer for the 1936 edition of *Modern American Poetry*. His skill with traditional meters declined; it remained, now, mistrusted and for long periods unused, or used only casually and briefly. The Auden-MacNeice *Letters from Iceland* came out that year with a section of brilliant Byronics, and if Jim had had any intention of going on with *John Carter*—as I believe that he did not—those pages might have dissuaded him. Auden's unapproachable virtuosity may, in fact, have had something—not much, but inevitably something—to do with Jim's writing verse more seldom. And in the Bickford's Cafeteria at Lexington and 43rd, over coffee at some small hour of the morning, we read together and recognized perfection in a set of new lyrics by Robert Frost in the *Atlantic*; one was the short one beginning: "I stole forth dimly in the dripping pause/Between two downpours to see what there was . . ." Perfection of this order Jim scarcely any longer tried for in verse.

Under one strain and another his marriage was breaking up; I remember the summer day in '37 when at his suggestion we met in Central Park for lunch and the new young woman in her summer dress appeared. It seems to me that there were months of indecisions and revisions and colloquies over the parting with Via, which was yet not to be a parting, etc., but which at length would be accomplished as cruelly required by the laws of New York. Laceration could not have been more prolonged. In the torments of liberty all Jim's friends took part. At Old Field

Point on the north shore of Long Island, where the Wilder Hobsons had somehow rented a bishop's boathouse that summer, a number of us attained liberation from the *pudor* of mixed bathing without bathing suits; a mixed pleasure, to tell the truth.

One occasion in this period that I remember well was a public meeting held in June 1937, in Carnegie Hall, by a "Congress of American Writers," a Popular Front organization, for the Spanish Loyalist cause. Jim and I went to this together, and as we took our seats he turned to me and said, "Know one writer you can be sure isn't here? Cummings." MacLeish spoke, very grave, prophetic. Then he introduced Hemingway. It must have been the only time in his life that Hemingway consented to couple with a lectern, and as a matter of fact he only stood beside it and leaned on it with one elbow. Bearish in a dark blue suit, one foot cocked over the other, he gave a running commentary to a movie documentary by Joris Ivens on a Spanish town under the Republic. Jim Agee hoped for the Republic, but I don't think he ever saluted anyone with a raised fist or took up Spanish (my own gesture—belated at that). He had joined battle on another ground.

In October he put in his second vain application for a Guggenheim Fellowship. His "Plans for Work" give an idea of his mood at the time, maverick and omnivorous as a prairie fire, ranging in every direction for What Was the Case and techniques for telling it. I do not know how he lived that winter, or lived through it.

Not, however, till the spring of '38 did he take the Harper contract and settle down with Alma Mailman, in a small frame house at 27 Second Street, Frenchtown, New Jersey, to write or rewrite and construct his book. Jim wrote for the ear, wanted criticism from auditors, and read to me, either in Frenchtown or in New York, most of the drafts as he got them written. There isn't a word in *Let Us Now Praise Famous Men* that he—and I and others—did not ponder many times. Frenchtown was then quiet and deep in the dense countryside, traversable whenever and as far as necessary in an ancient open flivver; they had a goat, God knows how acquired, in the back yard; there was a tennis court in the town. Jim played an obstinate and mighty game, but wild, against my obstinate and smoother one.

He labored all summer and fall, through the Sudeten crisis and the international conferences and the Nazi mass meetings at Nuremberg and elsewhere that sent the strangled shouting of *Der Führer* and *Sieg Heil, Sieg Heil* in an ominous rhythmic roar over the radios of the country. He labored into the winter. I have found among his things a journal in which he noted on December 1 that when the rent was paid he would have $12.52 in the world and in the same breath went on with plans for his wedding to Alma later that month. In January or February *Fortune* came to the rescue with an assignment: the section on Brooklyn in an issue to be devoted to New York City. For the rest of the winter and spring they moved to a flat in St. James Place, taking the goat with them. When Wilder Hobson went to see them once he found that the neighborhood kids had chalked on the front steps: THE MAN WHO LIVES HERE IS A LOONY.

X

In the living room or back yard of that place I heard several drafts of his prose on Brooklyn, and by some accident kept two drafts, one a final editorial copy, in a file. Twenty-four years later these turned out to be the only vestiges of this work in existence. In this case, too, *Fortune* found Jim's article too strong to print, and it did not appear in the New York issue (June 1939). He had written about the borough of Brooklyn with enormous grasp and wrath and awe and a machine-gun fire of clinical detail. *Fortune*'s editor appreciated this labor. As epigraph to the tamer article (by someone else) that finally got into print, he lifted one lyric sentence from Jim's piece and quoted it, with attribution.

After the Brooklyn interlude, the Agees returned to French-town for the summer. Some weeks before we heard Mr. Chamberlain's weary voice declaring that a state of war existed between His Majesty's Government and Nazi Germany, Jim Agee's manuscript of a book he had entitled *Three Tenant Families* was in the hands of the publishers. The war began, and the German armored divisions shot up Poland. In the Harper offices Jim's manuscript must have appeared a doubtful prospect as a rousing topical publishing event. The publishers wanted him to make a few domesticating changes, but he would not, and Harper then deferred publication; they could live without it. Jim was broke and in debt, and in the early fall he learned that fatherhood impended for him in the spring. I had just been given the job of "Books" editor at *Time*, so we arranged that he should join me and the other reviewer, Calvin Fixx, at writing the weekly book section, and he and Alma found a flat far over on the West Side somewhere below Fourteenth Street.

Now for eight or nine months we worked in the same office several days and/or nights a week. Early that year or maybe late the year before, I can't remember precisely when, the Luce magazines moved to a new Time and Life Building in Rockefeller Center between 48th and 49th Streets. We had a three-desk office on the twenty-eighth floor. Each of us read half a dozen books a week and wrote reviews or notes—or nothing—according to our estimates of each.

Jim Agee of course added immeasurably to the pleasure of this way of life. If for any reason a book interested him (intentionally or unintentionally on the author's part) he might write for many hours about it, turning in thousands of words. Some of these long and fascinating reviews would rebound from the managing editor in the form of a paragraph. We managed nevertheless to hack through that barrier a fairly wide vista on literature in general, including even verse, the despised quarterlies, and scholarship. With light hearts and advice of counsel we reviewed a new edition of the classic *Wigmore on Evidence*. One week we jammed through a joint review of Henry Miller, for which Jim did *Tropic of Cancer* and I *Tropic of Capricorn*, both unpublishable in the United States until twenty years later. Our argument was that, if *Time* ought to be written for the Man-in-the-Street (a favorite thought of the Founder), here were books that would hit him where he lived, if he could get them. In all our efforts we were helped by T. S. Matthews, then a senior editor and later for six years managing editor and a friend to Jim Agee.

XI

Of the physical make and being of James Agee and his aspect at that time, you must imagine a tall frame, long-boned but not massive; lean flesh, muscular with some awkwardness; pelt on his chest; a long stride with loose kneejoints, head up, with toes angled a bit outward. A complexion rather dark or sallow in pigment, easily tanned. The head rough-hewn, with a rugged brow and cheekbones, a strong nose irregular in profile, a large mouth firmly closing in folds, working a little around the gaps of lost teeth. The shape of the face tapered to a sensitive chin, cleft. Hair thick and very dark, a shock uncared for, and best uncared for. Eyes deep-set and rather closely set, dull gray-blue or feral blue-gray or radiantly lit with amusement. Strong, stained teeth. On the right middle finger a callous as big as a boil: one of his stigmata as a writer. The hands and fingers long and light and blunt and expressive, shaping his thought in the air, conveying stresses direct or splay, drawing razor-edged lines with thumb and forefinger: termini, perspectives, tones.

He wore blue or khaki work shirts, and under the armpits there would be stains, salt-edged, from sweat; likewise under the arms of his suit jacket, double-breasted, dark blue, wrinkled and shiny. He was too poor to afford a lot of laundering, and he didn't believe in it, anyway. After the baby arrived in March 1940, I remember one big scene in which Jim was engaged in spooning Pablum into Joel. The father sat, all elbows and knees, in an armchair upholstered in some ragged and ancient fabric that had grown black absorbing through the years the grime of New York. The infant in his lap mouthed with a will at the Pablum but inevitably gobs of it splattered down even on the richly unsanitary arms of the chair, whence Jim would scoop it in long dives lest it drip—irretrievably, you could hope—on the floor.

The time was about over for all fragile arrangements and
lightness of heart. In those days the German air-borne troops
were taking Norway. There was nothing we could do about it.
One fine day in late spring, playing tennis with Jim on some
courts south of Washington Square, I broke a bone in my in-
step. *Life,* with a wealth of illustration, assured us that General
Gamelin was the flower of military science and the French army
the finest in Europe. Within a week or so it looked as though
Life had exaggerated. While I was still getting around on a plas-
ter clubfoot the British were evacuating at Dunkirk and the
panzers were going through the Ardennes. The dress parade of
the German army down the Champs-Élysées was reported by
the *World-Telegram* with a photograph of the Arc de Triomphe
and the headline ICI REPOSE UN SOLDAT FRANÇAIS MORT POUR LA
PATRIE. I looked at this and realized that so far as I was concerned a decade had come to an end, and so had a mode of life,
to flatter it by that term, that included working for *Time.* To see
what could be done about my *modus vivendi* in general, I
turned over "Books" to Agee, Fixx, and Whittaker Chambers
and departed, taking my first wife away to the west and eventually to Santa Fé for the winter. There I settled down on my
savings to do unnecessary and unpaid work for the first time in
five years. I had resigned. Taking no offense, and with great accuracy of foresight, the people at *Time* made it a leave of absence until a year from that October. I intrude these details because I am about to quote a few passages from Jim's letters to
me during the year. At some point in the spring or summer
Houghton Mifflin, to their eternal credit, accepted the manuscript that Harper had released to him. Well, from a letter in
December:

> . . . Excepting Wilder, whose getting-a-job has done him a
> favor as leaving-it has you, everyone I see, myself included, is
> at a low grinding ebb of quiet desperation: nothing, in most
> cases, out of the ordinary, just the general average Thoreau
> was telling about, plus the dead-ends of one of the most evil
> years in history, plus each individual's little specialty act. I
> don't think I'll go into much if any detail—for though I
> could detail it blandly and painlessly and some of it is of
> "clinical" interest, it could possibly have an intrusive and

entangling effect. So I can most easily and honestly say that
it isn't as bad as I've perhaps suggested, except by contrast
with health and free action—is, in fact, just the average experience of people living as people shouldn't, where people
shouldn't, doing what people shouldn't and little or nothing
of what people should. Journalists, hacks, husbands, wives,
sisters, neurotics, self-harmed artists, and such. Average New
York Fall.

The book is supposed to be published January or February—no proofs yet, though. I now thoroughly regret using the
subtitle (Let Us Now Praise Famous Men) as I should never
have forgotten I would. I am rather anxious to look at it,
finished and in print—possibly, also, to read it in that form—
but I have an idea I'll be unable to stand to. If so, it might be
a healthy self-scorching to force myself to: but that's probably
my New England chapel-crank blood. Mainly, though, I want
to be through with it, as I used to feel about absolution, and
to get to work again as soon as I can. I am thirty-one now,
and I can conceivably forgive myself my last ten years only
[by] a devotion to work in the next ten which I suspect I'll
be incapable of. I am much too vulnerable to human relationships, particularly sexual or in any case heterosexual, and
much too deeply wrought-upon by them, and in turn much
too dependent in my work on "feeling" as against "intellect."
In short I'm easily upset and, when upset, incapable of decent
work; incapable of it also when I'm not upset enough. I must
learn my ways in an exceedingly quiet marriage (which can
be wonderful I've found but is basically not at all my style
or apparent "nature") or break from marriage and all close
liaisons altogether and learn how to live alone & keep love
at a bearable distance. Those are oddly juvenile things to be
beginning to learn at my age: what really baffles me is that,
knowing them quite well since I was 15, I've done such thor-
ough jobs in the opposite direction. Well, nothing would be
solved or even begun tonight by any thing I wrote or thought,
or at any time soon: my business now and evidently for quite
a while to come is merely to sit as tight and careful as I can,
taking care above all to do no further harm to others or myself or my now virtually destroyed needs or hopes, and doing a
timorous or drastic piece of mending when or whenever there
seems any moment's chance to. I haven't been very intelligent—to say nothing of "good"—and now it's scarcely a
chance for intelligence or goodness—only for the most dumb
and scrupulous tenacity. On the whole, though, it's time I

had a good hard dose of bad going, and if I find I'm capable of
it the winter will be less wasted then it otherwise might be.
Meanwhile, though, I find I'm so dull I bore myself sick. A
broken spirit and a contrite heart have their drawbacks: worst
of all if at the same time the spirit is unbroken and ferocious
and the heart contrite only in the sense of deep grief over
pain and loss, not at all in true contrition . . .

I thought *The Long Voyage Home* quite awful . . .

I feel very glad you like the reviews. I wish I did. As a matter of fact I have hardly judgment or feeling, for or against,
and on the whole, not a bad time with the job, except a general, rather shamed feeling, week by week, that with real intelligence & effort I could do much better, whatever the limitations of space and place. Then a book as important as
Kafka's *America* can't even get reviewed, and I shrug it off
again . . .

The magazine you write of [an imaginary one] makes my
mouth water. I spend a lot of time thinking of such things
and of equivalent publishers. They really existed in France and
Germany and even in England. The fact that they don't here
and I suppose won't ever, by any chance, makes me know just
a little better what a fat-assed, frumpish hell-on-earth this
country is. Last stronghold of just what . . . But I do love
to think about magazines like that. And the writing *can* be
done—the only really important thing—whenever and wherever qualified people can cheat their inferiors out of the time
it takes. Thank God you're getting it . . .

That is the longest excerpt. A shorter one, from a letter of February or March (he never dated his letters):

. . . I'm in a bad period: incertitude and disintegration on
almost every count. Somehow fed up and paralytic with the
job; horribly bad sleeping rhythm; desperate need to live regularly & still more to do new work of my own; desperate knowledge that with all the time on earth I could as I spiritually
feel now be capable of neither . . . Alma is in Mexico—so is
Joel—nominally, presumably, perhaps very probably, that is
broken forever. And so far, I am not doing the one thing left
me to do if it is ever possibly to reintegrate: entirely leave knowing Mia. It is constantly in the bottom of my gut—petrifying
everything else—that I must, and will; and I still do nothing.
A kind of bottomless sadness, impotence and misery in which
one can neither move a hand nor keep it still without some
further infliction on one or another . . . For some doubtless

discreditable reason it is of some good to speak of it, but I hope I don't do so at your expense, in sympathy or concern (I've known such things to derail me) —There is truly no need; as I say, I'm only too detached and anesthetized.

I delayed 2 months in all this trouble, in correcting proofs, but all is done now so I presume the machinery is turning. Don't yet know the publication date though.

Another one from about June 1941:

Your last letters have sounded so thoroughly well in the head and health and so exciting in potentiality, that the thought of its shutting-off in a few more months, with your return to work, has made me probably almost as sick as it makes you.

I think this could be rather easily solved as follows:

What with one expense and another I shall nowhere near have paid off my debts by October and so will nowhere near be free to quit work and get to my own. So why don't I continue at this work and you continue at yours, for 6 months or 8 or a year (we can arrange that) during which I could send you and Eleanor $100 a month.

That would be very scrawny to live on most parts of this country; but apparently in Mexico would be: in Mexico City an adequate poverty; elsewhere an amplitude. This would, then, involve living where perhaps you might rather not; but a living, and free time, would be assured. And when I am able to quit work, if you are ready or need to come back, you could do likewise for me on some general equalization—

I think that by this or some such arrangement we & others might really get clear time when we are ripe for it, and it seems a better chance than any other—What do you think? . . .

Another a bit later:

. . . Nothing on earth could make me feel worse than that you should for any reason whatever have to come back now that you are ripe for so much.

As for the money, I feel as you do, that it belongs to him who most needs it at a given time—your need for it for the next year or so is far out of proportion to any I could have short of a year or so of freedom first, and greater too than you would be likely to have again, without a long stretch of preparatory freedom. I think neither of us should think twice about your later paying me back—that is a wrong conception of the whole thing. I'll be able to take care of myself, one way or another, when my time comes for it—meanwhile I'll be best taking care for things I care for most, if I can make freedom and work possible for you when you can make best use of it.

I'm talking badly out of turn in all this walking-in and urging—I hope you can forgive it. It seems terribly crucial to me that you stay free at this particular time, and criminal if you don't . . .

Chambers is still moving Books at *Time*—Stockley does Letters, and an occasional review. If you should come back— which God forbid—I imagine I could get switched to movies & you could replace me here . . .

XII

I hope an occasional reader will understand that the foregoing private things are quoted after long hesitation and at the expense of my heart's blood. I think I am aware of every way in which they—and he, and I—can be taken advantage of. Jim Agee's agonies and his nobleness are equally the affair of no one who cannot keep still, or as good as still, about them, and there is no chance that all of you can. But some of you can, and some of you are thirty or thirty-one and hard beset and bound to someone in brotherhood, perhaps in art, and you may see that the brotherhood you know is of a kind really wider than you may have thought, binding others among the living and the dead. It is best, at any rate, that you should have the living movement of his own mind about his New York life and the dissolution of his second marriage, and it is essential that you should see proof of selflessness in a man who often appeared self-centered, and often was.

Before the publication of *Let Us Now Praise Famous Men*, just before I returned to New York, I received the book in September '41 for review in *Time*. When Jim got word of this he wrote at once, airmail special, to make sure whether I had been consulted, whether I had time to spare for it, and whether if, consulted or not, I did have time and would write the review, we shouldn't agree that he would not read it. I wrote a review, but the editor who had invited it thought it was too stiff and reverent (he was right) and sent it back. He reviewed the book himself, recognized great writing in it, but classified it as "distinguished failure." By this he, as an old *Fortune* editor, did not really mean that if *Fortune* had done it it would have been a success, but that was true: it would have been objective and clearly organized and readable and virtuously restrained, and would have sounded well and been of small importance beyond the month it appeared. A failure on the contrary it consciously was, a "young man's book," and a sinful book to boot (as Jim called it in a letter to Father Flye) and was thereby true to the magnitude and difficulty of the case, including the observer. It is a classic, and perhaps the only classic, of the whole period, of the whole attempted genre. Photographs and text alike are bitten out by the very juices of the men who made them, and at the same time they have the piteous monumentality of the things and souls represented. Between them, Agee and Evans made sure that George and Annie Mae Gudger are as immortal as Priam and Hecuba, and a lot closer to home.

I refused to take about a quarter of Jim's already mortgaged income, as he proposed, and returned to work for *Time* from October '41 to May '43, when to my relief I joined the Navy. That October of my return he got "switched to movies," all right, and the last and perhaps the best phase of his life began. He and Mia Frisch, who was to be his third wife, moved into the top-floor flat on Bleecker Street where they lived for the next ten years. Before I went to Fort Schuyler I managed to revise my manuscript of poems and put them together in a book, but not until Jim had commented on each in the most minute and delicate written criticism I ever had.

How more than appropriate, how momentous, it was that after 1941 James Agee had "Cinema" for all occupation could scarcely have been realized by anyone, but a few of us at least felt uncommonly at peace about his employment. He loved movies more than anyone I ever knew; he also lived them and thought them. To see and hear him describe a movie that he liked—shot by shot, almost frame by frame—was unquestionably better in many cases than to see the movie itself.

He had wanted for years to do a scenario for Chaplin; whether he ever did more than imagine it, I have been unable to find out. By the late '30s he had, however, not only written but published two scenarios, both stunning exercises in what must be called screenwriting as literature. The first, titled "Notes for a Moving Picture: The House," was printed by Horace Gregory in a collection called *New Letters in America*, in 1937. Detailing every shot and every sound, second by counted second, with his huge sensuous precision and scope, he constructed a screen fantasy for the camera, his angelic brain, before whose magnifying gaze or swimming movement a tall old house disclosed its ghastly, opulent moribundity until blown and flooded apart in an apocalyptic storm. Compare this with the efforts of more recently "rebellious" young men if you want to see how close to artistic nonexistence most of these are.

His second scenario was published in the first number of a review, *Films*, edited by Jay Leyda in 1939. In this one he merely (if you could use that word of anything Jim did) transposed into screen terms the famous scene in *Man's Fate* in which the hero, Kyo, waits with other Chinese Communists to be thrown by the Nationalists into the boiler of a locomotive. I am told that Malraux, who thought he had got everything out of this scene, thought again when he read the Agee script.

Concerning his movie reviewing for *Time*, T. S. Matthews has told me of one incident. Matthews, as managing editor, late one Sunday evening received and read a cover story Jim had written (on Olivier's *Hamlet*), and in Jim's presence indicated that he found it good enough, a little disappointing but good enough and in any case too late to revise; he initialed it for transmission to the printer (*Time* went to press on Monday) and in due course left for home, presuming that Jim had also done so. At nine the next morning Jim presented him with a complete new handwritten version. Fully to appreciate this you would perhaps have to have felt the peculiar exhaustion of Sunday night at *Time*.

Jim Agee, however, had now found a kind of journalism answering to his passion. Beginning in December '42 he wrote the signed movie column for the *Nation*, every other week, that Margaret Marshall, the literary editor, invited and backed, and that in the next several years made him famous. He began to be called on at *Time* for general news stories to which no one else could do justice. Whatever he wrote for the magazine was so conspicuous that it might as well have been signed.

Enough, and perhaps more than enough, has been said by various people about the waste of Jim's talents in journalism. It is a consolation and a credit to his employers that on more than a few occasions he was invited and was able to dignify the reporting of events.

XIII

When I got back to New York in 1946 I found Jim in a corduroy jacket, a subtle novelty, and in a mood far more independent than before of Left or "Liberal" attitudes. He had become a trace more worldly and better off (I'm sure Matthews saw to it that he was decently paid) and more sure of himself; and high time, too. His years of hard living and testing and questioning had given him in his *Nation* articles a great charge of perceptions to express. His lifetime pleasure in cinema had made him a master of film craft and repertory. He had had some of the public recognition that he deserved. Most important of all, I think, this critical job had turned his mind a few compass points from the bearing Truth to the bearing Art. He was ready to take a hand, as he was soon to do, in the actual and practical making of films.

We were never estranged, but we were never so close again, either, as we had been before the war. The course of things for me (here I must intrude a little again) had not only broken up my own previous marriage and way of life but had brought me back in astonishment, with a terrific bump, into Catholic faith and practice; and, though Jim intensely sympathized with me in the breakup, he regarded my conversion with careful reserve. He saw an old friend ravaged and transported by the hair into precisely the same system of coordinates that he had wrestled out of in the '30s. Or, rather, not precisely the same. For in my turn I had reservations, now, about the quality of Jim's old vision. I wanted to lead a kind of life that he had rejected and, in his own and general opinion, outgrown; and there was (at most) one art that I might practice, the art of verse, that he had likewise left behind.

All the same, the memory of what he had aspired literally to be, in college and for the first years thereafter, could return now and again to trouble him. One day in 1947 when he and Mia brought their first baby, Teresa, to spend an afternoon with my wife and me, he handed me the two very sad and strange sonnets on the buried steed, published three years later in *Botteghe Oscure* and now included in the collection of Agee's poems. His hand at verse had barely retained and certainly not refined its skill, and there is a coarseness along with the complexity of these and other late sonnets. Two or three of the final poems are very beautiful, though. "Sleep, Child" certainly is, and so is the peerless Christmas ballad in Tennessee dialect (but I am not sure how late that one is, and have no clue as to when it was written).

The last verses that he wrote were some rather casually attempted drafts, by invitation, for a musical that in the late winter and spring of 1955 Lillian Hellman and Leonard Bernstein were trying to make of *Candide*. Both playwright and composer felt that these drafts wouldn't do, but Miss Hellman is not sure that Jim, who was more desperately ill than he knew, understood this before his fatal heart attack on May 16. "He was not a lyric writer," Miss Hellman says. "Good poets often aren't." At my distance I find the episode fairly astringent.

Helen Levitt has told me that only a year or so before his death in 1955 Jim seriously said to her that poetry had been his true vocation, the thing he was born to do, but that it was too difficult; on the other hand, work in films was pure pleasure for him. I think he had in mind the difficulty for everyone—not only for himself—of making true poetry in that time; I think, too, that what he was born to do, he did.

Jim's leaning to self-accusation gave him a certain largeness

among his contemporaries, most of whom were engaged in pretending that they were wonderful and their mishaps or short-
comings all ascribable to Society or History or Mother or other
powers in the mythology of the period. I gather that he got
cooler and tougher about everything in his last years, in particular about love. Before he went to the Coast, in the late '40s, he
wrote a draft scenario, never worked up for production or publication, in which with disabused and cruel objectivity he turned
a camera eye on himself in his relations with women.

After my wife and I moved away from New York in the summer of 1949, we saw him only once again, for an evening, in the
following spring. His last letter to me was from Malibu Beach in
1952: I had written to say how much I liked *The African
Queen*. Of his final years I can have little to say. (I had been in
Italy for two years when the shocking cable came to tell me of
his death.) I am told that young men in New York began hero-
izing him and hanging on his words, but late one night at a
Partisan Review sort of party a younger writer in impatience saw
him as "a whisky-listless and excessive saint." I myself felt my
heart sink when I began to read *The Morning Watch*; the writing seemed to me a little showy, though certainly with much to
show; and I wondered if he were losing his irony and edge. It is
pretty clear to me now that he had to go to those lengths of
artifice and musical elaboration simply to make the break with
journalism decisive. He never lost his edge, as A *Death in the
Family* was to demonstrate—that narrative held so steadily and
clearly in the middle distance and at the same time so full of
Jim's power of realization, a contained power, fully comparable
to that in the early work of Joyce. Let the easy remark die on
your lips. Jim arrived at his austere style fifty years and a torn
world away from Edwardian Dublin and Trieste; if it took him
twenty years longer than it took Joyce, who else arrived at all?

The comparison with Joyce is worth pausing over a moment
more. Each with his versatile and musical gift, each proud and a
world-plunderer, each choosing the savage beauty of things as
they are over the impossible pieties of adolescence, each concerned with the "conscience of his race." Agee had less ice-cold

intellect; he could not have derived what Joyce did from Aquinas. He had, of course, nothing like Joyce's linguistic range. His affections were more widely distributed and perhaps dissipated. He inherited the violence that Americans inherit: a violence, too (it will not have escaped you), no more directed against office buildings, employers, and bourgeois horrors than against himself. The cinema that interested Joyce in its infancy had by Agee's time become a splendid art form, a successor perhaps to the art of fiction, and who else understood it better than he? The record is there in two volumes. Joyce had more irony, but Joyce, too, sentimentalized or angelicized the role of the artist. In all Agee's work the worst example of this is in the scenario of *Noa Noa*, and anyone can see that script becoming at times a maudlin caricature of the artist-as-saint.

Jim's weakness and strength were not so easy to tell apart. Consider, if you will, his early story, "They That Sow in Sorrow Shall Reap." Through weakness, through not being able to do otherwise, the boy narrator brings the laborer to the boarding-house and so precipitates the catastrophe that leaves the scene and people in ruins. Or is it entirely through weakness? Is it not also through a dispassionate willingness to see his microcosm convulsed for the pure revelation of it, for an epiphany that he may record? Was it weakness later that kept James Agee at *Fortune*, or was it strategy and will, for the sake of the great use he would make of it? Ruins were left behind then, too, but in New York journalism of the '30s no one created anything like the Alabama book. Likewise, no weekly reviewer of the '40s created anything like the body of new insights contained in his *Nation* film pieces. Again, no writer of film pieces prepared himself to write for cinema with such clean and lovely inventiveness (barring the instance I have noted). Finally, no scriptwriter except possibly Faulkner exercised, or learned, in film writing the control over fiction that went into *A Death in the Family*. When you reflect on his life in this way, weakness and strategy, instinct and destiny seem all one thing.

In one of the best novels of the '60s, Walker Percy's *The Moviegoer*, I find a sentence running like this, of cemeteries that at first look like cities from a train passing at a slight elevation: "tiny streets and corners and curbs and even plots of lawn, all of such a proportion that in the very instant of being mistaken and from the eye's own necessity, they set themselves off into the distance like a city seen from far away." It is an Agee sentence, so I conclude that his writing has entered into the mainstream of English. But I share with him a disinclination for Literary History and its idiom. Jim may be a Figure for somebody else, he cannot be one for me. "This breathing joy, heavy on us all"—it is his no longer; nevertheless, I have written this in his presence and therefore as truly as I could. Quite contrary to what has been said about him, he amply fulfilled his promise. In one of his first sonnets he said, of his kin, his people: " 'Tis mine to touch with deathlessness their clay,/And I shall fail, and join those I betray."

In respect to that commission, who thinks that there was any failure or betrayal?

◐

In Silence Where We Breathe

from *Voyages*

As a boy he was so silent
she raged like a gnat. Summer nights—

Summer nights he stood at his desk
wrapped in a wordless soprano.

Once he constructed a clipper ship
to scale from the *Century Dictionary*.

All May they ran barefoot
through the stinging southern streets.

The air was like mercury,
a heavy silver ball.

And the river stank of salt
and rotten magnolia candles

down the end of the street—slot machines!
From their grandmother's veranda

she could hear the ring of life
start out through a swing door—

No one could tell such stories;
but he never cried, not once.

The River

from *Fire Exit*

we move from one
land
to another

my sister died
in the river

the cradle
on your sister's
back
is empty

& the water
rises

mother

why do we go
on

if we are
dying

my father carried
a fish over his back
its tail touched the ground

grandmother
used to chain herself
to the postoffice
for woman rights

DONALD FINKEL

◗

The Garbage Wars

from *New Mexico Quarterly*

*And he dwelleth in desolate cities, and in houses which
no man inhabiteth, which are ready to become heaps.*

The	The city wears about her neck a
prison is	garland of dead rats like an
the world	albatross where can we stow it?
of sight,	foul conglomerate the poor, whom
the light	charity corrupts brain-damaged
of the fire	infants marked for the heap by
is the	starvation the jails filled
sun.	to overflowing with the young, the
	drunken and the meek for walking
	on the grass for smoking it
	for stealing cars for lying
	in front of them snipers and
	pacifists

*headless dolls, bicycles without wheels, torn cushions
vomiting kapok, non-returnable bottles*

(from the alleys of history step
the garbage men   an army of dog-catchers
and exterminators   marching on the ghetto
armed with headache balls and sledges)

as an example the General nails
a nation to the stake   sets it
aflame   friend and foe alike
assist via satellite   they get the
message   plain as a head on a pike
dapper little man   glaring through
gunmetal glasses   into the heart of the flame
a silk scarf blooms like a lily at his throat.

The Greeks   They've thrown a wall round the ghetto
set back-   withdrawn behind it   the Governor's
fires to   doubled the guard   O happy complicity!
save their   on the hill the students have taken
ships.   the library   overturn ceremoniously
                files for the letters A through E
                one thousand billy-swinging fathers
                burst through the doors   thunder
                of tumbling books   catcalls in the ashes.

*And the fish that was in the river died; and the river
stank, and the Egyptians could not drink of the water
of the river; and there was blood throughout all the
land of Egypt.*

Did Hera-   And the General   time's ultimate
kleitos   garbage man   moves in to clean up
teach a   he rakes the streets with fire
general   wipes out the snipers' nests
conflagra-   (for the purpose at every corner great
tion?   municipal incinerators   and the smoke
                thereof   and the ashes likewise
                consumed   and the residue pressed
                into bricks with which to build
                new incinerators)
                                        in the ghetto
                the inmates have set fire to their mattresses
                black clouds of acrimonious smoke

appall the suburbs
                    the city
thrashes in her agony   the supermarket
shrieks through her broken teeth   ten thousand
bedrooms lift their burning eyes to the constellations
for a sign.

LESLIE EPSTEIN

◖

Playground

from *The Yale Review*

Wracked as it was by tumors, buckling and swelling in turn, the playground wire was hopeless as protection. Here and there it was hoisted feet from the ground, its spikes were blunted, and what had once been a forbidding gate at Highland Avenue now hung slack on its single hinge. Yet the fence still served as a boundary, separating the profane traffic from the particular rhythms within its sanctuary. A pale boy in skullcap and side-curls dawdled in the empty yard, pushing a stick across the asphalt. Behind him someone turned on a classroom light, whiter than the April fog.

The church was on the far side of Canner Street, a block and a half from Highland, above a wholesale-retail meat shop. The curb below was almost always mounted by the rear wheels of delivery trucks. In the mornings the Yeshiva boys bunched wild-eyed on the sidewalk, as the men, their heads stuck through chasubles of brown paper, their backs stooped, trudged over the sawdust from the trucks to the storefront where, straightening up, they jerked the meat onto hooks in the doorway. Judging pauses, the boys ran the gauntlet in groups; they were cut by the spilling exhaust.

What daylight remained outside sifted into one end of the church through burlap bags over the windows. The other end was lit by banks of candles behind a small, open coffin. Perhaps fifty Negroes faced each other at the darkened center. Parents looked across the room to their children, and the children, Avengers and Royals, glanced at each other or held their eyes down. The room was still. Only the shadows moved on the walls and ceiling and over the face and brow of Delmore, the dead child, while the motors of the trucks shook on the street below.

Delmore's father was a huge man whose skin bulged everywhere through the ropes of his mourning clothes. Not many people knew him, even now. He found it difficult, fat, a stranger, to move through the streets; and when he went he always kept to the pedestrian lanes, his heart racing when the lights changed or warned him, in a language he could not read, not to walk. So he stayed to his room, following the play of roaches, and ate the cooked street food—the slices of pizza, the corn and shrimp, the beans in a paper cup—that Delmore brought him, Delmore taking the steps three at a time so the pizza burnt the roof of his mouth, Delmore spreading out the sheets of newsprint over the bed, onto the floor: "Look here what's in the *Daily News!*" With one hand on the back of his own chair and the other on the back of the chair in front of him, the large man corkscrewed upward. It took him a long time, and no one noticed he had risen until he actually started to speak.

"Onct I had a dreams was a no fond wish," he began, "the worstest of my life." He spoke softly but brokenly, and with effort, as if the words were twisted through the course of his body, caught now between the two chairbacks he continued to squeeze in his hands. "I chucked up all I was, coils an' coils of me, chucked up my insides to the outside out on the lawns. An' this dogs, he came to my 'testines, he ate me, tore me, shook me with the teeth in his head." He did not move, except to let his eyes roll open when he paused. "Then I would wake up an' turn over for the same thing would happen again an' I was fall off a high hill or would dream about snake or that I was dead sometime. It happen again and again, sometime falling, an' I *could not* wake up, or wake up sick.

"But sometimes I would go to bed to dream I was have encors with a girls an' would tried not to wake up then but I would wake right when that would happen. Only the bad time I sleep a long time. Why, I ask." The room was very quiet. The candlelight and the daylight just picked out the sweat on either side of his face. "One night I went out with a girls and had encors and she me caught; then I came home and went to bed an' went to sleep and sometime I begin to get up walk in my sleep and would call her name."

An elderly woman in glasses murmured, "Amen."

"My mother told me that the doctor brod me in his pocket an' my cousin had a baby in the Hudson right there. But I knowed from that night, knowed for sure, and all nights I walk in my sleep and call her name an' call till she handed me Delmore, my dream child."

"Amen, amen," said the old lady, and called up an answer, "Amen, amen," in others.

"An' this girls went from me, an' all dream of snake, falling, the dogs at my insides, went from me, an' there was but Delmore, who bring food to me, read to me, take me by the hand over Nostrand Avenue pavements for New York is a fearful place."

"Amen, amen," the congregation repeated.

"Once he readed me the newspapers from New York how a boys pushed a boys his brother into a well an' held him down some time till he was dead. An' he shows me the way they pictured them, one lie bitter dead, his brother with the policemens. An' Delmore bended his face to the newspapers and kissed the bad boys and my heart turned over and I cry out, 'No, child, you kissed the wrong boys, the brother who is living!' and he says, 'Papa, he won't do that never again.' "

There wasn't a sound—even the trucks had killed their motors—until the untiring woman whispered, "Amen, Brother."

"He was, you see, an angel and eleven years old. All the things ends up too soon, or goes on too long why I don't know it. I wakes up sick. My baby is dead—"

"Amen, amen."

"He is dead, Delmore, my dream child."

"Amen-Amen," a chorus now.

Delmore's father twisted even further to his left and stared at the tight group of Avengers who sat beneath the windows.

"Who killed him? Who did that thing?"

The half of the room where the older people sat burst into exclamations: "Amen!" "You ask it, Brother, ask it!" "Say it to them!" Above the shouts and through the dirge that broke from the women, the fat man's soft voice, like his great bulk, remained distinct and ineffaceable:

"Who killed him?" he asked. "Stand him up. I wants to see who did that to my child, my baby, my one fond wish."

The Yeshiva boys could hear Jeremy scraping the surface of the yard as they rocked over their books. It was difficult to see outside. Kintzler, the melamed, was strict; the windows were dirty and steamed over; the sky was darkening. But despite these obstacles the boys now and then saw him—looping aimlessly behind his stick—before they lost him in the warp of a pane of glass or the mist-filled playground. The freedom of the spectacle bewitched them. No one touched or approached him; he could come in or go away, whatever he wished. Still, he remained, day after day, the second week in a row, with no end in sight, swirling without restraint, without a book, with a head clear of learning. What ease! Twenty-seven souls flew through the walls and clung to the end of the lopped-off broomstick, while twenty-seven bodies gradually fell out of rhythm and lolled disrupted as tufts in a breeze. What brought them into synchronization again was not so much Kintzler's warning that, well, well, Levine, I will give you something to dream about, as it was the thought that followed the flight out of doors, the clamp of pain settling over their shoulders: a mother recently dead! An unthinkable event! The spirits flew smartly home, and the boys rocked diligently, chastened by the lunatic circles of the orphan below.

Jeremy coasted at the whim of the asphalt and flung out behind him the contour lines of the fenced-in earth. He drew as well, and as intricately, the topography of his parents' lives—the father hardly known, "in diamonds and pearls," as his mother had told him; and that mother, in the box, in the ground, a thing he had seen—until, with a blow that knocked the breath from him, the stick struck into the pit of his stomach. He would lift it, then, from the crack in the surface where it had lodged and resume the tracery of the playground, and of his recollection.

It pointed him now, banking and turning about a lump of tar, once again to his mother's face, the entire graph of it, the crisscross lines, the dark eyes of brown and black; and his stick became, again, for the thousandth time, her cane, her walking stick, her furled umbrella, and he beside it, his hand inside her arm and knuckles on her dress, large step matched with small, as he took her out, again and again, for a soda. And he saw, again, the struggle in her face as they sat on the stools (the stick on the rail between them), the pleasure in her eyes, still brown and black, the worry at her mouth, as she wondered why—and for no one else, no other person, only for herself—why this lavishness. And finally, he knew, she would bend toward him—behind her the soda glass, one straw straight, the other bent and pink with lipstick—rubies!—and her face would grow, and her breath near his ear, laughing, delighted, confounded: "Tell me, Jeremy, what is it? What do you see in me?"

The stick ground along the side of the classroom building, caught in the space where a brick was missing, flexed, and flew from his hands. He clutched it without a break in stride, back to his hand, to the cane, the walking stick, the umbrella, back with his right fist between her elbow and dress, back walking with her, monomaniacal cartographer, son. Shopping in the neighborhood, his left arm aching, impossibly weighed, pinfeathers rippled over the edge of the sack; pulling this way, that way, pressing, balancing, every muscle—arm, shoulder, chest, and neck—collaborating in the elaborate disguise, burning off pain, so that she might see, on his face, relish only, pleasure in the little task, smiling Atlas! And then the flat flowers on the neighbor's dress; his hand falling, falling, as his mother released him to make some sign of greeting; the surreptitious shifting of the load, the long maneuver from her left side to her right. And as he stalked behind her and the lady came up to them (he knew those four red petals, the dangling green stem), crossing the airspace far above him, he heard the familiar words in the other's voice: "Meesus Solmon, Meesus Solmon, just a leetle smile, please, Meesus Solmon." And immediately the flowers, satisfied he knew, passed on; and they walked too, he now on the inside, near the stick, adjusting his step to let its point strike, almost strike, his toe; clip, clap, first the wood on the cement, then his leather sole, an inch, half an inch, a quarter of an inch away. Until the next dress—white dots, blue background, not so fancy —and the same request: "Meesus Solmon, smile! Make my life gay!" The same, always, every day. His mother had such a lovely smile they stopped her on the street.

The wake continued unembarrassed. The shouts and cries that had greeted the spoken elegy soon turned into a dozen requiems. It was the older people who sang. Their children sat across the room, silently brushing their knuckles over their thin silk ties, trying not to listen. The individual chanting continued, the volume rose, the scale diminished, and the various voices, wheeling separately, strove to syncopate. Suddenly, as a confused flock of birds will snap behind its pilot, the singers followed a very black man whose voice struck the notes of the dirge like hammers, and became a single chorus after a single song.

Delmore's father stood through the tumult. He did not join the singing, but remained clinging to the chairbacks to ease the weight from his feet. He stared at the young people across the room, at each of them, pausing at every face and looking into it, or at the brow and the dark hair bent toward him. Whether it was the music that unnerved them or the fat man's gaze, the younger mourners began to shift their positions. A few left. The rest segregated themselves, so that without perceptible movement—inching from seat to seat or leaning backward and slipping into the row behind—the entire section was rearranged. Gang member sat with—and lightly unknowingly touched —gang member. Opposite them the groups of singers had unified; but on their side knots of Avengers glared at clusters of Royals. All that time Delmore's father looked at them, down one row and up the one behind it, and he rested after each sweep at Tyron, Ray, Vernon, Major, and Ivanhoe, who sat together at the end of the room, far from his son's coffin, about which the candles had begun to gutter, making the child's face appear older and aquiline.

Past its climax, the singing tapered and eventually ceased. In the silence, the boys hunched their shoulders or pivoted their shining heels, not realizing that the gigantic man was no longer looking at them. Instead his eyes fixed that group beneath the window, which, in reflex, drew together like a hydra around Ivanhoe at its center. Tyron, closest to the window and so (save Delmore) the most distinct figure in the room, half stood, sat again, and whispered something to his neighbor. Major shook his head in reply. Elsewhere, a girl got up abruptly, side-stepped down her row, and left the hall. A moment later a boy followed her. No one else moved. New trucks had mounted the pavement below, or the old ones had started their motors. Steam rang in the radiator like bells, twice, stopped, rang again. Suddenly Tyron jumped to his feet.

"What's the idea of this? What's happenin' here?" he shouted, pointing wildly at the silent man opposite him. "You, Fats, who you starin' at?"

"Tyron, man, why you don't sit down and close your mouth man?" Ivanhoe said from his seat on the bench.

"I don't like all this going on and not ending, man."

"You got no idea *what's* going on," Ivanhoe replied in a low, careful voice. "You makin' a big disorder so sit down."

"I know this wake's draggin' on too long," Tyron said. "I mean, we paid our respects already plenty. Way more than enough."

Ivanhoe got to his feet. "Shit, Tyron, don't you understand nothin' fundamental?" He stood now on the bench and Tryon, overwhelmed, sat down. "This ain't no wake, man. You got to understand what's a basic thing like that, that this weren't never a wake from the beginning. You want to know what this is? Huh? You want to see like the *principle* behind all this, do you, Tyron and all Avengers?" Ivanhoe waited with his hands on his hips, tall, thin, his skin the color of neglected metal, slightly violet. As he grazed it with his elbow, the burlap shook down creases of dust on him.

"Yes, Ivanhoe," his followers murmured.

"All right, what the *prime* thing to understand is is that this
here's no wake but a trial, like what they call the inquest over
the body. Now I want my meaning got good before we step-by-
step proceed. Is it crystal clear to all Avengers?" The group
nodded that it was. "Good. Fine. Now like everything else, a
trial's got to have regulations and formalities. You got to have a
victim, that's right, and you got to have someone who broke the
law, who done the crime. Those there are the rules of the game,
we all know that. But"—and here his voice rose above its habitual monotone—"these rules are being violated."

"How you mean, man?" Major asked.

"There ain't no doubt but what we got a victim," said Ray,
with a gesture toward the rear of the room, where the ceiling
and walls flapped in the dying light.

"I don't want no more interruptions," Ivanhoe announced.
"You gotta appreciate what I'm telling you. Sure, step one, we
got a victim. But he's being misrepresented, *that's* the point
here. I mean, there's Delmore in that coffin, a nice cat an' all,
but no saint like his father inferred, only a little black skin-
popper like the rest of us. You got to rid yourself of sentimentality, you know, this idea of him bending down on his *Daily News*
an' all o' that. Sure, Delmore flew like an angel all right, right up
to Pitkin and Georgia Avenues, Wednesdays and Fridays, and
then flew back to console me with the figures. He was a *messenger*, Daddy, and all the rest is figures of speech, angels an' all,
'cause his heavenly reward was enough stuff to snort for a while,
oh, a day or two—an' sure, a handful of corn on the cob to run
up to you." Ivanhoe spoke directly to the older man, who went
on gazing abstractly at the group of five.

"Now, step two, the question that's arose about who killed
Delmore. I feel like laughin' at that one, except out of my
respect I don't. 'Cause a killin' takes, you know, killers, just like
a trial takes someone who violates the rules. But what there are
here are knights, Avengers, what's called the dutiful men, true
to the code. Now say one night there's arranged a cut-up, nothing unusual, a cut-up. I mean, it's arranged formal. So the square
is drawn on foreign territory and our four guards posted at every

corner. The man steps in. Well, then, that man inside there is in danger. He's fenced in. Royals around on every side. But he's dangerous too, all-powerful, a domineer, prince with his knife out. No one comes in for the cut-up, you're the paramount leader. Everyone knows that; those are the laws. And no one came, either—except Delmore. He must've been high or blown on an O.D., 'cause he steps over the line, just *steps over the line*, wavin' his slips like a flag, or like ribbons, and he's dancing. I see it's him, no enemy, no challenger, not even a regular Avenger: just this little country boy, this crazy kid Delmore. But the square is magic so he took the knife. That wasn't no killin'— what that was was the rules, see, the whole ceremony."

The two chairs Delmore's father had been leaning on flew away from him and he started forward. Mourners jumped from his path, scuttling their own chairs or abandoning them to the great man's elephantine descent. He had not meant to move so forcefully and swung sidewise in an attempt to be delicate. But he was too large for the aisle and his steady progress down each bank of chairs, a half-step at a time, left the choir demolished. When he reached the church floor he turned and headed diagonally leftward, toward Ivanhoe, who stood his ground on the bench. The four protectors were on their feet but remained unmoving as the sweating figure heaved up his arms to Ivanhoe's neck: they drew back astonished as the fat man placed on Ivanhoe's brow a kiss that burned.

The sun had disappeared behind the buildings on the opposite side of Highland Avenue. A strip of sky between two tenements turned green. It was at this time, or near this time—just before his class ended and his grandfather arrived to take him home—that Jeremy shifted the course of his exploration. Recent memory, his mother, the box, the pale shoots of grass in the turned earth, was rolled like a chart and there stretched out before him only empty waves of black asphalt, tinted here and there, iridescent with oil slicks and dried, overlapped puddles of rain. Upon this unmapped sea he sailed, without hope of destination, directionless—reminiscence, his needle, spinning crazily.

At last he zeroed in upon a nacreous depression in the surface, circled it, encroached with his stick deeper and deeper into the ruffles of its shoreline. Dizzy, he knelt and hung his head near the ground, which heaved about him. An old crust of spittle loomed like a whitecap, the purple and blue aureoles of the slicks shimmered like jellyfish, as he placed his cheek against the tar. There, among the damascene watermarks, blinding as the beacon on an ancient wreck, floated his father, in diamonds and pearls. Jeremy approached and struck him with his stick. Diamonds crashed like stars from his legs, pearls rolled off his arms; and with them faded the last light. As Jeremy—the sea beating in his ears—came closer and brushed the last jewels from the eyes, night fell, and once again he failed to see his father's face.

Tyron led twenty Avengers across the intersection of Canner and Highland. When he saw the boy alone in the yard he held up his hand and the others stopped, accustomed to such delays. Each Yeshiva boy carried some change in a special pocket and pretended it was carfare. The gangs who shook them down had no way of knowing the subway was forbidden, a violent, screeching machine. It was unheard of for anyone to refuse, or not to come when called. Thus when Ray entered the yard and shouted at Jeremy, and when his summons went ignored, everyone looked up in surprise. Ray took another step into the yard and started to holler again; but before he was able to finish, the schoolroom door opened and the last class of students raced the sabbath down the steps.

The Negroes, sullen from the recent wake, hesitated, not knowing what to do. From habit, a few sought for Ivanhoe, but he remained on the outskirts of the group, his hands in his pockets, pointedly ignored by the crowd of girls who had attached themselves to the gang. When he sensed his comrades' eyes upon him, he turned his back and stared at the spotted mongrel tethered to a hydrant across the street.

"What you lookin' at *him* for?" Tyron shouted. "He don't have nothin' more to say." And with a wave of his arm he led the Avengers into the yard and deployed them in a line between the classroom building and the avenue, where the jammed cars now hung to each other with their lights. The boys knotted together for a moment, then also thinned into a line facing their antagonists. Down the length of that corridor Jeremy danced, but when Ray stepped forward to grab his arm, he swiveled behind his stick and looped obliviously away. Tyron swung his belt in the air and lunged toward Jeremy's head. The buckle caught him above the ear and he fell without a sound, pouring blood. The two groups stared at each other. No one moved or spoke. Then a girl yelled, "Look at them, they don't belong in this country," and the line of scholars broke.

Some wheeled and ran for the building, others attempted to skirt the line of Negroes and reach the street. All were pursued. At one corner of the yard a group of boys were surrounded by a circle of Avengers, who began to flick at them open-handed, stinging their faces. Tyron stood not far from where Jeremy lay and allowed a small boy to strike him in the chest, repeatedly. Kintzler ran from his office, rallied three or four of his older students, and led them against an equal number of Negroes. The two groups closed, pushed each other in the chest and then withdrew, only to grapple again more seriously, fists closed. Major and Vernon raced to the Highland Avenue gate and easily wrenched it from its hinge. With others helping them, they swept over the yard with it, trapping half a dozen Yeshiva boys between the steel net and the classroom wall. This became the center of the struggle. A boy would be run down, cornered, and carried to the enclosure, then thrust behind it as more and more Avengers gathered in front. The Jews clung to the wire, but their hands were struck away. The frame pressed them to the brick. Someone began kicking at them through the interstices of the grating. Belt buckles were smashed against the gate, occasionally penetrating it, and, worst of all, the end of a broken bottle was scraped across its surface in huge Xs, making—with the taunts and shouts and whooping laughter—a sound that parodied music, or chimes.

Caught in the evening rush, motorists rolled down their windows to watch the battle in the playground, and a small crowd gathered in the street. It was difficult to make sense of what they saw. In the gloom it seemed as if the playground had become one dappled animal turning on itself. Then, without visible cause, like a mist parting, the two sides pulled away from each other. The attackers withdrew and headed toward the gash in the fence, where they stood huddled together. It had been too dark for the onlookers to notice the pious, bespectacled Jew shuffle into the yard and peer quizzically at the conflict. Whether it had been the daring of his approach, or whether the violence had run its course, the Avengers had thrown the gate at the little man's feet and retreated. It had taken the old Jew—bedeviled by cataracts—some time to realize what had happened. It had to be explained to him over and over, and still the Yeshiva boys' triumphant voices piped around him as he knelt over what he suddenly realized was his grandson's wounded body. Only then did he deliver himself. Straightening up, pinching his nose with one hand and waving the other at the blurred backs of the fleeing attackers, he hurled after them and into the sound of distant sirens the one great epithet of horror and disgrace the new world had given him: "Peeeyew!"

Ivanhoe had not joined the disorder of battle, nor did he flee with his friends when the police arrived. He remained in the crowd at the intersection, a gray hat pulled low over the place on his brow where Delmore's father had kissed him and caused, somehow, his head to ache. The crowd dwindled as the boys, and then the police, left the yard. The stricken scholar—his sidelock dyed red as an Indian's—was carried on a stretcher to the ambulance, which, without siren or lights, drove away, leaving the grandfather caught by Friday's stars. The few people left on the sidewalk went home. Ivanhoe drifted across the avenue and squatted on a tenement stoop, trying with smarting eyes to focus through the playground fence and upon the aged Jew, alone in the square, praying indiscreetly to the Master of the universe.

Ivanhoe did not understand the old man's prayers or why he stayed to watch them. But there was something in the saintly bows and windmilling gestures that shocked him to the tenement stoop. His strength was draining out of him. The veins along the side of his head arched and pounded. He was almost blind with the pain and sweat in his eyes; often the Jew was invisible to him, save for the glint of his glasses when he bobbed into the occasional headlight of a turning car. When the mongrel suddenly lay his head across Ivanhoe's knee, he was too exhausted to shake him away. Encouraged, straining at the end of his leash, the dog thrust his black-and-white muzzle beneath the loose flap of Ivanhoe's pants cuff. Ivanhoe's attention remained fixed within the perfect square, upon the sporadic glint of the old man's spectacles, the blurred shape of his prayer, until he felt with horror the tongue of the dog caressing his lifeless hand. Fearful and enraged, betrayed by his body, he sat transfixed, going numb; but, in his pocket, autonomously, his hand squeezed his blockaded knife. He picked the tuft on the animal's chest where he judged the lungs to be; but then the distant figure stepped through the boundary of the fence and headed up the street. Cramped and sore, Ivanhoe could barely pull himself to his feet and stumble after him to wherever he would be able to confront him alone.

The Jew took the long way back because at night, and without Jeremy, he could not see his way through the alleys and small streets that cut directly home. The two men walked for an hour, up Lafayette Avenue, right on Patchen Avenue, left on Fulton Street, right onto Marconi Place and right again on a small, dead-end street whose sign Ivanhoe was too confused to read. It was one of the last Jewish streets in the neighborhood: two dim and gloomy lamps, a third burnt out; a block of tenements on one side, small shops—most of them empty—on the other; a fouled, dying street, out of whose open end the night wind blew like a moan. Ivanhoe had to quicken his pace to keep up with the old man, who walked without any hesitation down this alley where his feet knew every stone, each break in the curb, where by day the people called out to him, Rabbi! Prince! Now he mounted the steps of a shabby building and passed through the unlocked door. The youth paused in front of the house. Sweat passed in unbroken sheets over his face, his hand choked the handle of his knife. He rubbed the sleeve of his coat over his stinging eyes, pressed his temples with his finger tips, and sprang after the old man.

Jeremy's grandfather was already far above him. Ivanhoe stood in the well, his head back, watching the Jew pass behind the ribs of the staircase. And as he went, each neighbor heard him, and each threw open his door, so that the strict and holy man should be able to see. Ivanhoe saw him move from stair to stair, from landing to landing, into and out of the slats of light, higher and winding higher until, at the top of the stairs, he pressed his lips to the doorframe, and disappeared. Then the doors closed, darkness descended, the pain left him, and he turned to go.

PATRICIA GOEDICKE

◑

You Could Pick It Up

from *The Virginia Quarterly Review*

You could pick it up by the loose flap of a roof
and all the houses would come up together
in the same pattern attached, inseparable

white cubes, olive trees, flowers
dangling from your hand
a few donkey hooves might stick out

flailing the air for balance,
but the old women would cling like sea urchins
and no children would fall.

even though it is small,
the people are Greek, and it sits
like an oyster in the middle of the Aegean

still it is tough, it reminds you
of wagon trains, prairie schooners
drawn up in circles by night

you could swing it around your head
and still nothing would happen,
it would stay

solid, the white walls
rising up out of the sea
the pillared crown of the temple . . .

for twenty-six hundred years
it has endured everything, but now
we who have forgotten everything,

we whose homes have all gone
to super highways, belt cities, long thin lines
our glittering buses snort into the main square.

the spider web with sticky fingers
glues itself to the town,
slowly it begins to revolve, faster and faster

tighter and tighter it is wound
till the young men cannot stand it,
they pack up and leave town

the sky is full of children
with wild eyes and huge faces
falling to the ground.

JONATHAN GREENE

◑

O they left me

from *Quarterly Review of Literature*

O they left me at
the gate of ivory
from wherein
the heavy smell
of the elephant graveyard
came

      'worldly wealth
of ivory'

       & they sd.
go in & from this
false-death-stink
build your tower
of ivory

        mocking voice
& then picked-up phrase:
in dreams
begin responsibilities

that no man rightfully escapes,
his 'ivory vision' polished
by the cuttings & shavings
he thought excluded

                         as if
one alone
could wed gate
of ivory

         & of horn

(the aesthetic
with the real?
               imposed symbolism
               ?)

         —Virgil
whom Broch
pictured on his death-bed
as the repentant aesthete

in another imaginary life
led Dante, & in another
trespasser of Homer's world

model-upon-model
where the World
bites in

         the Real
is given
grabs us down

the Marriage of the Gates
rises
under-earth

STANLEY KAUFFMANN

◑

A Year with *Blow-up*: Some Notes

from *Salmagundi*

I first saw *Blow-up* in early December 1966, and in the months since, I have broadcast, written, and lectured considerably about it. Here are some notes on the experience.

Quite apart from its intrinsic qualities, *Blow-up* is an extraordinary social phenomenon. It is the first film from abroad by a major foreign director to have immediate national distribution. It was seen here more widely and more quickly than, for instance, *La Dolce Vita* for at least two reasons: it was made in English and it was distributed by a major American company. There are other reasons, less provable but probably equally pertinent: its mod atmosphere, its aura of sexuality, and, most important, its perfect timing. The end of a decade that had seen the rise of a film generation around the country was capped with a work by a recognized master that was speedily available around the country.

So this was the first time in my experience that a new film had been seen by virtually everyone wherever I talked about it. Usually the complaint had been (by letter) after a published or broadcast review, "Yes, but where can we see the picture?" Or, after a talk at some college not near New York, "But it will take years to get here, if ever," or "We'll have to wait until we can rent a 16-millimeter print." With *Blow-up*, people in Michigan

and South Carolina and Vermont knew—within weeks of the
New York premiere—the film that was being discussed. This
exception to the usual slow-leak distribution of foreign films had
some interesting results.

A happy result was that people had seen this picture at the
local Bijou. Before, many of them had seen (say) Antonioni
only in film courses and in film clubs. This one they had seen
between runs of *How to Steal a Million* and *Hombre*. To those
in big cities this may seem commonplace, but in smaller communities it was a rare event and had some good effects. To some
degree it alleviated culture-vulturism and snobbism; *everyone* in
Zilchville had seen *Blow-up*, not just the elite; so happily, there
was no cachet simply in having seen it. Further, the fact of seeing it at the Bijou underscored those elements in the film medium of popular mythos that are valuable and valid—all those
undefined and undefinable powers of warm communal embrace
in the dark.

But there were some less happy results of the phenomenon.
There was a good deal of back-formation value judgment. Because *Blow-up* was a financial success, it could not really be
good, I heard, or at least it proved that Antonioni had sold out.
We heard the same thing about Bellow and *Herzog* when that
book became a best seller. The parallel holds further in that
Blow-up and *Herzog* seem to me flawed but utterly uncompro-
mised works by fine artists. I confess I got a bit weary of
pointing out that to condemn a work because it is popular is
exactly as discriminating as praising it because it is a hit.

Another discouraging consequence. Much of the discussion
reflected modes of thought inculcated by the American academic mind, particularly in English departments. Almost everywhere there were people who wanted to discuss at length
whether the murder in *Blow-up* really happened or was an
illusion. Now Antonioni, here as before, was interested in
ambiguities; but ambiguities in art, like those in life, arise only
from unambiguous facts—which is what makes them interesting. Anna in *L'Avventura* really disappeared; the ambiguities in
morality arise from that fact. The lover in *Blow-up* was really

killed; the ambiguities in the hero's view of experience would not arise without that fact. (A quick "proof" that the murder was real: If it were not, why would the girl have wanted the pictures back? Why would the photographer's studio have been rifled? Why would we have been shown the pistol in the bushes? Some have even suggested that the corpse we see is a dummy, or a live man pretending. But Hemmings touches it.) This insistence on anteater nosings in the film seemed much less a reflection on *Blow-up* than on an educational system—a system that mistakes factitious chatter for analysis.

On the other hand, an art teacher in a Nashville college told me, while driving me to the airport, that *Blow-up* had given him a fulcrum with which to jimmy his previously apathetic students into *seeing:* seeing how the world is composed, how it is taken apart and recomposed by artists. In his excitement he almost drove off the road twice.

The script is by Antonioni and his long-time collaborator Tonino Guerra, rendered in English by the young British playwright Edward Bond. It was suggested by a short story of the same name by the Argentinian author, resident in France, Julio Cortázar. Comparison of the script and story is illuminating.

In the story the hero is an Argentine translator living in Paris —only an amateur photographer. One day while out walking, he photographs what he thinks is a pick-up—of a youth by an older woman. There is an older man sitting in a parked car near by. After the picture is taken, the youth flees, the woman protests, and the man in the car gets out and protests, too. Later, studying the picture, the hero sees (or imagines he sees) that the woman was really procuring the youth for the man in the car and that the fuss over the photograph gave the youth a chance to escape. It is a story of the discovery of, in Cortázar's view, latent horror, the invisible immanence of evil. (It is incidentally amusing that the photographer feels no such horror when he thinks that the woman is seducing the boy for herself.)

Antonioni retains little other than the device of subsequently discovering in a photograph what was really happening at that moment. He makes the hero a professional photographer, thus greatly intensifying the meaning of the camera in his life. By changing from the presumption of homosexuality to the fact of murder, Antonioni not only makes the discovered event more potent dramatically, he shifts it morally from the questionable to the unquestionable. At any time in history homosexuality has varied, depending on geography, in shades of good and evil. Murder, though more blinkable at some times and in some places than others, will be an evil fact so long as life has value.

Most important, Antonioni shifts the moral action from *fait accompli* to the present. His hero does not discover that he has been an agent of good, in a finished action. His dilemma is now.

With his recent films Antonioni has suffered, I think, from two professional failings of critics. The first has been well described in a penetrating review of *Blow-up* by Robert Garis (*Commentary*, April 1967). Garis notes that Henry James' public grew tired of him while he was inconsiderate enough to be working out his career and sticking to his guns; that Beckett, after the establishment of *Waiting for Godot* as a masterpiece,

> has been writing other beautiful and authentic plays quite similar to *Godot*, innocently unaware of that urgent necessity to move on, to find new themes and styles, that is so obvious to some of his critics . . . If it is regrettable to see the public wearing out new fashions in art as fast as automobiles, it is detestable to see criticism going along with this, if not actually leading the charge. The Antonioni case is like Beckett's but intensified. There has been the same puzzled annoyance with an artist who keeps on thinking and feeling about themes that everyone can see are worn out—themes like "lack of communication" or "commitment." There has been the same eagerness to master a difficult style and then the same relapse into boredom when that style turns out to be something the artist really takes seriously because that's the way he really sees things.

Another point grows out of this. This impatience with artists who are less interested in novelty than in deeper exploration leads to critical blindness about subtle graduations *within* an artist's "territory." We saw a gross example of this blindness last year in the theater when Harold Pinter's *The Homecoming* was shoved into the "formless-fear" bag along with his earlier plays. The fact that Pinter had shifted focus, that he was now using his minute, vernacular, almost-Chinese ritualism to scratch the human cortex for comic purposes, not for *frisson*, this was lost on most reviewers, who were just feeling comfy at finally having "placed" Pinter.

So with Antonioni. He's the one who deals with alienation and despair, isn't he? So the glib or the prejudiced have the pigeonhole all ready. Obviously the temper of Antonioni, like that of any genuine artist, is bound to mark all his work; but even in his last film, *Red Desert*, as it seemed to me, he had pushed into new areas of his "territory," was investigating the viability of hope, and had—without question—altered the rhythms of his editing to underscore a change of inquiry (not of belief). The editing is altered even further in *Blow-up*. For instance, the justly celebrated sequence in which the hero suspects and then finds the murder in the photograph is quite unlike anything Antonioni has done before, in its accelerations and retards within a cumulative pattern. And the theme, too, seems to me an extension, a fresh inquiry, within Antonioni's field of interest. Here his basic interest seems to be in the swamping of consciousness by the conduits of technology. The hero takes some photographs of lovers, and thinks he has recorded a certain experience of which he is conscious; but, as he learns subsequently, his technology has borne in on him an experience of which he was not immediately aware, which he cannot understand or handle. He is permanently connected with a finished yet permanently unfinished experience. It seems to me a good epitome of same-size man vis-à-vis the expanding universe.

There are concomitant themes. One of them is success—but success *today*, which is available to youth as it has never been. The hero has money, and the balls that money provides in a money-society, about twenty years earlier than would have been the general case twenty years ago; and he is no rare exception.

Yet his troubles in this film do not arise from his money work but out of his "own" work, the serious work he does presumably out of the stings of conscience. (What else would drive a fashion-world hero to spend the night in a flophouse?) He can handle the cash cosmos; it is when he ventures into himself, leaves commissioned work and does something of his own, that he gets into trouble.

Along with this grows the theme of youth itself. This world is not only filled with but dominated by youth, in tastes and tone. (There are only two nonyouths of prominence in the film. One, a nasty old clerk in an antique shop, resents the youth of the hero on sight. The other, a middle-aged lover, gets murdered.) The solidarity of youth is demonstrated in the hero's compunction to "prove" his strange experience to *his friends*. When one of his friends, the artist's wife, suggests that he notify the police of the murder (and her suggestion is in itself rather diffident), he simply doesn't answer to the point, as if law and criminality were outside the matter to him. Ex-soldiers say they can talk about combat only with other ex-soldiers. The communion of generations is somewhat the same. The hero doesn't want Their police; he wants certification by his friends.

Color is exquisite in Antonioni's films, and it is more than *décor* or even commentary; it is often chemically involved in the scene. In the shack in *Red Desert*, the walls of the bunk in which the picknickers lounge are bright red and give a highly erotic pulse to a scene in which sex is only talked about. In *Blow-up* the hero and two teen-age girls have a romp on a large sheet of pale purple-lavender paper that cools a steamy little orgy into a kind of idyll.

This is the first feature that Antonioni has made outside Italy, and it shows a remarkable ability to cast acutely in a country where he does not know the corps of working actors intimately. (He discovered David Hemmings in the Hampstead Theatre Club "off-Broadway.") It also shows a remarkable ability to absorb and redeploy the essences of a foreign city without getting either prettily or grimly picturesque. But there are three elements in this film that betray some unease—an unease attributable perhaps to the fact that he was "translating" as he went, not only in language but also in experience.

The first is the plot-strand of the neighboring artist and his wife. (Several people asked during the year, why I call her his wife and not his girl friend. Answer: She wears a wedding ring. If it is unduly naïve to assume from this that the artist is her husband, it seems unduly sophisticated to assume that he is not.) This element has the effect of patchwork, as if it had not been used quite as intended or as if it were unfulfilled in its intent. The relationship between them and the hero is simply not grasped. The poorest scene in the entire film is the one in which the wife (Sarah Miles) visits the hero's studio after he has seen her making love with her husband. It is wispy and scrappy. The discomfort is the director's.

The second is the scene with the folk-rock group and the stampede for the discarded guitar. The scene has the mark of tourism on it, a phenomenon observed by an outsider and included for completeness' sake. Obviously Antonioni would not be a member of such a group in Italy any more than in England, but he would have known a thousand subtle things about Italian youths and their backgrounds that might have made them seem particularized, less a bunch of representatives en bloc.

The third questionable element is the use of the clown-faced masquers at the beginning and the end—which really means at the end, because they would not have been used at the start except to prepare for the end. Firstly, the texture of these scenes is jarring. Their symbolism—overt and conscious—conflicts with the digested symbolism of the rest of the film. It has a mark of strain and unfamiliarity about it, again like a phenomenon observed (partying Chelsea students, perhaps) and uncomfortably adapted. It is Cocteau strayed into Camus.

Much has been made of the clowns' thematic relevance, in that they provide a harbor of illusion for the hero after a fruitless voyage into reality. But precisely this thematic ground provides an even stronger objection to them, I think, than the textural one mentioned above. Thematically I think that the film is stronger without them, that it makes its points more forcibly. Suppose the picture began with Hemmings coming out of the flophouse with the derelicts, conversing with them, then leaving them and getting into his Rolls. At once it seems more like Antonioni. And suppose it ended (where in fact I thought it was going to end) with the long shot of Hemmings walking away after he has discovered that the corpse has been removed. Everything that the subsequent scene supplies would already be there by implication—*everything*—and we would be spared the cloudy symbols of high romance. Again it would be more like Antonioni.

All three of these lapses can possibly be traced to his working in a country where every last flicker of association and hint is not familiar and subconsciously secure.

On the other hand I think that two much-repeated criticisms of *Blow-up* are invalid. Some have said that Antonioni seemingly ridicules the superficial world of fashion but is really reveling in it, exploiting it. It is hard to see how he could have made a film on this subject without photographing it. One may as well say that, in exploring the world of sexual powers and confusions in *A Married Woman*, Godard merely exploited nudity. By showing us the quasi-tarts of fashion (sex-appeal, instead of sex, by the hour) in all their gum-chewing vapidity and by showing us how easily the Super-Beautiful can be confected by someone who understands beauty, Antonioni does more than mock a conspicuously consuming society: he creates a laughable reality against which to pose a genuinely troubling ambiguity.

Another widespread objection has been to the role that Vanessa Redgrave plays. The character has been called unclear. But this seems to me true only in conventional nineteenth-century terms of character development. In a television interview with me, Antonioni said that Miss Redgrave read the script and wanted to play the part because—he lifted his hand in a gesture of placement on the screen—"*Sta lì.*"

"She stands there"; she has no explanations, no antecedents, no further consequences in the hero's life. I take this to mean that she is an analogue of the murder itself, an event rather than a person, unforgettable yet never knowable, and therefore perfectly consonant with the film.

Purely professionally from an actress's view, the role was a challenge because she has only two scenes, and those relatively brief appearances have to be charged with presence at once satisfying and tantalizing. Miss Redgrave met this challenge with ease, I think, not only because she has beauty and personality and distinctive talent but because she played the role against an unheard counterpoint: a secret and complete knowledge of who this young woman was. There was almost a hint that she was protecting Hemmings, that if he knew all that she knew, his life would disintegrate.

Thus my year of recurrent involvement with *Blow-up* and some observations about it. Now Antonioni has announced that he will make a film in America. I have two feelings about this. I am glad: because I would like to see how he sees America, just as I was glad to see his view of London. I also have reservations: because he functions more completely where he is rooted. Fine directors like Renoir and Duvivier and Seastrom and Eisenstein have all made films away from home, all of which contain good things but none of which is that man's best work. Some directors, like Lean and Huston, have functioned at their best in foreign places, but they are not quintessentially societal directors. Antonioni (like Bergman in this respect) has been best in a society that is second nature to him, that has long fed and shaped him, that he has not had to "study."

It is a considerable miracle that he made *Blow-up* as well as he did. Its imperfections arise, I think, from having to concentrate on the miracle. Still, to say that I like *Blow-up* the least of his films since *L'Avventura* is a purely relative statement. I would be content to see one film a year as good as *Blow-up*—from Antonioni or anyone else—for the rest of my life.

RAMON GUTHRIE

◑

Cantata for Saint Budóc's Day

from *The Quest*

> *Nam et vere dictum est quod sanctus Budocus a Scotia in Armoricam in lapide navigavit.*
> DE SANCTIS CORNUBII

Says what? Whole swags and gaggles of 'em?
Mud-hawks and pismires half a spindle long?
And ye've feared of 'em? What be ye—many mice?
Spankers a-hoo! And did not Saint Budóc
sail a stone a-float from Ballyhack to Brittany—
dead reckoning no less, with neither binnacle nor helm?
Barong! I'll show ye how to proper up a bilge.
Lobster-long scorpiums, you say?
beetle-bugs that squirt snuff at ye?
swift-skittering spiders the size of griddlecakes?
A-back! Broom-room is all I ask,
and in a whisk . . .

           Hee-yipes! and here they come!
—Didn't ye'd ought of warned a man!—
swarming up broom handle and inside
sleeves and pants legs, cruftier than sprikes!
  Har-*rook!* Har-rook! and if aught a one
aver I'm not scairt flealess,
I'll daunt him to defend it. Har*rook!*
Stand clear! I'm out of here. Ye canna keep
a good man down—*and that's an adage!*
You with the leather beard!

You with the mink ear-muffs!
Take on where I left off. I'm needed elsewhere.
Urgenter deeds attend me.
Har*rook*, old hamster, ye honk-nosed janissary!
Hindle me not, ye horehounds, lest ye'd be holystoned.
Harrook! Can't ye not see I'm hasping down the halyards?
Harrook, ye meddlestrums. Unhook your harps from here!
Harrook!
Screech ears for Saint Budóc whose day it is.
Hark! Hark! Harrook!

◑

Thin Ice

from *Hanging Loose*

Now this paste of ash and water;
water slipping over ice, greenish

brown water, white ice, November ice,
thin as glass, shot with air.

The kinglet, soundless, against the yellow
grapeleaves of the arbor, smallest of birds;

shrill day, the blowing, oily Atlantic off
Strong's Neck; the salt smell drifts, blown

through the newish Cape Cod homes.
On such days children fall down wells,

or drown falling through thin first ice,
or fall reaching after the last apple

the picker neglected, the tree leafless,
the apple spoiled anyway by frost; toad freezes,

snake's taken his hole; the cat makes much
shorter trips; dog's bark is louder.

The green has floated from earth, moved south,
or drifted upward at night, invisible to us.

Man walks, throwing off alone thin heat;
this cold's life, death's steamy mark and target.

DAVID IGNATOW

◐

Against the Evidence

from *Kayak*

As I reach to close each book
lying open on my desk, it leaps up
to snap at my fingers. My legs
won't hold me, I must sit down.
My fingers pain me
where the thick leaves snapped together
at my touch.
                    All my life
I've held books in my hands like children,
carefully turning their pages
and straightening out
their creases. I use books
almost apologetically. I believe
I often think their thoughts for them.
Reading, I never know where theirs leave off
and mine begin. I am so much alone
in the world, I can observe the stars
or study the breeze, I can count the steps
on a stair on the way up or down,
and I can look at another human being
and get a smile, knowing
it is for the sake of politeness.
Nothing must be said of estrangement
among the human race and yet
nothing is said at all
because of that.

But no book will help either.
I stroke my desk,
its wood so smooth, so patient and still.
I set a typewriter on its surface
and begin to type
to tell myself my troubles.
Against the evidence, I live by choice.

ALAN FRIEDMAN

◑

Daughter of a Bitch

from *Partisan Review*

Mostly I ate out in Paris, the cheapest places. But the few
staples I did buy I bought in the store just downstairs from me,
so two or three times a week I got to talk to the greengrocer.
"You didn't know? But yes certainly." My greengrocer's eyes
and ears went up together, a child's fat face with a big mus-
tache, and he told me he hated her frothily: standing amidst his
lettuce and leeks, into the sawdust he spat freely. I gathered that
my landlady Madame Dijour was a rent-gouger. She owned four
or five houses in the neighborhood and she was charging me
three times the rent I should have been paying. "Miser and pig,
ah, she's well-off but you can get nothing from her, not if your
wall folds or your ceiling rips. But her husband, ah, that was a
jewel, a good man, a gentleman, and in this neighborhood a
friend, a leader. Well of course, yes in the Resistance, tortured
by the Nazis, killed. God will pay them back what they did to
him. But she, the one upstairs, the Queen, he left her all this,
and she's worse than the Nazis, you don't know the half, I assure you. The way she treats that little girl of hers, that alone,
they could hang her for."

I had heard noises downstairs, whimpering noises I couldn't
identify. My landlady had me worried. She was a dyed blonde
whose plump face must have become unappetizing somewhere
along the line. After I'd heard the story of her husband's tor-
ture, I seemed to see it in her face and voice. Each of her eyes
had a different shape, sagging and rimmed like two healed cuts
on a tree trunk. When she talked to me in her skeptical, twitter-

ing French—"Good evening? What time is it. Early for you?"—
question marks came out in all the wrong places.

The idea of going home at night began to make me nervous
because she seemed to be lying in wait for me. Regular as clockwork, after an evening of coffee and Pernod on the boulevard, I
used to start worrying about Jacqueline and her mother. I lived
on the top floor. I used to sneak in at the ground floor entrance
like a burglar—I'd wait one minute until the timer had turned
off all the lights on the stairs—and then I'd tiptoe upstairs, trying to slip past my landlady's door on the first landing. It got so
that I was afraid of the door itself—morbidly nervous about the
way it had of suddenly snapping partway open . . . because the
stairs would squeak, and Madame Dijour would catch me more
than half the time. "You're going to bed"—with that chopping
innuendo—"now?"

Her voice was bright, steely. She knew not one word of English. With her French participles she seemed to be snapping her
long-nailed thumbs; imperatives and subjunctives flashed round
me this way and that with a sneer and a controlled hiss. "Turn it
so, insert the key softly, incredible hour, I might suggest you
remove your shoes *before.*" Even matters of information were
delivered with hints and barbs—"Rushing in again, no, not you,
your countrymen, the news looks bad tonight?" And in her simplest phrases something vaguely indecent. "You're going to bed?
You're going to sleep? Everything all right?" Not seductive—
she'd never invite me in. She'd just begin by complaining about
the noise on the stairs, then switch to the international situation, her favorite topic—swaying there in that yellow door slit
of hers in her opaque nightgown at midnight or one a.m. and
asking me if I'd heard the latest news bulletins.

So it wasn't until the afternoon her door suddenly opened
wide and she invited me in that I finally got to see what the
whimpering noises were all about.

The gendarme in her parlor startled me. "It's all right," my
landlady said. "Don't stand there like a donkey. You've done
nothing wrong."

As usual, I was wrapped in brown burly secondhand clothes.

But I felt neither very warm nor well enough concealed. In the dry winter air the points of my hair stood out, dishevelled and electric like my thoughts.

"Monsieur," the officer inquired. "Monsieur *what?*" His voice wavered in its pitch, suggesting that my real name could hardly be whatever I was about to claim. I didn't think but I *felt* he had come to arrest me for my thoughts about Jacqueline: he held open menacingly at his waist a thick black book that was chained to his trousers' belt. "Perhaps we can walk upstairs to your apartment?"

"Please, not at all," Madame Dijour insisted. "Stay right here." Jacqueline said nothing, absorbed in her schoolwork. "You can discuss your affairs here."

I thought of objecting. But the police officer had already begun writing my answers before he began asking me questions. "Very good, you are a student? You are American? Age, please." He had been oiled: a half-empty bottle and a couple of glasses rested on the table.

There were two animals asleep in the apartment. The pregnant cat I had often seen on the stairs lay curled in a basket; on the chair alongside Jacqueline slept the little dog. "And you have occupied the premises above, renting from Madame Dijour, for three months?" Seated at the smaller table, Jacqueline dipped her drying sunflower face from book to book—evidently translation.

Twice a week for the last three months now I had been giving her lessons in English composition. In fact, when I had first tried to come to terms with her mother about the rent, Madame Dijour had insisted on English lessons for her little girl. These were not a favor, she had explained, not a voluntary matter; they were something I would owe above and beyond my rent. But I didn't regret the arrangement, on account of the little girl's dog-like pathos, and something else. I was nineteen, she was fifteen. And when she'd sit at my kitchen table and lean forward to look into my big dictionary, I'd lean too as her skirt rode up, and I'd study the cursive script her blue veins traced on the shaded dry yellow scrolls of her inner thighs. When she'd catch me by

glancing up unexpectedly, I always thought I was going to discover from the look in her eyes what went on downstairs at her
mother's. I kept thinking about her father. Jacqueline had eyes
like faintly tarnished medals earned for unknown acts of hero-
ism, and I looked at their large dry surfaces to discover what will
power, what hand-to-hand combat, what sacrifice, and I learned
nothing—or rather something else—that I'd been leaning too
far, and that she regarded me with suspicion. After a while she'd
go back to work, and while she scribbled, always with many little
elegant curls of her penmanship, I schemed to take and gently
guide the stamen of her pen and the little cluster of her hand
over the page so that her ink would flow in flawless English and
the angle of my elbow could touch the bell of her breasts. And I
did no such thing.

But at night I'd try to imagine what it was that Madame Dijour was doing to her, what it was that left Jacqueline looking
like a field of crushed flowers. Over the months my night life in
Paris had become a lively and depressing burlesque. Sometimes
I imagined Madame Dijour asleep in her warm bed and Jacqueline naked and shivering in a cage fixed into the wide-open
window, and I wanted to slip through my window and crawl
down the wall and sneak through her window and unlock the
cage and cover her icy flesh with my body, but I didn't, because
in my fantasy my own window, when I reached it, was stuck,
warped, and clotted with a luminous mold. Or sometimes as my
wits wandered toward sleep I imagined that Madame Dijour
had been in the pay of the Nazis and ratted on her husband for
whose murder she'd had her own daughter deliberately framed
and condemned to serve in the galleys, and Jacqueline there became a kind of Saint Jeanne Valjean, and she was rowing naked
and sweating, and I wanted . . . but I didn't. So maybe you can
imagine what an ordeal it was for me when the gendarme in her
mother's parlor quietly asked to see my passport and began
checking it against a list he kept in his thick black book.

I had no idea what he was investigating, but I was young
enough so that it actually didn't occur to me to ask. I simply
handed over my passport, which I always carried, and said to

Jacqueline in slow English, as calm and gay as you please, "Jacqueline, what country am I from?"

She didn't answer. She looked up—yellow skin and yellow-white eyes—sucked her underlip in, then looked away . . . immobile, suspicious features that would some day be jowled like her mother's but were now just short of ripeness, pale plentiful hair pulled very tight, and a thin throbbing throat. For all the yellow blossom of her face and those breasts which were already swaying flowercups, she was skinny everywhere else—stemlike, stalklike, her inflexible arms, her in-folding shoulders, the hardly-any bumps of her hips. But in my mind's eye an older Jacqueline, surprisingly honored at graduation for her progress in English, had been chosen to deliver the valedictory address (her theme, International Love); and God! it was my own tongue-tied Jacqueline, now speaking passionate English stark naked before a thrilled auditorium; and afterward I tried to rise with a splendid gesture to congratulate my pupil, extending not my hand but, "Your exact rent please? Per month, Monsieur."

Madame Dijour said loudly, "Eighteen hundred francs." She paused, then repeated the figure firmly.

This was one-quarter of the correct amount. So it was she, not I, who was threatened . . . a rent-control check. Was it a mere formality by now? . . . had the cop been bribed? . . . what would my grocer have answered? I saw now why she had always refused to give me rent receipts. But if I called her bluff now, I stood to lose my pupil. Jacqueline translated busily; so I nodded.

"May I see your receipts," the officer asked while writing.

Madame Dijour's eyes arched separately.

Jacqueline with one slow lean arm began to stroke the dog; it stirred. I stirred, the soft stroke on my skin. "I always throw them away."

The officer dipped his head slyly; we were all now in collusion. He finished the rest of his drink. He closed his book and his pen officially, patted Jacqueline's head genially, and closed the door: gone. "It is evident," Madame Dijour said, "that you know how to handle the police." Her mouth was rosy and gold-flecked.

"And now you will have your reward." You can imagine what I thought.

Her sagging eyes rose to a pointed pause . . . nothing happened . . . and *"Jacqueline!"* Jacqueline rose calmly, obediently, refilled her mother's glass, and filled a clean glass for me.

American students in Paris, the international situation, English composition—we talked about awful things. The first chance I could I said to Jacqueline in English, "How's your homework—easy?" Catching her eye, I tried to wink . . . but it didn't come off, and she only shrugged her thin neck. She motioned for the dog.

"Sss! Poupée!" The dog Poupée stalked obediently past the basket in which the pregnant cat lay dozing and growled. The cat's eyelids flickered; its jaws opened and it seemed to sigh. Jacqueline caught the dog—it wasn't much bigger than a cat— she scooped it up with a sudden, shy bend and played with its ears. She said in English (startling me), "She is Poupée." (A dirty mop of a dog.) And pointing to the cat, "She is Bijou."

"You see, you *can* speak English," I said. I felt better—gratified to hear her try.

"Jacqueline has never performed very well at school," her mother informed me. "A pity. Mathematics and languages are particular weaknesses, they require the kind of discipline for which she has no aptitude. But with an American in the house, it is a golden opportunity? And perhaps when the Soviet Occupation comes, she will have occasion to learn Russian—eh, Jacqueline."

It was an odd remark with a suggestion of malice in it—did she suspect something about me and Jacqueline? Did she expect a Russian billet in her upstairs apartment? I tried, "You expect war again in the near future?"

"Yes certainly, soon, very soon," she assured me, "though perhaps I will not be in Paris." She drank, then leaned forward and said in her most compelling, mocking tone, "Did you know— how could you know?—listen, at Poitiers in my mother's house I have a vehicle, an automobile, which I keep always stocked with provisions and with a loaded rifle. At the very first signs of trouble between the great powers, of which there have been many during the past years, I have always fled immediately to Poitiers. There at Poitiers I listen continually to the radio. Should there be a more serious sign, I would immediately flee with Jacqueline in the automobile along a route to the Spanish border which I have already planned, to a village in Spain which is already designated. I will not wait this time."

"You really expect to know in advance this time?"

"I don't ever wait to find out. Jacqueline and I and the animals have gone often to Poitiers, eh, little beast?" For an instant I thought she meant Jacqueline, but she clicked her fingers and the dog wriggled loose from Jacqueline and came to her at once.

She put it on her lap, saying, "Though of course we shall all be blown to bits by the new bombs, not even Spain will be safe. Tell me, monsieur, what do you think, are men beasts? Are they capable of reason and foresight? Or will fear make them intelligent—like my little girl here. Have you seen her tricks?" I thought she meant Jacqueline, but with one hand she took the dog by its collar. With her other hand she reached under her own collar, and the nightmare began.

"Please, mother," Jacqueline said, tilting her head.

There was a long pause . . . I cleared my throat . . . "Pastry," her mother said. "Quick." I remember I was sitting in a rocking chair and I began to rock in it nervously. My pupil disappeared into the kitchen and came out again in moments with a plate of pastry. She offered me a piece, offered her mother a piece, then put the plate down near me. Deliberately, she avoided looking at me.

I said, "May I offer Jacqueline some pastry?" I lifted the plate.

"Jacqueline has no desire for pastry, I assure you."

She stood by her mother's chair, a twig of her mother in a short skirt. I wanted to resist . . . though I had no idea yet what I was resisting . . . I said, "How do you know unless you ask her?"

Unruffled, quite sweet, Madame Dijour shook her blond head, then craned her neck round so that the flesh wrinkled like

a braid. "Jacqueline, there, you see, there are some extra pieces
of pastry, would you like one?"

Her tone was inviting. There was a split second in which Jacqueline tried to decide which way her mother wanted the tip-
ping situation to right itself. She bent and touched the dog's fur
with her lips. "No, mother." She took the dog.

"Give me that dog," Madame Dijour said. The dog was returned. "Eat that." Jacqueline took the plate. It all happened
rapidly and was said softly. "Now eat."

Self-conscious, with restraint, Jacqueline began to eat. She
kept her medal eyes pinned to her mother.

With the dog on her lap, Madame Dijour took a sewing
needle from just under the inside of her elegant lapel and said to
me, "Watch. I suspect you have failed so far to appreciate this
fine animal." Holding the dog down, she placed the point of the
sewing needle against the animal's black snout. She pressed, and
the dog began to whimper—no squeal, no bark, only a high-
pitched faraway complaint. "You see," she continued, "not to
cry out, that is the lesson, that is the hard thing." She withdrew
the point, the dog wrenched its head, she forced the point again
into the snarling snout—the black lips lifted into a snarl, nearly
soundless except for the remote whimper.

She said, "You can inquire of my husband."

Jacqueline had stopped eating.

In her basket, the cat's tail swept and twitched in an arc
against her sleeping body.

The needle approached again. The dog's helpless eyes, already
vast and rheumy, opened wider—the pincushion nose could
take it no longer—and suddenly the bitch barked. The noise was
stunning. Her head jerked sideways, then shot forward, teeth
snapping at her mistress's hand. The needle fixed itself in the
animal's upper palate, visibly.

The noise—the rapid motion—were instantaneous and repeated. Terrified squealing *with* terrifying barking—the sounds
of two separate dogs locked teeth to throat—the jaws bared, another lunge at the needle, and another, and always the teeth
closed over the shaft and the point sank into the half-open pal-

ate. Until finally no motion, no sound, and Madame Dijour could put the point into the dry snout at will. Poupée remained rigid. There was not even whimpering now, only the red-rimmed watching eyes.

"When the Germans were in Paris during the war," she said, "my husband cried out."

At the surge of barking, even Bijou the cat had begun to stretch. She had risen up in her basket on two legs at the sound, then stretched again. Too pregnant to bother, she curled heavily around, meaning to retire perhaps. But she came instead, evidently by long-established habit—many-teated, sagging, and shaking her paws as though wet—to the foot of Madame Dijour's chair. "If he had not cried out," she said.

There was no attempt to finish the phrase. She lowered the dog to the floor.

My pupil's yellowish cheeks were now white, veined over the jaws and red at the bones, as if she were out in the cold. I had begun a strange slow rocking in my chair—with what feelings I don't know—terror? compassion? hatred?—I had ceased to exist, I think, just as if from the very beginning the dog's torment had wiped me out. I don't remember myself there; I just remember It: It whimpering, It rocking, It mouthless, It freezing, It pushing a needle.

On the floor Poupée lay on her back, quite still, even her eyes still. Obediently, Bijou's left paw shook with that wet motion again, then the cat's bored claws came through their sheaths, and sank with electric viciousness into Poupée's undefended snout. Well trained.

The dog made no sound—in memory I see her staring at me alone, but probably that's only a trick of memory—eyes without a plea in them, without a hope, and paws folded rigidly against her gaunt protruding breastbone. I still see the cat's paw, always the same one, the left, the claws thin and spread like a spider's legs—the strike so fast it can hardly be seen. But felt, yes. And I am rocking faster. The rungs of the chair creak slightly. Besides that, there is only one sound in the room—a whimpering. Not Poupée's of course. Jacqueline's mouth is closed, she is slowly chewing her pastry, the sound comes from there. With all the life left in me I want to rise, to mother her, to marry her, to caress her, to love her. But I don't rise. Her eyes are yellow like Poupée's but smaller, and she is moaning. I hear it still.

Days later we sat through the next lesson in my kitchen, neither of us saying or doing anything out of the ordinary. But when she began as usual to recopy her composition, I took the hand that held her pen in my own hand. She looked at me in a way that seemed meant to end the lesson. We kissed. When her tongue came out suddenly to taste mine, I thought she'd be my first French girl, and I took her close . . . but no, she escaped right through the door of my apartment and downstairs in through the door of her mother's apartment.

A couple of days after that, when I came tiptoeing anxiously up to my place, key in hand, I distinctly heard the cat wailing. The laundry room from which the sound came was opposite my door. I went in cautiously.

My pupil was in there. She seemed excited, skinny, tired—leaning against one wall, her shiny elbows tight against her waist, her flowerbell breasts pressed between her arms. It was a bare room, just the big laundry sink, a bucket and mop, four gray walls, and a closet door. I sensed that the two of us must be alone in the house, and I began to have thoughts, concrete thoughts . . . would she feel less afraid of discovery here in the empty laundry room with . . . or could she be persuaded to come to my bed across the hall? Against the door of the closet, the cat Bijou rubbed its back peculiarly.

"Go away," Jacqueline said. "Please." Something had changed. Clearly I was unwanted. Yet in some way I couldn't fathom, she did somehow seem excited by my arrival . . . and yet exhausted. I went to her and touched the slope of her shoulder. I never touched her again after that. The moment I caressed her, the cat's wail modulated to a new pitch. My movement must have done something—increased Bijou's urgency—the gyrations against the closet door changed to a frantic clawing. Her claws audibly tore through the surface of the wood. She must just have had her kittens—I hadn't noticed any change in her heaviness, as a matter of fact. It was Jacqueline's face I'd read: emptied, sagging with fatigue and joy, as if she'd given birth in pain. I asked, "Did you lock her kittens in the closet?"

She didn't answer.

Slowly horrified at her expression, I said, "Did you drown Bijou's kittens?"

Her eyes were fixed on the closet door; she hadn't been crying. Except for an irregular swallowing, except for an almost imperceptible rubbing of her childlike wrists against her thighs, she was very still, she hadn't moved since I'd come into the room, I doubt if she'd actually looked at me more than an instant. But now—I was startled—she gently pinched my arm. It was slight, but evidently important; she had decided to share something with me. "No," she said finally, "they are alive. Six. Four black kittens and two gray-and-white. I have given them to Poupée."

I thought I hadn't heard correctly. "You gave the kittens . . . to the dog?"

"Don't be afraid. She wants kittens, too, yes, and she will love them as much as Bijou. But I have disciplined Bijou now, which she deserves." She was very happy.

I forgot all about Jacqueline. I tried the closet door. It was locked.

She was on her way downstairs. Had I wanted . . . ? I almost lost my voice. "Jacqueline!" Jacqueline was gone. "Give me the key!" The cat stood on her hind legs, straining for the knob as though to help me—I tried to force the door.

The new noise must have wakened them inside . . . the dog began to bark . . . a piercing maternal yapping sound . . . a bark of triumph . . . and the six newborn blind bits of kitten flesh began to pipe . . . shrill, faint, so many, with such energy . . . the cat went wild at the doorknob—and I heard Jacqueline's terrible loving vengeance, her motherly delight, the dog's brute throat exploding through the woodwork, proclaiming that there was justice on earth, that love followed patience, that after mutilation came six puppies.

EMMETT JARRETT

◑

Human Relations

from *Chicago Review*

Terry is sitting in the *kafeneion* writing letters to all his friends
asking for money. If everyone sends him what he asks for
he'll have two thousand dollars. A rich man in imagination,
he hasn't the money to pay for his *mikro kafe*
so he must sit and drink more and more coffee till he hates it,
waiting for me to come back and pick up the tab.
He secretly hates Annie for throwing him out in the cold
but he doesn't dare tell me because I might not pay for his
    coffee.

Annie is sitting at home in front of the little electric heater
hating the Mediterranean weather for being cold and damp.
She had a right to expect the sun to cooperate, she thinks,
with her image of Mediterranean weather.
Annie hates Terry the more because she threw him out in the
    cold,
which was illogical in the first place, neither her fault nor his.

I am the key to the whole situation,
a classic triangle, classically screwed up.
I invited Terry in the first place and Annie resents it.
I let her throw him out in the second place so Terry resents it.
And I pay for his coffee at the *kafeneion* every day.
Terry resents his dependence, and Annie,

who counts the drachmas in my pants pocket every night
after I'm asleep, resents every last drachma.

And here I am in the middle of nowhere
stranded on a broken down Greek bus.
The gears won't mesh. I'm late for work
but not disturbed in the slightest.
The driver has just picked up a large rock.
He is debating whether to bash in the motor
which he resents because it won't work,
or bash in my head because I sit here so calmly in the crisis
writing in my notebook in a strange language
while everyone else shouts helpfully to the gears to shift.

RODERICK JELLEMA

◑

Poem Beginning with a Line Memorized at School

from *Poetry Northwest*

Whither, indeed, *midst falling dew*,
Whither, Miss Pfisterer, black-dressed and balding
Teacher of English, lover of Bryant,
Whither did we all pursue
While glow the heavens with the last somethingsomething?

Bradley Lewis, I mean:
Who put aside with his cello and his brushes
Our lusty masculine sneers at his graceful ways,
Skipped the civics exam to make him a son
And now designs engines with Mozart turned up loud.

Kenny Kruiter, I mean:
Expelled from high school for incantation with wine,
Who bends the knee to his common daily bread,
Hacks every day at bleeding sides of beef
And cheers twice a week the college basketball team.

Michael Slochak, I mean:
He always stuttered every dull thing he knew
And walked home alone—past home, to one gold period
When, crimson phrase against the darkly sky,
His jet purred into a green Korean hill.

EDWARD W. SAID

○

Meditation on Beginnings

from *Salmagundi*

Where, or when, or what is a beginning? If I have begun to write, for example, and a line has started its way across the page, is that all that has happened? Clearly not. For by asking a question about the meaning of a beginning, I seem to have deposited a ghostly load of significance where none had been suspected. Lévi-Strauss chillingly suggests that the mind's logic is such that "the principle underlying a classification can never be postulated in advance. It can only be discovered *a posteriori*." To identify a point as a beginning is to classify it after the fact, and so a beginning is always being left behind: to speculate about beginnings therefore is to be like Molière's M. Jourdain, acquiring retrospective admiration for what we had always done in the regular course of things: only now, the classification seems to matter. Somehow, we know, we have always begun, whether to speak, to feel, to think or to act in one way rather than another, and we will continue to do so. If that is beginning then that is what we do. When? Where? How? At the beginning.

The tautology that tells us to begin at the beginning depends on the ability of both mind and language to reverse themselves, and thus to move in a circle, an ability which makes thought both intelligible and verging on obscurity at the same time. We clearly know what it means to begin, but why must our certainty be toyed with when we are reminded that in matters of mind beginning is not really a beginner's game? We deride the wishful thinker who pretends that the order of things can be reversed; yet at other times we avail ourselves of reversibility, if our case needs its effects. Swift's projectors in Book III of *Gulliver's Travels* who build houses from the roof down live a fantasy of reversibility, but who more than Swift the hard-nosed pamphleteer wanted readers of his political writings to see things clearly, from the beginning—which meant wanting to reverse the ruinous trend of a European war policy, or the cancerous growth in English of neologism and cant?

Thus, one beginning is permissible, another one like it, at a different time perhaps, is not permissible. What are the conditions that allow us to call something a beginning? First of all there must be the desire and the true freedom to reverse oneself; for whether one looks to see where and when he began, or whether he looks in order to begin now, he cannot continue as he is. It is, however, very difficult to begin with a wholly new start. Too many old habits, loyalties, and pressures inhibit the substitution of a novel enterprise for an old, established one. When God chooses to begin the world again he does it with Noah; things have been going very badly, and since it is his prerogative, God wishes a new beginning. Yet it is interesting that God himself seems not to begin completely from scratch. Noah and the Ark are a piece of the old world initiating the new world. As if in an oblique comment on the special status of beginnings, Descartes observes in *Règles pour la direction de l'esprit*: "The human mind possesses in effect a *je-ne-sais-quoi* of the divine, where the first seeds of useful thought have been thrown, so that even though they have been neglected and choked off by studies contrary to their well-being, they spontaneously produce fruit." Every human being is a version of the divine, Descartes seems to be saying, and what seems spontaneous in man is in fact due to the resumption of man's beginning connection with God. To begin is to reverse the course of human progress for the sake of divine fruits.

A beginning must *be thought* possible, it must be *taken to be* possible, before it can be one, especially at the formal or concessive opening of a literary work; the "trouble" with A *Tale of a Tub* is that its alleged writer does not really believe that he can get started. The mind's work, in order to be done, occasionally requires the possibility of freedom, of a new cleanness, of prospective achievement, of special and novel appropriation. It must have these in the course of its continuing enterprises, historical, sociological, scientific, psychological, or poetic. In other words, it must be possible that Paul's injunction to the Romans, "Be ye transformed by the renewing of your mind," *can* be obeyed.

Finally, and almost inevitably, the beginning will emerge reflectively and, perhaps, unhappily, already engaged in a sense of its difficulty. This is true whether one thinks of beginnings in the past, the present, or even in the future. Thus at a very practical level Erik Erikson wonders where to begin in writing the biography of a great man: "how does one take a great man 'for what he was?' The very adjective seems to imply that something about him is too big, too awe-ful, too shiny to be encompassed." Huizinga, in accepting that history in some way deals with "facts," still wants to know how to begin to distinguish a "fact":

> To what extent may one isolate from the eternal flux of disparate units, specific, consistent groups as entity, as phenomena, and subject them to the intellect? In other words, in the historical world, where the simplest thing is always endlessly complex, what are the units, the self-contained wholes [to give the German *Ganzheiten* an English equivalent]?

When Erich Auerbach sadly acknowledges that even a "lifetime seems too short to create even the preliminaries" for what he calls a work of literary and historical synthesis, he sees no hope, however, that an absolutely single-minded narrowness can accomplish the task.

> The scholar who does not consistently limit himself to a narrow field of specialization and to a world of concepts held in common with a small circle of like-minded colleagues, lives in the midst of a tumult of impressions and claims on him: for the scholar to do justice to these is almost impossible. Still, it is becoming increasingly unsatisfactory to limit oneself to only one field of specialization. To be a Provençal specialist in our day and age, for example, and to command only the immediately relevant linguistic, paleological, and his-

torical facts is hardly enough to be a good specialist. On the other hand, there are fields of specialization that have become so widely various that their mastery has become the task of a lifetime.

It might have been to all of this that Nietzsche, with his superb desperation and infuriation, said, *"Ich habe meine Gründe vergessen"* (I have forgotten my beginning). The wish to have a good grasp of how it is that one's activity either has started or will start forces these considerations, and sometimes an impatient response like the one given by Nietzsche; nevertheless, such a grasp always compels us into a rational severity and asceticism, an understanding of which will be a major task in the course of this discussion.

In this essay, therefore, I hope first of all to draw attention to, perhaps even to exacerbate, the problem we face when we begin an intellectual job of work. My view is that an intensified, and an irritated, awareness of what really goes on when we begin—that is, when we are conscious of beginning—virtually transforms, corrects, and validates whatever the project in a very complete way. And this transformation ascertains both the direction of our enterprise and, also, its true possibilities.

Second, I should like to understand, however stutteringly, what sorts of beginnings really exist: the word "beginning" itself is, and will remain, a general term, but like a pronoun, it has a specific discursive role or roles to play, but these are as much in the control of reasonable convention and rule as they are in the control of reasonable assertion. I should like to examine all this as it bears on the possible kinds of beginnings available to us.

Lastly, I should like to record a part of the rational activity generated in us when we deal with a beginning: and rational activity, it will become clear, includes rational sentiment, passion, and urgency.

The beginning as primordial asceticism has an obsessive persistence in the mind, which seems very often engaged in a retrospective examination of itself. We all like to believe we can always begin again, that a clean start will always be possible. This is true despite the mind's luxuriance in a wealth of knowledge about ongoing actuality, about what Husserl calls *leben-dige Gegenwart* (the living present). There is a significant attention paid by the mind to a terminal in the past from which the present might have evolved, as well as a nervous solemnity— *when the question is thought of*—in the choice of a point of departure for an actual project.

Indeed, in the case of the great modern rethinkers the beginning is a way of grasping the whole project; Marx, to consider only one example, attacks Proudhon not only because of Proudhon's uncritically good intentions, but because of his misplaced priorities. "For M. Proudhon," Marx writes in *The Poverty of Philosophy*, "the circulation of the blood must be a consequence of the theory of Harvey." As Lukacs surmised in 1923, it was the job of Marx to show first that beginnings hitherto accepted by the forms of bourgeois thought contributed to, rather than lessened, the separation between man and his proper nature. Then Marx went on to demonstrate that, as Vico had demonstrated before him, man was in fact the beginning of all study, but man for whom "the *social* reality of nature, and *human* natural science, or the *natural science about man*, are identical terms." Clearly there has been a *radical* displacement of traditional thought, for in order to see man as the true origin of social change a new fusion between man and his activity must become possible and thereby rethought in man's mind. The very act of beginning must no longer set man apart from his end, but must immediately suggest connections with it. Marx has cemented his own interpretive activity with man's human activity at a common revolutionary point of departure.

Formally the mind wants to conceive a point in either time or space at which all, or perhaps only a limited set of, things start, but like Oedipus the mind discovers at that point where all things will end. The beginning implies, or rather implicates, the end. If the search is a more modest one, the mind will look for a *possibility* in the past and will therefore propose the present and the future to it for reflection: the result will be three varieties, or stages, of possibility, linked in continuous sequence. This sequence, however, seems to be *there* at a distance from me, whereas my own problematic situation is *here* and *now*. For one rarely searches for beginnings unless the present matters a great deal. It is my present urgency, here and now, that will enable the sequence of beginning-middle-end, and transform it from a distant object *there*, into the subject of my reasoning. So conceived and fashioned, time and space make a drama realized according to an immanent text of significance and not a scenario contemplated in a way that will keep actor and text intact and separate. Ever the dialectician, Lukacs writes that "as the consciousness is not consciousness bearing on an object there, but the object's consciousness of itself, the act of being conscious overturns the form of objectivity of its object."

The verbal problems are very acute. A beginning suggests a) a time, b) a place, c) an object—in short, detachment. *My* beginning specializes all these a little more, and when I say *the* beginning, they are theologized, as Kenneth Burke very cogently argues in *The Rhetoric of Religion*. Once made the focus of consciousness, the beginning occupies the foreground, is no longer a beginning but has the status of an actuality, and when it cedes its place to what it pretends to give rise to, it can exist in the mind as virtuality. In all this "beginnings" vacillate in the mind's discriminations between thought beginning and thought about beginning, that is between the status of subject and object. Paraphrasing Hegel, we can say that formally the problem of beginning is the beginning of the problem. A beginning is a moment when the mind can start to allude to itself as a formal doctrine.

In language we must resign our thoughts to what Nietzsche saw was "something [that] impels them in a definite order, one after the other—to wit, the innate systematic structure and relationship of their concepts." Also, "the unconscious domination and guidance by similar grammatical functions," of which a system of concepts or words is only a strong disguise, merely leases the mind the right to a notion of formal beginnings. Language, as we perceive it in its universal use, has no beginning, and its origins are as marvelous as they are imagined, but they can only be imagined. Profoundly temporal in its self-evidence, language nevertheless provides a utopian space and time, the prochronistic and the postpositional functions, over which its systematic determinism does not immediately seem to hold firm sway. Thus "the beginning," as often belonging to myth as to logic, a temporal place, and a root and also an objective, remains a kind of gift inside language. I shall be returning to this notion a little later. Heidegger and Merleau-Ponty have made effective claims for the identity of temporality with significance, yet philosophically and linguistically theirs is a view that requires, I think, our recognition of the mind's self-concerned glosses on itself in time, the mind as its own philosophical anthropology. What sort of action therefore transpires at the beginning? How, necessarily submitting to the incessant flux of experience, can we insert—as we do—our reflections on beginning(s) into that flux? Is the beginning simply an artifice, a disguise that defies the ever-closing trap of forced continuity, or is it a meaning and a possibility genuinely allowable?

Literature is full of the lore of beginnings despite the tyranny of *in medias res*, a convention that allows a beginning to pretend that it is not one. Two of the wide and obvious categories under which to list types of literary starting points are, on the one hand, the hysterically deliberate, and hence the funniest, and on the other hand, the solemn-dedicated, the impressive and noble. The former category includes *Tristram Shandy* and *A Tale of a Tub*, two works that despite their existence cannot seem to get started; this is beginning forestalled in the interest of a kind of encyclopedic, but meaningful, playfulness which, like Panurge taking stock of marriage before falling into the water, delays one sort of action with another. The latter category includes *Paradise Lost*, a prelude to postlapsarian existence, and *The Prelude*, which was to ready its author "for entering upon the arduous labour which he had proposed to himself." In both works the beginning has become the work itself. When a literary work does not dwell very self-consciously on its beginnings— as the works I have just named do—its actual start, as an intelligible unit, is usually deliberately formal or concessive. (I must evade the question of whether it is really possible to begin unself-consciously, since I am convinced that it is not really possible. The issue is one of degrees of self-consciousness: *Tristram Shandy* is uniquely sensitive about getting under way.) Yet I would argue that points of departure grew increasingly problematic during the eighteenth century, a development eloquently testified to as much in the titles of Frank Manuel's *The Eighteenth Century Confronts the Gods* and W. J. Bate's "The English Poet and the Burden of the Past, 1660–1820" as in their matter.

The search for such points is not only reflected but carried out in and, it comes to be evident to eighteenth-century thinkers like Vico, *because* of language. Polytechnical as no other human activity, language is discovered as an "intelligible abode" in which questions of origin can profitably be asked for purely linguistic as well as social, moral, and political reasons: Vico, in the misery and obscurity of his position at Naples, sees the whole world of nations developing out of poetry, and Rousseau, for whom experience is clarified by words to which he is entitled, writes simply because he is a man of sentiments and a member of the *tiers état*. Kant's *Prolegomenon to Any Future Metaphysics*, to speak now of a beginning that really aims to strip away the accretions of academic philosophy, undertakes a description of radical conditions which must be understood before philosophy can be practiced; nevertheless the *Prolegomenon* fully anticipates *The Metaphysic of Ethics* and *The Critique of Practical Reason*—it is coterminous with them—and the critical method with which Kant refashioned European philosophy. And in the essay "On Method" (in *The Friend*) Coleridge takes up the theme as follows, echoing Descartes: method distinguishes a noteworthy mind in its work, its discipline, its sustained intellectual energy and vigilance. Method, however, requires an "initiative," the absence of which makes things appear "distant, disjointed and impertinent to each other and to any common purpose." Together initiative and the method that follows from it "will become natural to the mind which has been accustomed to contemplate not *things* only, or for their own sake alone, but likewise and chiefly the relations of things, either their relations to each other, or to the observer, or to the state, and apprehensions of the reader."

All such investigations have in common what Wordsworth called "a cheerful optimism in things to come." What is really anterior to a search for a method, to a search for a temporal beginning, is not merely an initiative, but a necessary certainty, a genetic optimism, that continuity is possible. Stretching from start to finish is a fillable space, or time, pretty much there but, like a foundling, awaiting an author, a speaker, or a writer to father it. Consciousness of a starting point, from the viewpoint of the continuity that succeeds it, is consciousness of a direction in which it is humanly possible to move, as well as a trust in continuity. Valéry's intellectual portrait of Leonardo divulges the secret that Leonardo, like Napoleon, was forced to find the law of continuity between things whose connection with each other escapes us. Any point of Leonardo's thought will lead to another for, Valéry says in the same essay, thinking of an abyss Leonardo thought also of a bridge across it. Consciousness, whether as pure universality or insurmountable generality or eternal actuality, has the character of an imperial ego; in this view Descartes' *cogito* was for Valéry *"l'effet d'un appel sonné par Descartes à ses puissances égotistes."* The starting point is the reflexive action of the mind attending to itself, allowing itself to act (or dream) a construction of a world whose seed totally implicates its offspring. It is Wagner hearing an E-flat chord out of which *The Ring*, and the Rhine, will rush, or Nietzsche giving birth to tragedy and morals by ascending a ladder of inner genealogy, or Husserl asserting the radical originality of consciousness which will support "the whole storied edifice of universal knowledge."

Husserl requires a unique attention because the almost excessive purity of his whole philosophic project makes him, I think, the epitome of modern mind in search of its beginnings. The course of Husserl's development is, in the main, too controversial, too technical a subject to warrant further analysis, at least not here. Yet the meaning of his philosophical work is that he accepted "the infinite goals of reason" while seeking, at the same time, to ground understanding of these goals in lived human experience. Interpretation, which is a major task in the Husserlian and Heideggerian enterprises both, is thus committed to a radical undermining of itself, and not only because its goals are pushed further and further forward. For also its point of departure, no longer accepted as "naïve"—that is, merely given, or *there*—stands revealed in the scrutiny of consciousness: as a result, the point of departure assumes a unique place as philosophy itself, "essentially a science of true beginnings . . . *rizōmata pantōn*," as well as an example of the science in action. Put differently, Husserl tries to seize the beginning proposing itself *to* the beginning *as* a beginning *in* the beginning. What emerges precisely is the sentiment of beginning, purged of any doubt, fully convinced of itself, intransitive, and yet from the standpoint of lay knowledge—which Husserl acknowledged to be "an unbearable spiritual need"—thoroughly aloof and almost incomprehensible. This kind of purely conceptual beginning is curiously reminiscent of these lines from Stevens' "Of Mere Being":

The palm at the end of the mind,
Beyond the last thought, rises
In the bronze distance,

A gold-feathered bird
Sings in the palm, without human meaning,
Without human feeling, a foreign song.

It is to Husserl that Valéry's phrase "a specialist of the universal" is best applied. But I shall return to this queer, intransitive, purely conceptual but important kind of beginning very soon.

What is important to modern ascetic radicalism is the insistence on a rationalized beginning even as beginnings are shown to be at best polemical assertions, and at worst scarcely thinkable fantasies. Valéry's Leonardo is a construction after all, and Husserl's phenomenological reduction temporarily "brackets" brute reality. The beginning, or the ending for that matter, is what Hans Vaihinger calls a summational fiction—and it is a summational fiction whether it is a temporal or a conceptual beginning—but I want to insist against Frank Kermode by stressing the primordial need for certainty at the beginning over the mere sense of an ending. Without at least a sense of a beginning nothing can really be done. This is as true for the literary critic as it is for the philosopher, the scientist, or the novelist. And the more crowded and confused a field appears, the more a beginning, whether fictional or not, seems imperative. A beginning gives us the chance to do work that consoles us for the tumbling disorder of brute reality, the exquisite environment of fact, that will not settle down.

Auerbach's retrospective analysis of his own work as a critic seems to suggest what I have been saying. In his essay *"Philologie der Weltliteratur,"* he at first rejects the possibility of making a continuity out of all literary production merely by endless fact-gathering; the immediate disorder of literature is too great for that. Then he proceeds to the description of a synthesis performed by the critic, a synthesis that depends on the choice of an appropriate *Ansatzpunkt*, or point of departure. "Myth" or "the Baroque," Auerbach stipulates, cannot be suitable points of departure for they are concepts as slippery as they are foreign to true literary thought; rather, a phrase like *"la cour et la ville,"* for instance, fully embedded in the verbal reality of an historical period, will itself *become* present (since it is an actual phrase, not a constituted one) to the researcher's mind, and will thereby link itself to the regulating, inner movement of the scrutinized, reflected-upon period. What is essential to Auerbach's meditations is the critic's willingness to begin with the proper instrument of discovery, one forged by language in the act of being locally itself.

Auerbach felt the *Ansatzpunkt* to be a term in the mind's operation. It appears at first as a simple, single digit: he uses the word *"figura,"* for instance, because it is found to have a special place in many Latin texts. Subtracted from history because of an insistence that attracts the researcher's puzzled attention, key words like *"figura"* seem suited, when strung together in sequence, for a new addition to our knowledge. Yet a mechanical arithmetic is avoided when the *Ansatzpunkt* is revealed as a symbol in a formidable algebra. A point of departure is intelligible, as X is intelligible in an algebraic function, as *figura* is intelligible in Cicero's orations, yet its value is also unknown until it is seen in repeated encounters with other terms in the function and with other functions or texts. Thus the importance of a word like *"figura"* or of the phrase *"la cour et la ville"*: in the research, both emerge from a catalogue to enter history, which Auerbach construes as ready in his mind to incarnate them; ready, that is, to change them, and be changed by them. No longer mere words or unknown symbols, in Auerbach's writing they enact "the enchainment of past and future woven in the weakness of the changing body." A mute term, relatively anonymous, has given rise to a special condition of mind and has evoked the poignancy of time. The beginning is an effort made on behalf of continuity: thus a term is converted into history, a unit into a synthesis.

At first a recurrence amongst other sentences, Auerbach's *Ansatzpunkt* turns into a question that asks the reason for its persistence. *Nihil est sine ratione.* And persistence will give the critic the opportunity to view a literature, or a so-called period, as an interrogator acting for a mute client. Interrogation itself creates notable effects, of which one is the phrasing of answers that are given *in terms* of the question. Thus the disparities between a text by Racine, by Corneille, by Vaugelas or Molière are reduced in the interests of an overriding code of significance—embodied in a repeated phrase like *"la cour et la ville"* to which these texts seem directed—that links them all. The evidence Auerbach marshals, however, has a form and an economy that is as particular as the forms of events in a nineteenth-century novel, say a novel by Zola. It is not a mere collection of examples, but a synthesized shaped whole. Elsewhere, Auerbach commends Zola for his daring, not to say his hopeless task, in attempting to deal with the tremendous complexity of the modern world; and this same world offers a panorama of warring "facts" faced no less by a literary critic of Auerbach's learning, or by a philosopher of Husserl's energy. In the latter's *Cartesian*

Meditations he charges that "instead of a unitary living philosophy, we have a philosophical literature growing beyond all bounds and almost without coherence. Instead of a serious discussion among conflicting theories that, in their very conflict, demonstrate the intimacy with which they belong together, the commonness of their underlying convictions, and an unswerving belief in a true philosophy, we have a pseudo-reporting and a pseudo-criticizing, a mere semblance of philosophizing seriously with and for one another." Yet only with the voluntary imagining and the radical asceticism of a *formal willingness* to undertake the bolus synoptically can the researcher, whether novelist, critic or philosopher, even begin his task.

Beginnings and continuities so conceived are an appetite and a courage capable of taking in much of what is ordinarily indigestible. Sheer mass, for example, is compelled into a sentence, or a series of sentences. Books, names, ideas, passage, quotations —like the ones I have used—follow the sequence postulated for them; this is why Swift's "A Modest Proposal" is so perfectly illustrative of itself as a cannibalist tract, as well as of the operations of criticism, understood as rethinking. For the obduracy of Irish peasant bodies that are coerced into a marvelously fluent prose is no more than the obduracy of books and ideas coexisting in something we call either verbal reality or verbal history. A literary critic, for example, who is fastened on a text, is a critic who, in demonstrating his right to speak, makes the text something which is continuous with his own discourse, and he does this by first discovering, then by rationalizing a beginning. Thus the critic's prose—like Swift's as it mimics the cannibalism it propounds by showing how easily human bodies can be assimilated by an amiable prose appetite—the critic's prose swallows resisting works, passes them into passages that decorate its own course, because it has found a beginning that allows such an operation. The beginning therefore is like a magical point that links critic and work criticized. The point is the meeting of critic and work, and it coerces the work into the critic's prose. In finding a point of departure invariably in the meeting of his criticism with the text criticized, is the critic merely re-finding his vision, his biases, in another's work? Does this entail the hope that "prior" texts have prepared one's validity or right to exist with charitable foresight? That *Ansatzpunkte* exist with one's name on them? What, in fine, is the critic's freedom?

These are difficult questions. Let us examine Auerbach a little more. His *Ansatzpunkt*, as I said above, is a sentence or phrase, once spoken or written in a distance we call the past, but now mute: *la cour et la ville*, for instance. Yet the recognition of its wanting-to-speak, its importance in the present, transforms the *Ansatzpunkt* from an uninteresting but recurring motto into an instrument for the critic's work; like Aeneas's moly, it guides the critic through previously unnegotiable obstacles. There must of course be an act of endowment or assertion on the critic's part before an innocuous verbal "point" can turn into the privileged beginning of a critic's journey. The critic's belief, as well as his reflective examination of the point, together germinate into a criticism that is aware of what it is doing. Since a beginning of this sort projects a future for itself in cooperation with the protocols of critical prose—nowadays we speak of texts, meanings, and authors as coexisting in "literature"—the critic would like to devise a means for working with this set of conventions. He would also like to preserve what is unique and possibly strange in his own work. At the sheer level of the writing itself, the critic accepts the determination of linguistic and critical convention while hoping to retain the freedom of possibility: the former is governed by historical and social pressures, the latter by a point of departure that remains exposed to its contingent, and yet rational, status, one that encourages interrogation and retrospection. In the critic's work therefore a vigilant method and a record of that method's accomplishments are being produced together.

The point of departure, to return to it now, thus has two aspects that interanimate each other. One that leads to the project's being realized: this is the transitive aspect of the beginning—that is, beginning with (or for) end, or at least continuity, envisaged. The other aspect retains for the beginning its identity as *radical* starting point: the intransitive and conceptual aspect, that which has no object but its own constant clarification. It is this second side that so fascinated Husserl (I spoke earlier of a beginning *at* the beginning, *for* the beginning) and has continued to engage Heidegger. These two sides of the starting point entail two styles of thought, and of imagination, one projective and descriptive, the other tautological and endlessly self-mimetic. The transitive mode is always hungering, like Lovelace perpetually chasing Clarissa, for an object it can never fully catch up with in either space or time, the intransitive, like Clarissa herself, can never have enough of itself: in short, expansion and concentration, or words in language, and the Word. The relationship between these two aspects of the starting point is given by Merleau-Ponty: "Whether it is mythical or utopian, there is a place where everything that is or will be is preparing, at the same time, to be spoken." (*"Qu'il soit mythique ou intelligible, il y a un lieu où tout ce qui est ou qui sera, se prépare en même temps à être dit."*)

Mythical or a utopia, this place of which Merleau-Ponty speaks is probably the realm of silence in which transitive and intransitive beginnings jostle each other. Silence is the way language might dream of a golden age, and words, Blackmur says, are sometimes "burdened with the very cry of silence," with their very opposite and negation. Yet we do speak and we do write. We continue to use language, its burdens and confusions notwithstanding. The capabilities of language are not beggarly. For articulated language is also a way of apprehending, of alluding to, and even of dealing with what is unknown, or irrational, or foreign to it, whether we call the unknown a myth, a dream, utopia, or absolute silence. We never know, Eliot says, in any assertion just what or how much we are asserting. The unknown can even be called a beginning insofar as the beginning is a concept that resists the stream of language. Since in its use language is preeminently an actuality, a presence, any reference to what precedes it and what is quite different from it is an unknown. If, as I speak, I refer to a beginning, I am referring to what is not immediately present, unless I am referring to the transitive, useful beginning, the beginning defined as present for the purpose of the discourse. The intransitive beginning is locked outside of language: it is unknown, and so labeled. And yet I can and often must refer to it as Husserl did, even though it seems perpetually to refuse me.

Let me try another way of explaining this. When I read a page I must keep in mind that the page was written, or somehow produced in an act of writing. Writing is the unknown, or the beginning from which reading imagines and from which it departs in what Sartre calls a method of guided invention. But that is the reader's transitive point of view which is forced to imagine a prior unknown that the reader calls writing. From the point of view of the writer, however, his writing—as he does it—is perpetually at the beginning. Like Rilke's Malte, he is a beginner in his own circumstances. He writes for no real sake but for his writing: he writes in order to write. What he has already written will always have a power over him. But it too, while he writes, in the presence of his act of writing, is an unknown. It is felt but not present. The writer is the widow of an insight. Eliot says:

> It seems to me that beyond the namable, classifiable emotions and motives of our conscious life when directed towards action—the part of life which prose drama is wholly adequate to express—there is a fringe of indefinite extent, of feeling which we can only detect, so to speak, out of the corner of the eye and can never completely focus; feeling of which we are only aware in a kind of temporary detachment from action.

The unknown absence, felt by the mind, is represented by modern poets, critics, and novelists as an antecedent power that incriminates and is refracted in the present: its mode of being, whether as horizon or as force, is discontinuous with the present and partial in appearance. The great prior reality—whether we call it history, the unconscious, God, or writing—is the Other (Milton's "great taskmaster's eye") present before, and crucial to our Now. The unknown is a metaphor for felt precedence that appears in glances backward, as an intimation of surround-

ing discomfort, as a threat of impending invasion, always ready
to wreck our tenuously performed activity. It is Eliot's backward
look, "the partial horror and ecstasy," Conrad's darkness, seemingly at bay yet ever closer to springing forward and obliterating
mind and light, Kafka's trial that never takes place, but is
planned before K can do anything, an endlessly circumvented
trial but oppressively present in its very impingements, Borges's
ruins that gradually reveal themselves as part of a terrible plan
whose entirety one can never fully perceive but can always be
felt as immortal. Or, in radical criticism, it is the deep anterior
claim of the writing, sometimes willfully forgotten, sometimes
deliberately attenuated, but always haunting the critic whose
reading abuts the mountains and the caverns of an author's
mind-at-work: such critics write critical poems imitating the behavior of the mind. At its best, radical criticism is full of its own
changing, and haunted by its opposite, by the discontinuities of
the dialectic of writing, which it must re-enact and record. Thus,
according to Blackmur, "criticism keeps the sound of . . . foot-
steps live in our reading, so that we understand both the fury in
the words and the words themselves."

Here, it seems to me, Freud's little essay of 1910, "The Antithetical Meaning of Primal Words," is very relevant. In the
work of the philologist Karl Abel Freud found linguistic and
historical confirmation for his views that signs or words in a
dream can mean either their opposite or something radically
different from their appearance. Words in ancient Egyptian, according to Abel, contained a simultaneous recollection of their
opposite and even of their negation. "Man," he goes on, "was
not in fact able to acquire his oldest and simplest concepts except as contraries to their contraries, and only learnt by degrees
to separate the two sides of an antithesis and think of one without conscious comparison with the other." Abel, unlike Freud,
was a meliorist: Freud believed that words continue, in fact, to
carry a recollection of their opposite, the known carrying with it
a considerable freight of the unknown. Reading thus sends us
back in a regressive movement away from the text to what the
words drag along with them, whether that is the memory of the

writing, or some other hidden and perhaps unknown opposite.

Because we must deal with the unknown, whose nature by definition is speculative and outside the flowing chain of language, whatever we make of it will be no more than probability and not less than error. The awareness of possible error in speculation, and a continued speculation regardless of error, is an event in the history of modern rationalism whose importance, I think, cannot be overemphasized: it is to some extent the subject of Frank Kermode's *The Sense of an Ending*, a book whose very justifiable bias is the connection between literature and the modes of fictional thought in a general sense. Nevertheless, the subject of how and when we become certain that what we are doing is wrong *but at least original* has yet to be studied in its full historical and intellectual richness. Such a study would, for instance, show us when and how a poet felt what he was doing was *only* writing poetry, how and when a philosopher attributed to his philosophy the power to predict its own invalidation, and when a historian saw the past dreaming about itself in his work.

Let me recapitulate some of the things I have been trying to describe. The choice of a beginning is important to any enterprise even if, as is so often the case, a beginning is accepted as a beginning after we are long past beginning and after our apprenticeship is over. One of the special characteristics of thought from the eighteenth century until today is an obsession with beginnings that seems to infect and render exceedingly problematic the location of a beginning. Two kinds of beginning emerge, and they are really two sides of the same coin. One, which I called "temporal" and transitive, foresees a continuity that derives out of it. This kind of beginning is suited for work, for polemic, for discovery. It is what Émile Benveniste describes as the "axial moment which provides the zero point of the computation" that allows us to initiate, to direct, to measure time. Auerbach calls his *Ansatzpunkt* a handle by which to grasp literary history. We find it *for* a purpose, and at a time that is crucial to us, but it can never presume too much interrogation, examination, reflection unless we are willing to forego work for provisionality. It is a formal appetite that imposes a severe discipline on the mind that wants to think every turn of its thoughts from the beginning. Thoughts then appear linked in a meaningful series of constantly experienced moments.

There is always the danger of too much reflection upon beginnings. In a sense, what I have been doing in this essay proves the hazards of such an undertaking. In attempting to push oneself further and further back to what is only a beginning, a point that is stripped of every use but its classified standing in the mind as beginning, one is caught in a tautological circuit of beginnings about to begin. This is the other kind of beginning, the one I called intransitive and conceptual. It is very much a creature of the mind, very much a bristling paradox, yet also very much a figure of thought that draws special attention to itself. Its existence cannot be doubted, yet its pertinence is wholly to itself. Because it cannot truly be known, because it belongs more to silence than it does to language, because it is what has always been left behind, and because it challenges continuities that go cheerfully forward with *their* beginnings obediently affixed—it is something of a necessary fiction. It is perhaps our permanent concession as finite minds to an ungraspable absolute. Its felt absence has, I think, seemed particularly necessary to the modern mind, mainly because the modern mind finds it exceedingly difficult, perhaps impossible, to grasp presence immediately. To paraphrase A.D. in Malraux's *La Tentation de l'occident:* we lose the present twice: once when we make it, and again when we try to regain it. Even in the midst of powerful impressions upon us we find ourselves resorting to intervening techniques that deliver reality to us in palpable form. We are peripatetic converts to every mediation we learn, and learning, the process Vico described as autodidactic philology, then seems more and more to be a matter of submitting to various linguistic fatalisms. A critic, for instance, cannot take in literature directly: as Auerbach said the field is too minutely specialized now, and too vastly spread beyond our immediate ken. So we create sequences, periods, forms, measurements that suit our perceptual needs. Once we have seen them, these orders are left alone: we assume that they go on ordering to time's end, and there is nothing we can do about it. These mediating orders are in their turn commanded and informed by one or another moderately intelligible force, whether we call it history, time, mind, or, as is the case today, language. In *Le Visible et l'invisible* Merleau-Ponty writes:

> If we dream of regaining the natural world or Time by our coincidence, our absolute identity, with either or both, if we dream of being the identical zero-point we see there, or the pure memory which within us governs our remembering, then language is a power for error, since it cuts the fabric that connects us vitally and directly both with things and with the past: language installs itself like a screen between us and things. The philosopher speaks, but that is his weakness, and an impossible one at that: he ought not to speak, he ought to meet things in silence, and in Being to rejoin a philosophy that has already been articulated. Yet despite that the philosopher wishes to verbalize a specific silence within him to which he listens. That absurd effort is his entire *oeuvre*.

> (*Si nous rêvons de retrouver le monde naturel ou le temps par coïncidence, d'être identiquement le point 0 que nous voyons là-bas ou le souvenir pur qui du fond de nous régit nos remémorations, le langage est une puissance d'erreur, puisqu'il coupe le tissu continu qui nous joint vitalement aux choses et au passé, et s'installe entre lui et nous comme un écran. Le philosophe parle, mais c'est une faiblesse en lui, et une faiblesse inexplicable: il devrait se taire, coïncider en silence, et rejoindre dans l'Être une philosophie qui y est déjà faite. Tout se passe au contraire comme s'il voulait mettre en mots un certain silence en lui qu'il écoute. Son "oeuvre" entière est cet effort absurde.*)

Everything that is left after these orders of mediated presence are accepted we call unknown. But, as I have tried to show, the unknown remains with us to haunt us from its horizon. When we hint at the unknown we are involuntarily borrowing the words of our experience and using them to gesture beyond our experience. The archetypal unknown is the beginning. Newman called such a beginning an economy of God, and Vaihinger called it a summational fiction. We might call it radical inauthenticity, or the tautology at the end of the mind, or with Freud, the primal word, literally, with an antithetical meaning. Such a beginning is the unknown event that makes us, and with us, our world, possible as a vessel of significance.

The most peculiar thing about such an unknown beginning —aside, that is, from its enduring shadow in our minds—is that we accept it at the same time that we realize that we are wrong, that it is wrong. It is useless, except when it shows us how much language, with its perpetual memories of silence, can do to summon fiction and reality to an equal space in the mind. In this space certain fiction and certain reality come together as identity. Yet we can never be certain what part of identity is true, what part fictional. This is the way it must remain—as long as part of the beginning eludes us, so long as we have language to help us and hinder us in finding it, and so long as language provides us with a word whose meaning is as certain as it is obscure.

GALWAY KINNELL

○

The Bear

from *The Sixties*

1

In late winter
I sometimes glimpse bits of steam
coming up from
some fault in the old snow
and bend close and see it is lung-colored
and put down my nose
and know
the chilly, enduring odor of bear.

2

I take a wolf's rib and whittle
it sharp at both ends
and coil it up
and freeze it in blubber and place it out
on the fairway of the bears.

And when it has vanished
I move out on the bear tracks,
roaming in circles
until I come to the first, tentative, dark
splash on the earth.

And I set out
running, following the splashes

of blood wandering over the world.
At the cut, gashed resting places
I stop and rest,
at the crawl-marks
where he lay out on his belly
to overpass some stretch of bauchy ice
I lie out
dragging myself forward with bear-knives in my fists.

3

On the third day I begin to starve,
at nightfall I bend down as I knew I would
at a turd sopped in blood,
and hesitate, and pick it up,
and thrust it in my mouth, and gnash it down,
and rise
and go on running.

4

On the seventh day,
living by now on bear blood alone,
I can see his upturned carcass far out ahead, a scraggled, steamy
    hulk,
the heavy fur riffling in the wind.

I come up to him
and stare at the narrow-spaced, petty eyes,
the dismayed
face laid back on the shoulder, the nostrils
flared, catching
perhaps the first taint of me as he
died.

I hack
a ravine in his thigh, and eat and drink,

and tear him down his whole length
and open him and climb in
and close him up after me, against the wind,
and sleep.

5

And dream
of lumbering flatfooted
over the tundra,
stabbed twice from within,
splattering a trail behind me,
splattering it out no matter which way I lurch,
no matter which parabola of bear-transcendence,
which dance of solitude I attempt,
which gravity-clutched leap,
which trudge, which groan.

6

Until one day I totter and fall—
fall on this
stomach that has tried so hard to keep up,
to digest the blood as it leaked in,
to break up
and digest the bone itself: and now the breeze
blows over me, blows off
the hideous belches of ill-digested bear blood
and rotted stomach
and the ordinary, wretched odor of bear,

blows across
my sore, lolled tongue a song
or screech, until I think I must rise up
and dance. And I lie still.

7

I awaken I think. Marshlights
reappear, geese
come trailing again up the flyway.
In her ravine under old snow the dam-bear
lies, licking
lumps of smeared fur
and drizzly eyes into shapes
with her tongue. And one
hairy-soled trudge stuck out before me,
the next groaned out,
the next,
the next,
the rest of my days I spend
wandering, wondering
what, anyway,
was that sticky infusion, that rank flavor of blood, that poetry,
    by which I lived?

MARY NORBERT KÖRTE

◗

Beginning of Lines:
Response to "Albion Moonlight"

from *Ephemeris*

At the end I went down into
the sea
   and found a cave
   my love was there
       white with waiting
   his hand to trace
   a path for me among
   anemones

     frightened creatures
       grew in entrances
    for me to embrace first
    as one must embrace people
    careful of the arms

and my lover took me down
into the baptisms
of dark jewels
far into the other side
      of light

his silence washed me
turned to warm the shy reaching

so that I musiced with him
        his being
        his now
        the melody of touch

And the slow fuse burst
as Greek Fire
        against the outline of eyes
        looking in   looking in

        hard and deep in the passion thrust
        surely true

and our meeting roared as the surge of hemispheres
spinning to numbness
           the flamed rockets
           of embraces

(God takes   unaware of choice
you go where it is given to go

not following   going with
locked in a flame far under the sea
down in the dark folly of his shadow

           knocked down
           in the clumsy tears
           of looking   for answers

O it is worth it
        the nights of my fighting
        with anger
and the antiphons question each mid-day
where the sun is most insistent
              there I kiss
              the lips of sacrifice
              and taste

> more than Solomon's
> woman could want

there I am known
(abandoned to grace)
in the dark centre of his fire
that becomes my only womb

> the curve of things pulls out
> from under
> > and I am shafted
> > through to stiffness
> > end over end
> > slowly through to

full length
traversing the scope of all desire
coming at last to rest in
> peace

> peace
> there is no
> peace
> > comes falling
> > from that Light
> > where I see
> > I am
> > > the light
> > > because I am
> > > God

◗

"Afternoon" from The Journals of Robert Lax (Vol. I)

from *Hudson Review*

Kos
march 20 1964

this is the afternoon and so it is time to make a poem
of the afternoon, to come up from under it with a long
sigh and to swing into it from above: the afternoon, the
golden time: to have no subject but the world, life
and the world, life in the world, the texture of
life the texture of every minute as it passes

this is the afternoon and so it is time to make a poem
of the afternoon (the afternoon is making a poem of itself)

afternoon, the afternoon, the people stand on the sunlit
quay and wait for the canaris.

they stand on the quay and wait for the boat: the canaris
to arrive . . .

a long afternoon; an afternoon in the sun

the people stand in a kind of hushed silence; waiting
for the boat to appear on the (blue) horizon

an afternoon of hushed sunlight

a time of afternoon: the people stand in classical poses
waiting for the traditional return of the boat to the island

and wait for the boat to appear on the blue
horizon

a golden afternoon: when sunlight like honey is poured
on the land

they stand in hushed silence and nobody speaks

they are all there, all there, everyone from the town
is there

they stand on the quay in a hush of waiting and
look toward the (blue) horizon

this is the afternoon, a time to make a poem (of
the afternoon)

the afternoon is making a poem of itself.

the sunlight pours on the land like honey

(the sunlight lies on the land like a
tender regard)

this is the afternoon (a time for its music)

sun, the sunlight is the (music)
the music the music (the music) the
music (the music) the music the music

of (this time) of the
a (fter-noon)

the sunlight pours itself on the land and lies on
the land like a tender regard

they stand about and wait for the boat,

they wait for the boat, the canaris, to

come in

◗

Aristocratic Mouse

from *Sewanee Review*

The next day I was in Sewanee. There was quite a change
among the colored people. Many of them that I knew had gone
north. Some had returned. Many New people from the low
lands had come in. There were no baseball teams, no sport
among the colored people. A pool hall, a dance hall, that was all.
I spent the first three hours with Mama. She was so proud of me
the way I looked. I hadn't ever seen her as happy as she was
today. She said I am so glad you went away. If you had have
stayed here no doubt you would have been like John Will, your
cousin. He has killed two men. He is now in the penitenary for
ten years. You both were a like. The difference was you didn't
want to take law from a white person, John Will just wanted to
be a bully. His father died from broken heart. He spent every
cent he had trying to save John Wills neck. The old man used
to stop and talk to me. He thought you were the cause of John
Will being so mean, that he want to be like you. He said you
wasn't afraid of anything. You were so hard to understand. No
one ever knew what you were thinking. You talked things that
we just couldn't answer. Whites seemed to. Father Guerry and
Father Eastern understood you and you understood them.
Every body was glad especially the men when you left. I am glad
you came to me before going to war, because I wanted to tell
you that I didn't know that the grass rope I whiped you with
had cut you as bad as it had. I was scared for the first time in my
life when the men taken their guns off their horses. And thinking I had broke up your gun I knew we were helpless. When

Jack Prince walked to the porch, he said to the men, you ride. Dont attempt to harm not one thing here. He said to McBee take away from here if you value your job. Ely hasn't done any wrong. You know the white people of the University is fond of this boy, and you can catch plenty hell. She said I never knew why Jack was fond of you. He stops once and while to ask about you. Then I told her when I was taken to court to witness for Prince when he killed McBees dog, they begged me to swear that I saw the dog bite Henry. Mama I lied. I didn't no I was sinning. That is why McBee don't like me. Jack became to be my best friend. I will never lie for no one again under oath. I have prayed and prayed that God would forgive me. Henry won the case on my testimony. There is no good blood between Jack and McBee. They knew Jack was armed. That was why McBee taken them away. I forgive you. I knew why you whiped me. I didn't move one step. I taken it for our benefit. It was Gods plan. Father was right when he tole me to leave today. You knew I was in hot water. No one wouldn't have given me a chance with my gun. I had build a repertation of being good with a gun. Mama I still carry that repertation yet. I want to loose it. I haven't had a gun in my hand but once in four years. It don't fit my hands any more. I want to love people. I am being taught to respect the laws of man. I want to love everybody like Father Guerry and Father Stoney taught me. She said Mr. Colmore and the other white people said you didn't have to leave. I didn't realize how much these rich people were interested in you and you well fare. I explained to her why I was going France and to Chicago. I will come back and fight for the right of law in the south. For the colored people as man and women. To the flag of the United States. When I come back I will be discharged a man to the flag. That I will live all my life. I will loose the name of slave which is the name Negro. I was born free. She said you have talked like this all your life. I don't understand you and your dreams. You always said you were never alone. I said that is right Mama. I shall never travel alone. She said what you want for your dinner. I said a huckel berry cobler. She laughed and said that your favorite.

Soon the news was out. I was in town. All my friends came to see me. I was amazed to see that I had grown and devaloped in four years. I was larger than any of the ones that had kicked me around before I left here. Now I can beat them two at a time. Instead of hateding them as I once did I wanted to love them. Willie Six had told them about me boxing when he came back from Texas. Soon many teen age boys came wanting to see me box and tell them about hunting. I had been given the name The Hunter. I was looked on by these boys as a Danel Boone. From my back I was seized by two strong arms. I didn't have to ask who it was. He my stepfather picked me up in his arms as if I was a baby. He and Six lead me into the house. Mama had dinner on the table. This was happiest reunion I ever experienced. Father twice placed his strong hand on my shoulder and said, Mat he is the boy I wanted to see him be. He has grown to be strong. That is what he wanted to be from a little boy. Father said to me, I know you want to go north to come back and try to be high hat like so many of our young men have done. When they go back north we have to send for them either dead or sick and nurse them to health or death. Most of them try to play night life and work. This soon breaks them down. When they were penneless they had no friends. They knew they were always welcome here at Sewanee. As I sat here looking into these honest faces of these two strong black men, so strong physically with phisique of Greek God's. They were two of the kindest men I ever knew. I hadn't ever know either of them to have a cross word with any one. Every body black and white love them. They only knew Sewanee. Father hadn't been fifty miles from here in his life. Six he traveled with the varsity team. I don't think he spent any time away from them when traveling. He stayed with the team where ever they stayed.

I reviewed all this as I listened to them talk. I said nothing to them of my experience of this four years in Texas. They seem to think I was living on the flowering bed of roses. Instead each day I was traveling with my life riding on a prayer. This was the last time I saw these three love ones of mine together. I told them that I was going north on a visit for three weeks. Then back to Texas. I will live in Texas as long as Judge Dunlap lives. I asking about my white friends to learn that Father Guerry had gone to South Carolina. Father Eastern had been very ill. Father Tison was in New York at this time. That narrowed my visits down to one man that I would go to see. That was Mr. Robert Colmore. He and his two daughters and Miss Jonnie Tucker and Miss Sally Milhado. These people had been most kind to me in my young life. It was now four o'clock. I told them I wanted to go today to see the Colmores. I rose from the table to get dressed. I wanted to be on the University street at five o'clock to see the people taking their walks before supper. This was what I used to do when a boy. Father said when are you going to let me give you a boxing lesson. I said tomorrow if we can find some gloves. Six said he would bring them from the gymnasiam tomorrow. I ask Father did he still play football. He was now forty five years old. Six answered saying, he is still to tough for his opponiants. When I came out of the house I found the yard filled with boys and dogs. There were both colored and white. They want to know how to train their dogs to hunt. Some wanted to learn to box. I told them to be back tomorrow at noon. I would tell them at all I knew.

I left them. I was soon up on the main street at the supply store where the Hacks waited for rentals. There were many people on the promanade before supper. I saw many men I knew. They were excorting ladies. I didn't approach them. I had decided to go to Mr. Colmores. I heard the sound of the feet of a fast trotting horse on the slag stone road. I hadn't forgotten the sound of Maudes feet. It was Miss Sally Milhado and her horse. There was room for another vehicl. There I waited for her to pull in, which she did in dust. Maude had to stop like she had four wheel brakes to keep from crashing Henry Haskens hack. I bowed to her. She was wearing a tweed coat suit with a skidoo style hat to match. It was tipped on the left side of her head. She sat for a moment, looking at me. Then she said to lady Elliot sitting by her I will be darn if that isn't that little aristocrate whelp Ely. I haven't seen him since heck was a pup. I ask her could I asist her from the carriage. She held out her hand. I braced her arm as she steped to the side walk. She said you have grown to be a fine young man. I like your courtesy. She looked under her carrage. Then said you have the darnest habit of poping up when you can be of service. Will you please take that rattle snake off the rear axel of my carrage. I ask who killed it. She said I was coming from Natural Bridge. He was in the road. He refused to let Maude pass. I whiped the life out of him with my buggy whip. Then I thought the students might have use for him in there labitorial work. Lay him on the rock wall. I did. People gathered around to view him as enemy no. one of the mountions. He was a fine species. He had shedded and was near four feet long with eleven rattles and a button. Every body around wanted the rattles. I did to. So I pinched them off and ran across the street and down the lane to the Colmore home. I never saw Miss Milhado again. I kept those rattles over twenty years, to remember her and her brave ladyship.

All of the colored people and students call Mr. Colmore General. He was like a consolar for the colored people. He was a English born nobleman. His crest was a Afraican head with a bonds. Of course he would always be a English nobleman where ever he went. He was much interested in the well fare of the colored people. He encouraged them to play football and baseball. He attended all their games. When their was trouble among us he had a small court that tried us. No one had gone to the penitennary nor been tried by a county Judge. Sewanee had its own laws. He looked after that. He had four children which was all grown up. Two boys, two girls. One of the men was a minester, the other a doctor. He had sent the beutiful young ladies to England for lady ship training. They kept house for him. Miss Dora was considered the hostess. She gave me my first training as a butler. She was the finest cook I have ever known. She had given me my first lesson on etique and curtesy. At first I was like a bull in a china cabinet. She was always patient and kind. She often had to repermand me for my carlessness. She would always finish with some words of encouragement. No one ever carried a burden of regret. I had profit much in the outer world from her training. This I was thinking as I walked to their

home. I knew I owned them many thanks. As I entered the gate
the thought came of the day Sally Woods the cooks house
burned which was a quarter of a mile from here. Through the
woodlands. Sally got the news before any one. She call to lady
Dora who was up stairs telling of the burning. She started
through woodlands running. Miss Dora called me from the
terres where I was picking flowers. Telling me of the burning.
She ran into woods after Sally. I in a dead heat of three at Sallys
gate. The house was in a mass blaze. Sally wanted to go in it for
something. Miss Dora caught her around the waist. Sally struggled to free herself. Miss Dora was stronger of the two. She press
Sally against the fence. Tears was streaming down their faces.
She said to Sally, I can't let you take the chance. To loose you
would be a great loss to us. Don't worry, I will give you
everything you have lost. At this moment the walls fell in, spout-
ing ashes an live ember over us. We retreated to the middle of
the road. Sally was so bewildered she went to her knees. Miss
Dora knelt beside her holding her head against her breast, saying you see I almost lost you. I have you thats all that means to
me. I will give you your losses back to you. Everything. A month
later Sally had resumed house keeping with finer things than she
had ever owned. This was a family of high charater. That I
couldn't forget. I was received by the family with a warm welcome. I told them of the fine family I worked for in Texas. I
thanked for the training they had given me in the past. Here I
learned that Frank Gailor had gone to England and joined the
British Forces. It was close to suppertime. I bade the ladies
good bye. General walked to the gate with me advising me to be
a christion and try to advance in ever way. He shook my hand
with warmth and said good bye. I never saw this noble man
again.

Every thing here was happiest of thoughts untill I thought of
the rattles I had taken from the snake and how some of the
other people wanted them to. I knew I would not let any one
have them. So to prevent having and argument I would go by
the Hunt Spring and Cross the Street at the Hotel. I stood at
the turn off road untill I realized it would be best to go bye the

Hotel. Trouble was the last thing I wanted to have. When reaching the Hotel the vorando was clean of people. I knew they were having super. My mind went back to nine years ago when Bert Campbell kick me down those steps and caused me to be cripple for two weeks. I lied to white man who thought Bert had kicked me. I lied to him because I just couldn't stand to see a white man kick a Negro around. Because he couldn't afford to fight back, becuse he had no right of law. All though Bert needed to be kicked around. Any man that would abuse children need it. I had told him when I was a man I would kick him like he had done me. This I will do now. I went in to the Hotel to look for him to find that he didn't come here this summer. This was the only revenge that I had in my heart against any one in Sewanee. I left the Hotel and went pop calling among the colored people. By ten oclock I was home with Mama, drinking sasfras tea an eating fried pies. Mother was laughing when she said, it has been a long time since I have seen my house and yard full of people. You have had many visitors this evening. There has been many young ladies that hasn't been to my house before. There will be a dance tomorrow night. All the girls wanted to know if you danced. I answered them by telling them all my children dances.

I taken a comfarter out on the porch and made a palit with it. I slept untill six oclock the next morning. I smelled coffee. I knew Mama was up. She alway had her coffee at five thirty, like many of Southern colored people do. I put on my short road working pants and shoes. I told her I was going for a run down the mountion and back. She said don't stay to long. I am ccooking beaten round steak on onions, gravy, biscuits and fried apples for breakfast. She said can't you wait for breakfast. I told her it would be better for me to eat when I came back. Then she said you have always been different from most of our people. This I hadn't heard many times in the last four years. I threw a kiss to her saying I'll try to change before I get back.

I had a mile to go before I reached the mountain edge. On the way I stoped at Uncle Rufus Mosleys house I wanted to ask about his son Conzie. He had been a close friend to me when I lived on the north side of town. He was three years older than I. During the spanish american war a troop of soldiers on their way to Chicamoga Park camped two day out on the edge of town. He told me that we could run away with the soldiers and we could be like the cadets. He wanted to be a cadet like I did. He explained to me this is the only way a Negro can become to be a cadet. Quiet natural I was for it. When we arrived at the camp a sentry ask us what we wanted. Conzie told him we have come to join the army. The sentry called the corpal of the guard and told him, I have two recruits for the army. These soldiers were all white calvery man. Conzie told the corpal that he wanted to speak to the commander of the troops. He led us to a tent where there were six officers, one was a major. They laughed at us and joked with us. Conzie plead to the major to take him with them. He said he was seventeen year old. I was intirly to young. I went out of the tent to look at the soldiers how they camped. A few minutes later Conzie came to me saying I am going with them. I am going home and get some clothes and join them tonight when they are ready to leave. Don't you tell any body. When we got to the Quintard Momoreal we split here. He lived on one side, I lived on the other. That was the last time I saw Conzie. Three days later Uncle Rufus came to our house telling Mama about Conzie going away with the soldiers. He tried to find Conzie. He had no luck. For two year no one heard of Conzie untill he had become to be a soldier in uniform. He sent his picture to his family, telling them he was carrering in the army. And he was studing to become a cadet and become to be a commision officer. That he has done. He is a first Lueitenant. He is to come home before going to France. I wanted to see him if I could wait long enough. When I came out of the woods Uncle Rufus was going from the barn to the house with two buckets of milk. I yelled out who owns Rightous Man. He turned around as if a bit puzeled over this statement. He set the milk down and came to meet me. Saying I learn yesterday evening that you were in town. You taken the rattles off of the snake and ran to the Colmore home. Every body around there wanted those rattles. Then he said I know the General was glad to see you. He said

lets go in to see Mama. She should have breakfast ready. Then
he said, I don't have Righteous Man any more. He left me a
year ago. You know I drove him fifteen years. He said do you
remember what General Colmore told us one day about Rightoues Man. I said yes. He coated some poetry by Kipling saying,
The rightoues man diveling him through out heaven. He always
got a kick out of you calling the horse Righteous Man. Then he
said you know the General thinks a lot of you boy. We went
into the kitchen. Mama Mosley was friening ham and did it
smell good. She was the sweet easy going type of woman. They
tried to make me eat breakfast. I began asking about Conzie.
They told me Conzie would not be hear untill the tenth of Oct.
Three weeks from now. I could see they were most proud of his
success in the army. I was proud of it to. To me it looked at it
like this. Here was a milatary school that was honored as the
tenth most efficient military training school in the United States
credited by the Government. Conzie was a patrotic military
minded young boy denied of the oppertunity of entering in to
this highly honored school of training men to be service to the
government. He had the guts to support his ambition. To
struggle for ten years to make the grade that a cadet was supposed to be. He has been warrented as a commesended officer.
At this time, that is about the highest honor that a Negro could
have placed on him. This I told them, I only hope that luck
could favor me, that I could serve under his comman. Tell him I
hope to see him in France. Then I told Mama Mosley good bye.
Uncle Rufus walked to the gate keeping his arm around my
shoulders. I ask him didn't he buy a farm in the valley or some
where. He said yes, he bout a five hundred acreas. I ask why
don't you live on it. He said you know son, I am going to die
hear in Sewanee. You know your grand dady use to say there is
no white people like these Sewanee people. Then he said, I read
a lot. Here we don't live in fear of anything. Then he said, I am
glad to see you go north, if you are not going to live here.

I went back home to Mama Mat thinking I would take a road
work tomorrow morning. I had breakfast with Mama. I knew
their were kids in the yard waiting for me to talk to them. They

could wait. This day I felt closer to her than ever. I could see she had broken much in five years. She favored her right foot which she had suffered with for ten years. I told her I had decided when I go into the service I will make the allotment to you. I will allot my private pay to you. I will be an N.C.O. after the first month. That extra pay will be all I will need. I will have a ten thousand dollar insurince made to you. Mr. Hodgson will look after your Buiesness. I will write to him about it. Just then a dog fight was underway in the yard. I ran out to stop it. To find there about ten dogs, with string or rope leases. Had gotten in the fight. They had become so entangled with the leases they couldn't free themselves. I threw a bucket of water on them. That stoped the fight. I was five minutes cutting the string and ropes to free the dogs. Then I had to veiw each dog one at a time. They wanted to know if their dogs could make a hunting dog. These dogs breed was from dog to dog. I meant they were crossed from pamaranione to pot licker hound. I just couldn't tell them that they were not a hunting breed. As I looked at them siting on the ground with their dog, holding them so close I knew these dogs was close to their hearts. My mind went back when I was their age. Tepsy was my first dog to own. What a pal he was. They ask what was the first thing to teach a dog. My answere was to love you. This is done by you loving the dog. Spend time talking to him. He will soon understand much of what you have to say. He will try to give you love in turn. He will try to do everything he thinks will please you. When you see a animal you chase it and encourage him to chase. As soon as he learn you want to chase it by instenct he will start to track it down. When this happens it is up to you to make him the dog you want him to be. A colored boy ask what was the first animal that I and my dogs killed. This was one thing that caused me to tell a white lie and now I will tell the truth to you boys. Then I said wait untill I get Mama. I want her to hear this because she was the first one that I told the lie to. I want her to hear the truth. She came out and sat in her rocking chair.

Then I told them that a student had give me a bow and arrow. We were living below Tremlett Spring, beside the brook that flowed from the spring. This was backyard of the General Kirby Smith home. I had found that umberello staves were better arrows than wood. I sharppened them so they would penetrate wood, and very acuret for forty feet. It was a very small bow. Mama had told me not ever to use the steel arrows. That they were dangerous. When she caught me using them, she gave me a licking. After that I kept them hid in the edge of the woods, where I take them with me when Tepsy and I went out trying to learn to hunt. It was eleven years ago. On a foggy morning late in March I told Mama I was going hunting back of the ball park. I went to the log where I had my steel arrows hid. I taken one arrow. We started to climb to the top of the hill which had lots of trees and much under grouth. Just at the top of the hill Tepsy barked and ran into the shurbery and began fighting something. When I got to him he locked in battle with a animal larger than he. I didn't know what the animal was. He had Tepsy down. I began beating it with my bow. Then he turned his back to me. I gave him a kick in the back. This started them to rolling down the hill. Locked together. I ran after them, thinking if I could get a hold of the animals tail I could pull them a part. Then I would shoot it. Just as I caught hold of his tail I lost my footing falling on top of them. We three went rolling down hill for fifty feet before I could get to my feet. They kept rolling faster, I ran after them. They crashed into the trunk of a hickory tree so hard that both holdts were broken. Tepsy went to one side the animal to the other. Tepsy rooled far down the hill. The animals claws checked him. He stood up on his hind feet looking like a tiny bear. I was ten feet of him. I pulled the bow string as far as it would go and let it go into his breast. It was a luck shot. He tumbled over and went rolling down the hill. Tepsy latched on to him as he was passing by they both roll off the bank of the stream on the sand. Tepsy chooded and shooked it far several minutes. Then he pricked up his ears and tail looking up at me as if he was saying I have killed him. I bent over and pated his head. He started to chew the animal again. He knew he had done what I wanted him to do. Here I began to think of what I will tell Mama. How we

killed it. If I tell about the steal arrow she will whip me. This I
don't want her to do. I knew Tepsy thought he had killed it so
that is the way it will be. I have the bravest dog in the world.
We drug it home by the tail. I laid it on the porch and called
you, Mama, and ask what kind of animal it was. You said it was
a big ground hog, the biggest I have seen. How did you kill it.
Then I told her Tepsy killed him. She said he is bigger than
Tepsy. Then I said I helpt him. I ask her wasn't he good to eat.
She said yes, but I wont cook him. So get rid of him. I ask could
I take it to grandpa. She said yes he is fond of them. This hog
weighed over twenty pounds. I had to go a half mile to Miss
Emma Tuckers boarding house to meet my grandfather. I
would carry it on my shoulder a while then I would drag it.
Every body on the street would stop and ask questions. No one
could believe that this small dog killed it. Many people examined the animal. They couldn't fine where he had been shot
because their hide is tough and thick. The arow was small and
went through with such force the hole was so small he didn't
bleed. No one could not prove that Tepsy didn't kill it. So the
story has been that Tepsy was the best animal fighting dog in
Sewanee. Tepsy died two years ago at the age of 16 years old. I
know he died still thinking he had killed that ground hog. Now
you can see he will fight against great odds for the one he loves.
Love your dogs.

Then I told them I would be back after the war and hunt
with them. As these young boys filed throught the gate they
were carrying their dog in their arms as if they were afraid the
dog wouldn't know how much they loved them. I was sharring
my share of this love to, like any dog lover which I am. Then I
said Mama this is one whiping I missed. She said, every lick I
gave you you needed it even the ones I missed. Then she said
you wouldn't have been the good boy you are if I hadn't kept
you strait. She patted me on the cheek and said, I made a pot of
vegetable soup. Come and eat. While she was dishing up the
soup there was someone calling from the gate. Saying, hello old
yellow gal. Mama said do you recognize that voice. I said yes
Mama. I have heard it all my life. It is John Statum. She said

you wait here. I want to surprise him. She went to the door saying what are you two old bottle lappers doing here. If you think you are going to drink up my peach wine, if you do you are crazy. John Statum said you know I always come by and sample your wine. Mama filled two wine glasses and said to me, stay back of me. I want you to surprise them. When she gave them the wine in small glasses John said, I don't want to take sacrement. I want a sample of wine. Mama said if that don't please you I will have you put out. Statum said whose big enough to do that. Mama motioned me to come out. I said Hello Mr. Statum and Mr. Fry. Statum came to his feet quickly as surprised grasping my hand asking when did this red mountion mouse come back, after shaking hand with he and Jim Fry. These two were partnors in the maintainence work for the people that lived in the corporation. They done all the painting, paper hanging and hand man work. They were the oldest white men that had worked inside the corporation. And was loved by every body. They had taught me how to hand paper, when I would be around to clean up behind them for five cents an hour. When I was small they tried to give me something to do. John Statum said Mat do you know why I call this boy a mouse. He use to be the busiest boy around here. I have run into him in all parts of the mountions and nearly all the mountineers liked him. He never talked about any thing he saw are heard that didn't concern him. One time I told him not to tell anybody about what he saw. I can tell it myself now. He came on us when we had a keg of beer in the stream from Bubbling Springs to keep cool. I made him take a drink of the beer. I don't think he had ever tasted beer before. John Statum then ask me was that the first beer I had ever drank. I said yes. Then I told Mama that there were eight of these men. They had pushed a sixteen gallon keg of beer in a wheel barrow a half mile around the bench of the mountion and dug a hole in the stream of Bubling Springs, deep enough to surmurge this keg to cool off the beer. They were drinking out of tin cans that looked like empty tomato cans. I had been to Elk river fishing. I came this trail because of the spring water. I wanted to drink. When I found the stream muddy I followed up to see why. This was what I found. I was standing looking at them before they saw me. I could see all of them dizzy. When I said hello men, they looked at me as if to say I don't give a dam who. I can't move anyway. Statum pumped a tin rusty can half full of beer and told the men not to worry this mouse don't talk to nobody. Then said to me you drink this beer. I said no, I want some clear water. He handed me the rusty tin can with white foam running over the sides. I tried to gulp the foam. John Statum taken a deep breath and blew into the can sending the foam in my face. He was laughing at me rubing my eyes. He said drink it dam it. All the others were laughing. Statum said, you know old Ned has given you toddys every since you was born. I knew he wasn't lying. I had to do it to please grandpa. So I will drink this to please Statum. To my surprise it was cold and tasted good. I was very hungry. It tasted like food. I drank all that was in the can. I want to tell you this. I am not a drinking man. Although I have tasted beer many times since that day, no beer has tasted like that beer. Some day I am going to try drinking beer again from a rusty tin can. This caused Statum and Fry to laugh hardyly. Slapping each other on the shoulder because they realized I knew the cans came from the trash pile. Mama then told them they should be ashame to try and make a drunkard out of her boy. Then she to told them that was all of the wine. For them. She said you old bottle lappers will be here Christmas morning expecting ginger bread and wine, so I don't open that Jimmy John for no one untill Christmas.

Then Statum began talking about how the old people had died. There use to be six of these white familys and twenty of the colored. For thirty years these old familys had been close as could be. Ther hadn't been a cross word among them. Soon many of the older colored men came all of them I always called Uncle: Taylor Bryant, Pink Sims, Henry Woods, George Garner. These older men had been my friends all my life. As I sat looking at these older people enjoying the freedom of the law of Sewanee, these people had served in returned of good faith to each other. Mama had been a mid wife for many of the poor white familys. This is why all of the poor white people loved her. Dr. Looney has come for her to wait on a child birth at all hours, and this was one thing she really liked to do. She had some real women friends among these poor white people, like Sadie Hawkins, Ann Ferris, Anna Odear, Mabel Hall who done the sewing, she and Sadie Hawkins, for the colored people. All this afternoon I hadn't heard the word nigger or negro used. No one hadn't spoke of race. This was so different from other places I had been. Where all poor white people wanted a colored person to know that he supported white surpremacy and by him being born white he has eighty per cent of every thing over the Negro because the Negro has to get along with him. Only because no one has any right of law in the south except a white man. This event to me was food for thought that confirmed my opinion firmer than ever. That I would go on trying to fight for the right of law for the black man in the south. I had read where it said programs of law has often had to be schooled for many years before being accepted as a law. This I will do all my life. I may have to fight in a small way. I believe if I fight hard enough that I will gain enough that some educated man will put it over. Now I must prove that a Negro is not a citizen of the United States. That he is still a slave. When this is done I will be on my way to the right of law. I have got to go to France reguardless of what the Judge thinks. These old boys were discussing the athelets of Sewanee in the past. This had always been their hobby for years. You could believe that Sewanee had the only teams in the south. I found myself just as lonely as I had ever been in Sewanee, years ago. I had no one to talk to on what I wanted to talk about. This was no place as before to talk of the Negro problem.

I walked from them to the gate to see Willie Six and two young men with him. He had a set of boxing gloves. He said I brought you to oponents. These two young men were students at Fisk Univ. They were working at the Hotel. They were doing some boxing. I had a good work out just being defencive. The old boys got a big kick out of it. I proved to be much faster than my opponents. This caused John Statum to say that red mouse has always been the fastest animal in these mountions. No wild hog ever got away from he and his sheperd dog. All the mountioneers was fond of that boy. He was laughing as he said, you two have been boxing men, he not a man. He is a mouse. You have been looking for him from the start. Hugh Hill, the barber, he came up tell us that we would not have a dance tonight. That the Hotel at Mont Eagle was letting the colored people dance in the Hotel dining room. The Hotel orchestra would play for the dance. This meant all of the young people would go by hacks. I told all of my friends goodbye. Mama had gone in and had supper ready. I promised every body I would be back after the war. Most of them had said they would see me tomorow. I looked at them as they departed. I stood wandering why couldn't these people been kind to me ten years ago. I hadn't expected to have this kind of home welcome. I couldn't get John Statum out of my mine. He had always called me a mouse. Here I decided that I was just a mouse. That was all I had ever been. God made mice. They were the most lugurious living animals in the world. He eats every thing the rich man eats. He enjoy the crumbs that falls from the tables. I am gathering every crumb of wisdom I can that drops from the lips of the wise white man. This I will be a thief to do this all my life. I know I will always be a servant to man. I am going to be the aristcratic mouse. Miss Milhado had once called me a aristocrat.

I was leaning against the big oak tree in front of our gate, enjoying the late evening mountain sun. I heard Mama say come to super. Then she said what are you worried about. She said, I've called you twice, you didn't answer. I ran to the porch and stoped beside her saying, Mama you know that John Statum is a character. He has called me a mouse from a little boy. And now I can see that he is right. Mama brought both of her hands up to my face with a push slap. Holding them against my face saying are going to let that old bottle lapper get you down by calling you a mouse. I answered no. He gave me a good name. A mouse isn't a bad animal. God made them for some use. That use I don't really know. He don't destroy that he can't use. I have been stealing all my life. Not for myself but for my people. Thats much of my job in Texas. This is just about the use I can be to my race. By me being a good mouse I helped cut the rope that was to hang a colored man named Johnny Johnson. This I done by pleading for justice of law. I used the words of wisdom. That was like crumbs that fell from white lips. These crumbs I returned back to them with a plea for Justice. Some people refused to listen to my plea. I had to be humble. Father once told me when you humble often we receive our greatest blessing. This was my greatest. If I don't get back from France Mama please live hear the rest of your life. This is our home. You have more freedom among this class of white people than any place. I have been in the outer world. Last night I was thinking. John Will and Sam Donell were the only two people that has gone to the penetentary from here. No one has been hanged. Very few towns has this record. Over fifty years. John Will a Negro, Sam Donell a white man. Both commited murder. It seemed I had to witness too conflicts of Sam Donells. I had gone to the depot to meet you the day Phill Collins shot Sam twice in chest with a pistal. They had and argument over a passenger. Both were Hack drivers. Every body in Sewanee I believe prayed for Sam Donell to survive. He was shot through the lungs. For a week his hopes were dim. By being in such care as our hospetal gave, Dr. West our fine surgeon pulled him through. He regained his normal health. In three years he had his own stable. He owned a fine saddle horse. Lidge Harrison the black Smith lamed the horse when he shoed the horse. They had a argument about it. Sam rode away. Later Lidge started home to dinner. This day Mama had sent me to the villadge to buy ten cents worth of sugar and a package of tea. I went to Mr. Brooks store to get the tea because Mr. Burt his son always gave me a whistle. They were so kind to me. This is why I went as far in to the vilidge as I did. Just as I came out of the store, I saw Lidge Harrison walking along the road. Then I saw Sam coming in full tilt on his horse. Holding his gun a double barrell strait up. He stoped his horse just past Lidge and said I am going to kill you. Lidge stoped by a ox wagon that was standing by the road. He had a croker sack in his right hand. He waved it at Sam saying go home go home you are crazy. Sam raised his gun and fired. Lidge turned half round then crumbled down on his face. Sam sat there for a minute then rode away in full speed like he came. As if he had done and honorable deed. There were two white men standing close to me they went to Lidge and turned him on his back one said to me get that sack of fodder on that seat which was used for a coushun. I gave it to them an lefted his head the other pushed it under his head. Then I began to realize what had really happened. This was the first man I had seen killed and the first friend. Lidge was loved by every body. Just two weeks ago he had welded the nuts on the axel of my tin wagon so the wheels wouldn't come off. As large a boy as I were I ran home crying as if it had been my father. Sam served a short term in the penitentuary and returned and reestablished his business. He was never as popular again. He tried to be friends with colored people. He encouraged a colored man to have his own hack busness. He was the only colored man in Sewanee that ever owned a hack. His name was Holland Crutcher. He had worked several year when just a boy as feed man for Haskins and Donnell. There were two of these colored men that drove hacks, Fate Williams the Haskins had raised. There were many decensions between hack drivers. I never heard one between these two colored men.

I had review all of this past with Mama. We had been alone over and hour. She said it is seven oclock. If you are going to Mont Eagle you had better be moving along. I caught the eight oclock train. I was in Mont Eagle in thirty minutes. I went into the hotel to the servants dinning room. The help was having dinner. There was brother who was very young to carry a tray. He was a very good looking boy. He was glad to see me. He got me something to eat. I was please to see the two ladies we called the Stone sisters. They were from Nashville. They had been coming to this Hotel for years and always brought a staff of young school girls to work in the Hotel. They were like chaferones for the girls. The head waiter was from the Side Bottom Hotel in Nashville. He always brought young men students from Meharry coledge and Fisk. Some of his staff he would send to Sewanee. It was a beutiful dance. So many of the white were by standers that we were cramped for space. There were at least a hundred couples. This was a dancing lot. The guest apploded the dancers most often. Mont Eagle had this year the largest attendant of guest that I had seen and Sewanee had the least. I rarely got close to brother. He was busy with girls. I didn't care to dance very much. Three time I waltzed. I had come to see my brother. I learned from one of the waiters that there was a club room on the grounds where they played games. I went to look for it. There I would wait for my brother. I wanted to talk to him about going to Texas. It wasn't hard to find because men were going and coming. There were two white men boot legging moonshine whiskey. One dollar a half pint. I sat and waited until the dance broke at twelve oclock. Then a crap game started. I tried my luck. That was bad. I was soon broke of the five dollars I had brought with me. My brother came and joined in the game. Then the bootleggers accused one of the men of using crooked dice. They had lost all the money they had sold whiskey for. One of them had pulled a gun. He was holding a dice in his hand. Just then two young men rushed in saying where is that Cull. This is the name they call my brother. One passed by me saying didn't I tell you to stay away from my wife. My brother said she's not married to you. They both started swinging their fist. The other man was standing by me with a knife in his hand. He said to his brother beat hell out of him. I'll take any one that don't like it. I was already trying to controll my hand while looking at my brother try to handle a man twenty five pounds heavier. I had to admire him for doing as well as he was. He struck the blow. Some how my hands wouldn't stay put. I let go a short hard hook that landed on the button of the one with the knife. He droped to his knees, droping the knife. I grabed the knife. In the scramble the table was over turned that the lamp was on. There was mad scramble. Some one hit me on head breaking my hard straw hat. I didn't know who I was fighting and didn't care just then I backed against the wall. Stabbing with one hand and punching with the other. When I came to my good sence there was no one in the hut but me. I was still in the dark. I struck a match to find my hat. It was tramped flat. I picked up the coal oil lamp an lighted it. I see blood on my clothes. I found I hadn't been hurt. Then I felt sick. I knew I had hurt somebody. Just then my brother came in asking are you alright. I said to him why do you people have to fight. This is the first fight I have had with a negro since I left Sewanee. I use to have them two or three a week about you. I came to see you thinking I might take you with me. That I wont do. You Negro are crazy to fight each other. I wont be back to see you again. If I do we will be to old to fight. I went to him put my arm about his shoulders and said we are the only two of Mamas blood lets keep it alive. Then I said good by.

I walked to the station. I knew there was no train untill six a.m. It was six miles to Sewanee. I will walk it. I looked at my watch to see it two thirty. There was a man driving a mule and sulky. I ask will you let me ride. I got in hoping that he wouldn't be any of the ones that I used to know. We got a long fine. Where he let me off I had three miles to walk. I was home at four thirty. Mama was awake. I manage to keep her from seeing the blood on my clothes. I told her I was leaving on the six oclock train was why I came back tonight. She said I will cook breakfast while I packed and dressed. We had eggs, a slice of shoulder of pork cured, biscuits, huckle berry preserves and sasfras tea. This meal I could never forget with a darling you call mother that had shed many tears the only one for me. She walked to the gate saying son come back to me. I kissed her cheeks and told her you will come to me as soon as the war is over. I started on the trail through the woodland. There were roots I had stumped my toes on thinking it was a penilty for killing a frog. As I passed the butcher shop Agnes Ruef yelled wait you snassy. She came to the door smoking her pipe. Said are you running a way again. Shaking my hand said you are the best looking snassy ever raised in Sewanee. In ten minutes I caught the train.

The Lost Angel

from *Kayak*

Four little children
in winged costumes—
it has something to do

with raising money.
Children are hungry,
the one says, the one

who can talk.
And they go down the drive
in the driving rain, and there's

no car
to collect them, no
one waiting, and the bills

and coins spill
from his trailing hand
and float like pieces of light.

Wait! Wait!
I yell, and run
to gather what I can,

and he turns,
the one who can talk,
holding his empty fists

as offerings,
two shaking hammers,
and gives me back my life.

1966

from *Apple*

one time riding the subway last year I
found in the faces of men and women
despite their ugliness a kind of clear
singing overtone struck by the bodies
against each other (as a tuning fork
struck on the wrist is painful   but still yields
a long bright sound standing in the air)   but
today nobody was touching   instead
like cousins meeting at a funeral
embarrassed at forgetting each others'
names   they sat apart   pretending to be
concerned with the unalterably dead
reading   in their papers   that this morning
each stamped U S A   Marshal Ky's tanks rolled
into the city of Hue to crush a
clamorous rising of priests and children.
I saw no recognition of life or
death in these faces   saw in the air no
vibration or pain from touching   but the
silence of death spinning in the air.

RICHARD SCHECHNER

◑

Theatre and Revolution

from *Salmagundi*

This essay was written on two sides of a historical watershed in
the U.S. When I first sat down to write, in January 1967, the
possibility of armed revolution in America was remote. I could
foresee only the brutal suppression of revolutionary ideas and
activities by a reactionary government corroborated by an
equally stubborn and shortsighted population. Now it is August
1967. Newark and Detroit have happened. Rap Brown seems to
speak for many Negroes; a minority, but revolutions are fought
by minorities (ideally in the interest of majorities). Guerrilla
warfare—either open and violent or more sophisticated—seems
a real possibility. The Vietnam War has so divided Americans,
and so clearly revealed the contradictions within this society,
that those who felt a peaceable solution to our problems was
possible no longer think so.

How can we possibly reverse the trend toward colonial imperialism abroad and genocide at home? America has already
picked up the marbles dropped by the European colonial powers, and even deeper world divisions are apparent. Russia, the
U.S., and Western Europe seem partners against Africa, Asia,
and Latin America. The conflict can be stated in several ways:
(1) Western technology vs. peoples who do not yet have, but
who are seeking, that technology; (2) white people vs. yellow,
black, and brown people; (3) the great industrial centers of the
Northern Hemisphere vs. the overwhelmingly populous peoples
of the Southern Hemisphere (with India and China identifying
themselves with the South); (4) comfy commodity-oriented

peoples vs. overpopulated subsistence-oriented peoples. Certainly there is a convergence of circumstances which all point to a catastrophe of inconceivable proportions, warfare of murderous intensity. I do not mean nuclear annihilation, though that is a live possibility. I mean a series of confrontations, both political and military, in which millions will die by bullets, bombs, and starvation.

Seen in these terms this essay may be an expression of decadence, as my life perhaps is an expression of decadence: to foresee catastrophe and to speak of art is to fiddle while Rome burns. Be that as it may. I do not yet have within me the conviction of violence; I am not setting down my books and leaving for Harlem or Hanoi. But I wish to say that I know a war is under way and I feel my obligations. The extent to which I am unable to underwrite these obligations with action measures either my commitment to a life of intellect or my cowardice—or both.

The Poverty Program, we now see, was never meant to alleviate poverty. Its strategy was to buy off those who were articulate enough to frame in demands the hurt of have-not. In a society that is accustomed to converting everything into money-exchange, it was only logical to expect that social unrest could be purchased and neutralized; that the agony of the ghettos could be reified, isolated, and eliminated through official bribery. The assumption of the Poverty Program was that American society was "basically" sound: those who are not heard from do not matter. Clearly we know now (as many knew then) that our society is unsound. America as it is now constituted thrives on war and exploitation and in our ghettos we have an inverse model of America's relation to the world at large. At home an oppressed minority is fed palliatives followed by armored personnel carriers. Abroad an oppressed majority suffers under the whip of American industrial and ideological oppression. The same machinery which provides first "foreign aid" and "advisory groups" and later—when the population still refuses to see it our way—puppet governments, American firepower, and finally troops—this same machinery operates domestically. A decade ago we were told that America was a novice in international diplomacy and that our ruthlessness was because of our "innocence" abroad. This is a rationalization. Our ruthlessness comes from our need—a political and economic need—to exploit. We do no better than we have done because we do not care to do better; it is in our "national interest" to do as we have done. Thus we need a re-examination of that national interest.

Such a re-examination, I guess, would make us traitors. Because we would find that we have acted criminally to protect and enhance our material wealth; that we have frightened our population with "Communism" the better to keep them in line; that, by and large, we don't care what happens to the niggers in the ghettos or the billions of niggers abroad; that internationally we need these niggers (of many colors) to keep our industrial machinery going and that domestically our home-bred niggers are a pain in the ass that we wish to have done with, by mass murder if nothing else works.

Knowing these circumstances, traditional political activity appears fruitless. New Leftists reject the thinking and strategies of their elders, and Old Leftists lament the radical style of the sixties. Irving Howe writes:

> The "new leftist" appears, at times, as a figure embodying a style of speech, dress, work and culture. Often, especially if white, the son of the middle class—and sometimes the son of middle class parents nursing radical memories—he asserts his rebellion against the deceit and hollowness of American society. Very good; there is plenty to rebel against. But in the course of his rebellion he tends to reject not merely the middle class ethos but a good many other things he too hastily associates with it: the intellectual heritage of the West, the tradition of liberalism at its most serious, the commitment to democracy as an indispensable part of civilized life. He tends to think of style as the very substance of his revolt, and while he may, on one side of himself, engage in valuable activities in behalf of civil rights, student freedom, etc., he nevertheless tacitly accepts the "givenness" of American society, has little hope or expectation of changing it, and thereby, in effect, settles for a mode of personal differentiation. Primarily that means the wish to shock, the wish to assault the sensibilities of a world he cannot overcome.
>
> ["New Styles in 'Leftism,' " *Dissent*, Summer 1965]

Another older, if not old, Leftist, Leslie Fiedler, celebrated elements of the same style Howe berates. While discussing Peter Weiss's *Marat/Sade*, Fiedler referred to the "Road Vultures," a gang of motorcycle-riding Buffalo youths.

> I find in them a refreshing and terrifying confounding of old political categories, a confusion of the classical Right and the classical Left. And especially I find a rejection of what the Left has become; for instance, the sentimental identification with John F. Kennedy—that kind of faceless success symbol manufactured by prep schools, ivy league colleges, and PR experts—which ex-radicals of my own generation have fallen into so abysmally and pitifully. I find myself thinking, as I reflect on the Road Vultures and the *Marat/Sade*, that anyone who really hates, as I pretend to myself on most days, the indignities of living in the comfortable world which I inhabit, must in his heart find it much easier to identify with Lee Harvey Oswald and Jack Ruby, those real Mama's boy nuts, with those absolute lunatics, with their fantasies. [. . .] Anybody who doesn't really find it easier in his heart to identify with Ruby and Oswald rather than with Kennedy is not really honest in claiming to be disaffiliated with the world in which we live.
> [*"Marat/Sade* Forum," *Tulane Drama Review*, Summer 1966]

Fiedler's observations are much nearer to the heart of the matter than Howe's. In the less than two years that have gone by since Howe published his complaint, the New Leftists have become steadily more radical and organized. But they are not liberals, and the world they propose may be just as perilous as the one we now have. In fact, a split has occurred within the ranks of those who call themselves Leftists. An entire group— the hippies—have disaffiliated themselves; their political program, such as it is, is ideal communism. The Black radicals are arming themselves with guns. The white radical student groups sympathize with the blacks and adopt the styles of the hippies. What unites the three groups is a profound dissatisfaction with the American way of life; each group proposes models of social reorganization beginning with the dismantling of the capitalist economy and ending with a reconstructed consciousness. Taken together the radicals look tiny compared to the great inert (and incipiently vicious) American majority.

The deeply depressing thing is that no radical program seems destined for success. America may get out of Vietnam, and life here would "return to normal." A domestic Marshall Plan may be enacted permitting many ghetto Negroes to become middle class. These programs would alleviate the immediate pressures on the system. But the straightening of dangerous salients does not touch the central complex. Protests within institutional frameworks—from university rules to city ordinances to elections—are harmless games: the choices are never real. And truly insurrectionary activity is suicide.[1]

I find it more difficult in August than I did in January to turn at this time to the theatre. The theatre is a game I play well and it may simply be my strategy for avoiding more difficult problems. But at least I know that if our society is to change, our arts must change too. And the arts can, in a limited but important way, sponsor and provoke change. The social event of the theatre offers to its audience a direct participation and involvement that no other art can approach. Theatre is an acted event, a series of transactions, a visual-verbal participatory game. Its closest formal relations are sports and, in nonliterate societies, ritual. It can be celebratory, orgiastic, and communal. It can funnel social energy and redistribute it; it can generate action or neutralize the impulse toward action. In the hands of either oppressive governments or radicals it can be a major weapon.

Most primitive societies are rich in theatrical lore and exercises. The theatre is the natural way to celebrate birth, marriage,

[1] My thoughts on this are in flux. I have come a long way in a few months, and don't know how far I have yet to go. Can we fight a forty-year guerrilla war in America? Would it achieve anything? Is there any other way of changing our system? Must America go through a "fascist phase"? Are we headed toward fascism no matter what? Can any power be generated in an alliance between university students and black power people? Will students or Negroes support such an alliance? I don't know the answer to any of these questions. The thing is now to begin thinking in these terms. I would, of course, prefer peaceable solutions and orderly —though profound—change. However, taken as a whole, America may be too wealthy and self-satisfied to sanction any change from within. But then there is the possibility of being overwhelmed from without. In a generation, by a hostile world led, let us say, by China. Or we may hang on as Rome did, totally corrupt and slave-powered.

and death; to commemorate house-building; to retell events of national importance and personal terror and joy. That we in the West have reduced theatre to a differentiated spare-time entertainment does not exhaust theatre's potential or diminish its world-wide traditional functions. The Western theatre—from Aeschylus to Ionesco—is not the major theatrical tradition, but a most important offshoot that is now losing its relevance; and even within the Western tradition there were long periods of communal theatrical activity. The most important of these periods was in medieval times, when the Greek model was sufficiently weakly defined to permit a broader range of theatrical experience than Peloponnesian classicism sanctioned. Most essentially, theatre is structured events and transactions the collection of which may reconstitute the perceptions and conceptions of those watching and doing.

What does that mean, "reconstitute the perceptions and conceptions"? Simply, after one has participated in a theatrical event the world looks and means differently. Of course this may not happen; and just as naturally this reconstitution of experience is the aim of all art. I suggest only that theatre is better equipped for this task than literature if only because literature demands literacy; theatre is better equipped than the visual arts because painting and sculpture are passive and can engage viewers only through the operation of secondary mechanisms. It is, in fact, the recognition by nontheatre artists of theatre's unique possibilities that has led many of them recently to "theatricalize" their work. Paintings now perform, poets once again sing. Such activities, we know, are not modern but very ancient and they remind us of the time when art was a single, synesthetic whole.

A reconstituted perception is watching *Marat/Sade* and never looking at a bucket of white paint (or a gashed finger) the same way again. A reconstituted conception is seeing *Mother Courage* and then joining an antiwar group. These are intentionally pale examples because we have all but lost touch with theatre's power. Peter Weiss and Bertolt Brecht are fine playwrights but they but weakly incorporate this power. The difficulty is that

Weiss and Brecht write plays, a special kind of theatre in which identifiable characters enact a story in a space which separates the audience from the performers and the stage from the auditorium.[2]

One need not look far to find another kind of theatre. Of many examples I will cite just one, reported by F. E. Williams in his *The Drama of the Orokolo*.

> *The Fire-Fight*. The bathers, men, boys, and girls, were seen gathering for a moment about the bright fires by which the scene was illuminated. They seemed to be drying themselves, and as they did so they joined spontaneously in the chorus which rose to tremendous power. But they had something else in view, and this was merely an interlude. All were arming themselves with bunches of dry, inflammable coconut leaves, one in each hand, in readiness for the Fire-Fight.
>
> Now they divided themselves into two parties according as they were associated with the east and west sides of the *eravo* [ritual and communal men's house], and faced each other across the fifty yards of open space directly in front of it. Across this space a rough hurdle of bamboo poles had been hastily run up while the bathing was still in progress, and it now stood as a very flimsy frontier between the two forces.
>
> Suddenly on the east side all the torches seem to flare up simultaneously, and a moment later those on the west also, making perhaps 200 in all. The foremost on either side dash forward and shatter their torches on the hurdle, so that they seem to burst into a shower of sparks. Reinforcements charge in regardless. In a moment the barrier is broken down and the two sides mingle in a welter of flames and flying sparks. They pursue one another round and about with screams of laughter,

---

[2] There are probably many reasons why the proscenium stage developed, and why the notion that stage and auditorium should be separate spaces persists. However, surely one of the most important is the increasing identification during the seventeenth to nineteenth centuries of theatre with literature. The most notable formal characteristic of literature is the absolute separation of reader and work. The theatre, which mixed with its audience in the middle ages, and which existed on the wooden tongue of the Elizabethan stage, moved behind the proscenium with its curtain. There the players could be "seen" and their actions "read." The curtain was the book's cover and its opening and closing signaled the beginning and ending of "chapters." I thank Paul Epstein for this insight.

striking, dodging, and clashing their weapons together, while lighted torches, flung spear-fashion from the hand, travel through the darkness in blazing arcs, like meteors. For a few minutes the battle rages in the village, and then with one consent the combatants turn on to the broader spaces of the beach and the black distance is soon alive with darting and circling points of fire. Meanwhile the village constables have been blowing their whistles in a well-meant effort to restore order, though happily they are completely disregarded and their shrill bleats only succeed in adding a frolicsome tribute to the revels. But in a few minutes more the thing is all over. The remaining torches are dashed out on the sands, and all return to the village.

Village conceptions are changed by the Fire-Fight. Williams reports that the Fight "is possibly to be viewed as a last ritual license in the use of this dangerous element. For now the participants, or some of them, were to receive [. . .] a formal gift of fire together with appropriate warnings as to its use." Obviously certain parallels exist between some recent intermedia events and the Fire-Fight. Other parallels can be drawn between the Orokolo and our urban rioters who loot with a "carnival spirit" and sing "Burn, baby, burn." The Fire-Fight is part of a thirty-five-year ritual drama cycle which the Orokolo stage with superb relentlessness: it is a mirror of their life and a repository of their beliefs. Our art is less well formed and our urban fire rituals more primitive.

Closer to our traditions are the Greeks. I fear we have lost forever, converted by Aristotelian reasoning, the sense of the Greek chorus which Nietzsche, of all moderns, seems to have understood. Describing the Dionysian nature of the chorus, Nietzsche observes:

[. . .] the cultured Greek felt himself absorbed into the satyr chorus, and in the next development of Greek tragedy, state and society, in fact all that separated man from man, gave way before an overwhelming sense of unity which led back into the heart of nature. The metaphysical solace (with which, I wish to say at once, all true tragedy sends us away) that, despite every phenomenal change, life is at bottom indestructibly joyful and powerful, was expressed most con-

cretely in the chorus of satyrs, nature beings who dwell behind all civilization and preserve their identity through every
change of generations and historical movement.

[*The Birth of Tragedy*]

Dionysus, Eros, tribalism—the terms differ depending upon
whether you are Nietzsche, Marcuse, Brown, McLuhan, or an
ethnographer, but the sense is the same: Underneath whatever
repressive or suppressive machinery civilization generates to
keep itself intact, a counterforce of great unifying and orgiastic power continues to operate. At certain times in an individual's life, and during certain periods of a society's life, this counterforce is activated. Its show can be marvelous or ugly. It seems
to me that today in America (and in other parts of the Western
world) this counterforce is surfacing. There is a qualitative connection between the New Guinea Fire-Fight, the Greek chorus,
and our own folk-rock dances and light shows. LSD may be contemporary chemistry, but freak-outs are old stuff. I take this special quality to be the essential theatre.

It is no accident that Freud identified the unconscious (in
Marcuse's explication) as "the deepest and oldest layer of the
mental personality [. . .] the drive for integral gratification,
which is the absence of want and repression." [3] And this same
pleasure principle, translated and transmuted by organized fantasy, becomes, in Freud's view, the source of art.[4] The difference between art as we know it in the West and theatre as it has
traditionally developed throughout other parts of the world is
that Western art is individualized while traditional theatre is
communal. Western art, particularly post-Renaissance Western
art, has become a function of Protestant and capitalistic ideas; it
was inevitable that the individualization of art would lead to its
commercialization: nothing formally distinguishes the labor of
the individual artist from the labor of any other worker—and

[3] *Eros and Civilization*, 17. All utopian political and social programs
share this same goal. It would seem that the ultimate good is the free
expression and gratification of unconscious wishes. Whether the realization of this goal would truly be "good" remains to be seen.

[4] See *Jokes and Their Relation to the Unconscious* and "The Relation
of the Poet to Day-Dreaming."

labor is bought and sold by the piece or by the hour. Theatre most stubbornly resists individualization because even in its diminished Western version theatre demands the participation of at least two groups—actors and audience who together create the theatrical event.

But despite its inherently communal nature, Western theatre has been literaturized during the past four centuries.[5] A complicated process is now unfolding that promises to undo this literaturization. Artificial divisions among the arts and between art and life are being erased. Concerns for linearity and perspective are becoming less important, while our need for simultaneity, multifocus, and the total use of space is increasing. The tribal has been latently there all along and has survived the impact of Protestantism and industrialization. This tribal elation is emerging now not in the theatre itself but all around it in society.[6] The great unargued debate between Nietzsche and Hegel about the nature of tragedy is bursting on us again. Hegel felt that tragedy represented "a self-division and self-waste of spirit, or a division of spirit involving conflict and waste." Nietzsche, as we have seen, finds in the Greek chorus something "indestructibly joyful." It is perhaps the highest achievement of Renaissance theatre (and in some leavings since then) that both tendencies were precariously present in single works. Surely it is this double sense of waste and indestructible joy that gives Shakespeare's plays their greatness.

I suppose the Athenian community that saw *Oedipus* and *Lysistrata* (a community, we must remember, that predated Aristotle by several generations) sensed the affirmation—even in

[5] Footnote 2 was a discussion of one aspect of this process. There is other convincing evidence of this literaturization. We have come to "read" plays even in performance much in the same way as we read books: to obtain information. The text of plays, which was once merely an element of theatre, has become the core of the theatrical experience. The centuries after the Renaissance saw the participatory nature of theatre eroded by a demand for cognition. However, it seems as if this trend is now being reversed.

[6] Whether or not this tribalism can transform society and, if it does, whether the new society will be any better than that which it replaces is, of course, the subject of this essay.

terror and satire—which these events offered. Here in a single circular arena the whole community came to see its reality enacted. Although we have always known the topicality of Aristophanic comedy, we are just beginning to discover an equivalent topicality in the great tragedies. Aeschylus, Sophocles, and Euripides were not writing abstractly; their plays related most directly to the social life of Athens. *Oedipus* itself can undoubtedly be better understood as a drama of political choice than as one of religious significance. It is difficult to grasp this because Aristotle so profoundly shaped both our understanding of Greek tragedy and that Christian culture which chooses to accept these plays as pre-Christian Christian statements. Nothing the Greeks did in their arts was separated from the whole fabric of city life and that life was not organized according to Christian cosmogony. A Christianity infused with early European culture —pagan culture—reveals a sense of civic identity not unlike the Athenian. A communal and cosmographic harmony surely infused the cycles of York and Chester when townsfolk participated in those vulgar, beautiful, unapproachable panoramas of heaven, hell, and the commonest of men. Acted in the streets, continuing for weeks, these cycle plays unfolded a world history focused on the local community. The great theatrical events of fifth-century Athens and medieval Europe were community expressions. Reaffirming certain values, they questioned others, and were often merciless toward individuals. Aristophanes liked neither Athens' leaders nor the Peloponnesian Wars and he said so in his plays. Can we understand the society which sponsored these plays as sanctioned events? And need we remember that the wars went on, Athens lost, and her great civilization declined? (Even had she won, the system of alliances and conquests which she made would have insured her decline. Winning or losing wars is not as important as the social organization which develops under pressure.)

Were we today to sponsor such communal events we would probably discover subjects and forms too uncomfortable to permit public sanction. The celebration of the rioters in Newark and Detroit took on, at a certain point, the aspects of a performance. That, more than anything, outraged the authorities who responded with another kind of performance: the trigger-happy National Guard. Merely to think what it would mean to act out in Harlem or Westchester cycles of plays that truly represented the hopes and fears of our people, which accurately concretized our mythologies, and which steadily cast these hopes, fears, and myths in contemporary forms and activities—avoiding archaic and temporizing devices and seeking in the living values we act the images of our actions—even to think about such performances measures the repressive mechanisms deeply ingrained in our lives. Try as we might we would be unable to match Greek or medieval models. Our expressions become either innocent light shows or bloody riots.

In San Francisco this past year there was in Golden Gate Park a vast be-in, attended by nearly four thousand people. The slogan and fact of the be-in was "free grass and ass." The event was at once beautiful and ugly. It represented what those thousands of people wanted, but could hardly express in their formless dances, isolated scenes and dialogues, marijuana highs, speeches, and grab-ass. Many happenings have the same styleless expressivity. When the lid comes off we find that repression is our style, our myth-maker, and the source of our social order. Begin to remove repression and the result is not the "natural man," but confused milling about. It is a desperate situation socially and a distressing one aesthetically. During the heyday of rapid industrialization repression was the necessary tool for maintaining the social order so that certain technological skills could be developed and applied. Repression then became the major ideology of the West. The mechanism which Freud describes so well in *Civilization and Its Discontents* was accelerated by that particular civilization whose technology demanded alienated labor on a scale previously unimaginable. The ideology of repression became so deeply ingrained in our social arrangements that even now, when the demands of technology are becoming less ardent (for many whites and a few Negroes), we have very little to fall back on: we maintain repression not because we wish to but because we have nothing else. Our social life takes its shape from personal and institutional repression—remove repression and we find formlessness. After the rigor of Ibsen we have the amorphousness of Kaprow; after lynch-law we have Detroit. Perhaps it will take several generations for us to achieve the sophistication of the New Guinea village that acted out Fire-Fight. And perhaps we shall never get there, our habitual civilization and its cops intervening long before.

But the be-in was not entirely styleless, and neither are happenings or riots. The new theatre and its accompanying social behavior are styleless (and even destructive) in terms of what we expect of art and public behavior. But who can quarrel with Erving Goffman's profound platitude that all elements of social life "exhibit sanctioned orderliness arising from obligations fulfilled and expectations realized." It remains for us to discover and understand what obligations and what expectations.

Be-ins, happenings, light shows, and riots all witness—both by opposition and confirmation—life styles which are repressed, aggressive, and murderously self-destructive. I do not deny that some aspects of these events, and some entire, though isolated, events represent perhaps a breakthrough to a hedonism that is no longer hedonistic, toward a celebration of life; but much as I would wish it otherwise, the new art and most of our rebellious social behavior is a reaction against existing cultural forms and not yet a self-sustaining new culture.

But going still further down the road we have set out on, going much further, might bring us to the point where the creation of a new culture is possible. There will be a lot of shit before then. But it is necessary, good shit. To act out our social routines—to suggest public psychodramas for the allegedly sane —would be to open to public view the madness of American society. We have skirted the edge of this program for some time. What *Any Wednesday* insinuates The Fugs say. We are dissatisfied with the way we live, we have no adequate means of expressing our wishes. We can either clamp the lid back on or blow our minds.

Freak-outs, happenings, the wild collage of TV, be-ins, Detroit—these are already theatrical events. These daily theatres have erupted among us and we are scarcely prepared for them. Theatre professionals resent these intrusions and speak of tradition and retreating into performing-arts palaces and subscription theatres which resemble the great aristocratic forts of the French Bourbons. And our repertories, playing to fewer and fewer people, echo the cry, "Let them eat cake"!

Outside we live in a histrionic world. We no longer expect meaningful information from newspapers, radio, or TV. That information has been rehearsed and staged for us, invented each day to keep us entertained. We have become part of the media, extensions of our TV sets. They no longer exist to tell us about the world. Rather we exist to feed them material. We know that even a minor asocial act or major sanctioned activities, or pure chance, can get us into the papers, on the six o'clock news. We view ourselves each evening and automatically accept ourselves as part of world-wide programing. The spectacle of the Vietnam War or our Great National Space Adventure Complete With Thrills and Death poignantly illustrates this. Here events of immense barbarism, complexity, and sophistication are staged at a staggering cost. We are told that our "national security" depends upon these adventures. But how much of their function is pure entertainment? In what way are Cape Kennedy and Vietnam staged responses to our histrionic needs? As seen on TV they have all the formal characteristics of entertainment; they are exhibited at peak hours and bought by sponsors; and I expect that the affective response to these real-life shows is not significantly different from the response to the Superbowl football game. The hippies are dressed for performing, and the college kids, the SNCCs, the businessmen. Role-playing has become very important: could an ugly son-of-a-bitch with a lisp get elected President? What else should we expect when on TV there is no difference between a "real" war and one performed by John Wayne?

Fully exploring the histrionic quality of everyday life would mean creating theatre. But to propose such a theatre is to ask for an aesthetic and social upheaval of the most profound kind. It would mean bringing out in the open a set of attitudes that have been unstated; it would mean provoking America to paroxysm. Pursuing these thoughts into realities is taking Genet, Artaud, and Pirandello seriously. Should we then relegate such a theatre to the professionals, permitting only artists, and them but tamely, to explore the theatricality of everyday life? These activities would then be "represented" in our theatres, circuses, and dance halls; they would be filmed and videotaped. Obviously we have gone beyond this already. Or we could attempt to neutralize what's happening by officially organizing and carefully staging our be-ins, riots, and wars. We could arrange our riots with trained arsonists and looters (if the government trained them it would be entertainment; if they were self-trained and organized it would be guerrilla war). But even this is behind the reality. The Vietnam War is already being staged by professionals and frequently directed by newsmen. Of course we have the means to further sophisticate our methods. And to sit home scanning our screens. "There's a war on channel five," Mommy says. But Daddy insists on the riots on channel six.

This conscious and public programing would at least clarify the kind of world we are living in. It would result either in the total pacification of our population or in revolution.

What else is there? We could attempt a radical staging of our experiences, one which is neither officially sanctioned nor comfortable. We could attempt to create an antiofficial media system. Or, to put it in positive terms, we could stage the madness of our society so as to better avoid being trapped into living that madness. And we could show what celebration means.

Honestly, I must pause here. The foregoing argument about our officially staged media/reality, and the logical following out of those implications have not been pleasant. I believe that much of our communal life is already being arranged for us, and it is very nasty because many Americans live under the illusion that they are free. The only advantage of a still more conscious and planned staging of wars, riots, and the like is that patterns can be changed only when they are consciously grasped. Perhaps writing about these things will be enough. But I doubt it. And were we to more consciously stage our already histrionic lives I do not really believe things would improve. I think people would accept that staging and rather apathetically watch on TV the incineration of millions of people in camps—or in whatever new means of genocide our very resourceful technology offers. I continue this essay to write of more pleasant things with the consciousness that I am looking for a hope I cannot yet deeply believe in. I am frightened and therefore art will gallop in and rescue me. Upon such fantasies societies twiddle while destroying themselves.

The arena for a new media system is not TV but the streets. There the public space has already been invaded by demonstrators and hippies, tourists and shoppers. Work like that of Peter Schumann's Bread and Puppet Theatre is a beginning. But finally one has to go to the demonstrators, the students, the hippies, the ghetto dwellers on their doorsteps, the shoppers in the supermarkets—all of those who are consciously alienated from American society, and some of those whose alienation has not yet been self-articulated—and organize them to act out what they are already acting out. To touch more completely the nerve already exposed, and to nourish more vigorously the sensibility already visible. It is a species of aesthetic radicalism that I am proposing: a class-consciousness that is based not on income or education but on alienation and which takes as its first goal the awakening of consciousness, the expansion of awareness. I assume, perhaps unwisely, that persons alienated from our society can be turned on to a different social structure. It is a radical assumption, but some of the recent development of political thought among the hippies—an unlikely repository of social activism—indicates that there is a phase beyond dropping out: not getting back in but living out and demonstrating new patterns of social organization.

Such an undertaking—an alliance among students, artists, hippies, black nationalists, some educators—would mean, in theatre, fewer plays and more happenings, fewer stories and more events. It would mean constructing modern cycle plays and processions, be-ins and street dances. It would mean the exchange of radical leaders: send Luis Valdez to Spanish Harlem for two months to organize there a Teatro Campesino; have Joe Chaikin go to St. Louis and train cadre in the techniques of the Open Theatre (as Sydney Schubert Walters went from the Open Theatre to Minneapolis to lead the Firehouse Theatre); bring a leader of the Provos from Amsterdam to New York or San Francisco to organize demonstrations; have Peter Schumann go to New Orleans to show some people there how to make a Bread and Puppet Theatre. This kind of work is somewhere between union organizing and guerrilla warfare. The aim is to provide temporary expert leadership in cities across the country so that local groups can learn the techniques of radical theatre. The result will be a sustained and relentless attack on our official media and the government and system for which they stand. And the art works themselves will be positive presentations of new theatre techniques.

On another level teachers, students, and experimental artists could begin the important task of dismantling and reconstructing the great repertory. These plays—from Aeschylus through Shakespeare to Chekhov and Genet—constitute a tremendous burden and opportunity. Insofar as we merely accept them as written and as traditionally staged we are preserving modes of thought and action which have fossilized. If the universities have become a watershed of radical thought and activity, they also are the strongest bastion of conservative thought. To pass on our heritage without radically changing it is helping perpetuate the moral and conceptual base of the system that oppresses us. Therefore we must accept the work of Jerzy Grotowski in Poland who tells us that "no technique is sacred; any means of expression is permitted provided that it is functional [. . .]." Grotowski has shown us that it is possible to reconstruct texts treating them as materials for the art work to be created (rather than as models from which the work derives). This is a very important theoretic point. Because once we are ready to treat our repertory irreverently we can reassemble the fragments into designs that suit our present mood and needs. Our heritage is exhausted. The only way to use it is to eat it up, digest it, and come out with something else. Such was the Renaissance strategy that transformed Europe in several generations.

Thus the artist and educator have a special responsibility and opportunity. They, more than anyone, keep and confer the cultural heritage. And if economics and politics are two pillars of society, the cultural heritage is another—and perhaps a more basic one, providing as it does both the starting point and goals of society. We shall not be ready for new forms of thought until we have destroyed the old forms. To hell with Irving Howe's "intellectual heritage of the West, the tradition of liberalism at its most serious." This tradition, like the Universal Church at the end of the Middle Ages, needs total revision. It is our essential cliché: once it was glorious but it no longer works—the intentions and explanations our heritage offers do not control society; nor is there any hope that they can be propped up and made functional again. The work which the cubists and abstract expressionists did on perspectival painting needs now to be done on a more general level. The job is no longer to pass on an ancient inheritance, but to transform that inheritance into something it perhaps never intended to be. Such is the nature of revolution.

New Orleans–New York
January–August 1967

EUGENE McCARTHY

◗

Indiana I: Three Bad Signs

from *New Mexico Quarterly*

The first Bad Sign is this:
"Green River Ordinance Enforced Here.
Peddlers Not Allowed."

This is a clean, safe town.
No one can just come round
With ribbons and bright thread
Or new books to be read.
This is an established place.
We have accepted patterns in lace,
And ban itinerant vendors of new forms
                    and whirls,
All things that turn the heads of girls.
We are not narrow, but we live with care.
Gypsies, hawkers and minstrels are right
                    for a fair.
But transient peddlers, nuisances, we say
From Green River must be kept away.
Traveling preachers, actors with a play,
Can pass through, but may not stay.
Phoenicians, Jews, men of Venice—
Know that this is the home of Kiwanis.
All you who have been round the world
                    to find
Beauty in small things: read our sign
And move on.

The second Bad Sign is this:
"Mixed Drinks."

"Mixed Drinks."
What mystery blinks
As in the thin blood of the neon sign
The uncertain hearts of the customers
Are tested there in the window.
Embolism after embolism, repeating.
Mixed drinks between the art movie
And the Reasonable Rates Hotel.
Mixed drinks are class,
Each requires a different glass.
Mixed drink is manhattan red
Between the adult movie and the
                              unmade bed.
Mixed drink is daiquiri green
Between the gospel mission and the sheen
Of hair oil on the rose planted paper.
Mixed drink is forgiveness
Between the vicarious sin
And the half-empty bottle of gin.
Mixed drink is remembrance between
                              unshaded
40-watt bulbs hung from the ceiling,
Between the light a man cannot live by,
And the better darkness.
Mixed drink is the sign of contradiction.

The third Bad Sign is this:
"We Serve All Faiths."

We serve all faiths:
We the morticians.
Tobias is out, he has had it.
We do not bury the dead.

Not, He died, was buried and after three
                                        days arose.
But He died, was revived, and after three days was buried alive.
This is our scripture.
Do not disturb the established practitioner.
Do not disturb the traditional mortician:
Giving fans to the church, for hot days,
Dropping a calendar at the nursing home,
A pamphlet in the hospital waiting room,
An ad in the testimonial brochure at the retirement banquet.
Promising the right music, the artificial grass.
We bury faith of all kinds.
Foreverness does not come easily.
The rates should be higher.

SANDRA McPHERSON

◑

Preparation

from *The Colorado Quarterly*

It was likely to occur during the happiest story
Or at the explosion of a brainstorm or as the product fused
From mere numbers. The blue sky we knew would go
Yellow and fearsick, then after the flash, white

As a bloodless Caucasian. What we had to learn was like
    dancing:
To follow. A desk, no protection from the teacher's C,
Would save our lives. There were times we wondered—would
    we
Go all at once, tightly curled little foetuses, roomsful

Of legal abortions? A brace of peace
Holding our shoulders back bent. We were suspicious
Of white dawns. We kept one ear ready always
For the voice of our siren mother.

We expect now the friendly alarm Wednesdays
As Sunday we depend on brimstone to quake the church.
Some say that God alone, though he doesn't laugh, is not scared.
    And that
There still are those who sing without government like birds

And are prepared.

◗

Dirge

from *Southern Poetry Review*

The learned masseur McLuhan says books are dead. Why not?
It's a trend. Theologians tell us God is dead. And any day now
ornithologists announce to the next of kin the demise of birds.
Imperialism is dead. Colonialism is dead. Isolationism is
dead and the frontier is dead and the white man's burden and
peace in our time and the open door all dead, along with
domestic tranquillity and nonviolence and blushing brides.
Gandhi is long dead and Einstein and Schweitzer and Ford and
free enterprise and clear streams and pure air are dead
and of course Puritanism is dead and good taste is dead and
Lake Erie dead as denial and Lake Michigan being administered
final rites. Oh yes the Establishment is dead and so is the
antiestablishment dead. Hemingway is dead and Frost and
Faulkner and romanticism is dead and naturalism is dead and
goodness knows how many liberals agrarians one-worlders free
traders and oh my god Jack is dead and we all died with him
a little. MacArthur is dead Hirohito is dead and Hitler and
Mussolini. Bertrand the Russell and Charles the Grand and
Norman the Mailer and Ayn the Rand and Allen the Ginsberg
and uncounted others all dead from the neck up and more than
I care to recall deeply dead from the neck down. Why be half
safe? Cigarettes kill you and alcohol kills you and drugs kill you
and automobiles and planes and taxis and trains. Running to
war will kill you and running away from war will kill you just
as dead and overeating will kill you and not eating will kill you
and if the high voltage doesn't do it and the carbon monoxide

misses and VD and a stroll through the park at night both fail,
there's always the ever-dependable cancer and heart failure.
Sarcophagus McAbre worked to death. Who's for one hell of a
wake? Buddy, you still there? Buddy??!!!

ELAINE KRAF

◐

Westward and Up a Mountain

from *Chelsea*

I

I took Clarence up a mountain. He was not developing here. Nor was I. By the time that Seymour came to visit us in December of nineteen sixty-five, we had begun to lose the essential language. Clarence was no longer attending school. And I had been dropped from lists of Office Temporaries and The Kelly Girl Service for serious typing errors. Lapses in usual knowledge of key verbs occurred. I forgot the verb "to be." I asked someone how to spell "are." She whispered about it. Thus with the disease the rumor spread. Seymour became alarmed or concerned and arrived in a hurry.

"It's from being with him all the time," he said with the partial authority of an alleged father. There are five men who might be Clarence's father. According to my calculation, Seymour is one. He is second violinist with the Pittsburgh Symphony Orchestra. Excepting this accomplishment, his every deed has the signature of nebula. Like Clarence and me, Seymour is inefficient with words. Manufacturing sentences from ideas is alien to him. Words come out malformed; pinched together or separated by pockets of air. But with the fiddle underneath his chin, Seymour is eloquent. When the Pittsburgh Symphony Orchestra came to Carnegie Hall, I took Clarence to watch him play; his bow jumping across the redwood with ease.

He could not share with us the musical language with which he replaced words. And we had none to use. In this way he did not help us. But he was as much a father to Clarence as the statistical possibility indicated, generously sending an allotment for his miscellaneous expenditures.

"Did you ever think of putting him in some kind of a home?"

At that moment Clarence came in. He was carrying the old violin that Seymour brought him. The bow with loosened hair hung around his neck. Plucking the strings, he danced kicking up his legs. Seymour smiled and promised to bring an old cello that someone abandoned in one of the rehearsal halls.

Clarence waved good-by to Seymour from the window. But I did not wave this time. I began to dream of taking Clarence somewhere far away.

Seymour's visit depressed me. I was not used to having company. Even visits from school officials were becoming less frequent.

In the beginning I was called to school for many conferences about Clarence. His retardation was a combination of factors, they thought. And in view of its being inconclusive we should wait. Much would depend upon whether or not he learned to read.

After a series of failures, the methods of attack were exhausted.

"We have tried," said Mr. Appledoom, the principal, "phonic attack, word attack, sentence attack, as well as tracing in the air."

Consequently he had "taken it upon himself" to put Clarence in the class for children with slower mental development.

"Let's give it a whirl," he said, certain that Clarence would "feel more at home" in Mabel Fogg's room.

I looked into the classroom. Five mongoloid children sat on the floor hammering large pegs with wooden mallets. A boy with arms outstretched circled the room making airplane noises. Two girls rocked their dolls to sleep in back of the room. Clarence sat by himself, on a chair that was too small, grimacing and twisting his nose.

There was another meeting two months later. Mr. Appledoom, Mabel Fogg, and Doctor Clement Forthwright, M.D., revealed their unanimous suspicion. The following Saturday

Clarence and I arrived at an office in White Plains, just above or below Port Chester. Wires were cemented to his narrow head as he smiled, gazing straight ahead undisturbed.

It took an hour to scrub the cement from his patches of kinky hair. Then we went to Finnegan's Parlor for ice cream cones. We went there because of the stools. He swung round, legs stretched out straight. Finnegan stared at Clarence's long legs.

"How old is he?"

It was a question Finnegan often asked but one I cannot answer. The records of his birth were misplaced. And all I can remember about the year or hour he came forth is that it was snowing. Nor can his probable fathers remember because they were far away. Except Joe Paliacco, the singing waiter. (Last year he played a gangster in a revival of *Winterset*, and now he is understudying someone's brother in *View from the Bridge*.) Joe agrees that it was snowing. And he remembers that some months after Clarence's birth, I was in an institution. He visited me there a few times. When I came out I took typing lessons on West Broadway to prepare me for Office Temporaries.

"The Electroencephalogram showed no indication of focal lesion. No abnormalities were recorded," said Doctor Forthwright with regret. He looked at me sympathetically. "I'd caution you against optimism," he warned. "Spinal fluid examination may disclose an intracranial tumor."

He took a deep breath. "We will return to this area of investigation later on. Meanwhile may I suggest *Thematic Apperception, Rorschach, Bender Visual, Motor Gestalt*, and the newly revised *Terman Merrill Stanford-Binet*. Ethel Edgewater, a dear friend, and an excellent child psychologist, would be delighted to administer tests and prescribe treatment."

Seeing no reaction on my face, or an inappropriate one, he continued with determination.

"I will mince no words with you. Nondifferentiated schizophrenia is its current title. Reversible, only if attended to promptly. There are excellent facilities as well as resources to be taken advantage of."

Clarence continued his studies in the class for children with retarded mental development. Cheek on his desk, eyes gazing into voids we know nothing about, he began refusing lunch that the retarded children ate at a table in back of the room.

"He eats only hard-boiled eggs," said Mabel Fogg despairingly.

I watched Clarence picking off pieces of shell and putting them into his mouth with the rest of the egg. Then he vomited.

"Feathers," he said later. It was his favorite word. He lay so still I felt his forehead.

"No school, mother," he whispered. He forgot the word "school" soon after. When I told him he could stay home, he ran for his box of feathers, and pasted one on my apron. He asked for feathers three years ago after seeing a hat or a bird. I went to a store on West Forty-sixth Street where elaborate costumes are made for actresses and belly dancers. I brought home fifty. He stapled orange plumes on the front of his shirt, and put one on his beret.

He sits in front of a mirror tickling his nose with each feather. And laughing. Clarence's room is lined with mirrors. Ferdinand, the tattooed man from Ringling Brothers' Circus, was Clarence's favorite father. He brought us distorting mirrors. And Ferdinand was the only one of the five that I continued a romantic relationship with after I came out. It was seasonal; whenever the circus came to town. These were our happiest times. Clarence had a peculiar rapport with elephants. Ferdinand wanted him to be in a special elephant act. But I objected. He became interested in oddly shaped hats, and I in bizarre costumes. We keep our collections in a big closet in Clarence's room. Our main interests come from our circus days.

Ferdinand almost became Clarence's legal father. He offered me a ring. But I didn't want to travel with the circus. In those years, after the institution, I dreamed of being part of respectable society's "mainstream."

It was Ferdinand who kept the language alive for us then by reading to us every night. He loved Clarence. His sulphur-colored skin and flat broken nose did not disturb Ferdinand's affection. Nor did his spastic gestures and elongated head. I wish we had taken the tattooed man for a father and traveled with the circus!

Last year Ferdinand died of something chronic and malignant that he had never mentioned. We planted a tree for him in Central Park.

Several months after I had withdrawn Clarence from school, Ethel Edgewater knocked at the door. When he heard the knock, Clarence hid under his bed. I sat perfectly still. We both feared the school authorities because of my illegal act. Frequent telephone threats had precipitated its removal.

"It is only I, Ethel Edgewater, friend of Doctor Forthwright." (She was in fact Mrs. Forthwright.)

Her voice was as nice as a sparrow chirp so I opened the door. She looked friendly too, dressed in green with pointed shoes. She was less than five feet tall. Even Clarence came out ready to entertain. When I took her in to meet him, he was sitting in front of a mirror making faces. She seemed to approve so he took out his collection of hats; gifts from Ferdinand, oddities I found at the Salvation Army Store or Witches' Thrift Shop. He liked to try them on and trim them with feathers. Ethel Edgewater was speechless. Squeezing his nose together upward, he laughed putting a pot on his head. Turning to see if she was laughing, he saw a suspicious stare. In vain did she try to coax him from under the bed, peeking, chirping to him from her picket knees. He stayed underneath for the rest of her visit tickling his feet with a feather.

At the time of Ethel Edgewater's visit, I was beginning to lose details, although I got the main idea. She spoke, I think, in detail. Crestfallen, her chirp disappeared and she sounded like the Mrs. Forthwright she was.

"Indeed it is a sad state of affairs when a mother unable to provide a father is consumed with guilt and compensates by allowing her son's impulses to control their lives abdicating adulthood she keeps him from maturation and retards herself regressing alarmingly detached from reality losing identity community forsaking language and conspiring so that her son shall not learn to speak withdrawing him from school thereby fostering degeneration."

She spoke thus, if in more detail that I cannot recall recommending prolonged institutionalization for Clarence and intensive psychotherapy for me. However, first she would administer the tests that Doctor Forthwright enumerated. We would receive them jointly to save time and expense.

That was the last time that Ethel Edgewater came inside. No matter how often she chirped at the door we remained rigid until her pointed toes descended the stairs. I no longer opened the door for anyone. I called Office Temporaries from a pay phone in Finnegan's Parlor. If they needed me, Clarence stayed in the zoo. But they rarely used me any more.

After Ethel Edgewater's visit, I began to see Clarence and myself climbing up a mountain. Words were slipping off rapidly so plans had to be made at once.

Seymour must have regretted some of the things he had said about Clarence. A large check arrived soon after. I bought two pairs of boots, plane tickets to Denver, and a yellow parasol for mountain rain.

II

My plan was to climb Aspen Mountain until I came to the writers' summer cliff dwellings. There I would stop to find Clarence's father; the one man to pierce the soundless thing around us. Or covering us already. He would clip the gladless hush deciphering to us our meaning.

Clarence's smile that fell past all unnamed would come through this man's brain a sentence. Darting of my eyes nowhere, my smirk or laugh between things he would walk through discovering some request I wanted to make. Or a desire I did not know. Never yielding to the heavy still, his fingers on my mouth would bring words. Proud too, he would be, as my fluency increased and one sentence flowered into the next like the conversations I heard, but did not know. Full of words, verbs, arrangements of thought, Clarence's father would come down to be with us.

I had no doubt that it would happen. My responsibility was to get to the airport on time without losing the tickets. And to take Clarence westward and up a mountain. There they would be waiting to greet us.

I felt guilty about withholding my plan from Seymour, who might worry not finding us at home. Or someone might go there by chance. Like Ferdinand. If he were living.

Naturally I could not arrive at the writers' cliff dwellings without a disguise. I made the ascent as a lady poet. On a rented typewriter, I constructed poems from old magazine ads; cut up sentences and pasted them together in different order. It was, in truth, the best I could do. Without written guides I could no longer construct a sequence of words. Those who respected my poetry will be chagrined by this confession. The poem that secured my reputation was made from an ad for American Airlines:

Theater-in-the-air
Hawaii
Malihini.　　Jet Clipper
Hawaii
Pan Am. Astrovision.

Another world
Malihini
Dancing under stars.　　Jet Clipper.

Jet Clipper
Hawaii.　Astrovision Hula.
Another world
Malihini.

Before taking off, I made in this way, ninety poems to verify my identity as a lady poet. But it was to search for a husband and verbal father, that I carried my rented typewriter to Aspen.

At Kennedy Airport we drank soda from tin cans cooled in a tray of ice. Clarence rubbed the ice against his cheek. Then he offered pieces of ice to elderly travelers waiting at K-13. Some smiled graciously. Others objected to him. The ice melted, leaving the few remaining cans soaking in spotted water. We boarded the Golden Jet to Chicago, where we would get our Continental flight to Denver.

O'Hare: mysterious castle with silent passageways, arches, secret numbers, letters in combination, all twisting slowly toward gallant airships with fan-jet engines. Sudden corners revealed aluminum pushcarts for wheeling props or children in crisscross directions. Four feet tall, he reigned in the upper basket, splendid with a navy jacket covering his feathered shirt. He wore cabbage-colored shorts and snakeskin mountain boots.

As we glided to tin music, clocks stopped moving. Shadows of men I had beckoned to; who came up the elevator when Clarence was asleep, and never returned, decomposed like fake hysterias into the unconditional presence of O'Hare. I shed dead parts, under the glare, for night workers to sweep up. There was not much left then. Light, ready to go upward, I danced with the cart, Clarence its king.

It was night then. Into a night of blue stars, silent as an enemy hiding in elephant grass, we rose for the second time. He rested against me surrounded by space. My eyes, sorrowfully, had nothing to tell the other passengers. It was for this we were going to Aspen, Clarence and I, to find something to tell; a dream, a few sentences, so that someone could understand it.

The Trailway Bus wound around the edges of mountains. It stopped, finally, to let us rest at Colorado Springs. We sat on a balcony watching the sun clapping on the pool below. It jumped back blinding us. Voices came and faded. Bodies moved like wax images coated with icy water. And had they looked up to the balcony, Clarence and I would have been invisible. It seemed that way. I trembled not knowing who would greet us.

The bus stopped at the foot of a mountain. Under a drizzle, our feet in mud, we saw things dance though the mountain was still. Signs, awnings, glimpses of white-haired girls broke up space. (No one knew us.) We swayed. And Clarence fell to the ground which was ooze and stone, wetted crust; a multitude of things. He was unable to breathe. I helped him through endless grit up to the writers' cliff. Pointed rocks tore the edges of our boots. Red dye came off the suitcase as we waded knee-deep to the first door. Inside the writers assembled to introduce themselves. (They didn't want to but they did.)

"Nero, semantic specialist from Illinois; on call twenty-four hours a day."

He had no beard, dressed in blue wool up to the ears, his owl eyes grinned. Wildcats chased each other around the living room over poets' knapsacks and mountain boots. Clarence stared ahead nearly rigid. From his throat came rasping noises.

"I'm sorry to bother you upsetting these mountain rhythms you are so fond of. And we will be too. But Clarence is afraid of cats. We are also ashamed to notice the scarcity of air," I said, picking out the words one by one.

"I don't understand," said one to the other and all to themselves. After whispering and conferring among literary figures, an empty cabin was found. We lay there indefinitely.

It was a dark room sinking further into the slime each hour. Yellow muck reached the window sill and fell inside. He would have put his fingers into it and smiled if he were stronger. Instead, he lay on his back staring at the ceiling. We hadn't eaten for days. If I knew the directions I might have gone outside to look for food. Other cabins were situated farther up, but rain made the mountain too slippery to climb. No one came to see us. And the mountain outside the window made the room black. I covered Clarence and he fell asleep. I lay in the dark not even knowing what to dream. It might have lasted forever if Ivan had not come.

He happened to pass our window one day, squeezing through the small alley between our cabin and the mountain. His eyes came up to the window. Seeing us lying thus, so uniquely, he became interested. He called others to observe us. Anaximenes, Norma, Lunar, Clyde Hoffritz, Timmy, Jill, Nero, Hussanah, Faringsworth, and Barnaby all descended or came from behind to look. They brought gifts of fruit and cheese. It was the welcoming ceremony I had been waiting for. But we had no breath with which to receive them.

"Who may he be?" queried the cruel poet Anaximenes.

"My son. But without his feathers."

Nero's eyes lit up owlishly with comprehension. And immediate insight. He talked to us with animation. Then he left, followed by his fat wife, Hussanah. Others, waving good-by, went to do important things. Some disappeared into the mountains laden with knapsacks and sleeping bags, never to return, Ivan left after urging us to acclimatize ourselves.

I tried to do this, getting out of bed and staggering about for practice. Then I made my way through flooded streets, past gay beer gardens, between fierce mountain dogs until I found Tom's Market. I grabbed cheese and a bag of apples so Clarence would not starve.

It all crisscrossed so it was impossible to pass the cluster of Bavarian Gardens without encountering a poet or a prose writer's wife. One thing led to another, I surmised, in a series of semicircles. Car horns honked in greeting. Though I doubt that they knew me. Hussanah, orange-clad semanticist's wife, liked to be everywhere, I soon found out. So did he. Ivan, white-bearded, drove all day either from one end of the crossing or just coasting. He gave me lifts back from Tom's Market. The others were married; Timmy to Jill, cruel Anaximenes to Lunar, Clyde to Lil, Nero to Hussanah. When they were not doing other things or writing, they sat apart. (There is no sex in Aspen.)

During my acclimatization, I became preoccupied with Ivan, forgetting Clarence, who was becoming less mobile. His pulse grew weak, and he slept most of the time.

Ivan and I spent our days catching butterflies or wading in scummy water. We chloroformed a variety of insects. And when they were still, he photographed them whole or in parts. We became entomologists. But I saw things without knowing their names. Ivan did not attempt to instruct me. He sent me into my dank room to write. I ripped apart Colorado newspapers and made more poems. Ivan read them to everyone. The poetic examiner, Anaximenes, rewrote them. Clarence shivered there, in the morning, sleeping on wet grass, his nose buried in poisonous pollen.

At night I went with Ivan, leaving Clarence sleeping in our

cabin. Ivan didn't like Clarence to be with us even when we went bicycling or wading.

I was disappointed because we didn't talk. But he embraced me with meaning I hoped would become words. That is why I brought Clarence. But it didn't happen. Even though I tried to say things when the sun was burning on us lying hand in hand. Or killing bugs. Kissing, making love like mutes—Clarence heard nothing. His pulse fluttered until it almost went out. And nothing happened. I couldn't write my own poems or teach Clarence words. It was becoming worse.

Everything changed when Clarence became ill. The doctor said it was "mountain sickness" after doing a blood count. But it was a lung lesion. Or inflammation.

He stopped breathing one night. I carried him, bluish, to Ivan, who owned oxygen tanks and a resuscitator. He awoke eager to help end Clarence. Or revive him. He wasn't certain at first, blaming the distance between himself and me on my son. Nevertheless, he rang the bell to wake up the gentle townspeople, writers, and mountaineers. Quickly they came, ready for any emergency; Anaximenes, Stryke, Butch, Poo, Gargantua, Clyde, Hoffritz, Nero, Israel, Barnaby, and the writers' wives Hussanah, Lil, Lunar, and Lamarr.

We made haste to the deep everglade where the morning seminars were held. It seemed the correct thing to do under the circumstances. Everyone walked in size places, single file chanting or praying until we reached the Cedar Grove or Black Leaf Swamp.

Clarence was placed on the splintered table where the morning readings were held. Around him stood poets, prose writers, townsfolk, and buccaneers. Each held a candle, as the stars were hidden. Ivan put the rubber mouth of his resuscitator to Clarence's mouth and nose. Oxygen was pumped into his lungs from tanks relayed down a line of visiting critics and neighborly mountainfolk.

His body responded in spasmodic gasps or jerks and then was still. Another response, then silence while the black leaves up high hung like medallions. Faces had leafy shadows on necks, bones or eyelids.

I felt myself go out at those moments when his body refused to jerk. For what was I without Clarence? Ivan looked up and saw me vanishing. He who had wished for a me without this incoherent creature at my side understood that without Clarence there would be less of me than before. He gave the resuscitator to Nero. Enough breath returned to Clarence's lungs so that he could be driven to the hospital.

Ivan was not the first man who had wished to separate me from my son; who mistakenly believed that free of Clarence I would step forth fearless and voluble. But only for him who, with gentle hands, embraced Clarence would real words come.

III

I spent my days empty of Clarence in the lobby of an old hotel. I could not bear the silence and drizzling beneath the mountain. Or the unpredictable blast of sunlight from which I fled. The sun disappeared whenever I reached for it.

Ivan passed my window at all hours of the day, peering above the slime. Having no words, fewer than before, there was no greeting. I heard scurrying day and night across or above where they typed or chatted. I could not go there. If I went, I returned deafer than before. (In the old hotel there seemed to be more oxygen between tall brown chairs.)

At dawn I rose to attend seminars on the damp grass, watching bugs lost beneath my feet. My shoulders became hot as the grass dried. Seldom grasping themes, I could not decipher, any better, the glances upon me. Ivan's eyes not seeing over or into anything, I thought. He was far away but seemed bulky enough to smother someone.

Drug takers lay entwined, tolerant of everything, who perceived tenderer meanings and connections between words. Appearing and disappearing with grace, they were gentle. (These were the mornings deep among grasshoppers and fleas waiting for Clarence.)

Afternoons, I withdrew to the dark lobby and dreamed of home; of my cabinets of jade, Orient silk, and brocaded coats. To cater to men's interest in the appearance of things, I wore violet underwear trimmed with gold thread. But sooner or later Clarence would appear, dusty from lying beneath the bed, greenish from sluggish digestion, oddly grimacing and smiling as a way of greeting. How can I blame them, these men into whose arms I sank, exotically perfumed, if they could not reconcile this image with Clarence. In the end I was deserted.

A final effort to reconcile these facts had brought Clarence and me to Aspen. Or had I brought Clarence only to murder him? Had I not exposed him carelessly to the dangerous mountain air, damp grass, and poisonous pollen. And he had suffered mocking and stares from the townspeople, relentless from their battles with mad dogs, slime, and half-filled lungs.

Whenever the writers' wives suggested a jaunt in the chair lift, I forced Clarence to go. I took him on long walks into the mountains though he gasped for breath and fell to the ground.

If Clarence died, I was his murderer. And who was I without Clarence?

Away from our cabin, in the dark hotel, I gathered strength for whatever I must do to make Nero mine. For I had known since the first day that he was the man I came to find. To fulfill my journey, without sacrificing Clarence, I must come down the mountain with Nero as his father. Then could we re-create Clarence, giving him a legitimate birth date.

But Nero was devoted to his wife, the healthy Hussanah. Mornings at Nero's seminar, where, seated by her side, he constructed original synonyms and antonyms, I plotted her demise. Should I shoot her in the back with Clyde's pistol. Or throw her off the side of a mountain. I debated the use of Ham's knife or Barnaby's sling. The possibilities were endless. I chose stones. (If I gave up, we could never make the journey back. It was my last chance.)

Fate saved me from homicide. A telegram came from Doctor Tic of Aspen County Hospital asking that someone donate a lung for Clarence, whose lung was torn. His other lung was too weak to suffice for two.

Everyone around the seminar table was silent. They knew that my lungs leaked. But no one was generous. Then Hussanah, full of wrath, but anxious to give an appearance of nobility to her noble husband Nero, offered her lung. She had the healthiest lungs of anyone we knew. Therefore even her husband's protest was weak. I was grateful and prayed for the transplant to stick. It did. But poor Hussanah; her other lung, too elastic for its own good, and anxious to better itself doing the work of two, overworked and broke.

Thus we were all crying on Monday, particularly Nero who led the procession to the seminar table under which she was buried.

I pitied Nero and ran to his aid, my recovered Clarence beside me breathing well with the Hussanah lung. Better than ever. Nero couldn't resist him. Or his lung. Or the sight of me in white silk pajamas with jade buttons. His idea was a wedding so that Clarence could be his own son. Nero had always wanted a son just like Clarence. And a wife who did not talk but listened to him recite.

Flying down from the mountain on the Astrojet, he held my hand knowing what I was thinking; making sentences from my silence. Clarence sat on his lap, uncomprehending, who was soon to be deciphered by Nero the magician.

◑

Hannibal over the mountains . . .

from *Sumac*

Hannibal over the mountains,
between the great blades of mountains leaning back on steeper
ascents of Hannibal's framed by sky—
how he would smash these to build a road.
Looking back, he sees enough to pity—
whole communities of moss, flowers fanned up in the crevices,
his own soul barely escapes a hammer still trailing a glove.
Yet, going forward, his mind fetches out among cities
where he manages to occupy beds, boats, markets, wheels,
smoke, hats, the faces of policemen reddened by cold.
And looking out one night on a scattering of men in dreary
    helmets
he is overwhelmed by their sky.
How clearly I see your costumes, my husband, to whom
    poems
keep occurring.

RICHARD R. O'KEEFE

◑

Mozart in Nova Scotia

from *Quarterly Review of Literature*

The sea records no judgment of the man,
But his lived syllables startle the neighbor birds
Out of music.

During music
The captive sea rests frozen in the glass
Eye of the mantel's stuffed judicious bird,

And abruptly voiceless trees with nervous hands
Mocking at music
Condemn all decoration through the glass.

After ecstasy the ear resumes the world:
The sea is rhythm and the birds are song;
Neither is music.

I could throw the taxiderm into the sea
And smash revolving rococo for the birds,
And yet music,

Music would move in the mind moving green among trees,
Would echo deep as the drop through the sea's deep green.
The man is music.

RICHARD G. STERN

◐

Events, Happenings, Credibility, Fictions

from *The Yale Review*

Every now and then, critics conclude that a species or genus of an art has been exhausted or superseded. William Hazlitt's "On Modern Comedy" and Edmund Wilson's "Is Verse a Dying Technique?" are well-known elegies of this sort. The most recent object of what we can call genrecidal criticism is prose fiction. The following excerpt from a piece of George Steiner's is a sample of a not uncommon burial service:

> It is not only the traditional scope of fiction that is in doubt, but its entire relevance to the present, to the needs and idioms of our consciousness. . . . As is now becoming generally understood, fiction has fallen well behind sociology and reportage.

Such genrecidal conclusions as Mr. Steiner's—whose own fiction, by the way, tends to document his thesis—are almost always worth careful study, for they almost always testify to a special sort of artistic crisis. The crisis goes to the source of the art, the methods and conventions used at a given time to render the actualities which are their sources. The crisis seems to occur when new techniques appear to take over some of the older genre's jobs. So, a hundred years ago, photography exerted enormous pressure on painting.

The fictional crisis described by Steiner is more complicated than that old crisis in painting. The reason is that the verbal medium serves such a variety of masters. Indeed, fiction is not the only form of licensed lying. When we study its crisis, therefore, we will do well to examine first the matter of credibility.

In various systems of thought and action, the problem of credibility is signaled by such terms as image, propaganda, cover story, camouflage, hypothesis, legal fiction, credit, myth, illusion, dream, and fantasy, terms which depend on their place in particular systems. They all stand for ways of dealing with actuality. Many are securely protected by operating within such isolated systems as games, but those which tend to leak from their systems into areas where their degree of utility or fidelity is unclear are under suspicion. They may conceal public mischief or individual sickness.

When an element from an open system, nature, actuality, the world, is introduced into one of these closed systems, the result is disconcerting. If a speaker explodes a firecracker on the stage, the audience shivers or otherwise expresses recognition that an element from an open system has threatened the security of the closed system, the public speech.

Talleyrand, hearing that Napoleon was dead at last, said, "That is no longer an event. It is a piece of news." Dead, Napoleon belonged to print, to a closed and controlled system, and Talleyrand was no longer in even remote danger from the man who had once called him *"de la merde dans un bas de soie."*

Talleyrand's awareness of the distinction between the open and closed systems is that of the artist. Artists consciously employ the distinction all the time, and from the beginning seem to have made it a subject of their work. One need not haul in such latecomers as Mallarmé or Joyce for evidence here; Homer seems to have been on to it. In the eighth book of the *Odyssey*, the disguised hero listens to the blind bard Demodocus sing about the heroes of the Trojan War (it amounts to the *Iliad*), but unlike the enchanted listeners at King Alcinous's court, he weeps. What was a closed system, a fiction, or at least an artful story for them, was heart-rending, still-existent experience for him, a form of event, not news.

This brilliant Homeric anticipation of the famous modern

subject of the story of the story, the play within the play, is given perhaps its ultimate statement at the end of this same part of the poem. To his unknown guest, the king says, "Tell us why you wept so bitterly and secretly when you heard of the Argive Danaans and the fall of Ilion. That was wrought by the gods, who measured the life thread of these men *so that their fate might become a poem sung for unborn generations*." This royal claim that reality exists for the sake of art marks the limit of artistic solipsism: the closed system embraces everything. Wordsworthian recollections or the *fin-de-siècle* boast of art's superiority to life are dwarfed by it.

One can, I think, subsume all distinctions between art and actuality, even this extraordinary one of King Alcinous, into an even more general distinction, that between *being* and *having-knowing-picturing-remembering-loving-possessing-converting*, what have you. Being, and its alternate mode, doing, are not aware of existing or performing. The baby exists, but is unaware of existence; the beloved does not enjoy what the lover enjoys in her; she *is*, her lover knows, enjoys, possesses her. (When she herself enjoys, she is lover, knower, possessor; the sweetness of love is just this double, reciprocal state.) The doer does, the observer marvels, the witness and artist chronicle and convert.

One of the recent alterations in the equilibrium between art and actuality is the discovery on the part of many "do-ers" and "be-ers" that they are also characters; more, that they are or can be their own chroniclers, analysts, even poets. Max Scheler wrote that "feelings which everyone nowadays is aware of having in himself once took poets to wrest from the terrifying muteness of our inner life." Scheler only marked the effects of the novel of analysis and perhaps of psychoanalysis. These had given the silent lives of the world mirrors, but the tape recorder, the camera, the roving anthropologist, the reporter, the psychological caseworker, and the social surveyor have shown the "do-ers" and "be-ers" of daily life that they are not only specialized segments of opinion, but proper subjects of biography, actors in potential newsreels, amateur sages, and semi-artistic performers in events, in happenings. It is in part this transformation of characters into self-conscious actors and then into storytellers which makes critics feel that professional inventors of stories are "irrelevant to the needs and idiom of our consciousness." When everybody bakes bread, who needs bakers?

The doer who tells his story, the reporter who puts it into a news context, the historian or sociologist who provides a more elaborate frame for it are artists, as the Greeks would have said bakers are artists. They assemble divers materials into useful, beautiful, and delightful objects. Yet one must distinguish their works of art—Susanne Langer calls them works of practical art—from works of imaginative art. It will be useful to do this by examining the sort of event mentioned above, the unexpected intrusion on the closed occasion, the firecracker-menaced speech. Such an event has come to be known as a happening.

A happening is an artistic performance in the guise of an event. It is a situation which attempts to incorporate into a closed system as large an amount of uncontrolled, *actual* material as possible. Delight in a happening rises from the contrast between the magic security of art and the potentially uncontrolled pressure of intensified—rigged—actuality. A successful happening is of course unrepeatable; a happening's success grows out of shock or surprise. Happenings do not originate in the nineteen sixties. They've always existed, particularly in times of leisured opulence. Johan Huizinga, describing the fifteenth-century Burgundian festivities which featured motet-singing bears, pies filled with orchestras, and forty-foot towers called them "applied literature."

Many happenings spring not from festive energy, Dadaistic wit, and opulent ennui, but from social and artistic contempt, emotional rigidity, shallowness, cruelty, and perversion. Few national histories fail to feature tyrants who converted human beings into the subject matter of art. Such happenings have been examined by historians, social psychologists, and anthropologists, but they may be studied just as fruitfully by aestheticians. When art and nature are confounded, no specialist is privileged.

Happenings are of interest to the arts because they stand for a desire to alter the relationship between art and actuality. Many, perhaps most artists, want to shake up an audience by violating its preconceptions about what belongs to art and what doesn't. The first-night performances or exhibitions of many fine works of art resemble happenings. The *premières* of *Hernani*, *Playboy of the Western World*, *Marat/Sade*, *Le Sacre du Printemps*, the first days of the Fauves exhibit, even some early reactions to *Les Fleurs du Mal* and *The Waste Land* exhibit the violent reactions characteristic of happenings. The violence springs from rage at the broken contract between art and actuality.

There is another artistic side of happenings. Art forms may be said to originate in happenings. When an old religious ritual was altered by a figure stepping from the laymen's section of re-spondents, Greek drama began; and when someone altered a kind of hunter's memorandum in a Cro-Magnon cave, it was the beginning of mural painting. More recently, when Andy War-hol decided that the manufacturers of Campbell's soup failed to realize that their product was as pleasing to the eye as it was to the stomach, and signed his name as an artistic pledge of the observation, he fused a happening to a new sort of sculpture.

What has taken place in all these instances is that an action or object which belonged to the realm of being-doing has been appropriated for the world of knowing-appreciating-loving. The appropriation is usually bold, primitive, and shocking. The shock is one of transition; the consumer, the worshiper, or hunter has been converted into the spectator or appreciator. He has postponed the satisfactions of appetite for those of amuse-ment, delight, emotional involvement in a nonworld. The shock itself, the happening element, can't be repeated. If Warhol went on to sign a can of Heinz soup, he'd be called either an epigone or a bad promoter. He has to go on either to other happenings or to the exploration, elaboration, and development of his insight into a form. He has to relate it to some traditional system of materials.

An artist makes works which are not exhausted by initial per-formance, works which do not depend on bold shifts between art and actuality, which validate themselves in an artistic tradition and do not require validation by shock.

The claim that such works of literary art are no longer relevant "to the needs and idiom of our consciousness" ignores not only the crucial distinctions between such works as happenings and imaginative art, but the difference between these and such works of practical art as the reportage of Truman Capote and John Hersey, the wonderfully edited autobiographies assembled by Oscar Lewis and Danilo Dolci, collections of heartbreaking letters like those found in the mailbags from Stalingrad, and hosts of splendid memoirs, biographies, reports, essays, and histories.

In my view, no matter how splendidly assembled, how fascinating in detail or how rich in linguistic, expressive, or speculative power, these works are, by their nature, limited in the same way all works of practical art are limited, and that is by the necessity to conform in sequence, place, number, and character to actuality. Our delight in works of practical art is crucially conditioned by our feeling that they are not fictional but real. They are forms of news; and though all of us know now that the cameraman selects, the camera angle determines, the reporter shades and dramatizes, the sociologist has a thesis, nonetheless, we are investing emotionally in credibility. If we find that we have been taken, our reaction is—properly—rage, and, despite his skill, we arrest the forger of Vermeers, we throw away the text with beautiful but inaccurate blueprints, we don't lie down on the handsome but back-breaking bed, and we refuse to buy the fake reporter's brilliant work on the Asian village. Works of practical art must be true; indeed, they usually begin with a statement of their credentials. Here are a few of them:

1. The tape recorder, used in taking down the life stories in this book, has made possible the beginning of a new kind of literature of social realism. With the aid of the tape recorder, unskilled, uneducated, and even illiterate persons can talk about themselves and relate their observations and experiences in an uninhibited, spontaneous, and natural manner . . . most of the recording was done in my office and home.

. . . Occasionally I recorded at [the home of the Sanchez] in the Casa Grande. . . . I used no secret technique, no truth drugs, no psychoanalytic couch. The most effective tools of the anthropologist are sympathy and compassion for the people he studies.

[Oscar Lewis, *Children of Sanchez*]

2. The editor believes the thing to be a just history of fact; neither is there any appearance of fiction in it.

3. All the material in this book not derived from my own observation is either taken from official records or is the result of interviews with the person directly concerned, more often than not numerous interviews conducted over a considerable period of time.

[Truman Capote, *In Cold Blood*]

4. Throughout our work on [this book], I have been continuously impressed by demonstration of the extent to which that much abused term "total recall" can be literally true. . . . I retraced with her, time and again, the threads of many of these episodes, always from a different vantage point. Each time they checked out even to the smaller touches of phrasing, style, figures of speech.

[Carleton Lake, Introduction to Françoise Gilot, *Life with Picasso*]

5. He left the custody of the following papers in my hands with the liberty to dispose of them as I should think fit. I have carefully perused them three times: the style is very plain and simple; and the only fault I find is, that the author . . . is a little too circumstantial . . . this volume would have been at least twice as large, if I had not made bold to strike out innumerable passages relating to the winds and tides, as well as the variations and bearings in the several voyages.

Five editor-authors delivering the real words of real people. Surely praiseworthy activity, whatever the motive, entertainment, enlightenment, moral exempla, what have you. All deny that fiction is in their pages; the first and third speak here or elsewhere of new forms of literature, but all deny that they are making anything up.

Now of these five claims, two are manifestly false. The second is the preface to *Robinson Crusoe*, the fifth some of the prefatory matter of *Gulliver's Travels*. How do these fictional claims differ from the truthful ones? The two fictional claims are part of a different contract, an eighteenth-century convention of the art—revived now and then—which licenses departure from the real world even as it claims to be a chunk of it. Readers of *Gulliver* will never be troubled as the readers of Capote or Lewis may be—indeed, have been—by the question of the accuracy of their books. Capote and Lewis must justify their books in terms of the truth of their descriptions and renditions: the fiction writer justifies his book in a completely different way. Warhol would not be arrested if he sneaked into the art gallery one night, siphoned off the tomato soup from his six-dollar sculpture and substituted soapy water for it; but the maker of the original seventeen-cent can would be. The artist Warhol is not bound to the same standard of credibility as the practical artist, Campbell's designer.

Talking of public opinion half a century ago, Walter Lippmann wrote, "A work of fiction may have almost any degree of fidelity, and so long as the degree of fidelity can be taken into account, fiction is not misleading." A credibility gap causes rage in the actual world, not the world of imaginative art. Yet the degree of fidelity should be known to the imaginative artist. The imaginative artist "does the same as the child at play; he creates a world of fantasy, which he takes very seriously: that is, he invests it with a great deal of affect, while separating it sharply from reality" (Freud, "The Relation of the Poet to Daydreaming"). The imaginative artist is—at least in his art—separate from the lunatic and the lover and, in direct contrast to the practical artist, he works out techniques to separate his art from reality. Systematically, he violates at least some of the schemes or procedures of remembered actuality: places, ideas, characters, time schedules, meanings. His art derives in a measure from the dissociation of given materials. Even those artists who minutely reproduce their vision, who check their time schemes with almanacs (Fielding), their place names with city directories (Joyce), their memories of houses and clothes against personal or newspaper accounts (Proust), are only accumulating powder for fictional explosions. Far more than the tellers of romance, the cryptographic fabulists, the algebraic comedians, or the heart-twitching parodists, these "realists" wish to assemble the world in order to control it. Whenever the remembered actuality will not suffer the explosive charge readied for it, it is thrown out or substituted for. Those biographies which draw parallels between the artist's life and his fictional version of it are wonderful sources of such crucial substitutions and removals. (This is the case even for those artists whose lives are in no small measure consciously arranged to provide material for their work.) The components of the artwork are changed whenever the artist sees that the pattern of his felt insight demands that they be changed. And that changes everything. It exempts the fiction writer from libel suits, and rightly so. A work of imaginative art really represents only those moments of an artist's life which were expressible in that period of isolation from the world in which he worked out what counts for him; in the process of working it out, it alters under pressure of his insight and his form; places, times, and details which originally stimulated his imagination come to belong more and more to each other, less and less to the world from which they came. The result can be so overpowering that the artist may say with Alcinous that the life was lived for the art, or at least, that only in art were the intensity and meaning of the life felt.

The art form surely helps provide this intensity and meaning, and the form constantly alters. As fiction altered its modes of handling its special data, writers found that the modes and alterations themselves became fit subjects for their work. Since Flaubert and James, fiction—like music since the sons of Bach and painting since Cézanne—has been in no small part about itself. That is, it deals explicitly with its modes of representation. It is perhaps in response to such incestuous concentration that the new works of practical art have risen to put pressure on fiction, as if to say, "Back to nature, boys."

Fiction writers have often been men of unusual emotional, intellectual, and sensuous energy, and great works of fiction thus contain reports from the borders of human complexity and intensity. If we are to see practical forms expand to include such reports, all the better. Engineers follow in the wake of the most abstruse theorists. But then, theorists arise from great works of engineering. From penny dreadfuls to *Ulysses*, *Ulysses* through John Dos Passos to Hersey and William Manchester, and these to something novel.

It is, I think, not a time for funerals but for weddings and christenings.

JOHN PAUKER

◐

Flighty Poem

from *Prairie Schooner*

*(My dark reply to Lyda Franzusoff's
question about Plato's theory of birds)*

The sins we commit, in act or in thought, become birds.
The billion birds you see darken the sky are our sins
Flying south.
    Aloft or at rest, the billion birds
Endlessly chipper about the sins we commit.
They tattle to God in the sky, in the south, they
Darken the sky with our sins, and then they fly back.
Some fall, but unfaltering sins beget new birds to
Darken the sky.
    Look.
     It is black.

GEORGE QUASHA

◐

Rilke's Sixth Elegy Transposed

from *Caterpillar*

      Figtree
How long it's been meaning for me,
how you almost wholly neglect flowering
   and into the early determined fruit
   unsung   thrust your
     purest secret   .
Like the fountain's reed your bent bough drives
   downward the sap   and on up : and it springs
     from its sleep   barely wakened   into the
       fortune of its sweetest
       attainment   .   Look
               like the god
                 into the swan   .

    . . . We, however,
    are lingering,
alas, we   glory in flowering   and into the
   delayed core of our final fruit we
     enter betrayed.
In few   rises incursion of action
   so strongly they're standing and
    glowing in fulness of heart when
     seduction to flowering   silken as night breeze
    touches   the youth of their mouths, their eyelids :

    Heroes, perhaps, and those fated early

in whom gardening death twisted the veins
        otherwise   :   these
plunge forth   forerunners
of their own smiles   like horses
        in Karnak's mildly
          molded reliefs
of the conquering King

        +

The Hero   is
    strangely akin to those young dead:
        continuance
  means nothing, his
      rising is Being,
        continually
he takes himself off and enters
    the changed constellation of his
    constant peril.
        Few can find him there.   But she
    who folds us in sinister silence   suddenly rapt   Fate
    sings him into storm in her uproaring world   .
I hear none like him   .
                All at once   thru me
  borne by streaming air his
        dark tone blares

Then, how gladly I would hide from such longing   : O that I, that
  I were a boy and might still become it   and were sitting
  propped on forthcoming arms   and reading of Samson
  how his mother at first bore nothing and, then,
                          everything

        +

Wasn't he Hero   already within you   O mother   beginning
  already there his imperious choosing   within you?
    Thousands were brewing in the womb   trying to be
        him   :   but see!

he seized and
released, chose and
could do.
And if he wrecked columns   then it was he broke
out of the world of your body   into the
narrower world   where he further
chose and
could do.
O mothers of heroes
O sources of ravaging rivers   You
gorges wherein
from high on the heart's edge   grieving
girls have already plunged
—forthcoming victims of the son

For the Hero stormed thru the holds of love, and
of each heartbeat meant for him   each one lifted him
further beyond :
turned away
he stood at the end of the smiles :
another

◑

The Code

from *Stony Brook*

I had to pull the little maple tree
close to the house.
                    It had leaves already.
And I saw a doe standing
                        in its romaunt
munching peacefully
                      while the wolf stalked.
Such is my confusion.
When I broke it,
only the moloch unthink
                        groaned.

The seed knew
                before Sinai
it would be a root
                but not the nature
of man.
It was coded
                to become a shade tree
sized for the Colossus
                        Rameses the Second
and entered the earth
                        zigzagging
after the radish and the worm.

Its necessity would have cracked my cement
and pierced a water main.
Yet it was coded
                    in the presence of the sun
to turn our breath and water
                           into deer food
and connect us to our nature
and give us peace from pursuance.

In our deadly assignation
I was coded to be contemplative
with a twig:
                out of the ground
only an hour,
                   yet so downcast.
Poor Yorick!

In the root I saw a miniature
                   crab-apple tree
twisting into Dada.
                        Insane ending.

Must all lead back to the thinker?
                       Is there no
germination in a cube
or sprouting in a sphere?

ADRIENNE RICH

◑

For a Russian Poet

from *Poetry*

Everywhere, snow is falling. Your bandaged foot
drags across huge cobblestones, bells
hammer in distant squares.
Everything we stood against has conquered,
and now we are part
of it all. *Life's the main thing*, I hear you say,
but a fog thickens between this landmass
and the one your voice
so long mapped for me. All that's visible
is walls, endlessly yellow-gray, where
so many risks were taken, the shredded skies
slowly littering both our continents with
the only justice left, burying
footprints, bells and voices with all deliberate speed.

JOHN RIDLAND

◑

Two Poems about Money

from *Tennessee Poetry Journal*

Money in the Bank

When the housebreaker knocked at my door,
I asked him, what was he there for?

To rob you of all your silver!
Shone his courteous answer.

Please? I said, will you take it
All? The solid, the plated,

The pseudo-silver settings
Presented upon my weddings?

Each piece has grown its tarnish
So long in the furniture . . .

And your black-and-white TV,
He interrupted demurely.

So together we swept the whole ticket,
And loading it onto his pickup,

So long, friend, I called, and a thousand thanks:
An empty house is like money in the bank!

New Concepts in Money

The whole country is hungry for money.
It has devised many new ways
Of preparing money. Of all these,
I prefer broiled money,
Though deep fried in butter
Is also awful tasty.

*

In the banks they are planning
New ways to disguise their plain cooking.
In the Savings and Loans, however,
They may be adding too much sauce and spice to the meat.
Meanwhile the Government is trying to breed
A whole new strain of money
On the dirt ranches; and deep in the cities
The police are out on bicycles cruising for money.

*

Our Negroes want to eat money *now!*
Even our Mexicans and Chinese want more money, because
Money makes a pretty good meal when a man is hungry . . .
Well, wouldn't *you* like a thick sandwich of new money,
Fresh from the mint?
Even if there were other things to eat,
What can beat a hot-baked roll of real money?

*

All this attention to food and appetite—
You must think it is overdone;
But here it is nearly lunch time,
And I too am hungry for my daily money—
Or even just a dime in a glass of water.

JOHN WILLIAMS

○

Henry Miller:
The Success of Failure

from *The Virginia Quarterly Review*

On July 4, 1845, Henry David Thoreau, who had been living in Boston, moved a few personal belongings into a hut on the edge of Walden Pond, a small lake near Concord, Massachusetts, the place of his birth. He was twenty-eight years of age. As he tells us in *Walden*, he had tried a number of things before he made his escape into what he thought of as the wilderness. He had gone to Harvard and graduated; he had taught school for a brief time in his home town of Concord, and was by his own admission an unsuccessful teacher; he had thought of going into trade, and had worked briefly for his father, a small businessman who manufactured pencils; he had lectured before cultural groups in Concord, apparently without great success; he had written a few essays for the *Dial*; in exchange for room and board, he had performed odd jobs for Ralph Waldo Emerson; and he had been a tutor in the New York home of Emerson's brother William. Until his decision to abandon the "civilized pursuits" to which he was born, his was the ordinary life that any moderately intelligent young man, of no means but with some culture, education, and talent, might lead, given the conditions of his time and place. "The mass of men lead lives of quiet desperation. What is called resignation is confirmed desperation. From the desperate city you go into the desperate country, and have to console yourself with the bravery of minks and muskrats. . . ."

Three generations later, in the year 1930, another Henry—Henry Miller, of New York City, the son of a lower-middle-class German-American family—sailed to Europe, where he had spent the year before as a tourist. He left behind him a first wife and a child, a second wife, and his other few worldly possessions. As we know from his many writings—*Tropic of Cancer* and *Tropic of Capricorn*, the five volumes that now constitute *The Rosy Crucifixion*, and scattered essays and narratives in dozens of books—he had tried many things before finally making his escape from America. For two months he had attended the City College of New York, and failed to complete the semester; he had worked at a variety of clerical jobs, and in his father's tailor shop; he had been for three years a messenger-employment manager for Western Union; and for about ten years, intermittently, had tried unsuccessfully to become a commercial writer of articles, stories, and novels. He was, in other words, a member of a vast underground of lower-middle-class Americans who wander beneath the surface or on the periphery of our increasingly complex society, unseen by the very society that dominates their lives; men who exist marginally upon our culture, who for one reason or another have been unable to find a place in the social order that strives to give their lives substance or meaning.

He was, in short, a failure; and in *Tropic of Capricorn*, the volume dealing with his pre-Paris years in New York, he announces that failure:

> I couldn't waste time being a teacher, a lawyer, a physician, a politician or anything else that society had to offer. It was easier to accept menial jobs because it left my mind free. . . . The stabbing horror of life is not contained in calamities and disasters, because these things wake one up and one gets very familiar and intimate with them. . . . You know with a most disturbing certitude that what governs life is not money, not politics, not religion, not training, not race, not language, not customs, but something else, something you're trying to throttle all the time and which is really throttling you, because otherwise you wouldn't be terrified all of a sudden and wonder how you were going to escape. . . . One can starve to

death—it is much better. Every man who voluntarily starves to death jams another cog in the automatic process. I would rather see a man take a gun and kill his neighbor, in order to get the food he needs, than keep up the automatic process by pretending that he has to earn a living.

One should recognize immediately that this is not the prose of prophecy or apocalypse, as it has often been taken; it is, in its peculiar tone of despair and in its very rhythm, the prose of the Depression. In a recent essay, "The American Left," Daniel Aaron quotes an anonymous letter published at the bottom of the Depression by one of the displaced; it might almost have been written by Miller himself.

I wrote letters, I tramped hundreds of blocks to answer ads, I tried for jobs as teamster, clothing model, wringer man, floor-walker, garbage collector, truck driver. I wrote a Civil Service examination. I made ten dollars painting the ceiling of a barber shop. I managed an interview with my former superintendent, but he didn't remember me very well. I lived on a loaf of bread for ten days and then my money was all gone. . . . If it were necessary—if there were a famine, if I were a genius, an explorer, a martyr—I could endure cold and hunger, even degradation and insults, without a murmur. . . . But it is all so unnecessary, there is so little for me to look forward to, that I am beginning to think that it isn't so worthwhile to keep straight. The best I could look for, as a reward for going through another winter, or three, or five, like the last two, would be a job somewhere, sometime. And then could I feel secure? Another depression might catch me with no more resources than I had this time.

That Miller was not in this country during the worst of the great Depression does not matter; the "depressions" out of which both these passages spring are ones that are endemically American, always with us to one degree or another, in one way or another; they are more than political or economic; and the historical depression out of which the anonymous letter was written was only an intense symptom of a process that is implicit in our values and which has been with us nearly from the beginning of our country.

At the center of American life there is a polarity that I shall specify as the polarity of success and failure. This polarity has been generally recognized before, yet it is one whose precise identity cannot be seen except in a specific context of American history and culture.

The question of success and failure lies at the center of Thoreau's *Walden*, and it lies at the center of much of Miller's work, especially his "autobiographical romances"—*Tropic of Cancer* and *Tropic of Capricorn*, *Black Spring*, and *The Rosy Crucifixion*. And the many statements of the two men upon the nature of success and failure are remarkably similar. Thoreau writes,

> I would rather sit on a pumpkin and have it all to myself, than be crowded on a velvet cushion. I would rather ride on earth in an ox cart with a free circulation, than go to heaven in the fancy car of an excursion train and breathe a *malaria* all the way.

In the opening section of *Tropic of Capricorn*, Miller writes,

> Everybody around me was a failure, or if not a failure, ridiculous. Especially the successful ones. . . . I think of all the streets in America combined as forming a huge cesspool, a cesspool of the spirit in which everything is sucked down and drained away. . . . The whole continent is a nightmare producing the greatest misery of the greatest number. I was one, a single entity in the midst of the greatest jamboree of wealth and happiness . . . but I never met a man who was truly wealthy or truly happy. At least I knew that I was unhappy, unwealthy, out of whack and out of step. That was my only solace, my only joy.

Some years ago, H. B. Parkes, in *The American Experience*, wrote of the polarity between American political and theological theory: "In their political ideals, men give expression to what they wish to believe; but in their religion they show what they really are. A theology is, in fact, a kind of collective poem or work of art that records the secret emotional history of a community." It is that "secret emotional history" of the early American community that I should like to examine briefly.

In the strictly determined universe of the early New England Calvinist, mankind fell into one of two groups—the elect or the damned. This division was ultimately mysterious, but one who had a certain faith in God might feel reasonably sure of his own election; and it was a sign of that faith that he felt it a profound duty to impose his way of life upon his less fortunate fellows— by force if necessary. Life was a moral arena, and the battle was between Good and Evil; where one stood in that battle would not in theory influence the outcome, but it could give one a hint as to where he stood in the eyes of God—of the elect, or of the damned. Goodness, ultimately, was faith in God; action was merely a sign of that faith. And faith in God was faith in something beyond man and nature; for man, in nature, was corrupt, and his only salvation was to be saved from nature by the Grace of God. Thus, every impulse of nature tended to be evil, and any spontaneous emotion, such as love or even an excessive regard for another human being, was probably sinful. God was an ascetic ideal, and man found him in contemplation, not action.

But these settlers could, in their daily lives, be neither ascetic nor contemplative, even though Calvinist doctrine inexorably pushes man in upon himself. Their environment forced them to materialism, and their struggle against the wilderness was an external one, though it might have internal implications. Thus from the beginning the American Calvinist dangled between his sense of the doctrinal importance of his internal life and the practical necessities of his external life.

By the middle of the seventeenth century, however, the theology—that "secret emotional history"—had changed to accommodate necessity; and in the dim beginnings of American prosperity, the New England clergy began to preach that obedience to God was the way to worldly prosperity, though nominally such prosperity was valuable only insofar as it afforded an outward sign of inward grace. But one who saw prosperity as a *sign* of virtue did not have to step far to see prosperity as a *proof* of virtue. And as dogma weakened, it was almost inevitable that the prosperous man be profoundly convinced of his own virtue, and that he attribute that prosperous virtue to his own merits rather than to God's election.

Almost from the beginning, in America, the question of

success and failure has been a religious question; and it remains
so, to some extent, even in the twentieth century. Thus Miller's
rejection of the standard American attitudes toward success is
actually a rejection of a lingering Calvinist ethic that still works
beneath the surface of our culture, though his rejection is not, as
we shall see, as unequivocal as one might expect.

The popular view of Miller is that of the American who has
rid himself of all that is most American; who has brought into
American literature the invigorating strain of European modernism; who has rescued American literature from provincialism
and brought the genuine *avant-garde* to our own traditional
shores. In some respects Miller seems to share this attitude
about his own work and to encourage it in others. Except for his
repeated admirations of Whitman, Emerson, and Thoreau, his
literary praise has always been for the figures of another culture:
he has at one time or another admired and acknowledged in-
debtedness to such men as Dostoevsky, Van Gogh, Nostrada-
mus, Dante, Nijinski, Elie Faure, Rimbaud, Nietzsche, H.
Rider Haggard, D. H. Lawrence, the Oriental mystical writers,
as well as to such modern *avant-gardistes* as André Breton,
Blaise Cendrars, Céline, Ionesco, Anaïs Nin, and a variety of
lesser Dadaists and Surrealists. And nearly all of his writings
make some gestures toward the European "modernism" of the
twenties: the highly charged but never quite believable dreams,
the long metaphoric flights that are simply extreme exaggera-
tions of present reality, the passages of induced hallucination,
the occasional excursions in automatic writing, and the literary
affectations of madness.

But these are only gestures, and perhaps small debts, and one
will not find the significance of Miller's work in them; for Miller
is a writer who is essentially American, and American in a particular sense of that word.

If it appears perverse to suggest that in many ways Miller represents a nineteenth- and twentieth-century transformation of
American Puritanism, it does so, I suspect, largely because of the
celebrated question of his obscenity. One might wish to say that
the issue of obscenity is in no way fundamental to Miller's work;

and though one can almost say that, one cannot quite. For if Miller's use of obscenity is the most overt sign of his apparent rejection of the Puritan ethic, it is at the same time the covert revelation of the incompleteness of that rejection.

It should be clear to any serious student of American Puritanism that first the avoidance and then the symbolizing of sexual matters is one of the more obvious symptoms of the Puritan dilemma; and like many symptoms, it disguises more than it reveals. For obscenity and sexuality, in themselves, have little to do with the essential dilemma of American Puritanism; and when the more naïve among us wish to reject what we think of as the Puritan ethic, we turn immediately to the no doubt pleasant task of rejecting the Puritan sexual ethic—as if the taking of morphine might heal the wound.

In some ways Miller's obscenity is the most nearly innocent aspect of his art. The words he uses—the so-called Anglo-Saxon or four-letter words—we all know, else we would not be shocked by them. It is not a moral question, but a social one. If we are shocked by Miller's language, we are shocked not because our morality has been threatened but because our social standing has been; we are forced to confront and to admit the vital existence of one whose social standing appears lower than our own— one who would use such language, and so affront polite society. Thus snobbery subsumes morality, taboo overrides reason, and we are revealed to ourselves in all our cultural primitivism. We are made uncomfortable.

But though the language Miller uses was probably the basis for the widespread censorship of his books in this country, there are other pornographic techniques in Miller that are equally useful to his intention. Aside from the words, the sexuality and scatology found in Miller are of two sorts. First is that which is found with some frequency in the rather long, arty, and often irrelevant surrealistic fantasies that interrupt the narratives and expositions. By and large, such passages are so badly done that we have a hard time taking them seriously. Second, and more characteristic, are the sexual exploits that Miller attributes to himself in the autobiographical romances. And even these passages are strangely innocent; for they have that pathetic braggadocio and exaggeration of the lower-middle-class masculine world of the deprived adolescent (ugly, relentlessly shy, or merely poor) who finds himself outside the easy security of the promises of his society, and thus is committed to longing, talk, and the compensations of imagining.

When Miller is not indulging himself in quasi-surrealist nightmare sequences, or in the half-fantasies of symptomatic longing, his attitudes toward sex are almost embarrassingly moral, though not necessarily conventional. In the more straightforward narrative sections of the *Tropics*, he reveals himself to be, if not altogether proper in sexual matters, at least not the monster that we might expect from the more literary passages; and when he speaks "seriously" of sex, in his role as latter-day sage, in his essays upon the subject and especially in a work that remained until a few years ago unpublished in this country, *The World of Sex*, his thinking is approximately as bold as that of a university-educated marriage counselor or sociologist—though the language in which he specifies this thinking is not likely to be found in either. Like Lawrence, he sees the role of sex as essentially religious, and he speaks sentimentally of its "mystery."

I do not wish to imply that Miller is a Puritan *manqué*, the archetypal American Calvinist in an outrageous disguise. I am, rather, suggesting that the dilemmas and polarities that have characterized American Puritanism are remarkably similar to the dilemmas and polarities that lie at the center of Henry Miller's most important and characteristic work.

As I have already noted, the Puritan doctrine of Election and Damnation has its secular counterpart in the American doctrine of success and failure. There are other counterparts, however, nearly as significant.

Fundamental to the Calvinist system was the notion that all men were by nature corrupt and wicked, and that only a few might be chosen by God for salvation. This was God's choice, not man's, and it was predestined and absolute. In theory, neither man's works nor his actions could influence this election. One might expect that such a system of belief would lead to

spiritual inertia, fatalism, and acquiescence; the fact of history is
that it did not. It led, rather, to a remarkable energy, an astonishing exercise of the will, and a forceful rejection of any sort of
temporal acquiescence.

To understand this apparent contradiction, one must interpret the experience that it reflects; we return again to that "secret emotional history" of which the Calvinist theology is poem
and text. The world and society tell man that only his works
matter, and that he shall be judged by them; the Calvinist theology told him that he would obtain salvation not by works but
by faith, and that faith was the free gift of God. Now, to the
man who has any kind of insecurity about his own worth, nothing can be so devastating or paralyzing as to feel that that worth,
in the eyes of his neighbors or of God, depends only upon the
quality of his works. Thus, the Calvinist theology offered a profound alternative to the demands of a social world; and, as
Parkes says in this connection, "Those persons who accepted
this doctrine and applied it to themselves had an astonishing
sense of liberation, as though a burden had suddenly fallen from
their shoulders; they were immediately freed from doubt, insecurity, and anxiety. This instantaneous experience of conversion
was, indeed, a kind of rebirth."

For the ten years preceding 1930, Henry Miller had engaged
in the pursuits that he must have hoped would lead him to success, and he had failed. It was only when he rejected the approval of his neighbors and his country, and when he renounced
the possible value of his works, that he came to feel himself free.
In one of his essays of the Paris period, entitled "Peace! It's
Wonderful!" Miller writes:

> Night after night without money, without friends, without a
> language I had walked these streets in despair and anguish.
> . . . In any case, the important thing is that in [Paris] I
> touched bottom. Like it or not, I was obliged to create a new
> life for myself. . . . In this life I am God, and like God I
> am indifferent to my own fate. . . . Just as a piece of matter
> detaches itself from the sun to live as a wholly new creation
> so I have come to feel about my detachment from America.
> And like all the other suns of the universe I had to nourish
> myself from *within*. I speak in cosmological terms because it

seems to me that is the only possible way to think if one is truly alive. I think this way also because it is just the opposite of the way I thought a few years back when I had what is called hopes. Hope is a bad thing. It means that you are not what you want to be.

This is the Calvinist formula in its nineteenth-century transformation, a transformation made possible by a weakening both of a specific sense of sin and by the inevitable deterioration of dogma. "God" or "Christ" becomes the "self," the "natural" or "social" world becomes "America," and "heaven" becomes the "universe." But the habit of mind is clear beyond the transformation, and it is Calvinist. Emerson, Whitman, and Thoreau had wrought the transformation, and Henry Miller inherited it.

The notion of rebirth is central to Miller's thought, and it usually is tied, directly or indirectly, to the escape from America to Paris, from hope to unhope, from success to failure. For Miller does not consider that his writing is in any sense of the word a "good work," whereby he hopes to earn the approval of his neighbors. In the first page of what is probably his best single book, *Tropic of Cancer*, he announces his rejection of literature.

> I have no money, no resources, no hopes. I am the happiest man alive. A year ago, six months ago, I thought that I was an artist. I no longer think about it. I *am*. Everything that was literature has fallen from me. There are no more books to be written, thank God.
> This then? This is not a book. This is libel, slander, defamation of character. This is not a book. . . . This is a prolonged insult, a gob of spit in the face of Art, a kick in the pants to God, Man, Destiny, Time, Love, Beauty . . . what you will.

It is, in other words, aimed precisely and destructively at all that we think of as Literature. In the biographical note at the end of *The Cosmological Eye*, the first book of Henry Miller's to be published in the United States, he declares:

> I use destruction creatively . . . but aiming always towards a real, inner harmony, an inner peace—and silence. . . . Ninety-nine percent of what is written—and this goes for all

our art products—should be destroyed. I want to be read by less and less people; I have no interest in the life of the masses, nor in the intentions of the existing governments of the world. I hope and believe that the whole civilized world will be wiped out in the next hundred years or so. I believe that man can exist, and in an infinitely better, larger way, without "civilization."

Art, then, exists, not for its own sake, nor for ours, but for Miller's; and if the man who is Henry Miller has failed to the world, he may yet have succeeded to himself, who has become the object of his faith.

I am not the first to remark that, as pure theology, American Calvinism is a mess, a maze of contradictions, a chaos of impossibly opposed forces, a jungle of unresolved conflicts. In these respects, it resembles Miller's work, about which we could say many of the same things. I shall not attempt to resolve the illogicalities, to reconcile the opposing forces, or even to diminish the conflicts. The most I can hope to do is to offer some basis for understanding the conflicts, and perhaps thereby to suggest the significance and value that such an understanding may offer us.

One of the great conflicts in American Puritanism was between a mystical view of experience and a practical one. We find both impulses existing side by side in the early Puritan— one part of him is drawn toward the mystical being of God, and the other toward what is clearly a projection of God's strange will, the world itself. The Puritan conflict between idealism and realism is perhaps only another aspect of this earlier polarity, but it does have a peripheral identity in itself; in the Puritan ethic, that which exists in nature tends to be in conflict with that which exists in God's mind—hence our half-conscious aversion to sexuality, to bodily matters, to spontaneity, and to those shapes of flux and change that we must observe in natural processes. Yet the American Puritan found himself confronted with a natural world that he had to take with the utmost seriousness, if he was to survive; and in America, at least, the reconciliation of God and Nature has been an uneasy one.

And so has been the reconciliation of the conflict between

aggressiveness and submission. Aggressiveness is supposed to be an almost exclusively American characteristic; and yet along with that aggressiveness, so often noted by foreign visitors, there is a deep strain of submissiveness that disguises itself in a number of ways. We may not willingly submit to fate, or even to simple fact; but we will almost without question submit to our neighbors' opinions of us. This, of course, is only a reflection of another pattern of aggression and submission; the Puritan had, by dogma, to submit to God's will; but, if he were to survive, he could not submit to the world—to nature, to the hostile environment that surrounded him; and, finally, in the historical evolution of Puritanism, he found himself in the curious position of becoming aggressive in the acquisition of worldly goods, the worldly goods being God's outward manifestation of inward Grace, and hence the sign of the aggressor's submission to God's will.

We need only to read in Cotton Mather's *Diaries* to find a recurring conflict between what might be called the apocalyptic vision and the practical vision, and between the impulse toward contemplative self-revelation and externalized activity. Certainly in a world view that is as rigidly deterministic as the American Calvinist's, the impulse toward the apocalyptic vision is inevitable; for if the course of the world is determined by God's will, and if that will is immutable, then one can predict events and make prophecies; for everything observable is a part of a meaning, and may be interpreted; a mouse gnawing through a Bible is a portent of whatever Mather can make of it, and the simple incompetence of a servant affords a prophetic view of things to come in the world at large.

But perhaps more important for our purposes is the Puritan conflict between self-examination, self-appraisal, and introspection on the one hand, and toward practical, externalized activity and an examination of the world on the other. Such a conflict sprang out of a psychological necessity imposed by the tenets of Puritanism itself; for if man's fate, his election or damnation, heaven or hell, was wholly at the mercy of God's whim, or his arbitrary will, and if the only evidence of that fate were those hints that God might place before the consciousness of man himself, then man inevitably would find one of his major occupations in constantly examining the state of his own soul, and at the same time examining those manifestations of the external world which impinged upon him and offered some hints as to his salvation or lack of it. Thus the external world, to the Puritan, was in one respect intimately linked to man's own internal being, and he tended to see the external world in terms of himself.

This view of the self and the world is everywhere observable in Henry Miller's work. It is not too much to say that virtually everything worthwhile and genuine in Miller is involved with Miller himself. George Orwell, an early admirer, praised Miller extravagantly for his social criticism, especially in the early *Tropics*; but what Orwell failed to understand, or at least to mention, was that Miller's social criticism was vital and worthwhile only when Miller himself was personally involved in the conditions of which he was writing. When he writes abstractly against social conditions in which he is not involved immediately and directly—as, for example, when he writes about war, which he is against—his remarks have all the depth and intensity of those we might find in a Sunday supplement article, or in a *Time* magazine essay. Unless his own person is immediately concerned, he is likely to be trite, unimaginative, verbose, or excruciatingly literary.

Everyone who has read the *Tropic* trilogy, and especially *Tropic of Capricorn*, has no doubt remarked the almost mechanical alternation of method—the rather long, naturalistic passages interspersed with equally long passages of self-revelation and self-exploration. Narrative and introspection, scene and reverie; this is the structure, insofar as the books have a very definable structure. And part of the point I am trying to make about this structure is that the two modes are never really integrated; they remain in tense opposition, no doubt because the impulses remain in some opposition within Miller himself.

If one is still unsure of this matter, one has only to read Miller's so-called travel book on Greece, *The Colossus of Maroussi*;

it is one of the most extraordinary travel books ever written, surpassing even Lawrence's study of *Etruscan Places* for its egoism and self-concern. Though passages of self-revelation and description are alternated, we soon become painfully aware that Miller is really concerned only with himself, and Greece is important insofar as that country and its landscape are capable of eliciting responses from him upon love, death, sex, the peasant, war, life, literature, time, poverty, America, or whatever else Miller might have within him, needing release.

And there are dozens of other confusions, or conflicts, or polarities in Miller's work that have been noted, and condemned or justified, by nearly everyone who has read him. The most vulgar, low, and colloquial language that we can imagine exists immediately alongside the most intellectual and literary language that we can also imagine; I take it that this is, among other things, a reflection of that conflict between idealism and realism that I mentioned earlier. Apocalyptic vision, nightmare, and fantasy exist immediately alongside passages of the utmost practicality and naturalism; this, I take it, is a reflection of that Puritan conflict between mysticism and practicality. And passages of the utmost sentimentality jostle passages of utter cynicism: Miller is almost endearingly American in his view that all prostitutes—at least all French prostitutes—have hearts of gold, and he is capable of rhapsodizing for pages upon their essential virtues; and at the same time he is capable of describing with relish his bilking them of their earnings and of viewing their degradation with pitiless and sometimes eager enjoyment.

Like the Puritan, he feels himself to be an alienated being, a man on the outside, looking for a way in. As the Puritan made a kind of occupation out of self-examination and an elaborate questioning of his relationship to God, so Miller's whole work is an occupation of self-examination and elaborate questioning of his relation to—what? Miller cannot say, and neither can we. But we can say this: whereas the Puritan, in his effort to allay that deepening sense of alienation, moved closer and closer to the world as it was, and felt less and less the theological impossibility of doing so, Miller has seemed to move farther and farther away from the world and its dictates and its demands—has moved deeper and deeper into himself, into his own impulses, his own wishes, and his own visions. He has moved aggressively upon the world, in what he has called an act of creative destruction, so that he might become more submissive to the dictates of himself.

It is customary in a paper such as this, which attempts a general survey of the work of a man, to arrive at a simple critical judgment of the value of that man's work. I must confess an inability to arrive at such a simple judgment, and I make the confession with a little chagrin, though I must admit that the chagrin is tinged with irony. For it is a judgment that should be easy, one way or the other. After all, several things are unequivocal and clear. Miller is, and has been for several years, one of the most extravagantly praised (and damned) of all modern writers: for Lawrence Durrell, "American literature today begins and ends with the meaning of what Miller has done"; for Karl Shapiro "Miller is the greatest living writer"; and for Kenneth Rexroth he is to be "ranked with Balzac, Goethe, and Baudelaire."

But beyond this praise it is clear that Miller as a writer is guilty of virtually every major fault that it is possible for a writer to be guilty of. Stylistically, his work is a botch: he is incredibly prolix and repetitive, and many of his best effects are lost in jungles of approximate language; he is capable of an elephantine diction that sometimes makes Theodore Dreiser seem almost Flaubertian; the so-called "experimental" passages in his works often appear to be the kind of parodies, intentional or accidental, that the editors of a popular magazine might make upon some of the lesser Dadaists and Surrealists that in the twenties appeared in *transition* magazine; and he is capable of sentimentalities that would make a virginal New England schoolteacher of a certain age blush with shame. He has almost no sense of structure, in either his longer or his shorter works: his work suffers from literary giantism, or disproportion, and one often has the dark suspicion that a passage is long or short, according to whether or not Miller might have been interrupted while writing it; and his solutions to structural problems are naïve to an extreme degree. Apparently conscious of the disorganization that dominates his work, he evokes the metaphor of a river, declaring that he "loves everything that flows," and attempts to justify his garrulous prose by that sentiment. He is incapable of constructing a dramatic scene, and he has no sense of character —except his own—and no ability to transmit the sense of another human being—except himself—to his reader. He is at his worst when he is most serious—that is, when he wishes his "ideas" to be taken seriously—ideas which are, beneath the sometimes outrageous verbiage, so commonplace and old-fashioned as to be almost bewildering. And of the various costumes he wears—that of the innocent pornographer, the American abroad, the raucous prophet, the apocalyptic comedian, the outsider, the rebel, and the clown—none seems to fit him really closely. It is as if he had picked each of them up at some vast metaphysical rummage sale to wear as his mood suits him.

But after all this has been duly noted, and after we have read Miller, none of it seems really to matter; for cautious as we may be, we are left with the disturbing suspicion that we have been in the presence of an authentic genius, though a genius unlike any we have encountered in literature before. For in one respect, at least, we must take Miller at his word: he is not engaged in the act of writing literature. His work is, indeed, at bottom antiliterary, and antiliterary in a profound way that the Dadaists—those cultivated, highly educated, most humorous nihilists—could never have understood.

Miller's task has been, quite simply, to reveal himself, and to reveal himself as immediately and fully as his time and energy will allow him to do. Himself is the only subject he has ever had, and most of the time he has had the wit to know this, and not to pretend otherwise, at least to himself. He is not a novelist, and could never have been; for a good novelist must, perhaps, be offensively egotistic—that is to say, filled with pride and perhaps irrationally convinced of his own powers; but he cannot be egoistic—that is to say, so obsessed with the exclusive sense of his own identity that other identities have little reality, except insofar as they impinge upon him. And Miller is so consumed with a sense of his own identity that the question of his powers, or even the usual pride in his literary abilities, never really occurs to him. Nor, given his egoism, could he have been a philosopher, a social critic, an essayist—in short, he could not have been a writer, in the ordinary sense of that word.

Thus, seen in terms of its subject, the formlessness of his work begins to take on a new significance, so that the question of justification hardly arises. In a very real sense Miller is not engaged in writing books, or essays, or stories, or romances, or autobiographies, or whatever—he is engaged in writing, or revealing, himself, just as he is, or just as he thinks he is, at a given moment. And in Miller's view, to commit that self to a given literary form would be to betray it most profoundly; for finally he is not concerned that we see what he, Miller, *thinks* is true about himself; he wants us to see the thing itself.

And out of Miller's colossal, almost heroic egoism, the subject, Miller, is shown to us, not as a symbol of anything, not as a kind of everyman, but simply as itself. Miller never allows the integrity of his subject to be vitiated by lowering it to the level of myth or symbol; had he done so, it is likely that his work would have been without value to us.

It remains for me to suggest something of the nature of that character, that presence which constitutes the real subject of all that Miller has written; for it is in the nature of the subject that the significance of Miller lies.

I have said that at the center of Miller's work, and hence at the center of Miller himself, lies a set of polarities that curiously resemble the polarities found embedded in historical American Puritanism; but in saying that, I was not attempting to do anything very special, nor to imply any "mythic" quality to Miller's work. For the Puritan dilemma lies very near the center of the American experience, particularly at the center of what we might call uninformed American experience. And the polarities that we see in Miller are versions of the polarities that we encounter every day, in ourselves and in the life around us.

Miller's character is extraordinary in only one respect: and that is that it is so ordinary. This darling of the *avant-garde*, this prototype of the twentieth-century rebel, this almost legendary man, this candidate for the Nobel Prize—he is the most ordinary figure that we can readily imagine. Except for the fact that we have him on paper, we have seen him everywhere in America, if we have cared to look: the son of lower-middle-class immigrant parents, who for the first forty years of his life lived a lower-middle-class life, on the periphery of a middle-class society, with the usual ambivalent attitudes toward middle-class values and aspirations—a man indifferently educated, whose reading is scattered and eccentric and not really very wide—a man who had that most common of aspirations, to be a successful writer (what more middle-class ambition can there be?), and who, like most who have that aspiration, failed—and a man, finally, who, confronted with the failure that his life had become, found within himself a deep and compelling reservoir of indifference to all that he had been taught that mattered. We see such men around us every day—men who finally have been forced to the great freedom of genuinely not giving a damn; and we look at them with our ambivalence of contempt and envy.

But within the ordinariness that is the character of Henry Miller, what a vast humanity, finally, we find; and what a vast generosity of spirit. With the compulsive honesty that is possible only to the heroic egoist, Miller shows us this fleck of humanity in the chaotic arena of kindness and cruelty, sentimentality and cynicism, pretension and simplicity, tenderness and obscenity, suffering and ecstasy, hypocrisy and sincerity, falsity and truth, that is humanity itself. And if finally we are shocked by Miller we are shocked because we see, in unflinching and crude and graphic terms, written upon the page, beyond our evasion, simply ourselves, our selves that we hide from others and too often from ourselves; we see what we have made of ourselves, out of our time and circumstance; our real shock comes from nothing other than a glimpse of our persistent, affirmative, essentially amoral, and unhomogenized humanity.

In what we may think of as a typically American way, with what we may even call Yankee ingenuity, Henry Miller has made a success of his failure. The ten years of his life in America before he went to Europe, ten years when his sense of worldly failure steadily increased into his saving despair, and the ten years he spent in Europe as an itinerant menial, beggar, and hack writer—these years are the vital center of his work, and hence of his life. He made of these years of failure his great success, which is his work, which is himself. And he has shown us the degree to which a man can be free, even in the prison of his ideas and attitudes, his time and circumstance.

As has Thoreau, whose name I evoked at the beginning of this essay. But the parallels I have drawn between certain aspects of the thought of the two men obviously break down; and the dissimilarities in the later stages of both their careers are perhaps even more enlightening than the early resemblances. Miller left Europe and returned to the United States in the winter of 1940; Thoreau left Walden Pond and returned to Concord in the summer of 1847. For both men, the times away from their homes were the climactic periods of their literary lives, and their significant and vital work comes out of those times of exile.

But the end of Thoreau's life was dramatically unlike these late years of Miller's life. During his last two years, Thoreau was ill with tuberculosis, and he spent much of this time preparing a last group of essays for publication in the *Atlantic Monthly*. He did not live to see them appear there, but had he done so, he would have noted no untoward response to their publication. His first book—*A Week on the Concord and Merrimac*—was a failure from the beginning, and even *Walden* found but a very small body of readers during Thoreau's lifetime; most of his poems were not published, and those few that were went unnoticed; and his other essays were read as fugitive pieces in magazines. Thoreau died with the kind of worldly failure that he had, out of principle, courted for nearly all his life.

For the last several years, Henry Miller has been living in California. He is now a famous writer; he is moderately wealthy, sought after, widely admired and read; there is even a Henry Miller Society. Recently he was made a member of the American Institute of Arts and Letters, an eminently distinguished affair, our nearest equivalent to the Académie Française; I understand that he was pleased by his election. Miller has been living in a large modern house near Los Angeles; the house is most comfortably furnished, and like many southern California homes it has a large swimming pool on the spacious grounds. In his new prosperity, Miller has written almost nothing. But he is comfortable now, and I suppose at last he has earned his ironic success, which a few years ago he might have thought of as his damnation.

◗

A Man's Life

from *Folio*

to Martin Luther King, Jr.

The plastic spider under the table
has lost its power to frighten;
all mechanical voices, guns of complaint,
voices of war, have lost their claim on us.
This is the day when trees begin to shelter
threads of life, blossoming like hands.

Long, bare branches of a shadow
tremble gently and evenly
like the breathing of a flower
that will never be born.
The mountain rests on the horizon, dark island,
and slipping away like sleep
the fear of storms,
fear of tornadoes, fear of the prisoner
escaped from a work-gang on the highway.

Even when I am alone
the songs of sorrow support me.
The delicate spider of fear is gone forever.

JEROME ROTHENBERG

◐

The Student's Testimony

from *Caterpillar*

                        he was the last demon of ostrow
                come back to visit & play
on my mind blowing delicious
                        bubbles of red soap into
                the corners of the room
a furry singing little
                        demon with bulging eyes big
                bulging balls & all
animal twisted into shapes
                        like rubber
                "I love my demon" I would sing
& we would share the backroom of
                        the synagogue guzzling
                the gentiles' beer &
snapping paperclips
                        against the rabbi's silks reliving
                the poland of old friendships pork & fish
boiling & stinking in a single
                        pot we would dip our hands
                into & make our bellies
shine
                        what grease
                what aromas from the bookshelves
what smells of jews ripe for the sabbath
                        "fur" I would cry to him or "snot" & he
                would wrap me in his sleeves & let

their velvet warm me
                    nightly the books were opening
          in my dreams the letters
black as coal danced off
                    the page & fell on me I saw them
          cross my hips & write the double
yod upon my cock
                    "never had Polish child felt
          greater warmth beside her
mother than I felt there"
                    later the telephone came voices
          reached us from "the kingdoms"
messages of love
                    vibrated there were calls
          from warsaw krakow moscow kiev odessa
paris berlin new york london
                    buenos aires hongkong yokohama bombay
          melbourne juneau tombstone perth
detroit johannesburg topeka east st louis
                    homesick we dreamed "freedom" meaning
          that our hands could touch our feet reach
even the dirt between
                    the toes
          & breathe its essence
(of a hundred slaughterhouses
                    the sweet fat of the sabbath
          in our teeth we waited until the women
came to us bearing the bloody eyes
                    of cows & lambs
          they piled up on the table crying
"hosanna to the gentiles")
                    buckwheat for dinner
          in the lonely diner
eating globs of fat congealed
                    we played games near wealthy
          homes pretending that we were children
"the luck of the jews"

"constantinople nights"
"making the devil's mark on parchment"
also "the hair & beard of macroanthropos"
through which he led me his
furry body hidden under
three suits of clothes towards other
pleasures secret holes
he lived in
bathhouse partitions white with mold
& through a broken board the eye
watched the old women strove to behold
the slit the fiery entranceway
dissolve
the waters washing out the light the breath
that moves upon the waters
until the bulb above us splintered
"god is one"
we sang my demon clung to me
made of my tongue
his song
a master at pinochle sometimes
the deck flew in his hands
beautiful men wept like children
some shelled almonds for him
or filled his hat with vodka
the fat students loved him the dark ones
waited for news on the radio
"calm in the face of disaster"
pilgrims visited the tsaddik's court he sat
for seven days
dipped figs in wine
then lifted his milkwhite hands each
finger held a garnet
each eye a golden tear
electricity ran from his beard he wore
a neon caftan
thrice did my demon limp into his presence

                they were face to face neither
moving neither still in love
                        or heartsick
                theirs was a meeting of the upper
& the lower worlds
                        the "model of the universe" was always
                at their call an empty building windows
broken or taped-up with X's
                        in contrast to the tsaddik's its
                easy warmth stoves in perfect order
so even a stranger had a place to sit
                        forgetful of each other
                they let the time pass with singing not
with arithmetic
                        "a woman for me
                & a woman for thee" (he would order)
the one with a wen near her nipple
                        the other with a glass eye women
                with moist hair in their armpits
moister below
                        & furious
                reputed to be in love with great men they were
"nieces" to all the rabbis
                        breathless my demon would mount his
                from the rear the tsaddik
slept on in innocence of
                        heart & purpose
                barely
could feel her hand
                        betray him
                but blamed it on
the tightness of his linens while
                        wan allergic dreaming
                furry to his fingers
my demon
                        slept against the other's
                side forgetting

that the bride was always chaste the sabbath
                    always an interval
          between subscriptions
something cold but beautiful
                    not a mechanical process
          merely but responsive
to the touch
                    in satin slippers beneath
          a painted canopy
of stars each waited
                    for the bride
          each called her
sabbath but each had something else a different kind of sleep
                    in mind

.   .   .   .   .   .

                    (*coda*)

                    once in a lifetime man
          may meet a hostile spirit once
he may be imprisoned for his
                    dreams & pay for them
          lightning is like oil the motor
once it starts keeps
                    running
          such was their wisdom though we had
no use for it
                    only later seeing it
          reborn
in joplin on a billboard
                    his own shadow
          was more than he could bear the war
came & he ran from it
                    back in the cellar drinking
          too much he grew thin

the great encounter ended it
                        in flames the candelabrum rose did it become
            a heart
that broke into sparks & letters
                        a shower of ruined cities from which
            my demon
vanished fled from the light when I was born

NORMAN H. RUSSELL

◐

Two Poems

from *The Little Square Review*

because this is the way things are

a moose is lying down in a meadow
he is crushing some grasses and flowers
some small ants running out from under him
some birds nearby eating seeds
when he leaves the grasses will stand up
after a long time and the living ants
will carry the crushed dead ants away

some green fruits turning red on the bush
some birds come to feed upon them
dropping the seeds here and there in the grass
some lice in the feathers of the birds

in the night an owl flies crookedly
softly among the trees and some birds sleep
and over a great swamp clouds of mosquitoes
and many hungry bats

all the lives going along together
every life is a full life and it is completed
every moment it is completed or finished or over
every moment it begins all over again
because this is the way things are.

my fathers hands held mine

my fathers hands held mine
the first flint

now my hands alone
cut our arrows

the deer that dies from them
falls from both our hands

wife of my heart your mothers hands
help you sew my moccasins

my father speaks to me in many ways
i feel his hands on me

he is always with me
i will always touch my sons.

DAVID STACTON

Notes Written in the Self of a Man with a Singular Distaste for Writing Anything Down

from *Transatlantic Review*

I

Someone once asked me how the piano concerto was coming along. Since one has a duty to be witty and amusing, I said it was finished except for the notes. And yet it was a true remark. For though I can cast as glittering a net as anyone since Rimski-Korsakov, and each note a knot, sometimes it is a minnow in there, and very seldom a prize catch. And sometimes, alas, the net is empty.

Every artist is a fisher in his own seas. He begins by angling up a derivative creek. But as he gets older and so farther out to sea, not even he can tell whether there is anything down there or not. An arpeggio of sea gulls shows you there is something. There are movements below, and a mottle to the water. Or perhaps you may be so lucky as to steer your boat over the shoals of a major work, running swiftly to its feeding grounds, though shoal, alas, has two meanings.

For myself, I've always been a net caster. Some can hook a big fish with a simple line, but not many. I have always preferred a sample of the sea itself, and for that you need a net. Yet it is surprising: by baiting your hook with some flashing and unusual sound, you sometimes get a rise from the unconscious, a sample of what is down there. And sometimes, but only when the weather is calm and cool, you can lower your whole technique down into the sea of yourself, like a lobster pot, and it is amazing what you come up with, though it is usually a mixed catch, and very seldom a lobster.

Now that I can't compose any more, I can't help, from habit, recognizing the signs of what is down there, if only I were still able to lower my net: a song cycle about Joan of Arc; a fairy story more exact than *"Ma Mère l'Oye"*; *"Le Grand Meaulnes"* (one always comes back to the old house); and there is something, too, in the Fiori. I did just manage to draft a "Sermon to the Birds," those birds by whose chatter one knows which way the sea is running, or did before this happened to me.

II

I am told the fashionable thing to say of me, is that I am the Mozart of the Nightclubs. I suppose this was because the serious-minded found me trivial, for I made my own experiments, not theirs. It is true I did like nightclubs. I still do. One knows what the serious-minded are up to. But I find it difficult to believe that Karl Marx was musical. As for Schönberg, he tried to hide his sentimental streak by closing his eyes and counting up to twelve, but it did not work. It never does. One cannot change one's nature, even by copying the inevitable upside down, though many have become fashionable in that manner. All that effort to prove that one is not what one is, a minor follower of Wagner and Brahms, what is the point of it? It is better to make the best of what one is. One may deceive the devious for a while, but the arts are not devious. They are as straightforward as transplanting flowers from the unknown into the knowable once they have developed far enough to take root outdoors and do their growing in fresh air.

Schönberg has some interesting noises, but he did not love them. He has not found them, he has merely made them up.

Berg now is another matter. And though I do not happen to care for Webern myself, that is merely because I have larger hands. If one has small hands, naturally one carves a world in little, but true: it is the authentic silence he carves. He knew how to choose his materials. For a perfect craftsman, that is the only real task.

As a child, waking early, and hearing the first birds in the garden, it always seemed to me that somewhere there was a Creator who wound the world up every morning. The whole thing goes like clockwork. It is a mechanism. But that does not mean that the mechanism is not a charming, endless, and diverting thing.

What child would ever question that his doll was more alive than he? What child would ever tell that secret to a trusted grownup? For the child knows that grownups are not to be trusted, and so does dolly. To children and to each other, for no child wholly dies, we are only strangers, to be circumvented, too big to be of importance, irrelevant, really, to all our own toddling concerts.

And now I can no longer sit at the piano, that chessboard at which our fingers move the pieces more than we do, in the endless game against the opponent silence, I can at least, though only, describe that stranger who is each man in himself.

The time comes, and you never know when it will, for the matter is decided behind one's back, when a white silence will have the first move. Then woe betide you, for to the artist it is his work must take the initiative, not he, though some, it is true, have managed a good defensive game on the block. The virtuoso by nature is always on the defensive, until he has won. That makes him canny: Liszt had a few extra keys installed behind a trap door at the bass end of the piano, in case of need, should he begin to lose out to silence. One can understand that sort of thing; but it is not the manner in which I chose to play the game.

III

Significant tactics from my previous games, which is to say, from the game itself:

On the piano at Montfort (I liked Montfort: it was my model of the universe. At Montfort it was possible to spend whole diligent mornings merely winding the creatures up) there was a mechanical doll under a glass bell. When she was bored, when the phrase led nowhere, one had only to wind her up, and she lifted her arms, she turned her head, she did nothing in particular over and over again, until she ran down. When I was really at work, and had not the time to wind her up, she was content to stand there and shake out of sympathetic vibration.

My biographer says (it is the sort of thing which passes for music criticism), that it is possible that "the macabre fantasmagoria of *'Gaspard de la Nuit'* " owes something "to the author of the *'Danse Gothique,'* the lover of castle keeps and turrets in bronze." Possible, but scarcely practicable. From this sort of thing Montfort was the perfect refuge: it had no footnotes, only footpaths.

It did, however, have some Norman buildings, some shrubs and trees, and a pool. It had a little boat on the piano made of sliced seashells, with a starfish to steer by. It had, above all, the gardens themselves, where you could take a nip and tuck at the shrubs as you passed by, with the secateurs. And at night you could lie in your bedroom for hours, listening to the insect orchestra of the night, or to the woodwinds of the birds at three A.M., if you woke early. What one does is not necessarily what one is. Sometimes critics forget that.

This biography, or whatever you call it, which someone has given me, has irritated me so much, that some of it has stuck in my head. What about "the tall slim fountains among the marble statues, formerly represented in Fauré," And now, we may presume, on tour. What about my "brief chords, unkind, tired, and prosaic"?

However, the work provides snapshots and a list of works in

chronological order, and about these I have done considerable thinking recently.

Thus:

It is curious what one has done, and what one thinks of it, if one remembers having done it at all. There are some works we row away from as fast as possible, but here they are on the chart, anyhow. We all have to sail through at least once, to find out where the shallows are, where the barrier reefs, there is no disgrace in that. And if we tear up the charts, there is some danger we may forget and so run aground on the same course again.

IV

1899. *"Pavane pour une infante défunte."* I wrote it when I was twenty-four. I wish I hadn't. It is a piece for young ladies who do not play the piano properly, but I suppose my young self meant something by it. I wonder what?

1902. The "Quartet." Nothing wrong with the "Quartet."

1901–1902. Cantatas: *"Myrrha"* and *"Alcyone."* These were written to win the Prix de Rome, for Rome is an agreeable city. They did not win me it. Later those who did win it went on to fresh triumphs, and so wound up as teachers of harmony and the piano, in small provincial cities, in which it does not seem to me that *"Myrrha"* and *"Alcyone"* can be frequently performed.

In short, I did not win the Prix de Rome. In 1901 and 1902 that was all I knew of tragedy so far.

In 1906 Misia Godebski took me off on the family yacht. The company was stimulating and I like yachts. It was only a tour of the Dutch ports. I wrote *"Une barque sur l'Océan,"* the *"Alborado del Gracioso,"* *"La Vallée des Cloches,"* and *"L'Oiseau Triste."* I am told they are considered better than *"Alcyone"* and *"Myrrha."*

1907. *"L'Histoires Naturelles."* Jules Renard, who supplied the text, was a curious man. Toulouse-Lautrec, who did some illustrations to it, was even more curious. I suppose I am curious. Anyone who ever tries to do anything, must always seem a little unnatural not only to those who don't, but to that part of himself which doesn't either. What we do always seems irrelevant to what we are, except while we are doing it; then it is what we are that seems irrelevant. Thus the fascination of natural history: we reassure ourselves with what most men agree upon, which is not much.

1908–1909. *"Rhapsodie Espagnol." "L'Heure Espagnol." "Ma Mère L'Oye." "Gaspard de la Nuit."* 1911. *"Valses nobles et sentimentales."* 1912. "Daphnis and Chloë."

It was only a ballet, but boned, it made two quite acceptable suites. Diaghilev was a strange man, too, an aesthetic Svengali. No one who sang for him ever sang quite the same way afterward, and the lesser of them, not at all. One does not always have to warm one's hands before a fire: sometimes ice burns just as well. That was Diaghilev. He was a splendid host in restaurants and hotels. Seen in his own house, he behaved like a bad guest. His contempt for himself was quite remarkable, and looked like pride.

As for the *"Alborado,"* I see my critic mentions Gracián, who concludes a handbook to a practiced, suave hypocrisy, with the adjuration: be a saint.

That is what the *"Alborado"* meant. It was about that dismay with which we master reality. Such things can be tenderly done, for disappointment has the most exquisite manners.

As well as the apotheosis of the virtues, there is the apotheosis of absolutely nothing. "Daphnis and Chloë" was my contribution to the physics of hot air, caught in the silk meshes of a Montgolfier balloon. Among other things, I used to collect eighteenth-century engravings of ballooning. It does not get us to the stars, but it gets us closer.

1914. "Trio in A for Piano."

It was at about this time that in profile I began to resemble a distinguished rat. A well-bred town rat with an equally well-bred little place in the country, but still, unmistakably, a rat. I have also a picture of myself from this period, patiently enduring the discomforts of trench warfare. I must say I do not recognize the face. I look like one of those men in Hokusai or Hiroshige who huddle against the climate in a corn-shuck cloak.

1928, of course, was the year of the *"Bolero."* There seems nothing to say of the *"Bolero,"* except that I wrote it for Ida Rubinstein, whose style of dancing was equally monotonous. In street shoes, she was more agreeable.

"He's mad, he's mad," said a woman in the audience on opening night.

"She has understood," said I. Why do people so incessantly admire the least of us, as though that were all they were up to? It is what we do to others, of course, but then others do not count.

During the war the pianist Wittgenstein lost an arm. Like Christian of Brunswick in another war, he said *Altera restat* and proposed to go on playing. I wrote him a concerto and another for Marguerite Long. One tried for that sort of joy one feels when opening the shutters of an upstairs window at dawn, to let the bird song in. It is an emotion of middle age or of the crippled, of those who find it moving to be still alive, although the birds peck about on the lawn quite as usual.

After that, *"Don Quichotte à Dulcinée."* After that, nothing.

It was this disease. It might as well have been something else. The Universe, we are told, is self-contained and never still, a perfect work of art. But what about its Creator? He, too, must find it difficult to face the boredom of having done it all already. And one can't do it again. It is so hard, always, afterward, to recapture the mood.

V

So here I sit with this album of photographs and flip the pages. According to the chronology one lived from 1875 to 1937. The photographs are more informative.

Here is Fauré. He was the best of teachers. He insisted that you imitate neither yourself nor him. You might repeat yourself. Creative people often do. It is their way of getting their second wind. But to imitate one's self is a form of circular madness which was not Fauré's natural motion. Each time he unwound a little more of the original stuff, and though the pattern was the same, it was never the same piece twice. His works are full of pauses, rests, false feints, and dotted intervals. It was silence he loved more than sound, for silence is potential. From silence he unraveled his best works, and to silence he returned them. It was silence he had to teach. It made him Oriental.

Satie, of course, was different. He was the grand autodidact, and they always have a tendency to bustle. He made too much out of too little, and too little out of too much. He was a Paris Métro entrance to the arts. You descended into him in order to get where you were going, and you ascended out of him, with some relief, when you were there.

We are also given photographs of Chabrier and Liszt. These, says my biographer, were my influences. Unfortunately, I was that sort of artist critics find it impossible to admire, I was myself from the beginning. We all were, even Liszt. One could learn what one was, only by looking at what one had done; not that I have done much, and yet it has taken a lifetime. It is what one cannot bring one's self to do, that takes the time.

It is diverting to see what others thought of one, and of one's work. One can only hope that they are sometimes wrong, for assuredly they are not often right. In speaking of the sound of my "*Asie,*" my biographer says that I liked mechanisms that had gone wrong. Of course I did. Mechanisms always go wrong. As with human beings, one likes them for their failings, the way one likes the dead. On page 87 is a photograph of a windbell, attached to a door at Montfort. It is described as a *chinoiserie*. It is not a *chinoiserie*. It is a windbell. It was there because it made agreeable sounds. I was absorbed in the making of agreeable sounds. They meant what they were, no more, no less.

"Born March 7, 1875."

A picture of Mother, looming up like a tarsier. She has the same grip on her bough. She came from Aranjuez, and was a Basque. The bough sways and the creature is frightened to be seen, but it does not lose its grip.

There is also a picture of Father, who, in 1881, when I was six, seated me at that piano into which I have ever since fed my invincible questions, without which I cannot compose them.

For silence, too, has its code, and everything has to be translated into it. The piano is the control panel. The machine is one's self. It was set at birth to solve only some problems.

I find it amusing to see that in 1894 I wrote a piano piece called "*Ballade de la Reine morte d'aimer.*"

Later I reformed. I desisted. I no longer remember from what, from a lovely world which contains nothing but those ghosts called friends, perhaps. They are the ghosts of imaginary lovers, who in their turn, are the ghosts of imaginary friends.

It is only the blind who understand what they touch, and to be touched is for a moment to be blinded, and so to feel that worst of the emotions, pathos. Since one wanted neither to touch nor to be touched, one had one's ghosts instead. One had one's friends. One determined not to take the matter seriously, for that is the only way to enjoy it. And yet one does take the matter seriously, which means one cannot take it at all.

"In 1920 he created a considerable sensation by refusing the *Légion d'Honneur.*"

Who on earth would want it? It is the sort of thing one gives to a janitor.

It was too soon after the war. After a war, all honors seem posthumous. The medals and the citation are sent to the widow. The *Légion d'Honneur* is given to the corpse itself. He must sit up to receive it, and I am among those who believe Lazarus would have been better off where he was. Six of my friends were killed in the war.

When I am alone sometimes, and play the "*Tombeau de Couperin,*" of a warm evening, those friends come back, and one can scarcely remember how it feels to be dead any more, though one is dead. Once absence is permanent, it becomes a sort of return, like that room one sets aside for a friend who visits the house habitually. He may be away at the moment, but all the same, it is his room. You have only to go into it, to realize that. Having lost his own, he takes refuge in your body.

It is a squash-court game, to create. Given the right wall, the balls come back with a vigor we scarcely knew we could evoke. And so it is with the dead. One considers the nature of one's own abilities, the way an ordinary man jangles in his pocket his keys. One says for others what they would not dream of saying for themselves. And we create because we cannot help it.

That is why I keep the automata on the piano at Montfort. Like them, one performs when one is wound up, and one was wound up in the womb. From time to time, one toddles into an obstruction, and knees against it until one runs down. Or we stand with our face to the wall, until something jars us, and then we jog off in another direction again. For there is always a twist or two left in the exhausted spring. I quite understand why Fauré wrote "Dolly," or why he called it that. We are human because we are devil dolls. Wind us up, and we whirr off uncertainly toward our revenge. That we can move at all is the revenge we whirr to.

The literary classic held up to composers like a dusty mirror is Morike's "Mozart's Journey to Prague." The uncreative assure us that this is what the creative process is like. Morike has told them so. Mozart stops at an inn. He works as he travels in his carriage from engagement to engagement. And for some reason some plump Seville oranges give him the answer to everything.

At that, Morike is not wrong.

"No doubt God could have made a better berry than the strawberry," said someone once. "But God did not choose to." Synesthesia is out of repute. Yet one writes because one is ravished by the taste of sounds.

And I have myself tried to express the smell of oranges, of lemons, and of the lime. Alas, to express a lime is beyond my powers. What has moved me more is the mechanical blackbirds on an unmown spring lawn, under the apple trees, with their yellow beaks and their hunger, and the first *muguets de bois*, all designed by Fabergé, who also did the water and the glass they stood in, cleverly, out of rock crystal. God may have created the world, but knowing how unwise it is to rely on others, Fabergé created his own.

"In 1919 wrote '*La Valse*' for Diaghilev."

He was an aesthetic Fabergé, who knew very well what to make of other men's flowers. Some people are both too much and too little for you. We did not get on.

It was at about this period that Mme. Colette decided that

the one thing she needed from me was an opera. *"L'Enfant et les Sortilèges"* was the result. She had chosen her composer with care.

She was astute, that woman sitting upstairs in the Palais Royale, surrounded by glass paperweights. And yet in a way she was no woman at all, for she too, was the puppetmaster of herself. Though we collaborated, we did so at a distance. She preferred Cocteau, perhaps because Cocteau had not only given in to, but made capital out of, what he was. Whereas I could never face the vulgarity of doing either.

It is an agonizing work. It is "Dido and Aeneas" for children. Colette's fables were not always agreeable. A small boy, too young to be of either sex, is left alone to study his lessons, but decides to be wicked instead. So he is punished not by his Maman (there are few fathers in the works of Colette) but by the world. The tables, the chairs, the trees in the garden, and the animals, all tell him what they really think of him, and then feel sorry for what *they* have done. That's the real punishment in this world. He then returns to Maman. The moral of this is the difference between Dostoevsky and the truth. One does not prefer him to many people, but one does prefer him to the truth.

All works are taken out of ourselves in some sense. Most so when what we have to say in them does not concern us. *"L'Enfant"* was my *Trauermusik*.

The little boy has caused the curtains to be destroyed. They were figured drapes in actuality. They were only a world in two dimensions, but the little people printed on them could not survive anywhere else. The world in two dimensions was their home.

Il se commence un ballet de petits personnages qui expriment, en dansant, le chagrin de ne pouvoir plus se joindre, en chantant, les petits riens étonnants:

> *Adieu, pastourelles!*
> *Pastoureaux adieu!*
> *Les bras tendu, pastourelles,*

La bouche en coeur, pastoureaux,
Nos amours semblaient éternels.
Éternels, semblaient nos pipeaux.

L'Enfant méchant à déchiré
Notre tendre histoire.
Pâtre de ci, pastourelle de là,
L'enfant méchant qui nous doit
Son premier sourire.
L'enfant ingrat qui dormait sous la garde
De notre chien bleu.

So sing the shepherds and shepherdesses whose meadows the
child has just destroyed. A billowing of brown curtains into the
room, leaping like seals, as the warm storms of August sent a
gust of air through the French windows and across the rug, is
what one was after. Remembering that, one remembered so
many things.

. . . and then, at the end, out into the miracle of the garden.
What we do wicked we do in a room. For absolution we return
to the garden.

Frightened by what he has done, the little boy tries to undo
it.

Il a guéri nos blessures . . . groan the trees.

But nothing does. But no one does. Which of course is why
Colette said that someone and something could. She insisted
upon it. It is a fairy tale. It is something true.

I was a one-man procession. And now the procession is bearing me away, down a white-tiled corridor. One's whole life is a
rehearsal for that, so naturally one plays one's part. However,
one suffers that English pretense to human permanence with
patience only, for other races have not that much time. It takes
no patience to admire their hedges. Their bad weather gives
them an admirable high shifting light, like the light in a Tiepolo. I am told I am an artist for people who admire the Tiepolo
touch. But I do not think I have it. When one is back from that
arduous journey into the silence, one prefers smaller and more
definitive things.

Colette has set me thinking. She has forced me to define myself. "*L'Enfant*" is put on every Easter, for older children (the only kind that count) at Versailles. It is not a performance, it is a rite. But everything one writes is a rite, and I write for older children. They are the only ones to write for, for they have never quite lost the ability to see everything for the first time. They are still capable of wonder. What most people call maturity is no more than a refusal to carry one's own bags. I traveled light, but here are mine.

Besides, if one writes at all, no matter what the subject seems, one writes about Maman, Papa, Fido, and the garden, a cat, a rabbit, and the pool on which one sailed one's boats. What else would one write about? One is not one's self interesting, even though one is always interested in one's self. These thoughts come up from childhood. It is considered polite to show a concern for strangers, after all.

Maman and Papa persisted in telling us they were our parents. I have often wondered who they really were, in those moments when we were not there.

So now I compose no more. I wait.

But I wish I were at Montfort, instead of in this hospital. It is heartless and futile in a hospital. Whereas at Montfort, all the clockwork is wound up, and waiting to dance. The "*Valses nobles et sentimentales*" are better in the piano version, I think. They are an elegy. But then everything I wrote was a good-by.

When the child is tired and grows desperate in the garden, the squirrel is touched.

For once the child has been kind to him. "*Il a guéri ma blessure*," cries the squirrel, astonished that people should ever prove kind, let alone after they had as usual been cruel, and brings all the world round to his own gratitude. The trees take up the murmur. The powers of nature consult and decide they must help the little boy. The cicadas, the animals, pick up his desperate cry.

"Maman," he sobs.

"Maman, maman, maman," they amplify, into a suppliant shout.

It is dusk. The shutters fly back from a second-story window. The light streams out into the garden, not this hard modern light, but something warm as candleglow. The scent of *poudre-de-riz* and childhood and maternity swoons down into the garden, like the smell of moss roses in a conservatory.

"Mon enfant . . ."

I do not remember that to happen, from my own childhood. But it happens in the libretto Colette sent me. It happened to her. I suppose it will happen again, to someone. . . .

Yes, I would prefer to die at Montfort. But I suppose this way one causes less inconvenience.

This disease of mine, which has its symbolic aptness, first became apparent in 1933, when I was fifty-eight. I was bathing at Saint-Jean de Luz at the time. I liked to go there, for not only was it smart, it was close to Ciboure, where I was born.

Do you know that picture by Bakst of Nijinski on the beach, brown and strigiling himself? At least his arm is raised in that gesture. I tried to raise my arm so, and could not do it. I could no longer make certain movements with my hand. I stood there in the sun, with foam running over my feet, and for the first time saw that the machine was running down.

Apraxia and dysphasia, said the doctors, but why give our limitations a name? They were all the firmer about the name, because they could not find the cause. They found my case anomalous and therefore of interest. So did I. I could not write. I could not play the piano. I could not even reach out for certain things when I wanted to touch them. It was difficult to wind the automata up. I could still compose in my head. But there was no way of transcribing it.

I became a privileged person, condemned to hear complete performances of compositions no one else would ever hear. Unfortunately, a creative person is not so fond of his own works as all that. He would much rather write them out and get rid of them.

However, one soon learns how to die. Like everything else one does, it is a discipline, nothing more. So I went back to Montfort for a while.

Hélène Jourdan-Morhange asked me what I was doing one

day, when all I was doing was leaning over the balcony to look at a world I was no longer permitted to evoke.

"I'm waiting," said I.

Sometimes we say more than we meant to. For all our life is waiting, we never know for what. We only know that nothing that happens to us is exactly what we were waiting for. And so we go on waiting.

In 1935 I was sixty. At sixty, one is permitted to count what is left, to see how much bread and cheese one has for the final journey. And there is that nice young man to travel with, Hermes Psychopompos, the ghost of one's self when young, who now comes back to help an old man over. We are the best of friends, he and I. I never thought much of him when we were both young, but now I see he was my death.

And now it is 1937. My head is clear, though my body is confused. Beyond the walls of this room, Montfort is what I see. And all these tiled corridors turn into leafy paths.

There is a courtesy among doctors, and a precedence. So too between the patient and his illness. One makes it welcome, as best one can. One settles down with it, like two people in a house too small, each pretending the other is not there, except at mealtimes and in the evening. Since one's life was unsatisfactory, one ignored it. So, too, with one's death, no doubt. When one came out of that diamond surf at Saint-Jean de Luz, one found one's self walking back up the beach forever.

I think that if you listen to my music properly, you realize that it does not exist. It is only a form of listening. I wanted to decorate silence like a Christmas tree, with the shimmer of exciting baubles for the ear, until the whole thing shook with what it was. Not all joy is joyous: there is also the solemn kind. And that I wanted to pull down with some kind of sky hook to where it could be looked at, but it was too vast, and the aperture of our abilities is too small. It would never get through. It can only be poked at.

Silence is endless. It is we who dart in and out, with our scores, our snapshots, and our souvenirs, which prove to others we too made the trip. Laboriously one wove those phrases, by means of those symbols we call sounds, into a net to contain what could not be contained. Though the catch may be invisible, it is defined by the sudden sag and lurch of the net. No wonder one was ironic: one always knew what one had not caught. One was trying to do what cannot be done. There is no other way to do anything.

Now I compose no longer, my disposition has improved. Our talents leave us so little time to ourselves, and now I am like a businessman in a small way, retired on his rents. It is restful. It is what one had always looked forward to. But the waiting is a little long.

Bach without thinking about it, Beethoven by thinking about it overmuch, made models of the universe. Complete. I am incomplete. I wanted to admire the thing itself, not reproduce it. I had no world in me, so no wonder I have this fondness for automata and for anything small. We are small things ourselves. But wind us up, and we can smile with dignity until we run down. We can also smile with wonder. So it is not necessary to create a world. It is necessary only to set it down, as many have, and always the same one: only the handwritings vary.

One goes into a world without an owner, as a small child plays in the abandoned garden of the house next door. God moved away and never came back. Nobody seems quite sure who the present legal owners are, so at least the property cannot be sold. It makes a delightful playground, for no adult would dare to climb that wall. If you want an apple, and are a child, over the wall you go. And saints and artists are much the same. It is so easy. You need merely never say where you have been, and eat your apple, or your orange, by yourself.

Did Morike realize that, perhaps, with his fable of Mozart and the oranges? They were an exotic luxury in those days. But then, to a small child, any orange is a luxury, and the world a far-off, strange, and foreign place.

There are oranges in my apotheosis, I think, and citrons, and small methodically arranged dates. But there are not so many snapshots worth looking at in this biography of mine, after all, for most of them are out of focus.

In 1935 I was bundled off to Marrakesh. Sitting in pajamas,

on the terrace of the Hôtel de la Mounia, it was possible to watch another toy world down there, the drugged toy world of the Arabs. There was a trip to the Atlas Mountains. There was the music. And as in most dry countries, there was more water to be seen running than you would expect. In dry countries they like the sound of water running.

There is an attractive snap of me watching pelota at Saint-Jean de Luz, with Leon Lerritz. He was one of my private friends. I am wearing a paper hat, folded up out of the daily press. And though the shadow is too deep, one half of my face can be seen to smile. It is a happy picture: one does not see the other half.

Since it is December, the garden at Montfort will be frosted and sere. It is a garden haunted by an ancient music. And over those airs, which to some modern ears sound so strange, but which were so young, so vulnerable, you will be able to hear the electric sting to the spent edge of a wave, vanishing from the beach back into the sea it came from, and the rattle of water over stones.

The toys lose nothing for not being new. There will always be another child.

What a pity it is now considered improper to die at home. The hospital has come to insist on its right to replace a kind of kindness we no longer have the ease or means or will to express, with a brisk bureaucracy of its own. It has been decided to rob death of its privacy, for privacy is the enemy of the state. Besides, to die at home is to disturb the resale value of the house, and I only had a lifetime lease.

We experts at nothing hand our bodies over to these experts at something, who take such comfort from what they can do for us that I suppose we owe them this last comfort of robbing us of the last comfort we looked forward to.

You can have better care here, they say. But the care they give us is not the care we need.

At Montfort there is a rustle among the cabbages. I am there again. I look out.

What catches my eye is not so much that there are small orange oiled-paper lanterns under the trees, as that they are hung at a height of two feet. Out from among the boles of the trees there comes an ingenious company of the most grave and delightful people. They are the cool small pilgrims who through my music move away, farther and farther. They have come to dance me their *chaconne*. It is their good-by. For at the end of an artist's life, all his creatures come to say good-by. No doubt when a God dies, his creatures do so also.

From every branch, from every tree, from the house, from the garden, all small and glittering they come, while in the distance, a foot away, you can see a swarm of luceoles. Or are they luceoles? From *"Adélaïde,"* from *"Gaspard,"* from the *"Tombeau de Couperin,"* they come, fom the *"Valses,"* from the *"Rhapsodie,"* *"Ma Mère l'Oye,"* from *"L'Enfant."* With Colette for company, they have come to pay their respects. They come from Laputa. They come from the past. And will I please come away with them?

It is touching.

Is the world any the less real, for being perceived false? There is a grace we disguise with grace. We are always imitating some good quality we used to have. We all have two faces. Unfortunately mine, though facing in opposite directions in the conventional manner, were identical.

One is one's self the mask. It never slips away. It is we who slip away from it, and so leave the eyeholes bare.

It is the morning of December 28, 1937, in a quiet clinic in the Rue Boileau. I have gone away, but I have left behind my mask.

In my case it was called music. Pick it up, and it plays a tune.

◑

Our Willows

from *The Little Square Review*

I remember the waterside,
Standing under willows,
Where the yellow cottonbird
Came to sing. I remember.
Remembering, I weep,
    My little breath.

I remember the growing corn
Where we sat among green rows,
Where the little leafbird
Came to sing. I remember.
Remembering, I weep,
    My little breath.

I remember the wide meadow,
Walking among yellow flowers,
Walking through blue flowers.
Alas, how long ago
We walked among flowers,
    O little breath.

Alas, how long ago we walked
Among bloodred flowers,
Happily walking.
Alas, how long ago,
    My little breath.

I walk there now,
Walk in ugly sorrow,
Breathe in sighs,
   O my little breath.

"Tewa" (from a translation by Herbert J. Spinden, *Astrov, 223*)

◐

New England Love

or
A Gift
of Silences

from *Confrontation*

The sharp day declines
like the shadow of a sundial
   or a saint in profile.

Three oranges
on a plate
in winter
sunlight.

The fruit is chilly and tart;
the guest
his grained hand
on the table
waits.

(What is essential in the soul
is all in the stillness of the face.)

———————

A month ago
it was so cold

in the South
the fruit trees froze;

farmers burned tires
beside the frozen trees
in small bright fires
to keep the fruit alive:

they called in ten thousand
West Indians
to harvest the crops
before all was lost

(and under the Northern night
    cold carved like milk
roofs houses earth and trees.)

———————

Like a chessboard
    the light laid out
in which we turned
    with motions of the dance
        (you, the guest, and I.)

The fruit survived the cold
to come to a colder
clime.

The heart survived its silences.

And we survived the blinding
white
match of afternoon across a table
with a dancer's definition
and his grace
(when tenderness burned like a matchflame on a face.)

You may have thought I was unaware of your sorrow
but I was aware of little else.
(Agonized for words the spirit fails
    words)
        . . . . the wonder is that I should have seen
the fruit at all: how at the last the sun
touched the still globes of orange incarnadine.
It is the love within the silence tells
                all.

SYBIL WULETICH

◐

The Depraved Angel of Marat / Sade

from *Contemporary Literature*

Theater critics have reported their failure to find a positive moral philosophy in Peter Weiss's *Marat/Sade*[1] and, at the same time, have praised its spectacle of nonsense and obscenity as an effective expression of the "total theater" of madness, cruelty, and debauch. Apparently entertained by the sights and sounds of this play, these critics have not grasped some simple facts: that there is no genuine debate between Sade (evil) and Marat (good) in the work; that, in fact, Sade has been given complete authority by Weiss to write a play within the play and to present his own perverse philosophy illustrated by the spectacles that have been so widely admired. Taking advantage of the helplessness of the insane of Charenton, whom he summons to act out roles in his interior drama, Sade intends to please a callous, indifferent, and self-satisfied society that seeks novel and outrageous means of stimulating itself.

It was not Weiss's intention in impersonating Sade, to acknowledge Sade's genius for discovering and elaborating upon all kinds of perversions. In fact, Weiss implies that the evil within Sade was not his essential character, but a histrionic pose he had contrived to avenge himself against his jailers. Weiss reads all of Sade's work as his "attack against a corrupt ruling

[1] *The Persecution and Assassination of Jean-Paul Marat as Performed by the Inmates of the Asylum of Charenton under the Direction of the Marquis de Sade.*

class," his attempt to annihilate all moral principles its life and self-respect are founded upon by recording and celebrating the encyclopedia of crimes he has researched. These crimes, he prophesies, one day will undermine every society. The libertine Sade, displaying himself as a monster in his most impressive and evil work, denied that goodness, charity, and conscience are innate human characteristics; he insisted that man is essentially asocial, apolitical, and amoral, and that any protests to the contrary are lies. But beneath this persona is an altogether different man who discloses himself privately in his letters, a being self-doubting and guilt-ridden, who condemns the image of grossness, vileness, and depravity he parades in front of the world. Peter Weiss is after the whole man in his play, where angel confronts demon. The demon dominates the stage to carry out his final study of revenge against his final jailers and the final regime he lived to debunk. (He lived through four: Monarchy, Republic, Consulate, and Empire.) And the angel with a vengeance transforms the world into an asylum and his play into a psychodrama and digs "the criminal out of" himself and mankind. Putting everyone, including himself, on trial for murder, he relives the overpowering traumatic event of his life, the French Revolution, even as, with a triumphant sneer on his face, he turns the French national tragedy of 1793 into a terrifying laughingstock.

Some critics believe that the angel in Sade first came to public notice with his endorsement of the French Revolution. In a stroke of genius, however, after the "First Rabble-Rousing of Jacques Roux" in which Sade burlesques the demagogues' glorification of the motives and the aims of the revolutionaries, Weiss has Sade confess that there was no altruism or idealism in his longing for the Revolution. Quite simply, he depended upon the Revolution to express once and for all his boundless hatred of his jailers. How ironic, then, that when the violence of the Revolution was unleashed, the real-life spectacle of cruelty confounded Sade utterly. Witnessing scenes of plunder, rape, and murder that matched his own imagined projections in scale and savagery, he was racked with nausea. Psychiatrists and literary critics have argued that Sade was constitu-

tionally equipped to tolerate limited acts of cruelty; but to
Weiss, Sade's revulsion against violence was moral: Sade did
not cease political activity when he realized that he could not
sentence political prisoners to the guillotine; for a long time he
remained within the rank and file of the hard-core revolutionaries, trying to modify the "violent methods of the progres-
sives," as Weiss reminds us in his postscript. But he was
grossly outnumbered, and "like the advocate of a third approach, fell between two stools." Then in an irony of history
that surpasses any contrivance of literature, at the very moment
the angel in Sade came to life, those who had advocated noble
and humane ideals turned into beasts, and all of his sublime
pleading for sanity and restraint fell on deaf ears. Exhausted by
madness and cruelty about him everywhere, dispossessed of everything worth living for, he craved death and anonymity: "I
want all trace of my existence to be wiped out."

Still, as Weiss presents it in *Marat/Sade,* Sade's desire to
write and to affirm mankind survived even at Charenton, although the life instinct is blocked not only by Sade's uncer-
tainties of what kind of creature he is, but by the perverse and
ludicrous demands Coulmier, the director of Charenton, makes
upon him. Denying Sade freedom of speech, Coulmier expects
him nonetheless to supply outlandish and debauched scenes that
his Parisian audience has come all the way to Charenton to see.
And still Sade tries to do the impossible: to know and be honest
with himself, to reach his audience, to please Coulmier by giving
him the filth he wants, and to jolt him out of his complacency
through a kind of shock therapy. He moves in and out of the
scenes, now as the central character craving contact with the audience, now posing as Marat's foil, now histrionically advertising
his own depravity, now pleading for salvation and peace and be-
moaning the brutality and violence of war. At times he gives
stage directions to the actors, as though he were sanctioning the
purges and inciting the mob to violence. Then he "turns his back
on all the nations" and declares his indifference to human suffering. Although the feeling with which he writes betrays his
undying love of mankind, nothing in his play—not religion, sci-

ence, education, politics, God, freedom, reason, individualism, imagination, nature, life, not even death—is spared his mockery and denunciation.

The demon in Sade boasts a philosophy at worst depraved, at best nihilistic, and uses the inmates to burlesque the heroics of some of the revolutionaries. By casting them shrewdly, Sade knows he can rely upon their individual genius—their particular psychosis—to undermine the ideals they declaim. The paranoid actor who plays Marat shares his zeal in tracking down and exterminating the enemies. Railing against the moderates for "wearing their scruples as protective clothing," Marat steps out of the tub stark naked, as though to throw his physical weight behind the argument; but the mock heroic is abruptly silenced when a muddled, pathetic, and exhausted Marat "stumbles around the arena as if about to faint." The actor who plays Roux, priest turned revolutionary, screams freedom, strait-jacketed, and darts toward the audience like a jack-in-the-box. Duperret, trying to negotiate a coalition with Corday, is played by an erotomaniac who must constantly be restrained from pawing her. And the historical Corday, a woman of daring and determination, is played by a young girl who, on the verge of falling asleep, must be held up and prodded to action. The stage directions specifying lewd or uninhibited behavior indicate that Sade recognizes the needs of the patients but also that he is ready to exploit them to repeat the same argument again and again through their spontaneous gestures and grimaces: that civilization is a hypocritical fiction enabling a few to indulge themselves at the expense of the many poor, and that all noble endeavors to provide dignity and freedom both express and result in man's sexual abuse, mutilation, and murder of his fellow man.

Inasmuch as he is both guilty of perpetrating such crimes against humanity and himself a victim of others, he continues to stage (and sanction) spectacles of cruelty as a symbolic re-enactment of crimes he endorses, all the while condemning those same crimes with another, the angelic part of himself. As he confesses his sins and his guilt in the famous whipping scene

—which incidentally has been widely celebrated for its spectacle, but not for the eloquence and meaning of its poetry—whipping serves to exorcise the evil within him and to satisfy his continuing need for masochistic pleasure. And to the very center of his own conflict, Sade draws his audience by assailing us with the many insane whose grotesque and obscene antics horrify and sadden us, and cause us at the same time to gape and leer, to be perversely fascinated.

As Weiss imagines Sade's audience, it felt no conflict in its response; it came simply to see a scandalous show forbidden in any legitimate theater in Paris and in the meantime, with false modesty, disguised its motives by rationalizing, as Coulmier does at the beginning of the play, that Sade's drama is intended as psychotherapy for the benefit of his patients. But Sade, who went out of his way to call evil by its right name, will not tolerate hypocrisy and he never ceases to remind us that he can perceive Coulmier's innate vulgarity. Though Coulmier's censorship laws prevent Sade from insulting him openly, Sade's indirect means are effective; to mock and exaggerate Coulmier's pretense at decency, he devises outlandishly degraded scenes of murder and then cynically rationalizes them thus: since murder (the essential law of mankind) has been deflated in their times, made commonplace or "technocratic" by the cheapness and efficiency of the means and the uncountable numbers of the objects, one must reaffirm man by personalizing and meticulously staging mock trials and murders. And, to practice what he preaches, he stages with infinite care the persecution and assassination of Marat in his own play.

In their initial dialogues, Sade treats Marat with respect, indeed with genuine sympathy and understanding. Some of Sade's most eloquent lines are reserved for Marat in his explanation that "nature's indifference" has made him love mankind and answer men's pleas for help. Sade would never have permitted Marat to speak so persuasively at this point had he not strongly agreed with Marat; still he refuses to permit his own love of mankind to alter his view of reality as he sees it, and posing as the devil's disciple, he replies to Marat's defense of altruism by claiming that "nature's indifference" has taught him (Sade) to hate and destroy man. Later he is stricken by the sight of a patient who forgets where he is, begins to rave, and is forcibly restrained by the guards. With an involuntary resurgence of compassion, Sade asks sadly:

> Before deciding what is wrong and what is right
> first we must find out what we are
> I
> do not know myself
> No sooner have I discovered something
> than I begin to doubt it
> and I have to destroy it again
> What we do is just a shadow of what we want to do
> and the only truths we can point to
> are the ever-changing truths of our own experience
> I do not know if I am hangman or victim
> for I imagine the most horrible tortures
> and as I describe them I suffer them myself
> There is nothing that I could not do and every-
>   thing fills me with horror
> And I see that other people also
> suddenly change themselves into strangers
> and are driven to unpredictable acts
> A little while ago I saw my tailor
> a gentle cultured man who liked to talk philosophy
> I saw him foam at the mouth
> and raging and screaming attack with a cudgel
> a man from Switzerland
> a large man heavily armed
> and destroy him utterly
> and then I saw him
> tear open the breast of the defeated man
> saw him take out the still beating heart
> and swallow it.

Sade is anguished by the pessimistic answers that reality forces him to give to his own questions, while now it is Marat, self-absorbed, scratching himself, who does not hear Sade gently mocking his sudden indifference to human misery: "Marat I know/that you'd give up your fame and all the love of the people/for a few days of health/you lie in your bath/as if you were in the pink water of the womb."

In the following episodes, Sade takes Marat less and less seriously and the dialogue deteriorates first into a mock debate, then a mock trial. Clearly emerging as Sade's victim, Marat is attacked from all sides: from Sade telling him that he has squandered his energy on nonsense; from figures out of Marat's past, marshaled pitilessly to accuse him of being a bluff, egotist, and liar; from scientists, historians, and artists who denounce Marat's work as trivia, closing off one avenue after another of self-defense against his detractors; and finally from the unruly insane who completely surround Marat, crying for their freedom and for revenge against new oppressors, now that the Revolution has gone berserk and left them worse off than they were. Marat crumbles in the battering he receives, thus demonstrating one of Sade's laws: that no idealist is spared the fate of being reduced to a beast. (Weiss writes in the postscript that his Marat is a duplicate of the historical person; nevertheless, under Sade's direction Marat suffers a swift decline from idealist to madman.) Marat scribbles and speaks dryly of work he must do. His suspicions that enemies are plotting against his life mount and quicken into hysteria. And toward the end of the play, the paranoid actor consumes the historical Marat.

Marat's final degradation is staged in slow motion so that no one can forget the uttermost indignity reserved for him before his death: that he must see his political compact with Corday in what Sade protests is its true terms—a gross sexual alliance. Arranging the scene carefully, Sade has Corday enter Marat's apartment to stab him and instructs Marat to wake up and concentrate on lust: "Marat/forget the rest/there's nothing else/beyond the body/Look." Then, as he brings this tableau to an end with Corday caressing Marat—and here I believe the action on stage should be arrested for a full sixty seconds—Sade makes us now wonder uneasily to what new heights of perversity he will yet aspire.

Writing an epigraph to this tableau, Sade then orders the herald to announce that Marat's execution is to be postponed until "Marat can hear and gasp with his last breath" the significance of all of his life's work. And then in a horrifying parody of incantation and oracle, four singers, dressed in "the cap of the Revolution," recite a chronicle of chaotic events that followed Marat's death; that chronicle, mingling nonsense verse and nursery rhyme, makes unmistakable the failure of everything Marat hoped the Revolution would accomplish. Even his death would be no martyrdom, but rather the garish beginning of the purge which robbed (purified) the Revolution of all its meaning (its illusions).

> We're beheading them all (1793)
> Duperret
> and Corday
> executed in the same old way
> Robespierre has to get on (1794)
> he gets rid of Danton
> That was spring
> comes July
> and old Robespierre has to die
> Three rebellions a year (1795)
> but we're still of good cheer
> Malcontents
> all have been
> taught their lesson by the guillotine[.]

The message is devastating: the final end of all revolutions is a passionless, dehumanized repetition of murders, impelled by the same law, the principle of a repetition-compulsion in the unconscious mind that drives men to insane asylums. The death instinct, Sade implies bitterly, sadly, and sardonically, generates all noble, high-sounding ideals that can never improve things as they are, for men do not really desire the good and the beautiful, but only to kill and be killed. And finally to demonstrate the killer instinct, he stands by, making sure the lunatic who plays Corday executes her role exactly as he prescribed: that slowly, slowly the knife is driven into Marat's heart.

Satiated with horror, Coulmier extracts a platitudinous moral from Sade's play. But Sade is determined to have the last word. As though spontaneously demonstrating Sade's beliefs, the insane of Charenton, vaguely comprehending their roles as revolutionaries and unaware of the distinction between art and life, begin to march threateningly toward the audience. Coulmier, in hysterical self-defense, orders the curtain lowered. And, most likely, so would we, if for a moment we thought that the few actors who fly out into the audience after the play ends really intended to spring at our jugulars. In fearing the actors and relying upon Coulmier to draw the curtain, we implicitly align ourselves with the Coulmiers of the world who want to be entertained but not absorbed into the play. That is why, if we are to take the play seriously, we must try to understand what the insane in their gross and violent invasion of our safe world were pleading for, what claims the angelic Sade and Weiss believed they had a right to make.

In this play through the character of Sade, Peter Weiss has expressed his profound disillusionment with the Communist Revolution—a view he has since rejected—for the reason, it seems, that his faith in man's sanity and in the strength of his desire and capacity to survive is deeply shaken. Indeed, how many revolutions inspired by the wish to improve man's lot have ended in anarchy and bloodbath? An idealist tormented by history might find some relief from his nightmares in cynical answers to morally complex and tragic questions. And perhaps, therefore, like the demonic Marquis de Sade, Weiss tried from time to time to protect himself from massive disappointments and to take revenge against mankind for disappointing him, by denying that there was or ever could be any distinction between insanity and sanity, death and life. In Sade's passion for vengeance, he tries to forget that what really horrifies him are the thoughts that revolutions seem almost invariably to end in a reign of terror and that what he really yearns is to believe beyond belief in the possibility of man's devising creative institutions and laws to liberate and shape the life instinct. Not that those beliefs are explicitly advanced in the play. On the contrary, at the end, Sade laughs as he watches the insane incited to rebellion and Coulmier intimidated by his own patients. If one is forced to choose, then violence in a madhouse universe is surely preferable to the stupor to which the poor and helpless are subdued by the Coulmiers of the world. And yet to settle for violence as the only alternative to repression is cynical, since the price in human misery is so high. That is why the Sade who throughout the play ridicules all structures as pretenses of positive action and commitment and at the end, by inciting the actors to rebellion, implicity equates art and anarchy—that Sade must not have the final word.

In fact, the angelic Sade could never have endorsed so cynical, nihilistic, and detached a view of civilization and its discontents. It is true that Sade's dialogue and stage directions betray the cruel delight—perhaps his most contemptible trait—with which he incites in the mad a desire for self-expression that he constantly frustrates and that he knows is being undermined by their own half awareness of their grotesque failure to rise to the grandeur of the historical moment and to identify with the persons they represent. Yet at the same time, his play is a gift to the anonymous and discarded insane, given with a measure of love and compassion; through symbolic words and actions that ring true to them, he enables them to experience, if only during the time those lines are spoken, some connection with the world and offers them an alternative, however grotesque and transitory, to total withdrawal and suicide. Against the backdrop of buffoonery and slapstick that demeans the mad actors and against the grotesque and pathetic expression of their delusions of grandeur—Sade's monstrous and, under the circumstances, tragically ironic exaggeration of man's vanity, which makes them a bizarre picture indeed for any audience—Marat's eloquent declaration of love for mankind, Sade's self-lacerating confession of squandering his life on obscene fantasies of revenge, and Roux's desperate plea, late in the play and running against the tide of nihilism, to "take sides" resound in our ears and flood the heart with the shock and dismay that first assaulted us as we watched the mad silently moving on stage at the beginning of the play, in a thousand different contortions of misery and degradation. Undeniably, this play delivers a shattering blow to structure, language, and action—in a word, to art and life. But the sublime, however mangled, survives. The overriding tone, tragic and not burlesque, feeds our compassion for the angelic Sade (virtually eclipsed at the end) and our life instinct impelling us to confront the demon as antagonist, depose him, and answer the questions asked throughout—can Sade be saved? can mankind be saved?

At the end of the play, when the insane of Charenton negate the difference between art and life, *Marat/Sade* raises questions that concern the future of the theater of cruelty and our feelings on violence in general. Let the artist who wishes to pose as paterfamilias think long before he indulges his appetite for spectacle by rediscovering the madhouse as the arena of his play. And let critics explain why they are enthusiastic about the novelty and ingenuity in utilizing the defects of madmen as stage action. Thus far virtually every critic has affirmed the spectacle of *Marat/Sade* and called vices virtues in trying to justify pornography, cruelty, and barbarism on pseudo-philosophical or pseudo-aesthetic grounds. But I suggest that to permit oneself to be entertained under these circumstances is immoral, as immoral, in fact, as the enjoyment the demonic Sade gets in humiliating his actors, and as immoral as was the response of Sade's own audience, which Weiss, characterizing it as callous and hypocritical in the extreme, offers us as an example of what not to be. Furthermore, such entertainment is self-deceptive and potentially self-destructive. For pleasure obtained at the cruel expense of another's dignity dulls the edge of conscience, makes us forget, for example, that in his play the demonic Sade has gone out of his way to advance his murderous designs on mankind, on Marat in particular. Sade himself tries to entertain—but gives entertainment of a low order, as though he were throwing slop to pigs; and warning us again and again against being entertained, he reveals his conflicted desires to save mankind from coarse and immoral pleasures and conversely to savor the dramatic irony of watching the degradation of his audience whose destruction is part of his general scheme to annihilate mankind. One of Sade's main theses in this play is that man's tendency to exploit violence as a source of excitement generates and sustains violence. For was not this, in fact, Sade's own weakness and his vice? In one of the most powerful episodes in the play, "Marquis de Sade Is Whipped," Sade admits that he learned this bitter lesson when the French Revolution forced him to renounce the reality of violence which he had in his inimitable way made unreal, illusory, pleasurable in his fantasies. But now in this play, even while as the demon he feeds us violent entertainment with the intention of destroying us, as the angel he pleads that his play, which as illusion will insulate us from the destructive pain of real violence, may impel us to encounter the meanings of violence seriously. We might come to realize then that the genuine threat to our existence lies in the perception not of some external violence but of the inner violence of mind and soul he speaks of powerfully in the tableau, "Continuation of the Conversation Between Marat and Sade"—the kind of violence that can suddenly cause his respectable tailor for no reason whatever to spring upon an innocent man, kill him, then rip out and devour his heart.

Marat/Sade moves us with the realization that the knowledge of the abyss might save us from the abyss. To be saved, beside instinct, of course, one needs the intelligence to understand that survival with dignity and freedom requires not subduing and manipulating what might be construed to be external threats, but, first of all, before one even begins relating to others, knowing oneself and achieving an inner harmony and peace that Sade himself was denied, and, thereupon, it is to be hoped, the intelligence and honesty to call things by their right names. To be saved, we must be capable of humane responses, careful interpretations, and clear judgments, not casual and obscure affirmations and renunciations. Nothing perhaps is more difficult and more important. And, therefore, let us begin by understanding precisely why and how Peter Weiss intended us to renounce his own play.

JAMES TATE

When Kabir Died

from *Unicorn Journal*

They fought over his body.
The Mohammedans wanted to bury

the remains, while the Hindus
desired to burn them.

They argued so for days.
Then Kabir appeared before them!

and told them to go
to the casket and remove his

shroud. Both parties obeyed.
They found, in place

of the corpse, a heap
of flowers, half of which were

taken to Maghar by
the Mohammedans and buried,

the other half to Benares
and burned by the Hindus.

As Kabir himself has said,
we can reach the goal

without crossing the road.
Or, no: at the heart

of the Universe, white
music is blossoming.

JOHN WOODS

◑

Asking Directions
in California

from *Shenandoah*

1

I'm a stranger here myself, she said.
There's a banquet of streets
and I'm on a diet of discovery.
Hand over hand, I'm hauling myself in
through patience and a long memory.
I'm an uneasy tenant, gathering
mirror pieces from broken compacts
until in and out walk together.
One day at a time, one street
at a time. One of these nights
my cat won't come back.
Then I'll tell you where I am.
You can take it from there.

2

Farflung, diffuse, unstable,
hidden behind the dead end of swamps,
shut off by riots and hoses,
diving under channels and coming up roses,
following mail trucks to the morgue,
known by the deaf and dumb,
recently parachuted Armenians,
and drunks, who can't find their way

out of a bottleneck, models
with their heads in their hat boxes . . .

3

The women in our family
have always been artistically inclined.
We make strange maps
where it's always downhill.
You've plenty of gas; your oil's up;
but there's salt on your tailpipe.
You were weaned on a snowball, too.
Here, if you spit,
up yawns a national park, bears,
beer cans, bicycle paths,
and likelihood, a key word,
of being trampled by frosted baseball teams.
Drink Fornical, always bear right,
and you've got it.
Any end to a means,
there's a state flower for you.

4

I'm a stranger self than here.
You can't miss it.

◐

For Poets

from *Camels Coming*

Stay beautiful
but dont stay down underground too long
Dont turn into a mole
or a worm
or a root
or a stone

Come on out into the sunlight
Breathe in trees
Knock out mountains
Commune with snakes
& be the very hero of birds

Dont forget to poke your head up
& blink
think
Walk all around
Swim upstream

Dont forget to fly

JOHN WIENERS

◑

Invitation Au Voyage II*

from *Angel Hair*

Look, how rain fallen through the night
leaves woods hot, moist and calm,
how bird skims across grass
with no car in sight,
awaiting return.

This that promised land *au bout du monde*
where humid winds blow against your ankles,
dragon lilies on fences open to the sun,
Baudelaire's song heard again afternoon's vagabond.

Your lips a history of the heart,
your hands hot deserts on my brow.
Your eyes grey mirrors I would drown
for if to die would do it now

this kiss in my mouth,
your words the vow.

My dear girl, I know no way
to go on loving you
but this one. Our lives entwined
as a huntsman's bow.

Oh archer, skill my hands
land this arrow close to bounds

* See Preface, p. x.

that we cleave as wings on air
before transparent stranger appears
to take her away
in form of death or love

I'll take her away with me somewhere.

RICHARD BRAUTIGAN

◑

It's Raining in Love[*]

from *Hollow Orange*

I don't know what it is,
but I distrust myself
when I start to like a girl
　　a lot.

It makes me nervous.
I don't say the right things
or perhaps I start
　　to examine,
　　　　　　　　evaluate,
　　　　　　　　　　　　compute
　　what I am saying.

If I say, "Do you think it's going to rain?"
and she says, "I don't know,"
I start thinking:　Does she really like me?

In other words
I get a little creepy.

A friend of mine once said,
"It's twenty times better to be friends
　　with someone
than it is to be in love with them."

I think he's right and besides,
it's raining somewhere, programming flowers

* See Preface, p. x.

and keeping snails happy.
    That's all taken care of.

        BUT
if a girl likes me a lot
and starts getting real nervous
and suddenly begins asking me funny questions
and looks sad if I give the wrong answers
and she says things like,
"Do you think it's going to rain?"
and I say, "It beats me,"
and she says, "Oh,"
and looks a little sad
at the clear blue California sky,
I think: Thank God, it's you, baby, this time
    instead of me.

NOTES ON THE CONTRIBUTORS

A. R. AMMONS ("Guitar Recitativos") is Associate Professor of English at Cornell. First published by the *Hudson Review* in 1954, he has since completed six books, most recently *Selected Poems* (Cornell University Press, 1968). In 1969 he was awarded a Guggenheim Fellowship and the Traveling Fellowship of the American Academy of Arts and Letters.

JAMES APPLEWHITE ("House of Blue by the River's Curve") earned his B.A., M.A., and Ph.D. degrees at Duke University, completing his doctorate in 1964. His poems have appeared in four anthologies and in many small magazines including *Red Clay Reader, Carolina Quarterly*, and *Sou'Wester*. At present he is teaching a course on the English Romantic poets at the University of North Carolina at Greensboro.

JOHN ASHBERY ("Paris by Night") was educated at Columbia and Harvard. His poetry has been collected in four books: *Some Trees* (Yale, 1956), *The Tennis Court Oath* (Wesleyan, 1962), *Rivers and Mountains* (Holt, Rinehart and Winston, 1966), and *Dream of Spring* (Dutton, 1970). "Paris by Night" is a chapter from *A Nest of Ninnies* (Dutton, 1969), a novel written in collaboration with James Schuyler.

ELIZABETH BARTLETT ("The Walnut Tree") is the poetry editor of *E.T.C.*, a quarterly review of semantics. Her poems, essays, and stories have appeared in *Harper's, Saturday Review, Commentary*, and other magazines. "The Walnut Tree" will appear in her seventh book of poems, *Address in Time*, to be published by the Windfall Press, Chicago.

SCOTT BATES ("Fable of the Third Christmas Camel") is the author of *Guillaume Apollinaire* (Twayne World Author Series) and of poems published in numerous small magazines. He served in Europe during World War II and later received a Fulbright Scholarship for study in France. He is now Professor of French Literature at the University of the South at Sewanee. His anthology, *Poems of War Resistance*, was published by Grossman in 1969.

MICHAEL BENEDIKT ("The Wings of the Nose") lives in New York City, where he was born in 1935. He received his B.A. and M.A. degrees from New York University. A collection of his poems, *The Body*, was published by the Wesleyan University Press in 1968.

WENDELL BERRY ("10. [from Window Poems]") is a native and resident of Henry County, Kentucky. Since the fall of 1964 he has taught English at the University of Kentucky, where he received his A.B. and M.A. degrees. He has published a book of essays, two novels, and three poetry collections; the latest is *Findings* (Prairie Press, Iowa City, 1969).

JOHN D. BOYD ("The Dry Salvages") is a Jesuit priest and an associate professor of English at Fordham University. He is author of *The Function of Mimesis and Its Decline* (Harvard, 1968), and of many articles, poems, and reviews in such magazines as *Catholic World*, *English Language Notes*, and *Spirit*. Currently he is at work on a study of poetic theory, *Falcon in His Riding*, and a book of religious essays, *Redeeming the Time*.

RICHARD BRAUTIGAN ("It's Raining in Love") was Poet-in-Residence at the California Institute of Technology in 1967. He has contributed to many small magazines and his published books include *A Confederate General from Big Sur*, *Please Plant This Book*, and *In Watermelon Sugar*. At present he is working on a novel set in the American West.

DAVID BROMIGE ("Taking Heart") has published three poetry collections: *The Gathering* (Sunbooks, 1965) and *Please, Like Me* and *The Ends of the Earth* (both Black Sparrow Press, 1968). His work has also appeared in *Open Spaces*, *Occident*, and *Odda Tala*. Mr. Bromige reports that he "does not like his life written down." Anyone interested in further information, he writes, should contact him at Serendipity Books, Shattuck Avenue, Berkeley.

ROBERT GRANT BURNS ("An Exhibit of Paintings by George Inness") is a pianist living in Austin, Texas. A frequent contributor to small magazines, he has published two books: *Nettie Petty's Recollections* (privately printed, Austin, 1965), and *Quiet World* (Graficas Orion Press, Madrid, 1967). He writes that "the Inness poem was written after viewing a very large Inness exhibit held in Austin in 1966. I have a special interest in the faithful and perhaps even plodding artist who, after years of work, unexpectedly finds freedom and mastery."

CHRISTOPHER BURSK ("Adjust, Adjust") was born in 1943 in Cambridge, Massachusetts. A graduate of Tufts (B.A. 1965) and Boston University (M.A. 1966), he teaches English at Shaw University in Raleigh, North Carolina. His work has appeared in one book, *Three New Poets* (Pym-Randall Press, Cambridge, 1966), and several magazines—*Trace, Premiere,* and *Yankee.*

GRACE BUTCHER ("Some Sort of Death") is a former United States track champion—record holder in the half-mile (1958–1961) and winner of two cross-country championships. Her third book of poems, *In the Time of Revolution,* was recently published by Random House. A teacher of English at the Geauga County Academic Center of Kent State University, she serves on the staffs of both the *Hiram Poetry Review* and *Distance Running News.*

JACK CADY ("The Shark") earned his B.A. at the University of Louisville in 1961. His work has appeared in a wide variety of periodicals, from *Twigs* magazine to the *Atlantic Monthly.* At present he is Assistant Professor of English at the University of Washington.

GUY A. CARDWELL ("Time of the *Fermeture*") was born in 1905 in Savannah, Georgia. Educated at the University of North Carolina and Harvard, he served as Professor of English at many universities, currently the State University of New York at Albany. He writes, "I have published seven books, all 'scholarly,' including edited volumes; about twenty-five articles; many reviews. My major project for the next one or two years will be two volumes on ideas and images in the Old South, but I also hope to publish a volume of short stories."

WARREN CARRIER ("The Image Waits") is Dean of the College of Arts and Letters at San Diego State University. The founder of the *Quarterly Review of Literature*, he has published in many small magazines—*Poetry Northwest, Tiger's Eye*, and *Accent*, among others. The most recent of his five books is the poetry collection *Toward Montebello* (Harper and Row, 1966).

HAYDEN CARRUTH ("Sonnet") writes from Johnson, Vermont, "I have published five books of poetry, the most recent entitled *Contra Mortem* (Crow's Mark Press). I have also published a novel and a book of criticism. I have two books scheduled for publication in 1970: an anthology of modern American poetry (untitled), to be published by Bantam; and a collection of my own poems, titled (confusingly) *The Clay Hill Anthology*, to be published by the Prairie Press. I live here in farm country at the northern end of the Green Mountains, and make my living as a free-lance writer and editor."

JANE COOPER ("In Silence Where We Breathe") teaches at Sarah Lawrence College. In 1960 she was awarded a Guggenheim Fellowship, and in February 1969 Macmillan published her first book of poetry, *The Weather of Six Mornings*. She writes, "I'm interested in sequences of poems and long poems as well as lyrics. 'In Silence Where We Breathe' is in fact the sixth of a very loose sequence of eight poems, all concerned with coming to speech."

SAM CORNISH ("The River") was born in 1933 in Baltimore, where he went to Booker T. Washington Junior High School. His poems have appeared in many small magazines, among them *The Smith, Journal of Black Poetry*, and *Radical America*. To date he has published four poetry collections; *Chicory* (Association Press), *Sam* (Harcourt, Brace and World), *Winters* (William Young), and *Generations* (Bean Bag Press).

JAMES M. COX ("Edgar Poe: Style as Pose") is Professor of English at Dartmouth. He is the author of *Mark Twain: The Fate of Humor* (Princeton, 1966) and the editor of *Robert Frost* (a collection of essays on Frost for Prentice-Hall's Twentieth Century Views Series, 1961). He is now at work on a study of Hawthorne.

LESLIE EPSTEIN ("Playground") was educated at Yale, Oxford, and UCLA. " 'Playground,' " he writes, "was my first published short story; 'Disciple of Bacon' (*New American Review*, 4) was my second, and so far last. I have also published, not to perish, a good deal of criticism. Since 1965 I've taught English at Queens College in Flushing, where I'm now an assistant professor. I was married to a girl named Ilene in the fall of 1969. I own an Opel Kadette, which does not start on rainy days. I am working on a novel, half-complete."

DONALD FINKEL ("The Garbage Wars") is Poet in Residence at Washington University in St. Louis. In the early fifties he began publishing his poems in *Hudson Review*, *Poetry*, *Western Review*, and other magazines. Since then his work has been collected in five books, most recently *Answer Back* (Atheneum, 1968). "The Garbage Wars" is the title poem of his next book, scheduled by Atheneum for publication in 1970.

ROBERT FITZGERALD ("James Agee: A Memoir") was educated at Harvard (where he first met Agee) and at Trinity College, Cambridge. From 1936 to 1949 he was a writer for *Time*. He published his first book, *Poems*, in 1935 and has since published several other collections. His 1961 translation of the *Odyssey* won the Bollingen Award that year.

ALAN FRIEDMAN ("Daughter of a Bitch") was born in Brooklyn and educated at Harvard. His stories have appeared in the *New American Review*, *Hudson Review*, and *Mademoiselle*. At present he is at work on a novel which is to be published in 1970 by Harper and Row.

PATRICIA GOEDICKE ("You Could Pick It Up") was born Patricia McKenna in Boston and brought up in New Hampshire, where her father was resident psychiatrist at Dartmouth. She holds degrees from Middlebury (B.A. 1953) and Ohio University (M.A. 1963) and teaches English at Hunter College in New York. Her first volume of poems, *Between Oceans*, was published (Harcourt, Brace and World) in January 1968.

ELY GREEN ("Aristocratic Mouse") was born in 1893 in Sewanee, Tennessee. A hunter and trapper in his youth, he later became a sergeant in France during World War I. After the war he moved around the western United States until the mid-twenties, when he settled in California and worked as a butler and cook on private yachts and as a caterer to Hollywood parties. For a time he was butler to Douglas Fairbanks and Mary Pickford. In 1965 the Seabury Press published *Ely: An Autobiography*, covering the first eighteen years of his life. In 1970 the University of Massachusetts Press will publish his complete autobiography, which includes both the Seabury text and "Aristocratic Mouse." Mr. Green died in April 1968.

JONATHAN GREENE ("O they left me") is a designer for the University of Kentucky Press. Since 1965 he has also managed his own publishing venture, the Gnomon Press. He is the author of four books of poetry: *The Reckoning* (Matter Press, Annandale-on-Hudson, New York, 1966), *Instance* (Buttonwood Press, Lexington, Kentucky, 1968), *The Lapidary* (Black Sparrow Press, Los Angeles, 1969), and *A 17th Century Garner* (Buttonwood Press, 1969).

RAMON GUTHRIE ("Cantata for Saint Budóc's Day") was born in New York City in 1896. Self-supporting from the age of fourteen, he describes his education as "privately tutored by myself." He did, however, study at the Sorbonne and holds a doctorate in law from the University of Toulouse and an honorary M.A. from Dartmouth, where he taught French and comparative literature from 1930 to 1965. He has published two novels and six books of poetry, the latest of which are *Graffiti* (Macmillan, 1959) and *Asbestos Phoenix* (Funk and Wagnalls, 1969).

JIM HARRISON ("Thin Ice") has written two books of poetry, *Plainsong* and *Locations*, both published by Norton, and was awarded a Guggenheim grant in 1969. He writes, "I am currently living on a farm near Lake Leelanau, Michigan, with my wife, daughter, two dogs, and one horse, controlling the fish population of the lower peninsula."

DAVID IGNATOW ("Against the Evidence") teaches writing at the School of the Arts of Columbia University. Five of his poetry collections have been published by the Wesleyan University Press: *Poems* (1948), *The Gentle Weight Lifter* (1955), *Say Pardon* (1962), *Figures of the Human* (1964), and *Rescue the Dead* (1968). His *Collected Poems 1934–1969* is scheduled for publication in 1970.

EMMETT JARRETT ("Human Relations") was born in Louisiana in 1939 and educated at Columbia. He has published one small book of poems, *The Days* (Beanbag Press, Cambridge, Massachusetts, 1968), and is represented in Ron Schreiber's anthology *31 New American Poets* (Hill and Wang, 1969). He now heads the humanities program at St. Ann's School in Brooklyn Heights, New York.

RODERICK JELLEMA ("Poem Beginning with a Line Memorized at School") is Associate Professor of English at the University of Maryland. He is General Editor of a series of critical booklets, *Contemporary Writers in Christian Perspective*, published by Eerdmans Press. His poems have appeared in *Dryad, Nimrod,* and the *Harvard Advocate*.

STANLEY KAUFFMANN, born in New York City in 1916, is the film and theater critic of *The New Republic*. A former drama critic of *The New York Times,* he is a Visiting Professor of Drama at Yale University. He is the author of two collections of film criticism, seven novels that have been published here and abroad, and is currently editing an encyclopedia of film for the Thomas Y. Crowell Company.

GALWAY KINNELL ("The Bear") was born in Providence, Rhode Island, in 1927 and attended Princeton, where he received an A.B. in 1948. Houghton Mifflin has published his one novel, *Black Light* (1966), and three books of poems: *What a Kingdom It Was* (1960), *Flower Herding on Mount Monadnock* (1964), and *Body Rags* (1968). He has also published a number of translations, mostly from the French.

MARY NORBERT KÖRTE ("Beginning of Lines: Response to 'Albion Moonlight' ") was born and raised in California. At present she lives in Berkeley, where, she writes, "I make enough money to live on by working as a field assistant in a research project of the University of California Psychology Clinic, but I am primarily a poet. How could I be otherwise?" Her work has appeared in such magazines as *Aldebaran Review*, *dust*, and *Eikon*, and in five books, the latest of which is *The Generation of Love* (with pictures by Jess Villava; Bruce Publishing, New York).

ELAINE KRAF ("Westward and Up a Mountain") was educated at Hunter College in New York and at The New School, where she studied poetry under Kenneth Koch. "Westward and Up a Mountain" was her first published work. She expanded the story into a novel called *I am Clarence*, published in 1970 by Doubleday.

ROBERT LAX (" 'Afternoon' from The Journals of Robert Lax [Vol. I]") was born in New York City in 1915. In the past thirty years he has held a variety of jobs: movie critic (*Time* magazine, 1945); screenwriter (Hollywood 1946–1948); English instructor (Connecticut College 1948–1949). His work has appeared in many magazines —*Commonweal*, *American Scholar*, and the *Lugano Review*, among others. Since 1963 he has lived in a hut in the Greek Islands.

PHILIP LEVINE ("The Lost Angel") was first published in the *Antioch Review* in 1955. He is the author of *On the Edge* (Stone Wall Press, 1963), *Not This Pig* (Wesleyan University Press, 1968), and *Five Detroits* (Unicorn Press, 1969). He reports that his latest book, *They Feed the Lion*, is "now being fought over by various houses."

DICK LOURIE ("1966") is an editor of *Hanging Loose* magazine. He is also a musician, playing trumpet, guitar, and autoharp. He lives in rural New Jersey, where, he reports, "I'm self-employed in both poetry and music; as poet I do high-school and college programs, and as musician I work as a free-lance specialist with preschool children." In 1968 a collection of his poems, *The Dream Telephone*, was published by John Gill's New Press in Trumansburg, New York.

EUGENE MCCARTHY ("Indiana I: Three Bad Signs") is the senior Senator from Minnesota. He has published five books on politics, most recently *Year of the People* (Doubleday, 1968). In 1970 a collection of his poems will be published by Doubleday.

SANDRA MCPHERSON ("Preparation") lives with her husband and daughter in Portland, Oregon. She studied at San Jose State College and at the University of Washington. A collection of her poems, *Elegies for the Hot Season*, is scheduled for publication by the Indiana University Press in 1970.

RAY MIZER ("Dirge") is Professor of English at DePauw University in Greencastle, Indiana. His work has appeared in *American Bard, Western Poet, Fiddlehead, Galley Sail Review*, and elsewhere. A twenty-page section of his poems appeared in *Indiana Sesquicentennial Poets*, published by the Ball State University Press in 1967.

REBECCA NEWTH ("Hannibal over the mountains . . .") was born in 1940 and educated at Michigan State University. "Hannibal over the mountains . . ." is her second published work; her first appeared in *Essence* magazine. She is married, has two children, and lives in Guilford, Connecticut.

RICHARD R. O'KEEFE ("Mozart in Nova Scotia") was born in Pittsburgh in 1934 and was educated at Duquesne (B.A., 1957) and Pennsylvania State universities (M.A., 1959). His work has appeared in *Antioch Review, Northwest Review*, and *Little Review of the Pacific Northwest*. An assistant professor of English at Carnegie-Mellon University in Pittsburgh, he has finished a book which, he writes, "I can't get anyone to publish."

JOHN PAUKER ("Flighty Poem") was born in 1920 "across the street from the National Museum in Budapest." Formerly an editor of *Furioso* and currently an advisory editor of *Voyages*, his stories and poems have appeared in scores of small magazines. He has published two volumes of poetry, and his play *Moonbirds* (adapted from *Les Oiseaux de Lune* by Marcel Aymé) was produced on Broadway in 1959. At present he lives with his wife, Shoo-Shoo, in Washington, where together they "run at a snail's pace an art gallery known as the Fun House."

GEORGE QUASHA ("Rilke's Sixth Elegy Transposed") teaches at the State University of New York at Stony Brook, where he started the Stony Brook Poetics Foundation ("a nonprofit corporation with the central purpose of publishing poetry, translation, and poetics"). Quasha's work has appeared in *Poetry*, *Fire Exit*, and the *Washington Square Review*, and a group of his poems may be found in *Five Blind Men* (Sumac Press, 1969).

CARL RAKOSI ("I Had to Pull the Little Maple Tree") is Writer in Residence at the University of Wisconsin. Born in Berlin in 1903, he has lived in the U.S. since 1910. His early work, collected in 1941 as *Selected Poems* (New Directions), had appeared in many of the little magazines of the period, including Ezra Pound's *Exile*, the *Little Review*, *Hound and Horn*, and *transition*. "However," he writes, "I stopped writing in the late 1930s and did not resume until 1965." Many of his later poems have been collected in *Amulet* (New Directions, 1967).

ADRIENNE RICH ("For a Russian Poet") teaches in the SEEK program at the City College of New York. A 1951 graduate of Radcliffe, she lives with her husband and three sons in Manhattan. Her poems have been published in many magazines and collected in five books, most recently *Leaflets* (Norton, 1969).

JOHN RIDLAND ("Two Poems about Money") teaches English at the University of California at Santa Barbara. Born in London in 1933, he grew up in southern California and was educated at Swarthmore, Berkeley, and Claremont. He has published one book of poetry, *Ode on Violence and Other Poems* (Tennessee Poetry Press, 1969).

DEL MARIE ROGERS ("A Man's Life") lives with her husband and three children in Nashville, Tennessee, where she is completing work for her master's degree at Vanderbilt. Her work has appeared in *Epoch*, *Choice*, and *Perspective*. At present she is at work on a book of poems which, she hopes, "will soon find a publisher."

JEROME ROTHENBERG ("The Student's Testimony") is a graduate of the City College of New York (B.A., 1952) and the University of Michigan (M.A., 1953). He has published many books in the

United States and in England. The most recently published are *Narratives and Realtheater Pieces* (Pierrepont Press, Brooklyn, 1969), *The Seventeen Horse-Songs of Frank Mitchell* (Circle Books, London, 1969), and *A Summoning of the Tribes: Indian Poetry of the Americas* (Buffalo Translation Series, Buffalo, New York, 1969).

NORMAN H. RUSSELL ("Two Poems") is Professor of Biology at Central State College in Edmond, Oklahoma. The author of many scientific publications (seven books and sixty research pamphlets), he has also contributed poems to such magazines as *Prairie Schooner, Northeast,* and *South Dakota Review.* In 1969 his first poetry collection, *At the Zoo,* was published by J. R. Dicks Company of Smithtown, New York. Mr. Russell writes, "My Indian poems are inspired by my own experiences in nature and perhaps also by having had a Cherokee great-grandmother."

EDWARD W. SAID ("Meditation on Beginnings") was born in Jerusalem, Palestine, and was educated at Victoria College in Cairo, Princeton, and Harvard. He is the author of *Joseph Conrad and the Fiction of Autobiography* (Harvard, 1966) and of a forthcoming book, *Swift's Tory Anarchy,* also to be published by Harvard. He writes, "My interests—aside from literary ones—are philosophical and linguistic, as well as a political and cultural interest in Arab affairs." He teaches English and comparative literature at Columbia.

RICHARD SCHECHNER ("Theatre and Revolution") is Professor of Drama at New York University and Director of the Performance Group. He reports that he once won an award for having "defects of the teeth," corrected in 1948. In addition to this he has two books to his credit: *Public Domain* (Bobbs-Merrill, 1969), and *Dionysus in 69* (Farrar, Straus and Giroux, 1969).

JAMES SCHUYLER ("Paris by Night") was formerly a member of the staffs of the Museum of Modern Art and of *Art News* (to which he is still a regular contributor). A collection of his poems, *Freely Espousing,* was published by Doubleday's *Paris Review Editions* in 1969. "Paris by Night" is a chapter from *A Nest of Ninnies* (Dutton, 1969), a novel written in collaboration with John Ashbery.

JOHN SKINNER ("Our Willows") lives in Whittier, California, where he is a psychotherapist with the California Youth Authority. "Most of my writing," he states "has been professional, although I did contribute a study, 'Lewis Carroll's Adventures in Wonderland,' to the paperback, *Psychoanalysis and Literature*, edited by Ruitenbeek. A similar study was published in the *American Imago*, 'James M. Barrie, or, The Boy Who Wouldn't Grow Up.' "

DAVID STACTON ("Notes Written in . . .") died in Copenhagen in January 1968 at the age of forty-four. Though born and educated in the United States, he spent most of his life in Italy, England, and Denmark. The author of some twenty books, his best-known work was *The Bonapartes*, a best seller in 1966. At the time of his death he was nearing completion of a huge historical novel which has yet to be published.

RICHARD G. STERN ("Events, Happenings, Credibility, Fictions") is Professor of English at the University of Chicago. He writes that his novel *Stich* was selected as one of the ten important literary works of 1965 by the American Library Association, "while my novels *Golk* and *Europe* went unrewarded and scarcely remarked." "For the sake of my one-car wife and bairns," Mr. Stern recommends to the public his new collection of fiction, *1968* (to be published by Holt, Rinehart and Winston in 1970) and his first collection of poems, *Some Home Truths (Some Abroad)*, "prose in drag," as he confessed recently to Oriana Fallaci in *L'Europeo*.

LYNN STRONGIN ("New England Love") was born in New York City in 1939. Her poems have appeared in such magazines as the *Goliards* and *Galley Sail Review* and in three anthologies: *31 New American Poets* (ed. Ron Schreiber, Hill and Wang, 1969), *The Hand That Cradles the Rock: An Anthology of Writings on Women's Oppression and Women's Liberation* (Random House, 1969), and *Green Flag* (City Lights, 1969). Currently Miss Strongin is teaching English at Mills College in Oakland, California.

JAMES TATE ("When Kabir Died") was born in 1943 in Kansas City, Missouri. In 1966 he won the Yale Series of Younger Poets

Award with his collection *The Lost Pilot*. His verse has since appeared in the *Atlantic Monthly*, *Ante*, and *dust*. At present he is teaching at the University of California at Berkeley.

JOHN WIENERS ("Invitation Au Voyage II") was born in Boston in 1934 and educated at Boston and Black Mountain Colleges. His poems have been collected in four books: *The Hotel Wently Poems* (1958; 2nd edition, 1966), *Ace of Pentacles* (1964), *Pressed Wafer* (1967), and *Selected Poems* (1967).

JOHN WILLIAMS ("Henry Miller: The Success of Failure") is Professor of English at the University of Denver and editor of the *Denver Quarterly*. His essays, poems, and stories have appeared in a wide variety of periodicals from the *Nation* to the *Tiger's Eye*. He is the author of two poetry collections and three novels, the last of which, *Stoner*, was published by The Viking Press in 1965. At present he is "finishing a novel based on the life of Augustus Caesar."

JOHN WOODS ("Asking Directions in California") was born in Martinsville, Indiana, in 1926. His poems have been collected in four books, the most recent of which is *Keeping Out of Trouble* (Indiana, 1968). In 1969 he won *Poetry Northwest's* Theodore Roethke Prize. A professor of English at Western Michigan University, he lives with his wife and two children in Kalamazoo.

SYBIL WULETICH ("The Depraved Angel of *Marat/Sade*") teaches English at Hunter College in New York. She writes, "Recently I completed a book entitled *Poe: The Rationale of the Uncanny*, which was subsidized by grants from Smith and Hunter Colleges. This summer I received another grant from the City University of New York to work on a book entitled *Misericordia and Revenge*. I am married to Dr. Louis Brinberg."

AL YOUNG ("For Poets") was born in 1939 in Ocean Springs, Mississippi. The editor of *Loveletter* magazine, he has contributed to many others including *El Corno Emplumado*, *Journal of Black Poetry*, and *Umbra*. At present he is Visiting Jones Lecturer in Creative Writing at Stanford. Corinth Books will publish his first poetry collection, *Dancing*, in 1970.

NOTES ON THE MAGAZINES

ADVENTURES IN POETRY was founded by its editor, Larry Fagin, in 1968. Five issues, published irregularly, have appeared to date. At present the magazine is based in New York, where most of its contributors live. They include Ron Padgett, John Ashbery, Clark Coolidge, Lewis Warsh, Kenward Elmslie, and John Giorno. (c/o Larry Fagin, 437 East 12th Street, Apartment 18, New York, New York 10009)

ANGEL HAIR, a magazine of contemporary writing, was started in the spring of 1966 by Lewis Warsh and Anne Waldman. Later that year Angel Hair Books began, with the publication of *The Man with Blue Eyes* by the English poet Lee Harwood. To date, seven issues of *Angel Hair* have appeared, and eight volumes of poetry. Mr. Warsh states: "Editing a magazine casts a strange light on your relationships with other poets; it adds a dimension which enables you to connect whatever feelings of intimacy or distance you feel with them personally, as well as with their work. It also makes you see just what poems you like more than others and how much what gets into a magazine depends on where you are (both geographically and in your head) at a certain time." *Angel Hair* is printed by the Chapel Press in Williamstown, Massachusetts. (Box 257, Peter Stuyvesant Station, New York, New York 10009)

APPLE has published three issues to date, the first in 1967. Contributors have included A. R. Ammons, Wendell Berry, Howard McCord, "and lots of new poets, even two children." The editor, David Curry, writes, "Considering the neglects of which our Federal government is guilty, the spending of Federal funds for these anthologies is a kind of crime. But if the anthology is to be, I'm glad a poem as fine as Dick Lourie's '1966' will appear in it." (Post Office Box 2271, Springfield, Illinois 62705)

THE BELOIT POETRY JOURNAL, a quarterly founded in 1950, is owned, edited, and published by its editorial board: Robert H. Glauber, David M. Stocking, Marion K. Stocking, and John Bennett. In assembling the issues, Miss Stocking explains, "We take the best without regard to form, school, length, or reputation of the poet. About half of most issues turn out to be by people we'd never heard of before." The *Journal* has also published special issues devoted to Robert Frost, to Asian poetry, and to Concrete poetry. Christopher Bursk's poem, "Adjust, Adjust," was in a "Discoveries" issue of new poets nominated by writers who had already appeared in the magazine. Again in the words of Miss Stocking, "The light-hearted aim of *The Beloit Poetry Journal* is simply to share poems the editors enjoy. More seriously, we hope to keep our readers aware of new currents in poetry by assembling special issues (such as the Asian and Concrete ones) to display important work that wouldn't come to us in the ordinary run of submissions." (Box 2, Beloit, Wisconsin 53511)

THE BROWN BAG was founded in North Carolina as a quarterly in 1968 by William Newman and Peter Hanley. "However," writes Mr. Newman, "due to a conspicuous lack of bureaucratic efficiency, the magazine has since been published at haphazard intervals." He explains that in North Carolina "brown-bagging" refers to the "social drinker's" practice of bringing his own bottle to a "private club" concealed in a bag (and hence by-passing that state's law against liquor-by-the-drink). "We adopted the term for the title of our publication because we felt that good literature of a high proof, like good whisky, must be bootlegged, must be circulated and read in a covert fashion. *The Brown Bag* is a subversive organization, at least as subversive as Black Power. Masked beneath a nondescript packaging there is a Bolshie bomb, black, round, substantial, with a sizzling fuse, to disrupt polite literary salons and dignified autographing parties." (c/o William Newman, 203 Hall of Languages, Syracuse University, Syracuse, New York 13210)

CAMELS COMING, edited and published by Richard Morris, was founded in 1965, when the editor was a graduate student in physics at the University of Nevada. The magazine was originally published in conjunction with the *Camel's Hump*, a series of "poetry newsletters" distributed free, and *Quark,* "a series of mimeographed chapbooks." According to Mr. Morris the editorial aim of *Camels Coming* is "the publication of *intelligently raucous* antiestablishment or antiacademic literature and art." He also reports that "publication has been temporarily suspended because the editor has no money." (Post Office Box 8201, University Station, Reno, Nevada)

THE CARLETON MISCELLANY was started in 1960 by its first editor, Reed Whittemore, former editor and publisher of *Furioso.* The *Miscellany* is "published and supported by Carleton College and by the President and Board of Trustees of the College in Northfield, Minnesota." It has never, however, had an "administrative adviser" and has retained its autonomous status. Far from being regional in its interests, the magazine draws its material from all parts of the United States and from Europe. It features poetry, fiction, articles, and reviews, many of which are by authors previously unpublished. Now its editors are Erling Larsen, Wayne Carver, and Carolyn Soule. (c/o Carleton College, Northfield, Minnesota 55057)

CASSIOPEIA was founded in 1967 by C. Lewis Ellingham. As he explains, "The project began in New York with *Magazine* (six issues, edited by a variety of persons, myself as publisher, soon to be collected and reprinted by Abrams News Service). When I came to California in 1967 I retitled *Magazine "Cassiopeia"* and turned over the editing of the first issue to a young poet, David Schaff. We ended up working on the project, not fully completed until 1968, together, as we did on a second venture, *Cassiopeia II/ Ephemeris I*—the latter title being that of David's effort, a venture separate from my own. This issue appeared in October 1968 and a separate third part of *Cassiopeia* I hope will appear in the fall, under my own hand." (Post Office Box 317, Valley Ford, California 94972)

CATERPILLAR was founded in 1967 by Clayton Eshleman. It is a quarterly, in the tradition of *origin* magazine and the *Black Mountain Review.* According to Eshleman, "*Caterpillar* is less concerned with discoveries than with printing, regularly, in quantity, work by some thirty contemporary poets, providing a vessel for their work, for them to have a place for it, for other contemporaries to follow them with continuity." Some of the poets whose work appears regularly in the magazine are Robert Kelly, Jerome Rothenberg, Diane Wakoski, David Antin, Cid Corman, Charles Olson, Gary Snyder, Allen Ginsberg, Richard Grossinger, Carolee Schneemann, Armand Schwerner, Michael McClure, Ken Irby, and Will Petersen. *Caterpillar* is published and edited by Eshleman; Robert Kelly is a contributing editor. (36 Greene Street, New York, New York 10036)

CHELSEA began in 1958 as the *Chelsea Review*, making its headquarters on New York's West 25th Street "at a Greek cafeteria run by a Turk," according to Sonia Raiziss, coeditor with Alfredo de Palchi since 1966. In her words, the goals of the magazine have been "to break down the insular attitudes and quality of American prose" and "to introduce and stress current writing from abroad and so crossbreed native with foreign literature in two-way translations." *Chelsea* has also undertaken a number of special issues devoted to "themes, experimental styles, national or international styles of particular interest." An idea of the breadth of *Chelsea's* content is indicated by listing a few of its recent features: a technological issue guest-edited by A. R. Ammons; translations of William Carlos Williams into Italian; and special sections of poetry translated from the Spanish, Welsh, Danish, Greek, and Korean. (Box 242, Old Chelsea Station, New York, New York 10011)

CHICAGO REVIEW, "a quarterly journal of literature and ideas," was founded in the winter of 1946 at the University of Chicago. In the words of a former editor, Eugene Wildman, "the function of the magazine is to publish writers of merit who would have a difficult, if not impossible, time getting their work accepted by more commercially oriented periodicals." Subsidized by the University and staffed by its students, the *Review* published the early work of such writers as William Burroughs, Philip Roth, and Ronald Tavel. The magazine's 1967 *Anthology of Concretism* issue was the first volume of its kind to appear in this country. The present editor is Harry Foster. (c/o University of Chicago, Chicago, Illinois 60637)

THE COLORADO QUARTERLY was founded at the University of Colorado in 1952 as "a magazine of regional and national scope designed to appeal to the general reader." In addition to fiction and poetry, each issue contains a "diversified selection of articles written in nontechnical style by specialists in all fields." The magazine is edited by Paul Carter, assisted by Associate Editor Alex Warner. (Hellems 134, University of Colorado, Boulder, Colorado 80302)

CONFRONTATION was founded at Long Island University in 1968. So far two issues have appeared, edited by Eugene Arden, Dean of the Graduate Faculties of Arts and Science. Dean Arden writes, "We work under the aegis of Long Island University, but we accept encouragement and support from as many sources as we can develop." (c/o Dean Eugene Arden, The Graduate Faculties, Long Island University, Brookville, New York 11548)

CONTEMPORARY LITERATURE (known until 1967 as *Wisconsin Studies in Contemporary Literature*) was founded by the English department of the University of Wisconsin in 1960. According to the editor, L. S. Dembo, the magazine "has sought over the past decade to become a leading critical and scholarly journal covering the whole range of modern literature." Among *Contemporary Literature*'s regular features are literary interviews and reviews of fiction, poetry, and drama. In addition, special issues are periodically devoted to individual authors and to literatures of single nations. Most of *Contemporary Literature*'s contents are of a scholarly nature. As Mr. Dembo describes it, "Although the magazine is eclectic in its selections, it favors the rigorous conceptual article." (c/o Department of English, Bascom Hall, University of Wisconsin, Madison, Wisconsin 53706)

EPHEMERIS, edited by Davis Schaff, emerged from his collaboration with C. Lewis Ellingham on *Cassiopeia* magazine. The first issue, *Cassiopeia II/Ephemeris I*, appeared in October 1968. The second issue (no longer in collaboration with Ellingham) went to press in May 1969. For most of his material Schaff looks to the poets he knows around San Francisco. He explains, "Basically the issues have been formed around events here, locally, then outward. I would like to aim for as wide a participation as possible, but I don't want a collection, I want all the material in *Ephemeris* to come into a focus, by whatever means." (2156 Blucher Valley Road, Sebastopol, California 94752)

FIRE EXIT was started in 1967 as the periodical of the New Poets' Theatre in Cambridge, Massachusetts. The theatre folded one year later, but the magazine has survived. To date two issues have been published and a third is in the works. The four editors are William Corbett, Fanny Howe, Ben E. Watkins, and Ruth Whitman. In their words, simply, "We intend to publish the best poetry, fiction, and book reviews available." (9 Columbus Circle, Boston, Massachusetts 02116)

FOLIO was founded in 1965 by its editor, Adele Sophie de la Barre, and "sustaining patron," Dr. True W. Robinson. They had formerly collaborated on two other publications: *Off-Off*, "a group of poetry sheets," published in 1960; and *Token* (1961–1965), which was abandoned when, according to Miss de la Barre, "the word 'token' assumed political meaning which was uncongenial to us." The main interest of *Folio* is poetry, but occasionally the magazine publishes short fiction. Miss de la Barre reports that "in five years we have printed the writing of more than two hundred contributors, many appearing repeatedly. Our poets live in almost every state of the union and also in a number of foreign countries. The taste of *Folio*'s editors is clearly eclectic, and we try to shun prejudice." (Post Office Box 3–1111, Birmingham, Alabama 35222)

HANGING LOOSE is a quarterly magazine devoted primarily to poetry, "although we ocasionally publish songs, drawings, and short fiction." The magazine's name describes its format—unbound pages in an envelope which serves as cover. The first issue appeared in late 1966 (although the magazine is a direct successor to *Things*, which began in 1964) and seven issues have been published to date. Among the poets who appear regularly are Marge Piercy, John Gill, Victor Contoski, Dan Georgakas, Wesley Day, and Jack Anderson. The editors of *Hanging Loose* are Ron Schreiber, Dick Lourie, Robert Hershon, and Emmett Jarrett. (301 Hicks Street, Brooklyn, New York 11201)

HOLLOW ORANGE, a magazine of poetry, was started early in 1966 by Clifford Burke in San Francisco. "I started the magazine in order to combine my interests in poetry and in printing, and it has since evolved into Craniom Press, printer and publisher of poetry books, broadsides, pamphlets, and miscellaneous free poems and ephemera." Six issues of the magazine have appeared to date, and Burke continues as its sole editor: "In *Hollow Orange* I try to present, in a nicely done, pocket-size format, poems that please me." (243 Collins Street, San Francisco, California 94118)

THE HUDSON REVIEW was founded by William Arrowsmith, Joseph Bennett, and Frederick Morgan, and the first issue appeared in 1948. In it the founders sought to publish "the best available contemporary work in fiction, poetry, and criticism—with particular emphasis on the work of young and 'unknown' writers—and to explore cultural developments in their fullest implications." Moreover, they were determined to form a quarterly which would remain independent of the more academically and politically oriented journals of the time. *The Hudson Review* published the early writings of many younger Americans now well known, including Herbert Gold, Anthony Hecht, Galway Kinnell, W. S. Merwin, and Anne Sexton. The magazine's contributors have also included such figures as André Malraux, Thomas Mann, T. S. Eliot, Sir Herbert Read, and William Carlos Williams. Under the continuing editorship of Frederick Morgan, the magazine now publishes, in addition to fiction, poetry, and essays, regular sections of criticism devoted to music, theater, art, films, and ballet. (65 East 55th Street, New York, New York 10022)

KAYAK is "totally controlled" by the firm hand of George Hitchcock, the editor, publisher, and printer since he founded the magazine in 1964. *Kayak*'s list of contributors includes such poets as Donald Hall, Lou Lipsitz, Gary Snyder, John Tagliabue, and Peter Wild. Mr. Hitchcock explains that "*Kayak*'s aim is to bring down the great stuffed walruses of American poetry and to open a few paths among the icebergs. All decisions are made autocratically by its editor, who believes in God, mother, and the improbable, not necessarily in that order." (2808 Laguna Street, San Francisco, California 94123)

THE KENYON REVIEW was founded at Kenyon College in 1939 by Gordon Keith Chalmers, then president of the college. Under the editorship of John Crowe Ransom, the magazine's early contributors included such writers as John Peale Bishop, Lionel Trilling, Robert Penn Warren, William Empson, Wallace Stevens, and Cleanth Brooks. Ransom also published some of the earliest work of Leslie Fiedler, John Stewart Carter, Robie Macauley (a later *Kenyon Review* editor), and Robert Lowell. The current editor, George Lanning, endeavors to "steer an eclectic course among the fashions of the day." In addition to fiction and poetry, *Kenyon* is particularly interested in "belletristic essays about good writers who have had little or no serious attention in recent years, and we are especially receptive to the work of promising younger critics." (Gambier, Ohio 43022)

THE LITTLE SQUARE REVIEW first appeared, little and square in format (6" x 6"), in 1966. Its founder and editor, John Ridland, explains the magazine's purpose thus: "To match squareness of format by solidity of accomplishment, printing authors new or older (and sometimes both, men of forty or fifty new to writing or to publishing poems) who have not, in the editor's opinion, been granted sufficient recognition in larger publications. No platform this, other than an editorial judgment (whose basis would be sketched in a short editorial note, complemented by a short 'Note on Poetry' by the poet, in each issue): shaky planks for any 'correction of taste' on even a modest scale." (1940 Mission Ridge Road, Santa Barbara, California 93103)

THE NEW MEXICO QUARTERLY was founded in 1931 at the University of New Mexico. Its founders intended that the magazine "give to the faculty, advanced students, and all others who may have something worthwhile to contribute to the literature and scholarly thought of New Mexico an outlet for their writings and at the same time give to the thinkers of New Mexico a medium through which there may be an exchange of serious and disinterested thought on the problems of the state, regardless of their nature." Soon, however, the magazine abandoned this rather specialized localism. Through the years the pages of the *Quarterly* have seen the work of such diverse talents as Jesse Stuart and D. H. Lawrence, Robert Creeley and John Gould Fletcher. Recently denied its University subsidy, the magazine has suspended publication since spring 1969. (c/o University of New Mexico Press, Albuquerque, New Mexico 87106)

NORTHWEST REVIEW was founded in 1957 at the University of Oregon. In addition to local writers, the magazine has published the work of such authors as R. V. Cassill, Joyce Carol Oates, and Lewis Turco. Since 1965 the editor has been Ralph Salisbury, who reports that his *Protest and Affirmation Issue* of summer 1968 prompted the University to "state that there were insufficient press funds" to continue publishing the magazine. After a year's delay, however, these differences seem to have been solved. Now in the works is a special regional issue to be devoted to poets of the Northwest. (c/o University of Oregon, Eugene, Oregon 97403)

THE OUTSIDER, according to the editor, Jon Webb, has recently returned to New Orleans, "where the magazine was born in 1961 in an oval room called the Blue Room in an old building of the French Quarter." Continually beset by financial problems, *The Outsider* managed to publish three issues in New Orleans. But in 1963, Webb remembers, "Gypsy Lou, my wife and coeditor—artist, writer, typesetter, and bookbinder—developed a lung full of emphysema and we had to head west to Tucson, Arizona." In 1968 issue 4/5 was printed in Tucson and "sold out before we had sense enough to hide a few copies away in a trunk." Still in the red financially, the Webbs have already laid plans for *The Outsider* #6, to be published in New Orleans again. "We've got the strength and material. All we need is the cash." (629 Rue Ursulines, New Orleans, Louisiana 70116)

PARTISAN REVIEW was founded in 1934 "as an organ of the John Reed Club," but suspended publication in 1936. It was revised in December 1937 by a group of young writers who included F. W. Dupee, Dwight Macdonald, Mary McCarthy, George L. K. Morris, William Phillips, and Philip Rahv. It has published poetry, fiction, and essays on a variety of literary and political subjects. *Partisan Review* published the early work of James Agee, Saul Bellow, Ralph Ellison, and Leslie Fiedler, among others. In addition, its contributors have included such figures as Albert Camus, Franz Kafka,

George Orwell, and Jean-Paul Sartre. The magazine is published quarterly, and the editorial board consists of William Phillips, Chairman; Philip Rahv; Richard Poirier; and Steven Marcus, Associate Editor. (c/o Rutgers University, New Brunswick, New Jersey 08903)

POETRY was founded in 1912 by Harriet Monroe and has been published monthly ever since. There is virtually no major poet in English who has not at some stage in his career depended on *Poetry* to find a public for him. T. S. Eliot, Robert Frost, Wallace Stevens, Edgar Lee Masters, Edna St. Vincent Millay, Ezra Pound, Carl Sandburg, and Dylan Thomas are only a few of the poets that the magazine has published in its long history. Under the editorship of Henry Rago, who succeeded Karl Shapiro in 1955, *Poetry* was the first to offer major prizes to such poets as Alan Dugan, Robert Duncan, Thom Gunn, Denise Levertov, the late Sylvia Plath, Anne Sexton, and James Wright. Since Mr. Rago's death in 1969, *Poetry* has been edited by Daryl Hine. (1018 North State Street, Chicago, Illinois 60610)

POETRY NORTHWEST, which is subsidized in part by the University of Washington, is in its tenth year of publication. For its first six years the magazine was edited by Carolyn Kizer, with the assistance of Nelson Bentley, William Matchett, and Richard Hugo. Since 1966 the editor has been David Wagoner, assisted by Messrs. Matchett and Bentley. In Mr. Wagoner's words, "We publish nothing but poems, the best poems we can find; that has been and will remain our sole aim. Our 'discoveries' are those poems, which must speak for themselves." (Parrington Hall, University of Washington, Seattle, Washington 98105)

PRAIRIE SCHOONER was founded in 1927 by L. C. Wimberly at the University of Nebraska. In its earliest years the magazine was chiefly concerned with the work of local writers and poets. Its breadth and diversity since then are indicated by a few of its contributors: Randall Jarrell, Malcolm Lowry, Mari Sandoz, and Anaïs Nin. The magazine has always given special emphasis to the work of little-known writers, publishing some of the earliest work of Jesse

Stuart, Eudora Welty, and Jessamyn West. Currently edited by Bernice Slote, *Prairie Schooner* publishes fiction, poetry, "book reviews (by invitation), occasional humorous sketches, translations, and portfolio collections." (c/o University of Nebraska, Lincoln, Nebraska 68508)

QUARTERLY REVIEW OF LITERATURE was founded in 1943 "as an independent magazine run solely by its editors," Theodore and René Weiss. Since 1963 it has appeared not quarterly but semi-annually with double issues. The large issues permit the inclusion of the widest selection of writers, large selections from their works, and extended works: plays, novellas, and long poems. One issue each year is devoted to a single author and contains not only essays and critical treatments but often also new or previously unpublished material by the author himself. Among the writers so featured have been Pound, Montale, Leopardi, Valéry, and Marianne Moore. Literary innovation still interests the editors of the *Review*. However, they feel that today "the publishing of genuine work—the attempt to maintain basic standards—has become more important than ever. Discovery still deeply concerns us, but so does continuity and the reinforcement of accomplishments already arrived at." (26 Haslet Avenue, Princeton, New Jersey 08540)

THE QUEST was founded in the fall of 1965 by Alexis Levitin, Barbara Christian, and David Hartwell. The founding statement was: "We expect of the artist not only a well-wrought structure but, within it, a creative and meaningful reflection upon the essential truths of our existence. This emphasized interest in content, as well as form, is central to our quest." The magazine has published ten issues on a somewhat erratic quarterly schedule over the past four years and intends to publish "as many more as we can afford." Messrs. Levitin, Hartwell, and Thomas T. Beeler are the present editors, who report, "We have made a number of discoveries over the past four years, but none has been particularly rediscovered by anyone else. We intend to keep publishing them and anyone else we discover whose work merits publication." (Post Office Box 207, Cathedral Station, New York, New York 10025)

RENASCENCE was founded at Marquette University in 1948 by John Pick, who has edited the Catholic magazine ever since. He describes *Renascence*'s readers as "those whose literary interest is centered upon contemporary world literature possessing a spiritual dimension (Catholic or non-Catholic): T. S. Eliot and Dylan Thomas receive attention as well as Graham Greene, Evelyn Waugh, François Mauriac, and others. Our readers tend to be sophisticated in their orthodoxy. Our contributors steer clear of narrow parochialisms and naïve pietisms. Our articles are literary in their emphasis, and not primarily sectarian, and hence we like to think of our readers as intellectuals." (Marquette University, Milwaukee, Wisconsin 53233)

SALMAGUNDI is a "quarterly journal of the humanities and social sciences" which first appeared in the fall of 1965. Though founded by a small group of young writers, the magazine "is in no way limited to the discovery and encouragement of new talent." While *Salmagundi* has published "elaborate work by previously unpublished authors," it has also presented the work of established writers, encouraging them to undertake "particularly complex or lengthy" special projects. The magazine is "chiefly directed toward the literary community, combining literary criticism with radical political analysis, philosophical dissertations, original poetry, and drama." Edited by Robert Boyers, its most recent special issue was devoted to the work of Robert Lowell. (Post Office Box 768, Flushing, New York 11355)

THE SEWANEE REVIEW, founded in 1892, is the oldest literary quarterly in the United States. Since the early 1940s the editor has been chosen by special appointment at the University of the South, which publishes the magazine. Allen Tate was the first editor so appointed; since his tenure, editors of the *Review* have been John J. E. Palmer (now editor of *The Yale Review*), Monroe K. Spears, and Andrew Lytle, the present editor. *The Sewanee Review* carries on its long-standing interest and devotion to literary tradition by publishing not only "writing in all categories by new writers" but also the work of the more established authors and critics to maintain what it refers to as "the unity and continuity of the English language." (Sewanee, Tennessee 37375)

SHENANDOAH was founded in 1950 by a group of undergraduates and faculty members at Washington and Lee University. During the fifties the magazine was controlled by a revolving board of students and faculty and was published three times a year. In 1963 it began appearing quarterly, with James Boatwright as its first permanent editor. It continues to be published by Washington and Lee but remains editorially independent of the university. Since the fifties the magazine has published a wide variety of fiction, poetry, interviews, and critical work. Some of its recent contributors have been John Berryman, Robert Lowell, Monroe K. Spears, and Stephen Spender. It has published special issues devoted to the work of Sherwood Anderson, W. H. Auden, and Robert Graves. (Box 722, Lexington, Virginia 24450)

THE SIXTIES is edited by Robert Bly. He writes, "The Sixties (then The Fifties) was founded in 1958 to combat the literary forces that later came to edit the American Literary Anthology. Ave atque vale." (c/o Odin House, Madison, Minnesota 56256)

SOUTHERN POETRY REVIEW, a semiannual magazine of poetry and criticism, was founded by Guy Owen as Impetus in 1958 at Stetson University. It became Southern Poetry Review in 1964, when the editor moved to North Carolina State University, and is now published there in cooperation with the School of Liberal Arts. In 1968 the magazine celebrated its tenth birthday by publishing an anthology, A Decade of Poems, which included the work of Wendell Berry, A. R. Ammons, Louis Coxe, and over fifty others. Some of the poets the Southern Poetry Review was among the first to publish are James Dickey, Fred Chappel, John Unterecker, Miller Williams, Peter Wild, William Matthews, Dabney Stuart, and Vassar Miller. Many writers have also helped to edit the first ten volumes—among them are Max Halpern, Richard Goldsmith, Tom Walters, and William E. Taylor. (c/o English Department, North Carolina State University, Raleigh, North Carolina 27607)

STONY BROOK is published by the Stony Brook Poetics Foundation, which was founded by George Quasha in 1968. Only two issues have appeared to date because, as Mr. Quasha explains, "like most small publications, we are generally broke." Mr. Quasha edits the magazine with assistance from Managing Editor Roger Guedalla and Claudia Ott, who sets the type. *Stony Brook's* editorial credo is stated thus: "Our intention is to encourage participation in a multiphasic open forum, the dynamics of which are meant to symbolize, however modestly, the crucial struggle of our time: to unify human energies in rebuilding the human house; to evolve the spirit toward new principles of universal design for creative peace; in Blake's sense, to forever prolong mental and depress corporeal war. Our pretentions are grand because the need for action is great. Total struggle is necessary on every level." (Post Office Box 1102, Stony Brook, New York 11790)

SUMAC first appeared in the fall of 1968. The editors, Dan Gerber and Jim Harrison, had laid plans for the magazine the previous winter: "We felt there should be a magazine which would be a rather straightforward meeting ground of all 'schools' and groups in American poetry, and a bringing together of 'big hitters' and relatively unknown poets. Our aim is to print the best (in our opinion) poetry and experimental fiction we can obtain and to maintain an energetic catholicity." Among those whose work appeared in the first three issues of *Sumac* are Louis Simpson, Paul Blackburn, Ezra Pound, and Gerard Malanga. (Post Office Box 29, Fremont, Michigan 49412)

TENNESSEE POETRY JOURNAL was founded August 5, 1967, as a "private, nonprofit magazine" by Stephen Mooney. Two issues have appeared so far and a third is in the works. Mr. Mooney writes, "I am the editor, permanently, I suppose, unless I decide to give the magazine away someday. The aims of the magazine are to spread knowledge of national poets to this region and to give national distribution to Tennessee poets; to improve the poetic literacy of readers close to home; to find young talent and give it a chance to develop through the kind of criticism that results from national publication; to bring those on the outside in, to send those on the inside out. We have published the work of Robert Bly, David Ignatow, Harvey Shapiro, Leonard Nathan, and others nationally known; lesser-known regional writers include Scott Bates, Paul Ramsey, Frank Steele, Julia Randall, and of course many others." (Post Office Box 196, Martin, Tennesseee 38237)

TRACE was founded by James Boyer May, who has been its editor since 1952. One of Mr. May's original intentions in starting the magazine was to give special attention to the work of little-known, unpublished writers. And *Trace*, in his words, "continues to print the work of more hitherto unpublished persons than any other periodical." In addition to poetry and fiction, the magazine also publishes criticism, especially reviews of privately printed books and of little-known work in other small magazines. In 1963 a graphic-art section was added, and the magazine has begun to include theater and film criticism. Perhaps the best-known feature of *Trace* is its directory, published in each issue, of small magazines and independent presses. (Post Office Box 1068, Hollywood, California 90028)

TRANSATLANTIC REVIEW, related by name only to Ford Madox Ford's two-volume venture of 1924, was founded in the summer of 1959 by a group including George Garrett, Patrick Creagh, and J. F. McCrindle, who continues to be its editor. Since its first appearance in Rome in an edition of 500 copies, the magazine has grown considerably; it is now published quarterly and is edited in New York and London. The *Review* is composed mainly of fiction and poetry from the United States and Great Britain, with occasional translations of work by Asian and African writers. It publishes no critical studies, but it has featured a long series of interviews with film and theater directors and with producers and playwrights. Among the writers who have helped edit its more than twenty-five issues are William Goldman, Jean-Claude van Italie, B. S. Johnson, Heathcote Williams, and Eugene Walter. (Box 3348, Grand Central Station, New York, New York 10017)

UNICORN JOURNAL was founded in 1968 by Kenneth Maytag, publisher of the Unicorn Press, to "support humanistic values now threatened by our country's affluence and empire-building." It is published semiannually in both paper and hard covers, designed by Alan Brilliant, and edited by Teo Savory. The *Journal* consists of poetry, essays, folk tales, reproductions of art and photography, and translations, "with emphasis on non-Caucasian material." The contributors so far include Bienek, Goll, Hitchcock, Merton, Secunda, Vinh An, Vo-Dinh, and Vo Van Ai. Mr. Brilliant reports that *Journal* #3 is nearly complete and "promises to be the most ambitious editorial and design job we have yet achieved." (317 East De la Guerra Street, Santa Barbara, California 93101)

THE VIRGINIA QUARTERLY REVIEW was established by James Southall Wilson, its first editor, at the University of Virginia in 1925 "as a journal of liberal opinion and of literary excellence, Southern in location and sympathies, but national and international in outlook and contributors." Its pages have seen not only the work of such Southern writers as John Crowe Ransom, Robert Penn Warren, and Thomas Wolfe but also that of Robert Graves, Thomas Mann, and Luigi Pirandello. In addition to fiction and poetry, the magazine has published a wide variety of critical essays. Its sixth and current editor is Charlotte Kohler. (1 West Range, Charlottesville, Virginia 22903)

VOYAGES, in the words of William F. Claire, who founded it in 1967, is "the first of its kind ever to be published in Washington, D.C." Assisted by Frances Smyth, his graphic designer, Mr. Claire tries to "present accomplished writers who deserve attention they somehow haven't received." The magazine's principal advisory editors are Mark Van Doren and Anaïs Nin, which suggests the range of styles that characterizes each issue. Special sections devoted to Ben Belitt, Roger Hecht, Daniel Hoffman, and Hiram Haydn have been juxtaposed with work by young poets and by such writers as Thomas Merton, Pablo Neruda, and James T. Farrell. Mr. Claire hopes that under his editorship *Voyages* "will continue its journey for many years." (Post Office Box 4862, Washington, D.C. 20008)

THE YALE REVIEW, a quarterly journal, was founded in 1911 by Wilbur L. Cross, a professor of English at Yale and later Governor of Connecticut. The original purpose of the journal was to keep Yale alumni in a continuing intellectual relationship with their teachers, and the emphasis was on Yale faculty publication. This policy has long since been broadened to include work by a wide variety of authors in diverse fields. Under the joint supervision of John J. E. Palmer (editor since 1954) and Mary Price (managing editor since 1967), the magazine publishes literary criticism, fiction, poetry, and articles on a wide range of subjects, from international politics to classical recordings, as well as a substantial book-review section. (28 Hillhouse Avenue, New Haven, Connecticut 06520)